THE SHEPHERD

WINGS OF THE FALLEN

ANTHONY PRYOR

A PERMUTED PRESS BOOK

ISBN: 978-1-68261-093-0
ISBN (eBook): 978-1-68261-094-7

Wings of the Fallen
The Shepherd Book 2
© 2016 by Anthony Pryor
All Rights Reserved

Cover art by Christian Bentulan

PERMUTED
PRESS

Permuted Press, LLC
275 Madison Avenue, 6th Floor
New York, NY 10016
http://permutedpress.com

ACKNOWLEDGEMENTS

Thanks are again due to my writerly pals Dale, Danielle, Shawna, Garth, Rebecca, and once more to Rhiannon and Beth for their insightful critiques and commentaries. I further hope that I've managed to do justice to the rugged beauty of eastern Oregon and its inhabitants. This book was written with some very loud music playing the background and some very colorful imagery in my mind so I would also like to acknowledge the work of legendary album artists like Roger Dean, Rodney Matthews, and David Fairbrother-Roe, as well as the music of Metallica, Rob Zombie, Nazareth, Judas Priest, and many, many others who helped me to imagine a world of demons, swords, motorcycles, and heavy metal mayhem.

PROLOGUE

THE FALLEN

The first thing she perceives is the sound. It is distant, but recognizable—the full-throated scream of engines. Pistons rise and fall, powering drive belts, spinning chrome-plated wheels, sending machines roaring down the asphalt, past endless fields of rock and scrub grass, still and sere in the heat of midday, beneath a sky of cloudless blue.

The sound grows louder as a glint of metal appears on the horizon. The girl sees it and is—for reasons she cannot understand—afraid. Cowering on her porch, she watches as the machines draw closer—a double column, ten deep, of burly men in leather and iron, each mounted on a roaring beast of a machine, thundering towards her, spread unchallenged across both lanes. Their muscular arms are covered in wild tattoos, their heads bare or covered only in leather caps, hair in braids or streaming free in the wind, their eyes obscured by goggles. They wear leather riding outfits—chaps, heavy boots, and vests covered in constellations of pins and insignia portraying savage icons—demons, wings, hammers, swords, dragons...

She crouches behind the porch railing, peeking out tremulously, eyes wide. They are riding past her now, a whirl of glinting chrome, the roar of engines almost deafening. The noise of their passing vibrates through the ground, through the porch, through her body. Her cries are inaudible over the cacophony.

She does not see men now. She sees something else. Where once there were human riders, mounted upon raging machines, she now sees monsters—red, scaled things with horned heads and fanged maws, their brutally clawed hands gripping studded leather reins. Great weapons are strapped to their backs and thighs, things like axes, swords, and crossbows but huge and crafted of gleaming black metal. The machines are not machines now—they are monsters too, massively muscled, with metallic armor grafted to their black scaled flesh. Their broad heads toss back and forth and they scream, their eyes burning yellow and red. Their crimson talons rip great gouges from the asphalt as they bound along, driven by their nightmarish riders.

Then they're past, vanishing toward the far horizon, and they are men again, mounted on wheeled metal machines. The road behind them seems untouched, a normal stretch of weathered blacktop.

The girl stares after them, breathing hard, the terror slowly ebbing from her heart.

On their backs, the men bear a round embroidered sigil, portraying a disembodied pair of wings, pointed downward. Arranged in a semicircle above the wings are the words *The Fallen*.

There is a sign by the side of the road nearby.

It says *Flagstaff 70*.

The roar of engines fades in the distance, leaving only silence in its wake.

PART ONE

SHOUT AT THE DEVIL

"So tell me about the dead animals, Frank."

Frank Magruder took my question in stride, slowly sipping at his Coke, then staring out the window, across the Shari's parking lot, toward the landscape of dry grass and dark volcanic rock beyond.

He swallowed and looked back at me, his gray eyes steady and hard. He was a ruggedly handsome man of middle years, with salt-and-pepper hair and a weathered face.

"You know what bothers me most about all this, Mister St. John?"

"Alex," I said. He'd pronounced it right, too—insisting that it be said "Sinjun" is pretty snooty of me, I'll admit, but I like to be different. "Call me Alex."

Frank gave me a thin smile and put his drink down on the "Welcome to Oregon" placemat. His burger and fries sat untouched on his plate.

"What bothers me, Alex, is the thought that some journalist from Portland is here in town asking me about my dead animals, and that maybe he's thinking of writing some smartass little puff-piece about all the hayseeds out in Eastern Oregon and their weird cattle-mutilation problem. You know, to keep all the hipsters amused. Remind 'em of how dumb those hicks out in

Malheur County are. Give 'em a little laugh while they sip their lattes. That's what bothers me."

I looked at him as steadily as I could. Frank was a rancher, as unyielding as the Steens Mountains and like most people on this side of the state, he had little patience for tree-huggers from Portland like me. I'd tried to dress conservatively, my hair neat, my newly-grown goatee trimmed. It was probably all for nothing—Portland pretty much oozed from my every pore, at least as far as people like Frank Magruder were concerned.

"Frank, all I can tell you is that I take the situation out here very seriously, and I have no intention of making fun of you or doing anything but an entirely professional piece of reporting." I paused. A copy of my paper, *the Ranger,* lay on the table beside me. The cover story was *The 25 Best Places to Get Shit-Faced in PDX.* I probably should have picked a different issue. "I know we're not exactly the *New York Times,* and a lot of our stuff lacks in real journalism, but I'm trying to change that. We've run some very important pieces about Portland rebuilding after the Christmas Storm, about the homeless problem, about bridge safety..."

Frank nodded and held up his hand. "You don't need to tell me everything you folks have done for the world, Alex. I just wanted you to know that if I tell you what's been going on, I expect to be treated fairly. Like a human being, not something that belongs on *Portlandia.* I mean, it's a funny show and all, but that's not what we're like out here."

I smiled. "Understood. I have no intention of offending a man who drives around with a 12-gauge in his truck."

That got a chuckle at least. We fell silent for a few moments, letting the sound of clinking glasses and quiet conversation fill the gap. At last Frank spoke.

"First time it happened I didn't think much of it. I've got about five hundred head of beef cattle. They graze on land I lease from the government. I like 'em all to stay alive and healthy for as long as it takes to get 'em to the auction yard in Vale, but you're gonna lose one now and again. Accidents, coyotes, lighting, acts of God. We keep a close watch to make sure they're safe but we can't be there all the time."

He finally turned his attention to the lunch I'd bought him, taking a bite of his burger, chewing slowly, then swallowing. He finished his Coke and gestured at the waitress for a refill. "Core—that's my son—found a dead calf out on the range three weeks ago, up near Pinetree Bluff. Guess it died during the night. Coyotes had been at it and there wasn't much left. Ate the tongue, some of the organs. Ripped off the legs, cracked open the bones." He paused and looked out the window again. A breeze stirred the grass. Overhead the sky was almost blindingly blue, only slightly moderated by the tinted glass. "It was all chewed up pretty good, but it looked to me like the throat had been slit. Clean, like a knife. Like I said, I didn't worry about it—thought it was just some weird coincidence, or something that looked unnatural but had a reasonable explanation."

"I hear you." I sighed. He sounded like me three years ago. "Better to think it was disease or predators than a human being."

Frank accepted his refill and took another long sip. "Yeah, that's what it was, I guess. I didn't really consciously think about it. It wasn't 'til we found two more that I started to get worried. Those were full-grown beef cows, worth a lot of money. Slaughtered, left out on the range to rot. You know, when people go pick up ground beef at Albertson's they probably don't think too much about all the sweat and work someone puts in to produce it, or how close to the poverty line most of us live."

I understood that too. "If someone is out here killing cattle just for the hell of it, they could be costing someone their livelihood."

Frank's eyes met mine again and I saw a glimmer of acknowledgement, as if he was beginning to actually believe me. "The second cow, that one we found in the morning, maybe a few hours after it had happened, just off the access road east of Penny Creek. Must have been killed during the night and the coyotes hadn't found it yet. Some crows and buzzards, but we chased 'em off."

He stopped again and looked down at his hamburger as if seeing it for the first time. "God damn, Alex, it was horrible.

Someone had slit the poor thing from stem to stern, chopped off its legs, dug out its eyes... Hell... Spread the guts all over in a big circle, like they were trying to make some kind of pattern. I can tell the difference between what coyotes and crows and ants do and what a man with a knife can do. These cuts were clean. Those eyes, Alex. They weren't eaten or pulled out by a bird or something—they were *cut* out. You know how I know? They were lying there, not six feet away. Shit." He looked away from his plate. "God damn, I think about it, I lose my appetite, you know?"

I nodded. I knew very well. "Was that the last?"

"The last one we know of. That was three days ago. I reported it to the sheriff of course, but there really wasn't much he could do about it. Then I heard about other ranches that had the same problem. Sam Watson, Ben and Mary Bolling, even at Dan VanBeek's dairy farm... At least twenty cows and horses killed, exactly the same way—sliced up, guts spread out, left to rot. Hell." There was a different expression in his eyes now. Frank Magruder was afraid.

"No idea who did it?"

He shook his head. "Not really. Some say it was kids from the high school, some others think it was some drifter or something... Damn, Alex, if they're from here, who the hell could it be? And if they're outsiders, where the hell are they coming from, and where are they staying?"

"That's what I hope to help find out."

He looked down at the floor. The carpeting was a pleasant blue-green pattern, like waves at sea. "And that's not the worst thing, Alex. Not really."

I frowned. "What do you mean?"

Frank reached into his pocket and pulled out his cell phone. "I didn't tell anyone this, Alex. Not the sheriff, not Sam Watson. Nobody. I'm only telling you this because I think we need help, and no one else seems to be able to give it." He slid his fingers across the glass surface. "I took some pictures of the slaughtered cow at my place—the one we found fresh. Look here."

He handed me the phone and I squinted at the display.

It showed the tan flank of a fallen cow. The animal had been mutilated just as Frank had described—legs lopped off, throat and belly slit, entrails dragged out messily. But there was something else...

"You mean here, on the hide?" I asked.

Frank nodded.

I looked more closely. The image was fuzzy, but I could see them. There, finely cut, almost like handwriting, were a series of intricate lines and curves that seemed to form a consistent pattern. Almost like...

"Letters?" I stroked my chin. "You think these are letters?"

"Not any letters I recognize. Something foreign." He grunted. He looked like his old self again, steely and self-assured. "Some damned little teenager who watched too many *Saw* movies or something." With a suddenly renewed appetite he took an enthusiastic bite of his burger and spoke with his mouth full and a little more bravado than was necessary. "We'll find the little bastard, don't worry. And we'll string him up by his balls."

I forced a smile. "And make his parents pay for all the cattle?"

"Damn straight." Frank fumbled in his pocket. "Damn, I need a cigarette. But of course I can't smoke indoors, can I? Gotta make sure I don't pollute some liberal's sensitive lungs." He laughed. "Maybe I should just light up a joint, huh? Then no one from Portland'll care."

I let him talk. Everyone deals with fear in a different way.

"Mind if I send this picture to my number?" I asked. "I want to take a closer look at these cuts."

"Oh, sure. Have fun with it." The burger had disappeared in a matter of seconds, along with the rest of Frank's second Coke. Now he attacked his fries. "We're having a city council meeting about all this tonight at eight. You might want to cover that for your story."

"I plan on it." I waved at the waitress. "I think we're ready."

"Well, thanks for lunch." Frank looked a lot more relaxed than he had when I'd met him. "I appreciate what you're doing here, Alex."

I shook his hand. "I hope I can help, Frank."

The afternoon air was hot and dry as I watched Frank drive off in his massive white Chevy club cab pickup, a cigarette dangling from his lips. Sure enough, there was a shotgun mounted on the rack, visible through the rear window. I stood beside Yngwie, my '68 Camaro, taking in my surroundings and wondering what the hell to do next.

When most people think of Oregon they imagine snow-capped mountains smiling down on dense green forests, rivers and beaches, cities crammed with artistic types and flannel-clad guys who drink PBR. Well, that's true enough as far as it goes, but the entire eastern half of the state is a different animal altogether.

This was cattle country with grassy fields and craggy volcanic hills. The sky overhead was searing blue with only a few scraps of cloud, and a sun that beat down mercilessly. It was only June and the temperature was in the 90s.

The Shari's stood atop a low rise outside the town of Hayes, a cluster of old buildings surrounded by dark rock and a sea of sagebrush and cheatgrass, sprinkled here and there with stunted juniper trees. The weathered slopes of the Sheepshead Mountains rose in the west, the Bowden Hills to the south. Highway 78 passed nearby, and if I drove northwest on it for a few hours I'd be back in the world of shaggy trees and bearded chai-drinkers. But for now I was in Hayes, Oregon, staying with my editor Loren and his dog Beowulf at the local motel, trying to make sense of some very strange and seemingly insane events.

The truth was that I had every intention of writing a sympathetic article for *the Ranger*. It was all part of our new policy of occasionally attempting to do real journalism—slipping the odd serious piece in between cynical reviews of local bands no one had ever heard of and ads for strip bars. Ever since the Christmas Storm and its attendant devastation we'd been doing a reasonably good job of it.

Yeah, I was planning on being a serious journalist. But I had ulterior motives I wasn't willing to discuss with people like Frank.

The heat finally forced me to climb into my car, only to find its black interior to be about twice as hot. Wincing at the molten upholstery I started the engine and immediately cranked up the AC. It made Yngwie's gas mileage even worse than normal, but at this point I didn't care. Eastern Oregon has its charms, but the weather isn't one of them.

I called Loren as I drove down toward Hayes then turned the radio on, flipping past country-western and right-wing talk stations until at last giving up and slapping in a Finntroll CD. I find folk metal to be singularly relaxing, which probably makes me weird, but I'm used to that by now.

It was well past three by the time I rolled into town and the mercury was probably touching 98. Every building sported a bulky AC unit, including the old city hall where I stopped the car and got out.

Beowulf was sitting in the shade beside the steps, an empty water dish at his feet, his leash attached to the guardrail. He was a big dog, his ancestry located somewhere between lab and mastiff, with a jowly face and a stumpy tail. He was all black, and most people would have found him threatening, at least until they discovered what a massive marshmallow he is. He looked up at me as I approached, panting, drool trailing from his floppy lips.

I patted his head. "Abandoned by your master, huh? Don't worry, I'll take care of you."

"Hands off my dog, mister." Loren Hodges stepped briskly down the steps toward me, a bundle of printouts under his arm. He was tall and lanky, his hair slightly unkempt, his chin graced by a dark soul patch. He wore a t-shirt that said *$DO || ! $DO ; try try: command not found.*

"I should report you," I said. "Leaving your dog out here all alone."

"God, Alex." He seemed utterly unaffected by the heat as he untied Beowulf's leash from the railing. "This dog faced down the legions of hell for you, and you have a problem with me leaving him outside for an hour? Priorities, man. Priorities."

I nodded toward the papers he carried. "Find anything?"

"Some." Beowulf bounded toward my car and we followed. "There's some sick shit going down around here, Alex. They're having some kind of town meeting about it tonight."

"Yeah, Frank told me. Tough old bastard." I looked at my watch. I'd been careful to set it ahead—alone in Oregon, Malheur County was on Mountain Standard Time, not Pacific. I had no idea why. "Tonight at eight. I want to be there."

Loren chuckled grimly as I opened the car door and let Beowulf jump inside. "Yeah, me too. I guess they've got some kind of expert in occult crimes showing up."

I had a sinking feeling in my chest as I situated myself behind the wheel and started Yngwie's engine. "God damn. This I've got to see."

Our motel was on the edge of town, conveniently located along I-78, and it was probably as much of Hayes as most visitors ever saw. As Loren let Beowulf into our room I popped the trunk and pulled out my laptop bag, a heavy black duffel and an oversized gun case.

"You really think you'll need that thing?" Loren nodded at the gun case as I dropped my burdens on the floor. Beowulf dutifully jumped up onto Loren's bed and curled up, apparently exhausted.

I shrugged and unlocked the case. "It can't hurt. I'm not wild about leaving it behind while we're gallivanting about Malheur County anyway."

There were indeed guns in the gun case—two Glock 17 semiautomatic pistols and a reserve of ammunition, neatly tucked into foam cut-outs. In the middle, however, was my most prized possession.

My sword. Over four feet long, crafted of a glassy bluish material, with an elongated diamond shape for a blade and almost organic-looking spikes near the hilt. Even though it had been forged a long time ago for someone who looked nothing like me, its grip had molded itself to my hand so that it fit like a glove. I'd first touched it on a rainy night two and a half years earlier. A goddess had given it to me. She had called me Shepherd.

This sword could slay demons.

It was inert now, dark and shiny, its silver-blue inner light extinguished. I hoped it would stay that way, and that the bloody deaths of Frank Magruder's cattle would turn out to be a sick prank or the work of a demented high school kid who listened to too much Burzum or Celtic Frost. I closed the case.

Unfortunately, as Loren spread out a county survey map on the bed and I connected my laptop to the motel's pathetic free wireless, I was beginning to doubt it was as simple as a black metal-obsessed teenager.

"Magruder said there were twenty incidents," I said, opening my email and downloading the photos that I'd sent from his phone. "Several different ranches. Did you find that many?"

"I only found twelve." Loren read from a small notepad. "Maybe they didn't all report them."

"Maybe not. All the same?"

"Yeah, pretty much. Sick shit—cows cut up, guts spread all over the place. Some horses too. Usually worked over by birds and coyotes."

"Magruder said that the first calf was found near Pinetree Bluff. Where is that?"

Loren scanned the map and after a moment pointed. "Here." He uncapped a black Sharpie and made an X. "Where were the others?"

"There were two others, but he only told me about one. Along an access road near Penny Creek." I ran my finger over the map, looking at river names. I found a dotted blue line— *Penny Creek (seasonal)*. "Here."

"Right." Loren drew another X then looked back at his notepad. "They didn't all report exact locations. I've only got six more, and those are approximate." He frowned. "Hey, check this out. They're all west of town."

I smoothed out the map. The paper crinkled. "Interesting. Go ahead and mark them."

A few minutes later the map was decorated with eight black X's.

Loren sighed. His expression was one of weary resignation. "Shit. I knew it. I guess the sheriff never bothered actually mapping out where all this went down, huh?"

I didn't say anything. My hopes for a mundane explanation were fading fast.

The X's formed a rough circle ten miles across, centered about twenty miles west of Hayes. Since most of the locations were guesses, it wasn't a terribly neat circle, but it was there, plain as day.

"Damnation," I said under my breath. "What's in the middle?"

"Bumfuck, Nowhere, that's what's in the middle." Loren leaned into the map. "Well, there's something called Hauser Butte. Nothing else is even marked."

"I wager if we map out all of the cattle killings they'll all be the same distance from Hauser Butte."

Loren went over to his bed and threw himself down beside Beowulf. "No roads out there, either. I suppose you're planning on visiting?"

"Damn right." I started folding up the map. "Yngwie isn't up for cross country though. We'll have to rent a jeep or something."

"Yeah, well good luck with that. When I showed up at the town hall, they looked at me like I was with the Taliban. What makes you think they'll rent us a jeep?"

I closed the gun case, then stretched out on my bed. "We'll burn that bridge when we get to it." I reached for the remote. "Want to see what they've got on Pay-per-View?"

Beowulf abruptly sat up, whining and looking anxiously from me to the blank TV screen.

"Oh crap," Loren muttered. "We're missing *Ghost Stalkers*."

"God." I turned on the set and began searching through channels. "Can't your dog watch some other shitty reality show?"

Beowulf cast me a hurt glance.

"Sorry," I mumbled, finally locating the right channel. "Here's your damned show."

The Hayes town hall was lit up and surrounded by milling groups of locals as we parked nearby. We left Beowulf curled up on Yngwie's back seat with a bowl of water and joined the assembled citizenry in the gathering dusk. The heat was already beginning to lessen but still hung over us like an oppressive fog as the eastern sky faded from yellow to orange to red.

I spotted Frank Magruder, as serious as ever, smoking and chatting with a couple of friends and waved. To my surprise he favored me with a smile and waved back, excusing himself and walking towards us.

I shook his hand. "Good to see you again, Frank. This is my editor and photographer, Loren Hodges."

Loren smiled politely and accepted Frank's bone-crushing handshake. I'd insisted he wear a button-down shirt and leave the smartass tees at the hotel. *The Ranger's* best digital SLR camera hung casually around his neck.

"You should sit with me," Frank said as we mounted the steps. "I can at least tell you who's who."

"Good idea." I scanned the crowd. There was nothing especially unusual to see—men and women in jeans and plain shirts, some sporting caps with farm equipment logos, all looking stern, single-minded or worried. "Can you do me a favor?"

"Sure."

"Let me know if there's anyone here you don't recognize."

"You mean besides you two?"

"Yes, Frank. Besides us two."

He threw me a lopsided grin. I didn't mind—I consider sarcasm to be a neglected art form.

"Loren, if he spots anyone, try to get their picture."

Loren held the camera lightly. "Right, boss."

We settled down in the council chamber. It was standing room only and we got the last three unoccupied seats. The people around us seemed to defer to Frank, and when he sat down no one was inclined to dispute him.

"That's Chet Graham, the mayor," Frank whispered, gesturing toward the front of the room. "Used to run the dry goods store before the Walmart opened up in Burns Junction. Good man, but kinda slow, if you get my meaning."

It wasn't quite as imposing or pretentious as the city council rooms in other cities, nor did it really need to be. The mayor, a rotund man in a checked shirt, was seated behind a desk at the far end, flanked on either side by two councilmen. A slender Hispanic woman in a sheriff's uniform sat nearby. Beside her was a serious-looking man wearing a dark suit. There was a data projector on a table, attached to a laptop computer. As the room fell quiet, the mayor began to speak.

"I'd like to thank you all for coming out here tonight." His voice was nervous and reedy as if he was unused to public speaking. "I think it's important that we discuss what's been going on around here and get a handle on things before too many wild rumors start spreading. I've asked a couple of our fellow citizens to share their experiences, and then Sheriff Enriquez and her guest Dr. Forrester will answer your questions about cult crimes and Satanic activities."

Beside me, Loren sighed quietly and rubbed his forehead.

"Easy does it," I whispered. "Be professional."

Loren already looked disgusted, but shook it off and began to take pictures.

A couple of ranchers stood up before the council and told their stories, both similar to Frank's tale—they'd found cattle and horses slaughtered and mutilated, apparently by human hands, but never saw anyone actually committing the crimes. I made notes when they mentioned locations.

Beside me, Frank was busy searching faces in the room. He did so casually, his gaze never resting on anyone too long, his expression never changing. As one of the ranchers—Frank's friend, Sam Watson, soft-spoken, middle-aged and balding—described his own experiences, Frank pulled gently on my sleeve.

"Don't look." His murmur was almost inaudible. "Back wall, near the door. Tall man in a gray shirt, black hat. It's Jack Rafferty. Lives out on Goldfinch Road, never comes into town. Got a bad reputation. Don't even know what the hell he does for a living. I didn't expect to see him here."

I nodded and leaned over to whisper to Loren. "Get a panorama of the room. Make sure you include the back wall, near the door. Be casual."

Wordlessly Loren complied, quietly shooting. A few in the audience looked confused or annoyed, but Loren continued undaunted. Hayes wasn't the big city, and they probably didn't have to deal with news photographers in city hall very often.

"There's a kid standing next to him," Frank continued. "Never seen him before. Little bastard with a weird haircut. Doesn't look like anyone from around here."

I leaned back toward Loren. "Show me the camera when you're done."

Sam Watson sat down to a scattering of applause, and a short woman with graying hair stood and began to speak. Her name was Mary Bolling—she and her husband had lost four head of cattle, all mutilated the same way.

Loren finished shooting and handed me the camera. I scrolled backwards through pictures of the crowd until I found an image of the back of the room. I zoomed in on two figures and nudged Frank.

"Is this them?"

He nodded and I looked closer at the enlarged portrait. Jack Rafferty was an emaciated man with sunken cheeks. His clothes were worn, his dirty black hat pulled low over sharp, deep-set eyes. Like everyone else, he was staring intently at the front of the room where Mary Bolling was still speaking.

His companion seemed a little less absorbed in affairs. His hair was obviously dyed black and cut at a 45 degree angle across his forehead. His complexion was pale and unhealthy, and he wore a flannel shirt over a black t-shirt bearing the elaborate and unreadable logo of some band I couldn't identify. He had an earring, and I suspected that if he opened his mouth I'd see that his tongue was pierced. There was a wary look about him, and in the photos Loren had shot, his eyes were darting to and fro as if he, too, were scanning the room, looking for suspicious faces. I hoped that Loren's photography had looked sufficiently casual. As it was, I was able to memorize his features without actually staring. Thank God for digital technology.

Mary Bolling finished speaking and returned to her seat. There was no applause, only concerned silence as she sat down and Chet Graham introduced Sheriff Enriquez. She looked very sharp and professional in her gray and green uniform, a .38 revolver on one hip.

The sheriff stood to scattered applause, then waited for silence, inspecting the crowd thoughtfully.

"Now I know a lot of you are worried about what we just heard here tonight," she said. In contrast to the mayor's nervous voice, her tone was warm and reassuring. "I'm here to tell you that we're doing everything we can to find the people responsible and make sure they never do it again." That got a round of applause. A number of people began to smile, looking less tense and concerned. Enriquez indicated the severe-looking man sitting beside her, who smiled and nodded. "Doctor Mark Forrester is an expert in occult crimes and has generously offered his extensive resources to aid in our investigation. Doctor Forrester?"

There was more clapping. The tension in the room seemed to drain, as if now that an authority figure and a competent-looking man in a suit were involved, the case was as good as solved.

"Thank you, Sheriff." Forrester wore wire-rimmed glasses and didn't seem to have a hair out of place. "And thank you,

Hayes, Oregon. I really love this part of the country, and it's a real pleasure to get out here again, especially when I can give back something for all the good times I've had in the Pacific Northwest."

I resisted the urge to roll my eyes, but Forrester's audience was eating it up. All around me the townspeople were watching him with rapt, reverent attention.

Forester went on, stepping over to a data projector and switching on the laptop. "Lights, please?"

A deputy dimmed the lights and a screen lit up with a PowerPoint slide that read "Satanic and Cult Crimes."

"It's clear to me that Hayes is dealing with a series of ritualistic Satanic crimes. The characteristics of these incidents are unmistakable. As I have shared with Sheriff Enriquez, the threat of Satanic crimes is a very real and present danger, and many communities have been its victim. Though they reached their height in the 1980s, the entire country has been experiencing a resurgence in cult crimes over the past several years."

He changed the slide to a new one that said "Cult Membership" and went on. "First, we have to understand the environment in which ritualistic Satanic sacrifices take place. Law enforcement officials across the country are aware of a growing underground network of Satanic cults with memberships in the thousands. We believe that these cults did not disappear, as many had hoped, but simply went underground, waiting for public vigilance to lessen."

That got a gasp from the audience and an angry grunt from Loren. Beside me, Frank looked skeptical but didn't make a sound.

"How do people join these cults?" Forrester's delivery was tight and concise. He reminded me of my old friend Damien when he was making a particularly important point. "There are a number of ways. Some were born into the cult and indoctrinated by parents through systematic sexual abuse. Some women—so-called *breeders* are forced to give birth to infants exclusively for human sacrifice. Others are recruited with offers of rewards, or through occult activities. One of the most lucrative avenues of recruitment is among adolescents. Naturally rebellious and curious, teenagers are natural victims for Satanic predators, who use almost any means of getting a young person's attention—drugs, sex, heavy metal music, pagan religions, and seemingly-innocent games like *Dungeons and Dragons.*"

Beside me I felt Loren stiffen as if he were seriously weighing the consequences of striding up to the front of the room and punching Forrester's lights out. I put a hand on his shoulder.

"Occult crimes expert my ass," he muttered just loudly enough for me to hear him. "Fucking asshat."

By now Forrester had moved on to a slide that listed the "Warning Signs" of Satanic involvement.

"We're almost entirely certain that these cattle mutilations are the work of young converts, working at the behest of a larger network." His expression was grim but determined, dramatically illuminated by the light from the projector. "It's important that the parents of Hayes watch their children for signs of cult involvement." He began to check off bullet points. "Isolation. Lack of communication with parents. Rejection of favorite activities and friends. Abrupt changes in behavior—listening to heavy metal bands like Kiss, Motley Crüe, and Black Sabbath."

I silently facepalmed, and Loren seemed ready to explode. Frank was sat, arms tightly folded, looking as if he'd just bitten into a raw onion as Forrester's tirade continued.

"Also, look out for involvement in so-called alternative religions such as Wicca, Witchcraft, Buddhism, and Islam. Such things are sometimes just signs of normal adolescent rebelliousness, but Satanists are always ready to exploit such feelings to their advantage. Interest in so-called role-playing games. Interest in violent or satanic movies. Wearing punk or goth clothing and jewelry..."

Now *I* was ready to go clobber the moron. Tales of Satanic conspiracy were decades old, and Dr. Forrester's lecture would have been right at home in 1985, along with all the bands that he'd named. I wondered how someone like this could continue to make a living in the digital age, but nothing really surprised me anymore.

As Forrester moved on to a discussion on satanic cult graffiti, explaining that the peace symbol was actually anti-Christian because it used a broken and inverted cross, I risked a glance around the room. Our two friends were still there, but the young outsider's face bore the faintest trace of a smirk, in obvious contrast to the worried expressions of those around him.

I whispered to Loren. "This guy's an idiot. We can go at the break if you want."

Loren was too busy giving Forrester the stink-eye to reply. He was probably imagining tying Forrester in a chair and pelting him with 20-sided dice or something similarly sadistic.

When I turned to Frank, he nodded his head toward the front of the room and rolled his eyes.

"What'll you bet Chet's paying that egghead five hundred a day?"

It wouldn't have surprised me.

Apparently we were the only ones who felt skeptical about the eminent doctor (doctor of what, I wondered?). Everyone else seemed to hang on his every word, and by the time he cited statistics of 1,000 to 3,000 ritualistic satanic murders a year, a horrified murmur passed through the crowd. Satan had come to Hayes, Oregon, and here was the man who would help drive him out. I wondered desperately when we'd finally get a break and be able to leave this nonsense parade behind.

As Forrester droned on, I saw Enriquez reach into her pocket and pull out a cell phone—it was apparently on vibrate, for she began to talk on it quietly, a look of concern growing in her eyes. She turned and whispered urgently to the mayor.

Forrester hesitated, and blessed silence filled the room for a long moment before Enriquez gestured at one of his deputies. The lights came back, temporarily blinding all of us who had been sitting in the dark. A confused tumult followed, which Enriquez only partially stilled with a raised hand.

"Quiet, folks. Quiet please. I'm sorry, but something has come up and we'll have to end this meeting early. Thanks for coming, and we'll explain fully later. Good night everyone!"

With that abrupt and unexplained conclusion the crowd dissolved into a disorderly throng, half making their way to the exits, half standing there wondering what had just happened. Sheriff Enriquez was in discussion with Mayor Graham and the council members who responded with looks of shock and confusion.

I took the opportunity to rise and look toward the back of the room. Neither Rafferty nor his young friend looked especially concerned but were instead waiting for the crowd to thin enough to let them out. As I watched, Rafferty leaned over and spoke into the younger man's ear.

I'd gotten better at reading lips since my adventures began—maybe I was more aware, or maybe it was one of the little enhancements to basic performance that I'd gained since taking up the sword. No matter—I saw what Rafferty said.

He said, "Go get the truck."

Many times I'd thought about moments like this—a looming crisis, the need to act swiftly, coupled with about eighteen different things I had to do. This moment called for firm, decisive action, cold and deliberate.

Unfortunately I had no idea what to do, and wasted long precious seconds thinking about it. What I came up with resembled a plan about as much as a kindergartener's portrait of his teacher resembles the Mona Lisa, but it was the best I could do.

I listened, opening my ears to the ocean of voices around me. At first it was nothing but random noise, but after a moment I began to here individual snatches of conversation.

"...Claire Doyle is missing..." "...supposed to be staying with Laura Murphy..." "...Never showed up..." "The Murphy's didn't know she was coming over..." "She must have disappeared this afternoon..." "They didn't report it until after seven." "Jesus. Someone must have grabbed her out on Bellweather Road..." "Oh my God." "Do you think it was the Satanists?"

I'd heard enough. Frank was still standing, looking at the chaos around him. I put a hand on his shoulder and spoke as calmly as I could manage. "You hear?"

His grim gaze met mine. "About Claire Doyle? Yeah, I sure as hell did. It's those two, isn't it? Rafferty and that kid. Everyone else in the room, they all looked worried, or wondered what was happening." He cast a glance backward. Rafferty and his friend were just heading out the door. "All except those two. It was like..."

"Like they already knew what had happened?"

"Yup. Sure as hell." There was the faintest suggestion of unsteadiness in Frank's gray eyes. "Shit, Alex. I know Claire Doyle. She's only ten, for God's sake." Then the steadiness returned. "What do you need, Alex?"

"Go out and get your truck started. We need to follow Rafferty and emo-boy out of town. You know what Rafferty's truck looks like?"

"Sure. Piece of crap '88 Ford Ranger. Dogshit brown."

"Keep an eye out for them. I'll be out as quick as I can manage. Can we take our dog?"

That threw Frank for a momentary loop. "Dog?"

"Yes, dog. Can we take him?"

"I guess."

I nodded. "Thanks. I'll meet you outside."

Without another word, Frank made his way through the crowd. Rafferty and the kid were just heading down the steps.

I turned to Loren. "Come on. We need to get Beowulf. The gun case and duffel are in the trunk."

"Right, boss." Now Loren plunged into the crowd and I followed. There was no hesitation—we'd saved each other's lives enough that we trusted each other implicitly.

It was dark outside and the street was full of locals. Some were getting into cars and driving away. Traffic jams were probably a rarity here in Hayes, but they were on the verge of one now.

We stopped briefly to get our gear out of Yngwie's trunk, then headed toward Frank's big white truck, Loren leading Beowulf on his leash, me carrying my gun case and the black canvas duffel.

"Hurry up," Frank urged, waving me on. The engine was idling noisily. "They just drove past. Let's go."

Loren and Beowulf clambered into the club cab. I slid the case and duffel after them.

Frank looked at the case. "We going hunting?"

"Maybe. I hope not." I jumped into the front seat, slamming the door just as Frank pulled out into traffic, cutting in front of another car, drawing a chorus of shouts and honks.

"Screw you," Frank said, mostly to himself. "We got work to do."

* * *

The lights of Hayes vanished behind us. The air outside was turning cold and a crescent moon had risen as Frank guided his truck down I-78. A dozen or so vehicles had been ahead of us when we'd left town; one by one they had turned off into driveways and dirt roads, and now only three remained. Frank gripped the wheel tightly, his gaze fixed on one of those three, the tail lights of Jack Rafferty's rusty Ford Ranger.

Overhead the stars shone down, far brighter than anything I'd ever seen in light-polluted Portland. The Milky Way stretched from horizon to horizon, a backdrop to the parade of summer constellations. It would have been beautiful if not for the lurking dread that I felt and the grim urgency that drove us on. I had the beginning of a headache but tried to ignore it.

"You see that asshole Forrester cozying up to the mayor?" Loren demanded. He sat with his feet on the gun case, one hand holding the duffel and the other on Beowulf's head. The dog was curled up beside him, looking up periodically to make sure he was okay. "Where did they dig up that dickweed? Jesus. The eighties called, man. They want their outrage back."

Frank's eyes didn't deviate from the road, but his voice was calm and measured. "God knows. Enriquez is a good woman, but she's got a huge corncob up her ass, and Chet's still just a jumped-up salesman. What the hell was that moron talking about? I used to listen to Motley Crüe back in the day. Never made a Satanist out of me. *Shout at the Devil*—now *there* was a record. Not like the crap they put out after they hit it big. You guys listen to any of that old folks' stuff, or do you just like that alternative shit?"

I chuckled. "Nope. I'm kind of a metal-head myself. I play bass. Loren and I jam occasionally."

"I got a pretty sweet Strat clone," Loren added. "And a Mesa Boogie half-stack."

"Well, well." Frank seemed to like that. "You learn something new every day. I had a band once. Long time ago. Me and Jimmy Rodriguez and Dave Barnes. Power trio. I played lead. Had a nice Epiphone Les Paul Standard. We called ourselves Knightmare. You know, with a 'K'? Then we found out there were about six other bands with the same name so we changed it to Frightmare. Stupid name, huh?"

"Well, it *was* the eighties."

"Yeah, it was." Frank sighed. It was the first time I'd seen him do anything like that. "We were gonna get out of this town—Me and Jimmy and Dave. Go live in the big city. Seattle. Portland. Hell, if things had gone different I might be in Hollywood right now, fat and rich, living in a mansion married to an ex-playmate like all those assholes in Crüe."

Even as emotion crept into his voice, Frank's focus on the road ahead and the tail lights of our quarry didn't waver. "But my dad needed me when Mom had her stroke. Then Paula got knocked up and I did the right thing by her. Got married, had a second kid. I stayed and took over the ranch and here I am. Paula walked out five years ago. Emily's grown up and married now; Corey's getting' ready to leave. Maybe he's the one who'll finally get to move to Seattle and be a rock star. I dunno."

There was a long pause. Neither Loren nor I could think of anything to say.

Frank shook his head sadly. "That song, *Shout at the Devil?* You remember. It wasn't about Satanism or devil-worship or any of that crap those idiots like Forrester think. It was just about fighting back against the things that stood in your way. The things that keep you from your dreams."

The tone of his voice didn't change—it was as if he was discussing the weather or feed prices. "When you're a kid, you really dream big, you know? But then you grow up and you see that the world doesn't work like that. And you have to take all those things you wanted to do, all the ways you were gonna change the world, put 'em in a box, and bury 'em. Bury 'em real deep and never look at 'em again. That's what it's like living out here. Lots of people with lots of dreams and nothing to show for it."

Frank finally broke the tension with a laugh. "What the hell are you two so quiet for? Like it's a funeral or something. We're not dead yet, are we?"

"No." I felt myself smile. "No, we're not."

"And it looks like you've managed to make life out here a little more interesting anyway." He laughed again. "I don't know what's getting into me tonight, sitting here moping and complaining about crap I can't change. Never mind. It's a good life, really."

I nodded and let it go. My headache was still threatening, like the black sky before a cloudburst. People seemed to act like that around me lately—spilling their guts and telling me their life stories. God only knew why—I didn't think I was any more trustworthy than the next guy, and I've never had the inclination to be a bartender or a therapist. I was just a journalist, and not an especially noteworthy one.

But I did have a few secrets.

Forrester was a fool—that was pretty clear. Yet there was a core of truth to what he was saying. There were indeed groups to fear out there—cults, fanatics, demon-worshippers, call them what you will. But they didn't recruit kids by running D&D games or making them listen to 80s hair metal.

I reflected that if Forrester had bothered to at least glance at the Internet he'd have learned that there were real-life Satanist bands out there, names he could rattle off without sounding like a throwback to the Reagan administration. Of course a lot of them were *Satanist* in name only, adopting the moniker to piss off their parents or parole officers, like Frank and his friends.

As for me, I was of the opinion that Satan didn't exist. Other things did, however—things that made Satan look like a grade school bully.

I looked out the window at the starlit landscape, Frank's momentary lapse into confessional mode still replaying in my mind. Sage and rabbitbrush stretched out into infinity, interrupted here and there by patches of fescue and Oregon sunshine. The Sheepshead Mountains rose in the west—featureless masses of black that obscured the stars. I wondered what was out there.

Frank had favored me by telling one of his secret truths. It was more than I deserved—I'd only told him part of my own truth. I was indeed visiting Hayes as a journalist representing Rosenblum Media, publishers of *the Ranger,* but I hadn't mentioned to anyone that I also wrote an irregular column about occult phenomena called "Eye on the Unknown." It had originally been the work of my friend Damien Smith, but he was gone now, a casualty of the very forces he'd sought to investigate, and I was left with the task, along with my other jobs as writer, editor, and part-time demon hunter.

Loren and I had been documenting weird events for over two years now and either we were starting to notice them more, or they were getting more frequent. Serial killings, unexplained disasters, cult activities (real ones, not the type that Forrester and his friends imagined), strange new religions... It was no surprise that people were starting to look over their shoulders, wondering whether the devil really *was* there, lurking in the shadows.

Unfortunately, people like Forrester were always there to exploit others' fears. Strange forces were indeed on the rise, but his facile explanations and willful ingenuousness only made it harder to tell true from false.

My thoughts, and the relative silence, were abruptly interrupted by a fearsome racket from outside. A pair of motorcycle engines buzzed like angry bees, rising abruptly in pitch as they roared past us, one on either side. Frank swore and I caught a glimpse of two massive motorcycles and their leather-clad riders—helmetless, long hair streaming behind them as they flashed by, then they were swallowed up by the darkness, invisible save for a pair of red tail lights, thundering down the road, past Rafferty, and rapidly dwindling into the distance.

"What the hell was that?" Loren leaned forward, thrusting his head between mine and Frank's. "They're driving like morons."

"Dumbasses," Frank muttered.

I didn't reply. The unexpected explosion of sound had made my headache burst fully into bloom. I leaned back, closing my eyes and suppressing the urge to ask Frank if we were there yet.

It didn't look good. My headaches were usually a warning that something very bad was about to happen.

We'd been driving for nearly a half hour—at least twenty miles from Hayes. The two bikes were gone now, along with all of the other vehicles. Only Rafferty's truck remained, a pair of tiny red pinpricks in the darkness.

"We're almost to Goldfinch Road," Frank warned. "If he's going home, he'll turn off about... Now."

As if on command, Rafferty's tail lights veered left and bounced away toward the mountains, periodically obscured by puffs of dust.

Frank slowed. "I can't follow him or he'll see my lights. What do you think we should do?"

"Pull over for a minute," I said. "We'll figure out something."

Gravel crunched beneath our wheels as Frank brought the truck to a halt beside a tottering wire fence. The mountains were closer now, rounded and wrinkled.

I got out, followed quickly by Loren and Beowulf, who immediately began an intense personal effort to irrigate the desert.

Loren watched as Rafferty's tail lights grew fainter and fainter.

"I sure as hell hope we know where they're going." He kicked gravel into the brush. "I don't want to lose 'em now."

"Me either." I followed his gaze. The lights finally vanished. They knew something. I was sure of it.

I looked back at Frank. He was leaning against his truck, smoking a cigarette. "That road go anywhere besides Rafferty's place?"

Frank shook his head and took a long drag. "Nope. Goes right through a gap in the hills and down into the desert. No side roads. No nothing. He's the only one dumb enough to live out here."

I mentally pictured where we were in relation to Hayes and had an idea. "Frank, is Hauser Butte anywhere nearby?"

"Matter of fact it is—about four miles across the desert from Rafferty's place, right on the Harney County line. Why you asking?"

"Just a hunch." I looked down Goldfinch Road. "How close can we get to Rafferty's place without being spotted?"

Frank finished his cig and ground it out with his boot. "The road starts to dip a couple hundred yards before we get there. We can stop the truck right before the dip and walk the rest of the way. Hope you're wearing boots."

"Hiking boots," I said. "Loren?"

"Just my Nikes. Sorry."

"Well watch out for snakes. They'll be all curled up for the night and won't like getting walked on."

Loren looked unhappy at that. "Thanks, Frank. Important safety tip, everyone."

Beowulf finished his business and trotted up to Frank to accept a neck scratch.

"Nice looking dog."

That was about as much of a compliment as Frank was willing to give, but Beowulf seemed to appreciate it, leaning against his leg and looking up at him happily. His expression was deceptive. I'd seen those same teeth—the same ones he now bared in a canine smile—rending demon flesh in defense of both me and Loren.

Goldfinch Road stretched out ahead of us, a ribbon of lighter gray in the gloom.

I pulled open the door of Frank's truck and stepped up onto the running board. "Let's get moving."

III

G oldfinch Road was rough, studded with potholes. The darkness was, if possible, even deeper here; only Frank's headlights lessened the gloom, illuminating the strip of gravel that plunged out into the scrublands. It got worse as we went; eventually we were bouncing around like clothes in a dryer.

I looked back at the gun rack where Frank's Remington 870 rested.

"You got shells for that thing?" I asked.

Frank nodded at the glove compartment. "Box of double-aught. Think we're going to need it?"

"Just being careful." We hit a pothole and lurched suddenly up and down. "I'm still afraid I'm dragging you out here for nothing, Frank."

Frank laughed again. "I've done dumber things in my life, Alex, believe me." He shot a look back at Loren. "How's your dog doing?"

"Better than me." Loren looked slightly green. "I think I'm getting motion sick."

"Hm." Frank spared only limited sympathy. "We'll be there in a couple of minutes."

He turned hard to avoid another hole and now we all lurched sideways. Loren groaned.

At length the road turned sharply and began to dip, granite walls rising on either side. Frank hit the brakes and we pulled to a halt amid swirling dust.

Frank set the parking brake. "Last stop. Everybody out."

The air was still and the lights of Hayes were invisible here. Only the gravel beneath our feet gave any indication of civilization at all. It smelled of dust and dry vegetation. Loren clambered unsteadily out and Beowulf followed.

Frank was a gray blob in the darkness beside me. A tiny orange coal indicated he was smoking again.

"It's black as Satan's asshole down there and it's full of ravines and gullies. We're gonna have to be careful or someone'll break an ankle."

I pulled out the duffel and the gun case.

"Don't worry. I think we're covered."

I unzipped the bag and rummaged for a moment, then pulled out an elaborate contraption with straps, clips, and what looked like a short pair of binoculars fixed to the front.

I handed it to Frank. "Here. Try this on."

He accepted and after a little fumbling managed to fit the harness over his head so that the binoculars were suspended in front of his eyes. I reached over and flipped a switch.

Frank took out his cigarette and whistled, blowing smoke.

"Very nice. I've been hunting with these things." He looked back and forth. The contraption looked ungainly and vaguely silly, but he didn't seem to mind. "You came prepared, Alex."

"I was never a Boy Scout," I admitted, "but I take their motto to heart. The goggles are detachable if you want to use them as binoculars." I pulled out a second pair and handed them to Loren.

"You didn't happen to bring three of these did you?" he asked, adjusting the lenses. "You know—one for Beowulf?"

I donned the third pair. It was the cheapest of the bunch, bought at one of those spy supply stores that sells parabolic mikes and phone bugging equipment. It didn't have the range of the other two, but I figured I'd take up the rear anyway. When I turned the goggles on the world lit up in garish neon green.

"I'm working on that," I said. "Trying to find Beowulf some of that doggie ballistic armor that the SEAL teams use, too. No luck so far. Just be thankful I brought this one as a spare."

Frank finished his cigarette. "You got a couple of machine guns in there, chief?"

"Afraid not." The bag did contain combat knives, flashlights, a first aid kit and GPS unit, all of which I distributed to the others. "Of course you haven't seen what's in my gun case yet."

Even behind the goggles it was obvious that Frank had misgivings when I opened the case.

"What the hell is that?" he demanded. "It looks like a goddamned sword."

I pulled it out and held it up in one hand. "It is a sword. Not a damned one, fortunately."

Frank's head swiveled, leveling his grotesque mask at me. "Look, Sinjun—I'm starting to have some misgivings about you and this whole thing. I was willing to go along with you, but now you're pulling out swords like Conan the Barbarian and acting like it's the most natural thing in the world..." He turned away. "God damn. You almost had me, Alex. Almost had me thinking you took this all seriously."

I slid the sword into its scabbard. I'd had it custom made from heavy leather. It strapped across my back with enough free play to allow me to move and draw the thing with relative ease.

I spoke as seriously as I could. "Call it an affectation, Frank. Like I told you this afternoon, this is not a joke to me." I reached into the case and pulled out one of my Glock 17s. "How's this, Frank? Is this serious enough for you? I've got two of these in here along with four full magazines. You've got a shotgun in the truck. And yeah, I have a sword and, believe me, if I didn't think we'd need it I wouldn't be wearing it. You think I don't know what a huge tool I look like with this thing strapped to my back?"

Frank spoke cautiously and I imagined that behind the goggles his eyes were narrowing with suspicion. "There's something here you're not telling me, St. John. I don't appreciate being left out of the loop."

"Frank, please listen to me. Loren and I have been doing this for years now. We're here because it's important to us, and because we're worried about what's happening here. Contrary to what you might think, we're not just idle hipsters from Portland screwing around with the country bumpkins."

Loren spoke up. "We thought it was just the bullshit with the cattle mutilations. Now... Hell. Now there's a kid missing. Those two assholes down that road might have something to do with it. If they don't, well we're not any worse off than we were before. If we can help find out who's responsible for all this, then who gives a rat's ass whether Alex wants to carry around a sword?"

Frank breathed a disgusted sigh. "Christ, you Portlanders. Drive me fucking nuts." He leaned into the cab and unracked his Remington. "Come on, guys. Lock 'n' load time." His goggles focused on me again. "I sure as hell hope you don't cut yourself with that thing."

* * *

We walked in silence. Sensing the seriousness of the situation, Beowulf stuck close by Loren, who walked carefully ahead of me, pistol holstered at his side. Frank led the way, cradling his shotgun—he'd filled his pockets with shells—and still puffed at a cigarette as we went. I kept checking my holster to make sure the Glock hadn't fallen out—it was silly I knew, but I was beginning to feel an old and familiar sense of uncertainty and fear as we walked lower and the ravine walls rose around us, lit up in an unnatural green.

Fortunately no one stepped on a snake. We'd walked for about ten minutes when Frank raised a hand, bringing us to a halt.

He gestured ahead and spoke softly. "Down there. Near the mouth of the ravine. It opens up onto the desert after that and Hauser Butte's a few miles farther along."

I knelt beside Frank and scanned the road ahead. Rafferty's place was a rambling sprawl of weathered wood that might once have been a pleasant ranch house. Now it was in disrepair, shingles missing, the porch caved in, a rusting truck carcass in the front yard. A few potted cacti lay scattered about, among scattered pieces of junk and debris.

"See his truck?" I whispered.

Frank shook his head. "Nope. Not there."

Loren swore. "Shit. They went someplace else."

"Not possible." Frank pointed. "There wasn't any place else to go. No place but the desert."

"And Hauser Butte."

"Yeah, and Hauser Butte."

"They may only have stopped long enough to pick up something," Loren said. "Like a kidnapped girl, maybe?"

"It's possible." The fear and uncertainty were still there, coiled in my stomach like the snakes that lay hidden all around us. "I want to see what's in there first." I thought for a moment. "You and Frank go get the truck, bring it down. Beowulf and I'll go in and check out the house."

"Alex, are you sure that's a good idea? Never split the party, remember?"

"No, as usual Loren, I'm not sure. But if they've kidnapped the little girl we've got to go after them, and I still want to check that house out. If you've got a better idea I'm all ears."

Loren shook his head. "No, I don't. Just checking." He turned back up the road. "Come on, Frank."

Frank hesitated, then followed. "Don't do anything stupid, Alex, you hear?"

"Just listen for gunshots." I gestured toward Beowulf who sat patiently beside me. "Come on, boy. Let's go see what's down there."

Beowulf looked uncertainly after Frank and Loren for an instant then was on his feet, trotting after me.

My head still throbbed faintly, and the garish green images from the night vision scope didn't help matters. A few yards from the house I flipped the goggles up and stared into the starlit shadows. It was a mosaic of gray now, weathered and prematurely ancient in the dry high desert air. I smelled old wood and gasoline.

I lowered the goggles and gazed beyond the house. The land flattened out, covered in brush. Somewhere out there was Hauser Butte. And, if my instincts were correct, Jack Rafferty and his little friend.

And maybe, just maybe, Claire Doyle was there too.

I stepped carefully toward the house. Beowulf crept silently after me, head low, feet moving slowly but methodically, as if he was stalking something.

The front door was locked, but I'd spent part of the last two years learning basic breaking and entering. I took a set of lockpicks from my pocket and a few moments later the door creaked open. I slipped inside, followed a few seconds later by Beowulf's dark and reassuring form. His head was down and his eyes were wary.

The smell hit me instantly—unwashed dishes, old grease, filthy bedding, and the stench of rotting meat, pungent and unmistakable.

I wasn't inclined to alert anyone that I was inside by turning on the lights, so I killed the goggles and switched on my flashlight.

The front room was a pigsty. A filthy old sofa sat behind a battered coffee table. A TV and DVD player occupied the opposite wall with a stack of adult DVDs beside it. I prodded it with my foot and the stack fell over. Bondage, rough sex, extreme fetish, and the like. I wasn't surprised.

The coffee table was strewn with junk—dirty cups and plates, old hot rod and gun magazines, and tissues soiled with things I didn't want to know about. Only one thing stood out on the table—a clean, glossy three-fold flyer emblazoned *Pilgrim Foundation.*

I shone my light on the flyer. *The Pilgrim Foundation,* it said, *dedicated to outreach and support for America's homeless youth.* I frowned, trying to puzzle out what a hermit like Rafferty wanted with such a thing. I reflected that it was probably junk mail that he hadn't bothered to throw away, but I pocketed the flyer anyway.

In the kitchen the source of the dirty dish aroma and the grease was pointedly obvious. So far, I'd found nothing but the home of an antisocial slob who liked porno and hated housework.

Beowulf whined. He was troubled and my head still hurt. There was still no source for the rotting smell, and it was even stronger here.

There was a single narrow door in the kitchen. Mentally I reviewed the layout of the house. This would be the garage.

Carefully I turned the doorknob and pressed on the door. It refused to open, as if something inside were holding it shut. I pushed harder and it gave slightly. More pressure and...

The door flew open and the stink of decay swept over us like a cloud. There was a light switch just inside the doorway. I turned it on and off several times with no effect. Then I flashed my light around inside the garage and instantly wished I hadn't.

The organs and missing heads hadn't all been taken by the coyotes. Some of them were here, in Jack Rafferty's garage. Horse and cow heads were nailed to the walls, staring at me with filmy eyes, tongues lolling, their flesh blackening and peeling back from withering muscles and white bone. Organs, legs, tails, eyes were laid out on the floor in an elaborate pattern. A horse's head and neck lay on the floor—that's what had held the door shut. On the walls someone had painted intricate characters in black and white paint, characters that looked like the ones carved into the hide of Frank Magruder's dead cow.

There was a long folding table near the garage door. It was covered in dried blood, fat, and fluids. Several sharp knives lay there, along with candlesticks, bloodstained books, and a stone mortar and pestle.

I stepped into the room, keeping a hand over my mouth, my gorge rising. I carefully stepped over the offal, feeling my soles sticking to the concrete floor. Beowulf had gone stiff and was growling ominously, but he advanced along with me, step by cautious step.

The table was even more repulsive up close. I prodded the pile of books with my flashlight, not wanting to touch any of them. They were too befouled for me to read titles or any details.

An alarming sensation jangled in my brain—one that I hadn't felt in years. My right hand moved almost of its own accord, without conscious thought, drawing the sword from its scabbard. The pressure in my head was almost unbearable, throbbing insistently. It was as if opening the garage door had tripped some kind of arcane switch or set off an alarm.

Beowulf snarled. There was a rattle from behind me. I whirled, shining the light into the middle of the garage.

God...

The cow and horse heads that had been nailed to the wall had come to life, jaws working, tongues curling, producing wet hissing sounds. On the floor, the disembodied limbs and organs were crawling like worms, writhing and flopping together into a messy pile in the center of the room. Beowulf's barks grew almost hysterical.

Panic reflex gripped me. Even though the sword was in my hand, pulsing faintly blue, its glassy alien surface matching itself to the contours of my grip, and the pistol was at my side, undrawn, I remained frozen for a long instant, both fascinated and horrified by the untidy heap of disembodied flesh as it pulled itself together and rose up in a tall putrefied column.

Beowulf moved first, driven by savage instinct, launching himself at the thing, ripping at it with his front paws and grabbing a huge chunk of dead flesh in his jaws. He pulled it loose but it disintegrated in his mouth, sliding away and rejoining the main mass.

"Beowulf, no!" I charged after him, sword whirling. A meaty club of flesh lashed out from the thing's body. I tried to duck but it slammed into my face with a wet, numbing thud. I stumbled and my sword blow glanced off, slicing a slimy chunk of fat. My goggles went spinning away, crashing to the floor somewhere behind the bloody table. Then a second blunt clubbed limb flailed at me, sending the flashlight flying. It shattered against the wall and we were plunged into darkness.

Beowulf was still with me. He moved with senses I didn't have, and I heard another ferocious series of snarls and the wet sound of tearing flesh. I threw myself toward the sound, stabbing high so I wouldn't hit Beowulf. I felt my point plunge into something soft and yielding. It didn't make a sound—it had no mouth, no vocal chords, probably no brain to speak of, but it recoiled and shuddered as the blade cut into it.

The sword was particularly potent against demons and things that didn't belong in this world, but despite the unnatural engine that drove this particular pile of stinking flesh, it was made up of mundane substances. All it could do was chop off pieces. In the dark I felt them squirm under my hand, wriggling back to join the main body. My most prized weapon was proving singularly ineffective.

Something about the sword enabled me to move faster, jump higher, and strike with greater strength—but here, in the restricted confines of Rafferty's garage, none of those things seemed of much use. I could hit the thing, and did, chopping off more chunks without apparent effect, but it didn't care. There was no room to maneuver, and in the darkness I had no idea where it was anyway. The sword's blade gleamed faintly silver-blue, but not strong enough to penetrate the inky dark.

I stumbled, feeling something wrap around my legs like a steel cable, yanking me upward, swinging me like a tetherball, throwing me against the wall with bone-jarring force. The breath was knocked out of me and I crashed to the ground, barely managing to keep hold of the sword. Beowulf's barks grew louder and more frantic, then I heard another crash and a pained yelp.

Rising to my knees, struggling to draw a breath, red flashes alternating with the pitch black of the garage, I fumbled at my side, unsnapping my holster, pulling the Glock free. I had no idea where I or the creature was, but at least I had another weapon. On a sudden impulse, I fired a shot into the air, momentarily lighting up the room like a flashbulb. I saw the thing there, frozen in the instant of illumination, a repulsive pile of veiny flesh. A loop of stringy tissue was wrapped around Beowulf's neck, lifting him off the ground as he struggled, jaws snapping.

I fired instinctively, shooting at the place where I'd seen the column of unclean gray and pink and black flesh and bone. A second flash lit up the garage, and I saw a messy wound erupt in the creature's midsection. It shuddered again and in the darkness I heard Beowulf barking from the other side of the garage—he'd managed to break free.

I fired again, but another vicious blow struck me as I squeezed the trigger. My arm went numb and my shot went wild. Another blow buffeted me from the other side, tearing the sword from my grasp, driving me to my knees, fumbling for my fallen weapons.

"Oh fuck! What is that thing? *Alex!*"

A blaze of light filled the room, a tiny yellow sun shining in the doorway. The horror loomed over me like a gruesome tidal wave, towering up, ready to crash down and crush me like an insect.

I heard a confused angry chorus of shouts and the explosive blast of a shotgun. A quivering convulsion passed through the thing and it collapsed, squirming across the floor, shedding pieces, slime cascading from a half a hundred pellet wounds. I dove aside as it fell, chunks of slimy flesh falling around me.

As I rolled across the bloody floor, my hand found the pistol. Then I was on my feet, my finger tightening, squeezing off shot after shot at the disintegrating bulk as it wobbled and crawled away from me. It was smaller now, falling apart, growing tinier and weaker.

Loren stood in the doorway, flashlight in hand. Frank was beside him, chambering a shell in his Remington and firing on the thing again, splattering more chunks of gore.

It was over now. Whatever had created this monstrosity—held it together, made it move and attack—was draining away, leaving only a messy pile of organs, skin, and bone, shuddering and twitching for long seconds before they finally lay still.

I stood, panting, head down and holstered my pistol. A fat lot of good it had done me. There was a lesson here, I knew—

don't become too dependent on your tools, don't get complacent, don't think that there's a weapon for every monster. It was a valuable lesson to be sure, but right now I wasn't really in the mood for lessons.

Frank strode forward, shotgun trained on the now-still collection of dead organs and limbs. His face was screwed up in distaste—the stench was getting to him, but his hold on the gun didn't waver.

"What the hell *was* that thing, Alex? What the *hell* have you gotten me into?"

My breathing had slowed, but I still felt ill, on the verge of vomiting. Loren hugged Beowulf, who looked shaken but all right.

I retrieved the sword, then stepped painfully over to the table and gathered up the blood-covered books. I'd touched some pretty vile stuff tonight—a little more wasn't going to hurt.

"Let's get out of here before I puke," I said. "I'll explain outside."

No one objected.

* * *

The air smelled of dirt and sagebrush—pure scents of the earth, unlike the rancid reek inside Rafferty's garage. Frank smoked while Loren stood quietly with Beowulf, trying to make sense of what had just happened.

I dropped the books into the truck then loaded my pistol with a fresh magazine. "To answer your question, Frank, what you just saw was some kind of necromantic construct. It was a trap. An alarm. Or a security system. I don't know. When I opened the door, I triggered something. It might be in one of those books, I don't know. Something made all those dead animal parts come together into what you saw. It tried to kill me and Beowulf. If you hadn't showed up when you did, it might have succeeded."

"What do you mean, necromantic?" In the glow of the flashlight I could see Frank's glare, angry as a thunderhead.

It was pretty obvious his patience had run out. "Like magic or something? What the hell is all this, Alex? Come clean with me right now, or so help me I'm getting in that truck and driving away, and I'm leaving you and your hippy friend and his damned dog here to deal with whatever is out there on your own. You hear me?"

"Hey, who you calling a hippy, redneck?" Loren sounded deeply annoyed.

We ignored him. "I hear, Frank. Loud and clear." I took a deep breath. "You're right. For lack of a better term, it's magic. Like this sword. Only the sword wasn't very effective since the thing was made out of the flesh of real animals. It works better against supernatural things like demons that are bound to another reality."

"Demons? Jesus, Alex, what kind of bullshit is this?" He threw down his cigarette, stomped it, and lit another. At this rate, he'd be through six packs before morning. "God damn it, Alex, I'm trying to quit, you know? Who can goddamn quit goddamned smoking with this kind of goddamned crap going on?"

"I know. I know how it sounds. Listen, I'll explain as best as I can. This universe... The reality we live in... It's only one of an infinite number of others. And some of those others are close by ours, like bubbles in a bubble bath. They adjoin each other, overlap, occupy the same space. It's... It's complicated."

"Don't treat me like a four year old Alex. I understand words with more than two syllables."

"Okay, okay. Well, sometimes those bubbles leak into each other. And in those other universes there are other... things. Things that want to get into this world. Alien things. Powerful alien... beings. Gods. Demons. Kind of like..." I faltered. "Like, well..."

"Like Cthulhu?"

I stopped and blinked. Something had just flown out of deep left field and hit me squarely between the eyes.

"Yeah!" Loren jumped on it like a starving man on a burger. "Yeah, just like Cthulhu. You read Lovecraft?"

"All the time. Love it." Frank snorted. "And you thought I was just another Eastern Oregon yokel."

"That," I reassured him, "is the last thing I'd ever think about you, Frank. You keep surprising me."

"The feeling's mutual."

"Frank, I don't know how else to put this, but Loren and I, we... We try to keep those things out. Try to keep the doors to those other realities closed. And we use things like this sword to do it. We keep a low profile, since people would think we were crazy, and well, I'm afraid that if too many people start believing in those doorways, more of them will start to open. We have to hold back the avalanche, Frank. Keep people safe. Hold the line."

Frank nodded. In the east the sky was growing gray. We'd been out here for hours and this time of year dawn came early. "All my life I've wondered if there was more to it than what I saw. More than just getting up every day and doing my job." He rubbed the back of his neck. "I guess there is. I guess I'm glad you showed up and proved it to me. What's that line from Shakespeare? More things in heaven and earth than are dreamt of in your philosophy?"

"Five hundred years later it still makes sense."

Now Frank looked up. Overhead the stars were beginning to fade.

"My father told me to stop playing, you know? That dumbass reverend at our church said it was all music of the devil and Dad believed him. Somebody told him that *Shout at the Devil* was originally called *Shout with the Devil*, but the record company made them change it. I told him what I told you—it wasn't about the devil, it was about standing up to the things that hold you back. Standing up for yourself. He didn't listen to me. Just to those fools in church. He made me sell my guitar. Sure, if the kids are listening to it, it's gotta be bad. We gotta stop 'em and make 'em do something 'constructive' with their lives. What bullshit. Like that moron Forrester. They just can't stand it, those people. Just can't stand it when someone else is happy, can they?"

I took another deep breath and let it out. "So you're still with us?"

Frank snapped out of his reverie in an eye blink and instead of replying shone his flashlight at the ground under our feet. There were tire tracks in the dirt. "They were parked here then they drove off that way. Towards Hauser Butte. You were right, Alex. They're up to something." He looked angry and this time it wasn't at me.

The eastern horizon was pale with approaching dawn. I felt a pang of hunger. I looked at my watch. To my surprise it was only a little past four. Then I remembered.

"Shit. I keep forgetting we're on Mountain Time. Sunrise in a half hour, Frank. There might still be time."

Frank turned on his heel and strode toward his truck. "Then what the hell are you doing letting me stand around and whine about my father? What are you, my goddamned shrink?" He yanked the passenger door open. "Get in. We've got a hell of a drive ahead of us."

Weary, tired, bruised, craving food and a soft bed, I complied. In the back seat Loren had recovered his usual sunny disposition. He scratched Beowulf's chest and Beowulf grinned as we lurched along the road, and out into the desert beyond.

"Was that fun, boy? Necromantic constructs? Who's a good dog, huh? Who's a good boy?"

IV

There was a driving urgency as the truck lurched and rattled across the rough desert floor. No one spoke but instead sat, tensely bracing ourselves for each jarring bump, staring in the growing light toward the rugged low massif ahead of us. We were approaching from the east; I hoped that if anyone was there they wouldn't see us in the light of the rising sun.

I had a pair of 10x50 military binoculars in the bag. I struggled to hold them steady as we advanced, trying to figure out the distance with the range-finding reticle. I wasn't having much luck.

"Stop for just a second, Frank. I need to get a fix."

Frank grunted and we ground to a halt. Fortunately we didn't kick up much dust—this was hardpack, rocky desert, interspersed with gray-green brush and a few bright purple and yellow wildflowers, brighter now as dawn approached.

I leaned out the window and focused on the butte. A labyrinth of weathered granite, scrub juniper, gray-white sky, a single crow flapping up from a roosting place...

Nothing... A curse rose to my lips when I saw Rafferty's truck, dogshit brown, parked along a shoulder of the butte, almost invisible against the rock and obscured with piles of brush.

"They're up there. Hammer down, Frank."

Frank complied wordlessly, jamming the truck into gear and surging forward, rock and brush crunching beneath us, engine roaring, springs protesting.

I glanced back at our passengers. Loren was still struggling with carsickness but looked determined nevertheless. Beowulf sensed our urgency and was tense, poised and ready to leap out the moment the door was open.

"Ready to roll, Alex. Ow!" Loren yipped as we slewed sideways and his arm smashed against the door handle.

My Glock was secure in its holster, safety on. I had fourteen rounds. I gripped the scabbarded sword tightly between my knees.

Hauser Butte loomed larger ahead of us. We were climbing now, almost to the rocky jumble at its foot.

"I see Rafferty's truck." Frank's voice was tight, almost angry.

I unsnapped the scabbard and wrapped my fingers around the sword's grip. "Stop right behind him then get out as quick as you can."

"Hang on." Behind us, Loren grabbed Beowulf and hugged him tightly.

We were slammed forward, straining against our harnesses, then as quickly slapped back into our seats.

"Out!" I shouted, kicking my door open, unfastening my harness, and jumping away, pulling the sword free in a single action.

I led us single file up a narrow trail that wound around the shoulder of the butte, emerging on the other side. Both caution and urgency drove us on. My headache was back, stronger now, more insistent, ominous. Around me the growing light seemed to pulsate in time with the throbbing inside my skull, getting stronger and more intense as the dazzling rays of the sun shone from the far horizon, back toward Rafferty's house and the horrors inside.

There were voices ahead, murmuring, chanting, call and response. A single voice soared over them, babbling something I couldn't quite understand, and a ragged chorus replied, mumbling the same words, echoing off the granite rocks and walls around us.

Words echoed in my head now, pounding on my brain along with the incessant pain—words spoken on a stormy day, years ago as I took the alien sword in hand. *Shepherd. Nomeus. You stand in the doorway with a candle, holding the darkness at bay. Save those you can. Avenge those you cannot.*

Would we be able to save someone today, or would we have to avenge her?

We emerged from the trail just as the sun cleared the horizon behind us. The slope below us stretched back toward the desert floor, open and relatively free of debris. There were two more vehicles parked there—a battered Toyota 4x4 and an open-topped Jeep.

There were people there too—I counted seven. They stood in a semicircle, their backs to us, dressed variously in ragged jeans and t-shirts. They looked young—three girls and four boys, and on the slope in front of them, lying in the dirt, filthy, motionless, bound and gagged with duct tape...

"*Claire!* Oh, Jesus!" It was Frank. As they turned in surprise, I saw a shirtless Jack Rafferty standing over the bound girl. He was covered in tattoos, obscured by the blood running down his emaciated chest. In his hands he held a great two-handed weapon that looked like a cross between a scimitar and an oversized cleaver. He had just hefted it over his head, but his face registered shock when he saw us.

We were frozen for almost an entire heartbeat. The kids—none of them older than 18—were tough-looking and grim-faced, with various tattoos and piercings visible, eyes far darker and wearier than anyone their age had cause to be, and among them—yes, it was the kid from the town meeting.

They had weapons—a random assortment of knives, pipes and improvised clubs, but they made no immediate move to attack. I forced myself to stay calm. They were human beings. Teenagers. God only knew why they were here, but I wasn't ready to cold-bloodedly cut them down.

"Easy, Frank," I said softly. "Let's see if we can get out of this in one piece."

Frank nodded, but kept his shotgun poised. Loren had drawn his pistol and knelt down in firing stance. Beowulf was standing beside him, legs splayed, glaring at the kids with ill-disguised hostility, but he limited his reaction to a low growl.

I looked from face to face, brandishing sword and pistol.

"Sorry to crash the party," I said, forcing myself to stay calm. My heart was racing, and I had to struggle to keep the tremor out of my voice. "I think one of your guests doesn't want to be here."

From behind the line of teenagers, Rafferty spoke. He still held his weapon aloft, poised for a decapitating blow on his captive.

"Go away! This is no business of yours! You don't know what you're dealing with, mister!"

"I think I do, Rafferty," I shot back. His eyes widened when I said his name. "We just met the burglar alarm at your house. It's not working anymore."

Rafferty's mouth opened and closed as he tried to think of a rejoinder. Then at last he mumbled something inaudible and cast his gaze several yards off to his left where a great granite boulder towered forty feet high.

Pain stabbed through my head again and I felt the sword vibrate slightly. The rock seemed to blur and shift, and in the center an oval patch of glowing light grew, a whirlpool of unpleasant greenish light, a color with which I was all too familiar.

"*Rift!*" I shouted, and Loren was on his feet, racing toward the kids and at Rafferty beyond them. "They're opening a—"

Too late. The portal yawned wide, unnatural light flaring, and something that I could barely perceive shifted inside it, vast and disturbing like a glass jar full of octopi or snails or dead fish. Long ropes of green-glowing energy whipped forth, spinning and flapping madly.

The kids broke formation, coming at us from all directions. Loren and Beowulf charged, making straight through the crowd

43

toward Rafferty. A boy stood directly in their path, wielding a baseball bat. Beowulf was on him before he could react, leaping up and crunching down on his forearm, rending flesh and breaking bone. The kid screamed and dropped the bat, then Loren was past him. Beowulf released him with a disdainful snort and loped along after.

So much for diplomacy.

Frank and I exchanged a quick glance, then raced down the slope after Loren.

Two of the whirling masses of alien force struck at us, hitting Loren heavily amidships, sending him flying. He fetched against a rock with a cry, losing his gun. Beowulf stopped short and turned, whining toward his master.

Another tendril aimed itself at me, but I felt a familiar warmth flowing through my arm as—glowing bright and silver-blue now, intense even in the morning sunlight—the sword moved to intercept it, slicing it into two pieces that instantly dissipated, vanishing like spider webs. The tendrils withdrew, repelled by the sword, keeping their distance.

Beside me Frank's shotgun went off and a boy fell, howling and clutching his bloody leg. Thankfully he'd had the presence of mind to simply wound him.

I stopped short when I saw Rafferty. He was on his knees, holding Claire's recumbent form, the big chopper at her throat. The remaining teenagers—two girls, two boys, and the town meeting kid, stood back a few paces, weapons at the ready. They were lean and dirty, as overtly hostile as a pack of starving dogs.

Drool ran down Rafferty's chin. His eyes were wide, pupils dilated. "Get out! Get the fuck out or she's dead. You can kill me if you want, but she'll be dead and it'll all be for nothing."

"You talk pretty big for a man with a shotgun pointed at him," Frank growled. "You touch her and I swear you're all dead, every one."

"If we leave, you'll kill her anyway." I felt my anger growing—that old need for vengeance, the most sterile and useless of acts, yet one which I was sworn to carry out. "I can't let you do it."

Rafferty's face twisted as he sneered at Frank. "You got no idea what you're fuckin' with, Magruder." He looked at me. "And I don't even know you, asshole. Think that sword's gonna help you? Fuck off." He looked back at the kids. "Take 'em. Use what I taught ya. I'll finish the invocation."

As one, the teenagers turned their gazes on me, faces stony, eyes growing wild. As I watched, my head throbbing, I saw what looked like an intricate tracery of fine fiery orange lines, extending from each kid to Rafferty, and into the nearby rift, where the energy-tendrils still waved and writhed.

Desperately, I tried to raise the sword. If I could sever those lines, perhaps I could break whatever connection bound them together. But a stabbing pain shot through me and I cried out, stumbling. The energy flowing from the sword shielded me from the worst of it, but the pressure was still nearly crippling.

Frank groaned and collapsed, still holding his shotgun. I felt a growing pressure in my chest, as if someone was reaching inside me, squeezing and prodding, searching for some vulnerability, some weakness. My heart pounded and my headache grew until I feared my brain would explode. I tried to breath, but something clamped down on my lungs, tightening like a vice.

"Jesus, Alex... What the hell..." Frank's voice was strangled as he writhed on the ground beside me.

I fell to my knees. Shit... The pressure was overwhelming the sword's protection. I tried to raise my Glock, but it seemed as heavy as an anvil, dragging my arm down, urging me to fall to the ground and surrender to the horrific pressure, letting it crush the life out of me...

A pistol went off near me and one of the girls fell, shrieking, clutching her arm. Then Beowulf charged, grabbing a boy by the leg and sending the rest fleeing.

"You okay, boss?" Loren asked. His head was bloody and he stood unsteadily, but he held his pistol firmly enough.

The pressure on my insides suddenly vanished and I was back on my feet as the remaining kids scattered, their concentration broken. The power in the sword flared anew, and I prepared to throw myself at Rafferty.

He still held the cleaver against Claire's throat, but he was staring at the rift, where the energy tentacles still writhed, growing firmer and more material every moment. His lips moved silently—he was chanting something to himself, something that was affecting the gate he'd created.

The kids were fleeing now. The girl Loren had shot leaned against the boy who'd taken a blast from Frank's shotgun and together they stumbled down the slope, away from us and toward the cars. The others ran in different directions. The glowing threads were fading, growing thinner and shorter until at last they vanished altogether.

"Rafferty!" I shouted, brandishing the sword, hoping to somehow interrupt him or screw up his invocation, even though it was probably the most dangerous thing I could have done. "Give it up!"

Then the emo kid was in my path, knife in hand, eyes angry. His fellow cultists had deserted him, but he was apparently made of sterner stuff. He stabbed at me and I leaned aside. Inside me I felt the compulsion to swing the sword and slice him in half, but I managed to ignore it, raising my Glock and shooting him in the shoulder as he swung the knife back. He fell, but made no sound.

Goddam it... I gathered myself to jump over the kid at Rafferty, but a new pain shot through me. The headache was back, blindingly strong, tearing through my synapses like a jagged piece of rusty metal. I stumbled again, fighting to hold onto pistol and sword. Something was pounding inside my skull, hammering, trying to crack it open and suck out the brains inside. Jesus...

"Holy shit!" Loren's voice cut through the pain. "What the fuck is that?"

The buzzing wasn't inside my head now. It was in my ears, and it was growing louder, resolving itself into the thunder of engines, throaty and powerful.

I looked up and had to shake my head to make sure I wasn't hallucinating.

A squadron of at least twenty huge motorcycles was roaring up the slope, chrome gleaming in the light of the rising sun. Mounted on the cycles were burly blonde men who looked like... Well, like Vikings in biker leathers, jeans, boots, and goggles. I realized that we'd seen two of them out on the highway just a few hours before.

They rode past the parked cars, wielding an assortment of weapons—clubs, swords, hammers. As I watched, one of them swooped down on the two wounded teenagers, swinging a heavy black chain that wrapped around the boy's neck, yanking him off his feet and nearly decapitating him. His body seemed to desiccate and fall apart in the instant it took to hit the ground, leaving only a few weathered bones and scraps of cloth.

The fleeing girl screamed and fell as the cycle shot past her. A second cycle was on her an instant later, cutting gory furrows through her flesh, leaving behind another rapidly-disintegrating corpse.

Then the riders were on the slope, pulling their machines to a halt and dismounting, charging the remaining kids, slashing and clubbing.

I could barely comprehend what I was seeing, and as my head jangled and pulsated with pain I saw them with a kind of double-vision, like when you take off the 3-D glasses at the movies. At one angle they were what they seemed to be—huge, muscular Nordic men sporting long blonde hair and beards, hacking and tearing into helpless teenagers with brutal but familiar weapons.

Superimposed on this scene, however, was another that faded in and out, blurring and sharpening as my headache waxed and waned. In this view the Vikings were tall creatures with bestial, snarling visages, their bodies covered in crimson scales, their clawed hands gripping cruel and exotic looking weapons, cutting the kids apart and drawing the energies from their bodies, leaving only twisted husks behind. The motorcycles, parked on the slope below, were squat four-legged beasts with powerful black bodies covered in plates of riveted metal, huge horned heads, and yellow burning eyes.

Beowulf was having a fit, roaring and foaming like a mad thing, but at the same time staying close by Loren, sheltering behind his legs. I'd never seen Beowulf like this before, but it was pretty obvious he was terrified.

I was still frozen and trying to make sense of what was happening as Rafferty stood, looking desperately left and right, watching the bikers tear his followers to pieces. He glared at me hatefully.

"You! You brought them here, you fucker! You've ruined everything!"

He raised his chopper above Claire's head. He was too far away for the sword, and my gun was forgotten at my side. I desperately moved to take a shot, but I knew it was too late. I'd hit him, but not before he'd cut Claire in half. Only an instant...

Frank's shotgun exploded and a huge chunk of Rafferty's shoulders and midsection vanished in a red spray. The cleaver fell clanging to the ground, followed an instant later by Rafferty's corpse.

"Fuck you," Frank muttered. "Never fuckin' liked you anyway."

Three of the biker/monsters approached the glowing rift and the thrashing tendrils. They raised their hands in unison and shouted a single word that seemed to echo from the rocky butte above us.

"Ljúka!"

The rift shrank and vanished, leaving behind an ordinary boulder. The waving appendages were cut off as if they'd been closed in a door and faded away into nothingness.

It wasn't over. The boy from the meeting lay on the ground between me and Rafferty, clutching his wounded shoulder, his eyes wide with terror. Two of the bikers advanced on him with steady, measured steps. He reached out to me beseechingly.

"Help me, mister! Please... I don't wanna..."

That's as far as he got. The first biker yanked him off the ground and the second cracked his skull with a ball peen hammer. In my strange double-vision the weapon was a massive warhammer, inscribed with leering demon faces. The kid convulsed, his form withering away into dust, his screams fading.

The two bikers turned and stared at me. Even in their human forms they were scary, with bodies like weightlifters and faces like rock musicians. They wore jeans, leather chaps, and black leather vests over bare, muscled chests. I blinked, and they became the grim scaly monsters I'd seen before. Another blink, and they were human again.

Frank and Loren stared, and Beowulf growled uncertainly.

"Get behind me," I said, then raised the sword defensively. It was shining brightly now, urging me to fight the new threat.

I met the creatures' gazes, looking first at one, then the other. "I don't know who you are, but I'm not a helpless kid you can kill without a fight. Keep back and leave my friends alone. We're here to get the girl and go home."

The hammer-armed biker stepped forward. His vest bore a number of insignia—a dragon, a snarling tiger, a howling wolf. Around his neck was a leather thong, and on the end was a medallion in the shape of a spiraled triskelion. He looked from the sword to me, then back again. Then his eyes widened slightly and he seemed to recognize me.

"*Hirdir,*" he said, his voice a bass rumble. "Shepherd."

To my overwhelming surprise he took a step back and bowed his head slightly.

"Our pardon, Shepherd. *Fridur.*"

Then he and his companion turned and made their way down the slope toward their parked mounts, along with the rest of the riders. On the back of each of their leather vests was an embroidered patch in the form of inverted angel's wings and the words *The Fallen.*

I stared as they mounted up, kicked their cycles to life, turned and rode away. My headache was vanishing now, but I still saw flashes of crimson-scaled demons mounted on burly clawed monstrosities, bounding across the desert, vanishing into the distance.

Loren and Frank stared. Beowulf heaved a relieved sigh and trotted over to Claire who still lay on the ground beside

Rafferty's corpse. His was the only body left—there was no evidence of his followers save a few pieces of weathered bone and the two vehicles parked below.

"Holy shit, Alex. What the fuck just happened?" Loren's voice cut through the morning silence like a knife.

Abruptly the spell was broken. I rushed over to kneel beside Claire, cutting her bonds with the sword and carefully peeling the duct tape from her mouth. She seemed as tiny as a wounded bird, her blonde hair dirty, her arms bruised, but her thin chest rose and fell regularly.

"She's alive," I said. "Unconscious. They must have drugged her."

Frank knelt beside me, holding Claire's hand, checking her pulse.

"So what do we do now, Alex?"

I thought for a moment. "I'll tell you what we do now. You pack up Claire and we'll throw what's left of Rafferty into his truck. We'll leave the truck and his body at his house and you get the girl to a hospital. My guess is she won't remember a thing, and if she does they'll put it down to hallucination from the drugs. You tell Sheriff Enriquez that you saw Rafferty and thought he was acting suspicious so you followed him out to his house and found him about to sacrifice her, along with all those dead animals and the evidence that he's the cattle mutilator. He threatened the girl and you shot him. Tell the sheriff that, Frank. Later on, come back here and run those cars into a ditch where no one'll ever find them. Don't mention us, don't talk about the kids, don't mention the bikers or any of that. You did it. You."

Frank looked puzzled. "What about those kids? Who were they? Don't we need to..."

"Yeah, we need to find out who they were and what they were up to. But without any bodies to show the sheriff I wouldn't advise you tell any stories about cults and gates and strange Viking bikers. That's not something Enriquez is equipped to handle. We'll look into that part. It's more important than you imagine, but we can't tell anyone about it, not yet."

He nodded, seeing the logic of my argument. "Okay. I'll keep my mouth shut. Then what?"

"Then Corey knows his dad's a hero and you got to shout at the devil, Frank."

He swallowed hard. If I didn't know better, I'd have thought there were tears in his eyes.

"Okay." He gently picked Claire up and we began to walk back toward the truck. I scabbarded my sword and retrieved Frank's Remington.

We walked a few more steps before he spoke again. "Alex, if you need anything, let me know. I'll do whatever I can to help you. I won't tell anyone what happened, but if you need a friend in this part of the country, keep me in mind."

I nodded. "Will do, Frank. Will do."

Loren's voice echoed from nearby. "Hey, Alex! Look at this!"

"We gotta go, Loren. Claire needs to go to a hospital."

"Only a second, Alex. You gotta see this!"

I sighed. "Excuse me, Frank. I'll join you at the truck."

I sprinted over to where Loren stood, beside the great boulder where Rafferty had opened the rift. My legs hurt and I had bruises on top of bruises.

Loren pointed at the rock face. "Check it out, dude."

I stared for a long moment. There was an image carved into the rock. It had been left centuries previously, sitting here unseen ever since—a rough human figure with huge eyes in the shape of twin spirals, staring out at the desert like a raccoon.

"She Who Watches," I muttered. "Our mysterious patron."

"This must be one of those thin places." Loren leaned closer, staring intently at the image. "They were going to open a rift and kill that little girl. Why?"

I shook my head. "I have no idea. I think *we* just opened a huge can of worms, though."

"You're probably right."

I whistled for Beowulf and he came running. I looked after Frank, disappearing into the rocks with his precious burden.

"Come on," I said. "Let's get the hell out of here."

Loren smiled wearily. Blood was drying on his face.

"You don't have to tell me twice."

As we trudged back I went over the incident in my mind. Those things, the seemingly human bikers—I'd seen their true selves, their crimson demonic bodies. They'd ruthlessly killed Rafferty's cultists and would have killed him if we hadn't done it first. Who were they? *The Fallen*... What did it mean?

But they didn't even try to kill me and my friends. They had uttered words in another language—*Ljúka, Fridur*. They'd recognized me, and I was willing to bet that the word they'd called me—*Hirdir*—meant "Shepherd." It was a name known only by a handful—the name that She Who Watches had given me, one that had been carried over the millennia by only a few select individuals.

They knew who I was and had begged my pardon.

Again, the question—who were the Fallen?

And who was Rafferty? What scheme had we interrupted? Who were those kids? What was in the books I'd taken from his house?

In short, what the hell was going on?

As fervently as I might wish otherwise, I had no idea.

PART TWO

TEMPUS FUGIT

One of the problems with being a part-time demon hunter is that unless you're independently wealthy you have to have a day job. Mine was being the editor of a disreputable weekly newspaper called *the Ranger,* and as soon as I returned home learning the secrets of Rafferty's cult and the identity of the Viking-demon bikers had to share priority with our "Great Portland Sex Survey" issue. So while I set my automated search engines loose seeking any information on Rafferty, his little buddies, and bikers called "The Fallen," I also had to sort through thousands of emails from our eager and somewhat perverse readers.

"So should this story about doing it with the whole rugby team after the game be on the ballot for Kinkiest Experience or Best Fantasy?" Consuela stood defiantly at my desk, brandishing a ten-page printout. "Since I'm pretty sure it never really happened, and I'm going to have to edit the hell out of it either way."

I sighed. "Use your discretion, but I'd say give our readers the benefit of the doubt. If someone says that they banged the entire team... Hey, why not? It could have happened."

Consuela shrugged. "I just don't think we should be in the business of publishing fiction."

"Connie, what do you call our letters page? We published one last week from a guy demanding that the CIA stop controlling his mind with chemtrails."

"You're the boss," she replied, turning on her heel. "At least 'til Terri gets back."

I rolled my eyes. "Tell me again why I put up with you?"

"Because no one else will do the work for what you're paying me, that's why."

Then she was back at her desk, furiously editing down the rugby team story for publication.

I reflected that it wasn't likely Terri would be back any time soon. Our publisher, president of Rosemblum media, was on an extended visit to deal with family crises in New York and had left me in charge. Besides making me feel like the XO on the *Titanic*, it hadn't changed my duties all that much, save for requiring a few more late nights every month.

Of course it made the whole Shepherd thing more complicated, but that part of my life mostly consisted of endless waiting punctuated by moments of terror and violence. I now lived in the big Woodstock house that had belonged to my late friend Damien Smith. We'd fixed it up with a fresh coat of paint and a new roof. We'd organized Damien's chaotic piles of books and papers and let in fresh air for the first time in decades. The basement was now home to an extensive library and a hidden armory that was an NRA member's version of Disneyland. And upstairs we'd updated and improved Damien's servers, leaving them to run 24/7, endlessly searching, seeking out strange and inexplicable events all around the world, as well as information on our new friends from Hauser Butte.

There had been a suspicious incidents in the months and years since Onatochee had almost drowned the Pacific Northwest—mysterious animal attacks in New Mexico, a basement full of headless torsos and occult inscriptions in Las Vegas, swamp monsters in New Jersey, reports of sewer-dwelling humanoids in Los Angeles, and more events that would warm the heart of the average tabloid reporter or reality show producer. I had neither the time nor the resources to chase them all down, and so we'd filed them with all the other unsolved mysteries, for future investigation or *Eye on the Unknown* articles.

Then we'd read about the cattle mutilations in Malheur County. Some instinct told me that here, relatively close to home, was a story we needed to pursue, and that we had to go armed to the teeth. Sure enough, something major had happened, and we'd been in the thick of it. Unfortunately right now I had no idea what it was.

I was busy choosing survey questions such as "Which local newscaster would you most like to have sex with?", "I'm kind of ashamed to admit it, but I'm into..." and "What Portland business has the sexiest employees?" when Loren's eternally cheerful face appeared in my doorway.

"Quit your grinnin' and drop your linen," he declared, brandishing a printout and waving it around too fast for me to see anything on it. "We got a hit on Emo Boy."

I rubbed my eyes. "It's nice to know you're not letting boring shit like your regular job interfere with the important stuff, Loren. Now maybe you can close the goddamned door and say that again, more quietly."

Loren complied contritely. "We've got to stop doing this. Consuela will think we're having an affair or something."

"I think she already does, so what's the harm?" I waved him into a seat. He claimed that his injuries from Hauser Butte were healed, but he moved stiffly, and as he sat I saw him suppress a painful wince. "You got a hit?"

He nodded. "I just checked the VPN and your search engine got a hit. That kid with the shoe-polish hair had an arrest record." He handed over the papers. "Big shock, huh?"

"Hey, show some respect for the dead, okay?" I looked at the sheet. The boy who had died on Hauser Butte stared at me sullenly. "Wayne Richards, aka Jammer. Age 19. Charged with shoplifting, assault, and meth possession. Sounds like a fine, upstanding young man."

"Yeah, a regular All-American Boy. He copped a plea and got a suspended sentence. Then he turned up on Hauser Butte. Keep reading. There's a list of known associates. They call themselves the Couch Park street family. Only it's not really a family, it's a gang."

I flipped through the pages on the Family. It was quite the rogues gallery—a parade of grim mugshots, each with both their legal and street names. Dreads, aka Denise Weber, a tough, haggard woman in her early twenties with shaggy dreadlocks. Charles "Gadget" Lopez, a rat-faced youth with a hollow, meth-ravaged face. Nicole "Demi" Weiner, a girl who might once have been pretty before sticking her face full of metal. Slash, aka Darryl Cole, a pudgy, thick necked character with black-painted lips, dead-white skin, and a spiked black Mohawk who stared into the camera with angry, piggish eyes.

"Slash? Seriously?" I looked at the picture incredulously. "God. Guns 'n' Roses have really let themselves go."

"Yeah, I know," Loren replied. "I've been calling him Bozo the Goth myself."

I focused on two pictures—a boy with close-cropped hair and a tattooed spiderweb on his neck and another with sleepy blue eyes and a sneer. Douglas "Boner" Hamilton and Peter "Possum" Norville. I'd seen both of them, standing with angry expressions on the slopes of Hauser Butte. Boner had received a blast from Frank Magruder's shotgun and Beowulf had bitten Possum on the arm. Both had perished at the hands of the Fallen.

I finally came to the last page. This one was different—a man in his mid-fifties, with greasy graying hair, a sallow face, watery brown eyes and a dark moustache above thin, hard-set lips. Though he wasn't the prettiest guy in the world, he didn't seem especially dangerous either. His name was Thomas Kingman, aka Father Tom, aka Terrance Caine, aka Ted Rice.

"Hell, this guy looks like a real winner."

A hint of disgust crept into Loren's voice. "That's their Grand Poobah, Father Tom. He runs the whole family with an iron fist. Of course he says it's because he cares about his kids so much and wants to keep them out of the hands of the authorities, but he's just a sadistic motherfucker. There was an interview in *Willamette Week* with a girl who got out of the family. She said that

Tom has the older family members act as enforcers, beating or threatening anyone who tries to leave. The police know about him—they think he sexually abuses the kids too, keeps them in line by alternately terrorizing and coddling them. They've never gotten enough evidence for a conviction. The most he's done is a couple of nights in lockup. Anyone who's willing to testify ends up recanting or disappearing."

"Shit. What the hell were kids from a Portland street family doing in Eastern Oregon hanging out with Jack Rafferty?"

"I dunno. Maybe they were looking for new places to cook meth."

"Seems reasonable, except for the demon worship and human sacrifice."

"Hey, we all need a hobby. Homeless street kids have so much free time on their hands, after all."

Homeless. The word resonated, and I remembered something—glossy paper, bright colors totally out of place with the cesspit where Jack Rafferty had made his home.

I opened my desk drawer and pulled out the flyer I'd grabbed at Rafferty's. *The Pilgrim Foundation—dedicated to outreach and support for America's homeless youth.*

"Shit," Loren muttered. "Why the hell would that fuck Rafferty have a flyer from a Portland homeless organization?"

I glanced outside. It was a lazy early summer afternoon. Traffic in the street below seemed relaxed and unhurried. In the distance I could hear the faint sound of a motorcycle engine.

Was this the last peaceful moment, I wondered? A final breath of soft, comforting summer before the horror came on us again? Downstairs in the basement the sword hung on the wall, dark and quiescent ever since the fight on Hauser Butte. But now I knew it would come to life again soon.

Jack Rafferty. Jammer. The Couch Park Family. The Pilgrim Foundation. My instincts told me that there was a connection. We just hadn't found it yet.

"Screw the issue," I said at last. "I'll take care of it. I want you to learn everything you can about the Couch Park Family and the Pilgrim Foundation. And you'd better start now."

Loren grinned. "I knew you'd say that."

* * *

A day with Consuela had worn me out, and not in a fun way, but we'd managed to get the issue to bed. By the time I guided Yngwie out of the parking garage and onto the rush-hour streets of Portland, I was not in the mood for sex surveys, research, evil cults or demon bikers. Unfortunately, Loren's research had given me a hunch and I was about to follow it.

As I drove over the Steel Bridge toward the glass towers of the Portland Convention Center I reflected on what we'd learned so far. Up until today it hadn't been much.

The Fallen's words had turned out to be Icelandic, or a language very much like it. *Ljúka* was a verb meaning "to bring about an end," *fridur* meant "peace" and as for *hirdir,* I already knew what it meant. Demons masquerading as human bikers had called me by an ancient honorific then begged my pardon. They knew who I was, and we apparently had history, though I was damned if I could say what it was.

Icelandic is a very old language—virtually unchanged for millennia. A Viking raider transported to modern Reykjavik would have no trouble making himself understood. And that meant that for all we knew the Fallen were actually speaking in ancient Norse, not Icelandic.

The books I'd taken from Rafferty's garage were similarly frustrating. They were disgusting, covered in dried blood and possibly even worse things (I was careful to wear latex gloves when I looked at them). They looked old, hand bound in rawhide, with fragile ancient pages. One of the three was actually scribed on vellum. Many of the pages were stuck together, and those that could be inspected were covered with more of those strange runes I'd seen in the garage. Try as I might, I was unable to find anything that even vaguely resembled them.

I had no doubt that they were ritual or spell books of some kind, and that Rafferty and his buddies had used them to do horrific things—blood sacrifice and necromantic construction among them. But if Rafferty and the Couch Park kids could read the weird runic inscriptions then they were well ahead of me.

I needed to know more about the Couch Park Family. And a quick phone call confirmed that a very good source of information was currently sitting at the Convention Center Burgerville nursing a small coffee.

* * *

"Yeah, I know Jammer," Milo said, wolfing down a Tillamook bacon-cheeseburger. He was thin and wasted-looking, but as far as I knew he avoided drugs save for the occasional weed. A copy of Jammer's mugshot rested on the table beside him. "Ran into him at a couple of parties. He didn't do much for me, though."

"What do you know about him?"

Milo shrugged. "He seemed like a complete asshat. Not much besides. He hung out with those Couch Park fucks."

In addition to learning martial arts and transforming my basement into a survivalist bunker, I'd spent the past two and a half years making contacts among Portland's street kids. Despite my efforts, I'd had only limited success given their community's justifiable distrust of outsiders and the adult world. Nine times out of ten, an older man who took an interest in a clubber or a street kid was looking for one thing, and it wasn't intellectual discourse.

Milo was one of my few connections to that world. I'd first encountered him one night after a trio of letter-jacket jock types decided to have a boot party on his face. Milo, it seemed, had committed several sins, ranging from being a homosexual to not dressing in a socially acceptable fashion, and the Aryan bat-squad had decided that his penalty was a savage beating.

The appearance of a scary-looking guy wearing a black leather coat and casually wielding a shotgun tends to put a damper on your fun, and the three of them split after some impotent bluster. I'd cleaned the kid up and taken him home, where he'd spent the night on my couch. I think the fact that I hadn't tried to get him drunk and rape him scored some points in his mind—when people expect the worst of you it's not hard to make a good impression. Since then he'd been a useful contact, dropping tidbits about the local scene in exchange for the occasional meal and a pre-paid cell phone.

"You mean the Couch Park Family?" I asked.

"Yeah, those shitheads. Pretty fucked-up bunch. Them and their fuckin' Father Tom. Old fucking perv. They didn't really hang at Pioneer very much. They preferred O'Bryant Square."

"Were they homeless?"

"They had homes, some of 'em. Jammer and some buddies were squatting at an abandoned house out near Canby. I went to a party there once. And a lot of 'em had pretty cool clothes. Fuck if I know where they got that kinda money—a couple of 'em worked night shift at a convenience store, some of the chicks posed on the Internet, but otherwise they were as broke as the rest of us. Musta lifted all that shit they wore."

"Anyone else know Jammer? Any friends outside the family?"

He thought for a long moment. Outside the sun was just touching the horizon, lighting the city a warm yellow-orange.

"Yeah," Milo said. "Yeah, I remember he came to a party once with this tattooed chick. Red hair, Chrome Crawford piercing. She had tattoo sleeves and a big hourglass with wings on her chest. She was all over Jammer so I guess she was his girlfriend. She said she was a dancer. Called herself Crimson, but that's a fuckin' stupid name. I think her real name was Anne or something."

"A dancer? You mean like... an..." I tried to come up with a diplomatic term. "An exotic dancer?"

"I mean she took her clothes off for money. Fuckin' gross if you ask me."

I grinned. "Not your type?"

"Fuck, no. I got better things to do with my life than have some chick grind her twat in my face."

"So do I, though I can't imagine what."

Milo looked disdainful. "You're too fuckin' straight, you know that, Alex? You should expand your horizons."

I shook my head slowly. "When I do you'll be the first to know. I figure I owe you that much."

He laughed. "Anyway, I didn't see her with him again after that party. I think they broke up. I ran into her a couple of times. I think she dances in sleazy shitholes like Clem's and Doc Holiday's. Last I heard she was at some place in Overlook called Shanny's. Maybe she can tell you more about Jammer. Or maybe she'll just rip you off."

"My choice, I guess," I said. "Thanks, Milo. You've been a big help."

He drained his coffee and stood, slinging his backpack. "Yeah, you're welcome. And thanks for the burger."

* * *

The sun had set and the cloudless sky glowed cherry red as I parked downtown near the Pittock Building. I locked up and walked toward O'Bryant Square. It was a pleasant enough park, flagged with dark bricks, a great bronze fountain at the top of tiered steps at one end. It was supposed to be in the shape of a rose, but I couldn't see it. Idly I noted a bronze plaque that said "May you find peace in this garden."

In the dusk it didn't look like there were too many peace-seekers. A couple of homeless people huddled on benches, and there was a filthy bus shelter nearby that stank of trash and urine. Inside the shelter, several artistic individuals had gone to work with a spray can, tagging it with the enthusiasm of the young and the tweaked.

I looked up. The light was dim, but I could see characters there, painted with more care than the others.

I frowned, feeling a growing sense of dread. They looked exactly like the writing in Rafferty's book, on his garage walls and carved into the hide of Frank Magruder's cattle.

With shaking hands, I pulled my phone from a pocket and started to take pictures of the ceiling graffiti.

I heard a soft footfall behind me. I whirled to see two figures filling the arch of the bus shelter. The first was grayhound-thin, clad in jeans and an old army jacket. He had unkempt blonde hair and stared at me with overtly hostile blue eyes. I didn't recognize him.

The second I had seen the day before, staring at me from his mug shot—thick-necked, pudgy, and pale. His lips were painted black and his Mohawk was combed out. His girthy frame strained a black t-shirt and the waist of his baggy cargo pants.

Slash, aka Bozo the Goth.

"You takin' pictures, man?" he demanded, tiny eyes narrowing to black, hateful slits.

I didn't reply, but instead strode purposefully toward them, shouldering past one, then the other.

It surprised them a little, but not much. The blonde one turned and I felt an arm reaching for my neck.

I pivoted instantly, kicking the back of his leg, driving him down to his knees with a surprised "Hey!" then swung him by his shirt, slamming him into Slash, who yelped and stumbled ponderously backward. The whole bus shelter shook when he blundered into the frame.

I was across the street and under the awnings of the Pittock Building by the time they recovered. I'd succeeded in surprising them, but even with two years of martial arts I didn't think I could take a pair of street thugs alone. My eyes sought out Yngwie, parked a block away.

Glaring murderously, Bozo and his friend started across the street toward me. As they did, the glass and wood doors of the Pittock Building swung open and a trio of businessmen stepped out, jabbering about telecommunication networks and accounting software. I quickly fell in step behind them, leaving the two toughs behind, looking angry and frustrated.

As we turned the corner, I darted away, making for Yngwie, unlocking the door and speeding off without a backward glance. I was so busy trying to slow down my respiration that I forgot to turn on my lights in the growing gloom, until an irate pedestrian screamed at me.

"God damn," I muttered.

Slash was a member of the most ruthless street family in Portland, and I had no doubt his companion was as well. Had they merely been annoyed with me for taking pictures of their territory, or were they just looking for a fight? I slowly blew air through my teeth, thinking about what had just happened.

Things were starting to get weird again.

II

I regretted not bringing Loren the moment I saw the crowd hanging outside Shanny's. Dark figures milled around, cigarette smoke hung heavy, and a forest of discarded beer bottles gleamed under the single street light.

The building didn't look any better—I suspected that it was the type of place that changed hands every year or two, and it had probably borne numerous names in its long history. Presently the name *Shanny's* was applied in large pink letters across the front, with "beer" and "dancers" in smaller script beneath it. Music thudded harshly from inside and I wondered why the neighbors never complained, then decided that the neighbors were probably the ones outside smoking and drinking beer.

A closer look at the patrons left me somewhat relieved. There were a few middle-aged, slightly overweight biker types among the crowd, and none of them spared me more than a glance as I stepped through the black-painted glass door and into the stifling, dim-lit interior. A gut-heavy bear of a man in an undersized t-shirt and leather vest sat near the entrance. He gave me the once-over as I entered, then nodded curtly as I walked past.

"Welcome to Shanny's," he grunted. "The garden spot of Northeast Portland."

Yeah, that was it. The atmosphere was close and smelled like beer and the entire place had an air of a floating rave club that had wandered for months and finally found a semi-permanent home. Cheap tables and chairs littered the place—some metal, some wood, some resin—packed with shadowy figures, grouped according to social alignment—bikers here, Latino gangbangers there, black gangbangers over there, goths and street punks elsewhere. Under other circumstances I might have gotten all teary-eyed at the sight of all these disparate races and cultures united by beer and sex, but then I reminded myself that if the biker at the door hadn't patted me down, he probably hadn't patted any of these others down either.

The stage was a cleared section of linoleum with a pole in the center, surrounded by a low wall made of 2x4s. I remembered that it was called, without the slightest trace of irony, the "rack." A mixed bag of patrons had pulled their chairs up close, busily knocking back beers and gawping at the young woman strutting her stuff in the center to the deafening strains of gangsta rap.

She was thin, spare-bodied, and lithe, with small breasts and a cute, freckled face framed by short dishwater blonde hair. She was talented, spinning on the pole, then writhing on the floor with convincing simulated abandon. As I watched, a black gentleman held out a dollar bill and she took it in her teeth, grinning seductively.

I turned to the bartender, who seemed oblivious to his surroundings.

"Is Crimson dancing tonight?" I asked, but the thunder of the music drowned me out, and he did not seem to hear. Either that or he was ignoring me.

I gestured with a fiver and got his attention, buying an overpriced bottle of American beer with a German-sounding name. He opened it and it foamed over as he handed it to me. It was about as delicious and satisfying as I'd expected it to be.

"IS CRIMSON DANCING TONIGHT?" I demanded, and still got no response. I glanced at a nearby patron with a frustrated expression, and he grinned, revealing a mouth full of yellowed tusks.

"He don't listen to nothin'!" he shouted. "Just comes in and serves the booze! Great bartender, huh?"

I nodded. "Don't they usually offer advice and comfort to the lovelorn?"

"He don't, that's for damnsure." He looked at the stage. "Pretty cute, huh?"

I nodded again and for the third time asked if Crimson was dancing.

He frowned. "You mean Scarlet? I think she used to call herself Crimson. Yeah, she's here. She'll be out after Summer."

"Thanks." Anne, Crimson, now Scarlet. The woman seemed to have identity issues. I didn't consider Scarlet to be much of an improvement, but at least it was consistent.

Summer finished her set, gathering up discarded clothing and fallen singles (with the occasional five- and ten-spot), then bowed and sauntered away, striding confidently atop four-inch stilettoes as if she'd been born in them. Before disappearing into the back room, she turned, smiled sweetly and blew a kiss at her patrons, who responded by staring back like a pack of starving wolves. Then she was gone, and the crowd began to disperse.

I took the opportunity to cash in a twenty for a handful of bills and took my beer to the rack.

So far no one had bothered me. I was beginning to relax. I'm not a small guy, and I hoped that in my coat I was a relatively imposing figure. The men at this cut-rate dive had their own conflicts, and their own rivalries, and seemed uninterested in the affairs of a stranger who appeared content to sit alone, nursing a beer and waiting for the girls. Perhaps strip clubs were the low-life equivalent of Switzerland.

I turned my attention to the stage, waiting for the door to the dressing room to open, and for our featured performer to come out. I didn't have to wait long.

There was no announcement. The notion that this place might have anything approaching a PA system was too laughable to contemplate—the thunderous music came from a stereo system attached to an amp and four tall speakers. One of the bikers had probably taken it from a guy he killed.

Not that Scarlet needed to be announced—everyone's attention was riveted on her the moment she appeared. She wasn't tall—perhaps 5'4", clad in a black halter, vinyl shorts, thigh highs, and spike heels. The outfit barely concealed a figure that seemed a perfect blend of soft curves and athletic muscularity.

Her hair was a rich, dark red—everything about her seemed to complement it. Her skin was pale, but not unhealthily so. A single piercing glinted above bright red lips. In contrast, her eyes were pale blue, unexpectedly framed by a pair of ugly black glasses that she managed to make sexy.

Her chest bore the tattoo that Milo had described—a colorful hourglass with wings that spread across the tops of her breasts. A blue and yellow-rayed sun graced each shoulder, and identical, garishly colored sleeves made of seemingly random objects—paisleys, ribbons, Mexican-style candy skulls, cartoon cat's heads—covering both arms. A circle of Celtic knotwork surrounded her navel and on each side of her abdomen was an azure peacock, its feathers stretching around her hips to her back.

Her expression and demeanor as she stalked forward on black spike heels was that of a big cat on the hunt. A tangible sense of sensuality and menace rolled off of her in waves. I felt it, and so did the other guys who sat nearby, staring wordlessly.

Then the stereo blared to life and the soft opening chords of a Deadmau5 remix filled the room, a pulsing compliment to the hungry, dangerous look in Scarlet's pale eyes.

She began unceremoniously, as if letting the music itself move her. First she spun, and her back was to me. She was tattooed there as well. The tails of her two blue peacocks covered each side of the small of her back, and above them, between her shoulders, was a circular mandala. In its center was an elaborate, interwoven pattern, and around the outside was a series of strange characters.

It took me a moment to recognize them as the symbols from Rafferty's garage and his blood-soaked books.

She turned again and cast her burning gaze across the men who sat at the rack, staring lustfully through corrective lenses. She stood, legs spread apart, head thrown back, fingers twined into her hair, then thrust her hips as pounding drums and synths flowed through the room like a warm, caressing breeze. She scanned the faces at the rack, assessing us with a smoldering gaze, sliding her black-tipped fingers up and down her body.

Emotions flickered in my head and chest as Scarlet worked the room, slipping easily out of her few items of clothing and making love to the shiny metal pole—fear, lust, curiosity, bafflement, and flat-out terror. Every time she turned and revealed her naked back to me the mandala-shape was there with the same monstrous runes I'd seen daubed in blood and sliced into flesh.

Then when she turned back and her blue-white eyes met mine, still behind heavy hipster glasses, I felt something different—hints of warmth and comfort that I hadn't felt in years. I'd known it once, looking into eyes of a different color, and then again in the presence of a creature who was, for want of a better term, a goddess.

Scarlet wasn't exactly a goddess, but something in her eyes reminded me of a day on a windswept hillside when I swore an oath and took possession of an ancient weapon and an ancient duty.

Then she turned away and I saw the mandala and its cruel, incomprehensible runes and I thought of a bloody massacre on a lonely mountain in eastern Oregon.

Numbly I reached into my pocket and fished out a single, folding it lengthwise and setting it on the rack. When she turned back she saw me and crawled over, taking the bill in her teeth, and locked eyes with me for a moment. Again, the warmth and comfort of She Who Watches glimmered inside me. She rose to her knees, stroking the bill across her nipples. Each one was pierced with a silver bar.

I'd played the role of another lust-addled observer, a man to be teased and cajoled until he finally came across with cash, but my mind raced, wondering how a woman who exuded such almost divine grace had come by those alien symbols, permanently painted onto her pale flesh.

The music gave way to the dulcet tones of Skrillix. By this time she was down to fishnets, heels and a thong. Now she took her time, writhing and sliding around the stage with serpentine grace, and by the time the thong had vanished I was busy noting that she had one last piercing that hadn't been visible before.

Emotion, sensation, memory all warred with each other. There was horror and fear of the unspeakable mark she bore, but there were flashes of remembrance, of a love and sadness, hope and loss, and true adoration of a being I could not comprehend, but served anyway. It was as if Onatochee's evil, Tsagaglalal's power and Trish's sensuality and love were all born in the same person. And it also didn't help that I was getting aroused.

The human mind is a fragile thing, and the male mind is more fragile than most, particularly when it's fighting a war against a rising tide of sexual excitement. Here, in this unsophisticated dump, despite my dislike of strip clubs and surrounded by the dregs of society, I found myself actually being turned on by a dancer.

And this dancer bore the mark of something terrible that I had yet to identify, yet I couldn't quite help myself.

The rational side of my mind, the one that stared at Scarlet's mandala, feeling both fear and fascination, demanded that I learn more, that I find out what the hell was going on. I reached into my pocket again, almost robotically, and selected a twenty dollar bill, folding it and holding it up between my fingers.

She caught sight of the bill as she turned and she grinned at me fiercely, striding over to me with confident steps, her feet steady despite her impossibly high heels. Never taking her eyes from mine, she bent down, squeezing her breasts together and taking the twenty between them.

"*Tempus fugit,*" I said, loud enough to make myself heard over the music.

That got her attention. She looked at me in surprise.

"What?"

I nodded at the tattoo on her chest. "*Tempus fugit.* Time flies. Your winged hourglass."

She grinned. "You're the first guy who ever got that."

I glanced around the room. "Honestly, the clientele here don't look like Latin speakers."

"Yeah," she admitted. "They tend to be few and far between."

I tried to keep my gaze steady and not look away. "Someone told me there was a very pretty dancer here named Crimson. You wouldn't know her, would you?"

She laughed. "Asshole." Her tone was surprisingly friendly. "You're looking at her."

I grinned back. "I kind of figured."

The music changed again, to some random Daft Punk piece. She turned back to her other customers but shot me a coy glance as she did so.

Finally she finished, on her knees, back arched, arms extended, her pale breasts pointing toward the ceiling, piercings glittering, red hair bright in the spotlights. The beat faded and she stood, arms spread, bowing. She still wore her glasses and very little else. The gathered thugs clapped appreciatively as she began to gather up the scattered bills and stuff them into a small purse.

She didn't bother to put her outfit back on, but slipped into a short red silk robe with a dragon embroidered on the back and strode confidently from the stage. Instead of heading back to the dressing room, she sauntered toward me, moving on her heels with a rolling, comfortable step. Her black-rimmed eyes met mine again and once more I felt the chill of her predatory gaze combined with a sense of warmth and kindness.

"Hey big spender. Care for a lap dance?"

I tried to smile but I probably only looked distraught.

"Uh..."

Her sympathetic expression deepened. "Aw. You're new at this, aren't you?"

I nodded.

"Here's how it works. You give me another twenty and I sit in your lap and shimmy for a while. What do you say?"

I shifted uncomfortably. My clothes were feeling uncomfortably close. "That might be a bad idea right now. How about I give you another twenty and you just sit and talk to me for a while?"

She considered this for a moment then shrugged and settled gracefully into the seat beside me. "Jeez. I don't get that kind of offer very often. I guess you like me, huh?"

"I guess I do." I shifted. Nope. Still uncomfortable.

She looked quickly around the room. The gangbangers and bikers returned to their beers and were now focused on the next performer, a pert brunette called Tiffany. They didn't seem terribly upset that their dancer was paying attention to someone else.

"Shit, it's more than I get from this bunch of mental defectives." She shrugged. "But they tip pretty good. Do you have a name, or should I make up my own?"

"Alex. And is Scarlet your real name? Or should I call you Crimson?"

"Oh, screw that. When did you fall off the turnip truck? Strippers never use their real names."

"Can I ask what yours is, or is that considered rude?"

"Sure it is, but at least you asked." She beckoned me close, then whispered, barely audible over the pounding music. "My real name's Annabelle Lee."

I looked skeptical. "No kidding."

"No, really. Dad was a huge Poe fan. You can call me Anna, though."

I wasn't sure whether I believed her or not, so I just smiled. "Well, I like it. It fits your appearance."

She looked at me, as if not sure whether to be complimented or insulted.

"I'm glad you think so. It's not much of a stripper name, is it? I kind of need something more exotic if I'm going to dance for my supper and look like I belong in a Nine Inch Nails video. Otherwise, these assholes'd expect me to look like *that* little darling." She gestured at the brunette dancer, who smiled sweetly and flipped her off. It all seemed relatively good-natured.

We moved to the bar and I bought her a beer. Most clubs had pretty strict rules about buying drinks for dancers, but neither Mister Big and Silent at the bar nor the doorman/bouncer seemed to care. And now most of the patrons were eagerly gathered around the stage watching Tiffany bend over and wriggle. We were the only ones at the bar.

I sipped at my horrific bottle of foamy, urine-colored water, aka domestic lager. It was horrible, but I knew better than to order a pale ale or a *hefeweizen* in a joint like this.

"At the risk of sounding like just another drooling idiot sitting at the rack, I like your tattoos."

She nodded and smiled knowingly. "I can't fault you for that. They're great conversation starters."

"Any personal significance? Your peacocks are very cool." I wanted to ask about her back piece, but at the same time I needed to keep it casual.

"Not really." She looked into her beer as if she were reading tea leaves. "I saw the design at the shop and the guy at the shop suggested I put one on each side, so you could see the tails when I turned around. I saved up my money for months before I got them."

"Were you dancing then?"

"Nope. Waitressing and working the drive through at Burgerville. That's no way to go through life, son."

"How'd you get started performing?"

She rolled her eyes. "You may not believe this, but I don't get that question very often. By this time most guys are asking what my favorite position is."

"I usually save that kind of question for a third or fourth date." I grimaced. I was overstepping. "Not that I'm thinking of this as a date, of course..."

"Of course not. You're just buying a drink for a stripper with the pierced nipples 'cause your life is so boring and mundane."

I flashed a nervous smile. Oh, if only she knew...

"I had a friend who danced. Taught me the ropes. She was making four, five hundred a night. Of course she worked Gentlemen's Clubs." She made air quotes as she said it. "Those are the places that are just like this one, except the drinks cost more and the dancers wear evening gowns between sets. Not sexy little robes like this. Me, I'm lucky if I make a hundred a night. It's not bad, but if rent is due and you're only dancing two or three nights a week..."

"What about your other tattoos? Do they mean anything? The ones on your stomach and your back?"

She looked slightly surprised. "My, aren't we the curious one, Alex? The one on my tummy is from a book on Celtic knotwork. I really liked it. I was dancing by the time I got that one. The sleeves were the tattoo guy's idea, too. The back, well, I'd rather not talk about that one."

That got my attention, of course. I'd have to tread lightly.

"Bad memories?"

She shrugged, sipped her beer, and didn't reply immediately.

"It was my boyfriend's idea. He had one just like it. Thought it would be romantic if we both got the same tat. A symbol of our love, you know? He even paid for it."

I tried to look crestfallen, and succeeded. "Oh. You have a boyfriend?"

"Had," she said emphatically. "Had, had, *had*. We broke up after I got the..." She stopped, glaring. "Why the hell am I telling you all this? Who the fuck do you think you are? Can we *please* talk about something else?"

Shit. If she was telling the truth, she had no idea about the tattoo's significance. Unfortunately her generous boyfriend— probably the late Jammer—likely did. With growing distress I realized that there was another unfortunate aspect to this conversation. I was actually starting to like this woman, and not just because I'd seen her naked.

I felt a weight growing inside me like a stone in my gut. I tried to blink it away, along with the memories that swelled up along with tears.

I remembered eviscerated cattle and strange letters scrawled in blood. I remembered a bound and helpless little girl on Hauser Butte. I remembered young people dying at the hands of ferocious demon warriors...

From even deeper I remembered dark-painted lips, lustrous black hair, warm flesh writhing beneath me, and violet eyes staring lovingly into mine. I remembered those same eyes turned jaundiced yellow as she threw herself at me, knife in hand. I remembered thrusting my sword through the body of someone I had loved and watching her fall, lifeless onto a filth-strewn floor.

Wild, adventurous, sensual—I'd loved her. I had never known for certain whether she had loved me, but she'd fallen into darkness before I fully understood what we faced. She'd perished on the blade of my sword, but she'd been a lifeless husk long before I finally tracked her down.

She was dead by my hand and I had had to live with it for a year and a half now.

I couldn't let it happen. I couldn't face it again.

I looked directly at her and spoke quietly, doing my best to keep my words unhurried. "Anna, my name is Alex St. John. Please believe me when I tell you I'm a friend. I'm trying to help. Your boyfriend—he was called Jammer, wasn't he?"

Anna stared at me with an expression of growing horror. The throbbing music seemed to fade into the background, inaudible over the roar of blood in my ears.

"I know who he is, Anna. I know about his friends. If you knew them you're in serious danger. You've got to tell me about Jammer and how he made you get that—"

"*TODD!*" Anna's voice cut through the music, through the roaring in my ears. "Todd, *get over here!*"

Like Aladdin's genie, the big-gutted doorman was there beside me, his face as grim as an oncoming thunderstorm.

"Whaddya need, hon?" His voice rumbled angrily.

Anna glared at me, her tentative friendliness now replaced by burning anger. "This asshole is leaving, Todd. Now."

I felt growing panic and frustration. Some of the bikers around us had noticed and were watching, amused.

"Wait. No, wait. I..."

Todd slapped a meaty paw on my shoulder.

"You heard the lady. Out."

It was pointless to struggle. I let Todd take me out, holding one arm behind my back and pushing roughly.

"Anna!" I shouted back as he propelled me through the door. "Look out for those Couch Park bastards! They're dangerous! They're..."

"Shut the fuck up," Todd growled, planting one foot in front of mine and giving me a final shove. I went tumbling onto the pavement, to a chorus of guffaws and scattered applause from the smokers outside.

Todd glared at me as I lay on the sidewalk and thrust up a middle finger. "And don't come back, fuckwad."

I gathered up what dignity I could and stumbled away, a chorus of jeers and laughter fading behind me.

Yngwie was where I'd left him a couple of blocks away. I fumbled for my keys and pulled the door open, falling inside, and sitting at the wheel for several long minutes, panting heavily, trying to get a grip on my anger and humiliation.

It was almost midnight. If I went back I'd be asking for an ass-kicking, and there seemed no way that Anna, Scarlet or whatever her real name was would trust me. There had been anger in her words, certainly, but there had also been fear.

She knew more than she was telling. There had been real fear in her eyes when I mentioned Jammer and the Couch Park Family, and she was even afraid of someone who claimed that he wanted to help. I'd had a chance to learn more, perhaps even crack the entire affair wide open, and I'd blown it.

Grimly I started the engine and drove away.

There was nothing more I could do. Tomorrow, when I was thinking straight, when my heart wasn't running like a trip hammer and adrenaline wasn't racing through me, then I'd figure out what to do.

Right now, my elbow hurt where it had struck the pavement, my head was beginning to throb, and I felt like an abject failure.

✠✠✠

C old, unhappy, and depressed were inadequate terms to describe the state I was in by the time I got home. I'd screwed up my best chance to learn something new about Jammer *and* I'd probably made a permanent enemy of a very pretty and interesting woman. I was in the bathroom opening a bottle of melatonins when the compulsion hit me.

I'd felt it on the morning of *Hecate Trivia* nearly three years ago—the overwhelming need to do something, a fully-formed notion crafted in my mind. I hadn't really understood it then, but now... Now I knew more, and as the compulsion led me downstairs I followed it.

Damien's basement had once housed his book collection and spare parts for Yngwie. Over the last year we had expanded it significantly, adding flooring, reinforced walls, security doors, and a couple of extra secret rooms. The main room still held Damien's library, now housed in climate-controlled glass cases, a huge plasma TV with both X-Box One and PS 4 (those were Loren's idea), bass and guitar amps, a drum machine, my father's Ernie Ball bass, and Loren's pathetic fake Strat-o-caster. This was the public basement where we hung out, jammed, watched videos, and I let Loren kick my ass at various video games.

Through a locked steel door lay the armory—its walls covered with pegboard and hung with dozens of weapons, everything from stun guns to automatic pistols, rifles and shotguns. It was all legal, but we had more. Behind one of the shelves was a well-hidden security door that concealed the vault where we kept the illicit stuff. But that wasn't what had drawn me downstairs.

On the wall, gleaming faintly with silvery-blue light was the sword—the conduit between my world and the others. And now it was alive again, as it had been on Hauser Butte.

I reached out and my fingertips touched its glossy surface. There was a faint shock of contact, like a spark of static electricity, and suddenly I was no longer in my basement.

The stars above were strange. A road stretched endlessly into the night, a strip of deeper darkness against the shadowed landscape. There were lights moving down the road, arrow straight, a double ranked column at least a hundred riders. A chorus of angry screams cut through the night, a disturbing amalgam of animal and machine.

Behind the column a wall of flames spread across the horizon, miles distant but growing closer despite the riders' speed. There were vague shapes in the flames like racing horsemen and lithe dancing women with great evil scythes. It took me a long moment to realize that the riders were fleeing from the advancing inferno.

My vantage shifted like a movie camera mounted in a helicopter, zooming in on the riders... Scaled, crimson, powerfully muscled, with horned heads and bestial faces, alien weapons strapped to their backs, mounted upon jet-black coursers with metallic skin and burning yellow eyes...

The Fallen.

The flames drew ever closer, almost as if the Fallen were not even moving. The burning wall resolved itself into thousands of individual figures wreathed in flames, a pitiless firestorm that ravaged the land, leaving only charred ruin in its wake. The horsemen were there, followed by the scythe-dancers and flying things that spat orange flames, and behind them ranks of grim soldiers in rusty armor, wolves with wings and scorpion-tails, ancient gnarled giants and dragons, demons and cast-down gods with the heads of lions and jackals, the claws of birds, the bodies of serpents...

The horde was only a heartbeat behind the Fallen now. The back rank of riders screeched to a halt and dismounted, drawing weapons, their snarling metal beasts beside them. The rest of the Fallen raced on, toward the horizon, where the sky was growing lighter.

The flame wall swept down upon the rear-guard, but the Fallen stood their ground. Flaming horsemen tumbled to the earth, sliced apart almost effortlessly. The Fallen's black weapons rose and fell in unison, cutting through burning flesh and armor. Then came the scythe-wielders, skull-faced naked women with streaming tresses of fire. Glowing orange metal met black axes and swords, sparking and splattering in the darkness like fireworks. The riding beasts leaped about the fray, biting and tearing, clawing and slashing, roaring with animal-machine voices.

Some of the Fallen were cut down by the slashing demon-weapons. They were all doomed; they had stayed behind to buy time for their fellows, yet there was no sorrow in their actions—even in their demonic faces and burning eyes I saw the joy of battle, the exultation of slaughter.

The armored warriors threw themselves at the Fallen. A savage storm of combat raged on the road, quarter neither asked nor given. Swords, axes, lances, knives, claws, teeth... Anything that could be a weapon was used. When one of the Fallen went down he kept fighting, dragging himself along on hands and knees, ripping and rending until at last his scaled crimson flesh was punctured in a hundred places, gouting black and steaming blood, collapsing on the ground to move no more.

At last the rearguard was wiped out. The flaming host resumed its pursuit, but the surviving Fallen had raced ahead and gained a lead of miles.

They thundered along the strange black pavement. Ahead the sky was lightening—an oval portal that revealed blue skies, clean and cool in contrast to the crimson and black nightmare that they left behind. In a moment, the Fallen raced through, their ebon mounts' claws pounding, leaping into the rift, passing from the world of darkness into flawless blue.

And as they rode through, they changed. In an instant the red-skinned demons and their monstrous metallic coursers transformed into tall, handsome men with long flowing blonde locks, clad in mail, bearing spears and swords, wearing elaborately-decorated goggle helms, chased and engraved with serpents and dragons. The riding beasts became black horses, sleek and muscular, coats shining, their tack gleaming gold and silver.

Behind them, the rift closed and the world of ashes and flames vanished. Three score Fallen stood mounted upon their horses in the center of a vast stone circle, surrounded by rune-carved monoliths. Beyond the stones rose silhouettes of leafless trees, indistinct in a heavy mist. A fire burned in the center of the circle, and a lone man stood beside it, clad in a pale tunic, grasping a branch of mistletoe in one hand, a sword in the other.

The man spoke. It was another language, but I understood his words.

"Welcome, hosts of Valhalla, come in our hour of need!" He stepped forward and dropped to one knee. "Blessings of Odin upon you. By what name are you called, warriors?"

One of the Fallen urged his horse forward. Like the others, he was tall and bearded, his blonde hair woven into a single braid. His helm's crest was decorated with a snarling dragon and his eyes were cold and weary.

"I am called Arngrim." His voice rumbled like distant thunder. He looked back at his fellow riders, now ranked behind him and looking about at their new world. He paused for a moment, as if making a decision, then spoke. "We are called *Fordæmdur.*"

The priest looked puzzled. "The Damned? Surely not, warrior. Are you not emissaries of Great Odin, sent for the salvation of his people?"

Arngrim lips turned up in a dark and humorless smile. "If that is what you believe, then that is what we are. Yet ever shall we be called *Fordæmdur*, for damned we are, and lost, fallen from a higher place, sent here to do the gods' will." He held up his spear and addressed his men. "So it has been decreed. We are the Lost. Forsaken. Fallen."

Now his gaze turned again and it seemed that he looked straight at me, his handsome face framed by his beautiful helm, his eyes dark blue and sad behind a metal goggle-mask.

"*Fordæmdur*," he said again. "Until the day of our vengeance."

The fog closed over them, and all vanished, replaced a moment later by another scene, this one in a sylvan glade surrounded by lush trees covered in white blossoms. Arngrim was there, down on one knee, his helm resting on the ground beside him. The Fallen were ranked behind him, mounted upon their horses.

Another man stood above Arngrim, clad in mail and a white cloak embroidered with a black device—sword and shepherd's crook crossed. He too was helmetless. His face was lined and care-worn, but his eyes were gentle, looking down at Arngrim with compassion. In one hand he held...

I felt my dream waver and blur, as if wakefulness were stealing upon me. I focused on my hands and looked again.

In his right hand the cloaked man held a strange sword, crafted of shining glassy material, its hilt set with thorns, its blade like a long diamond.

He bore my sword. He was the Shepherd.

Arngrim spoke. "I swear to you, *Hirdir*, that I and my people will leave your people in peace, save to defend ourselves, and save to rid the world of the servants of the Great Enemy. The Fallen swear this." He turned to his assembled Fallen. "What say you?"

As one, the Fallen raised their weapons and shouted. "Aye!"

The Shepherd replied quietly, as if speaking only out of necessity. "I too swear, that on the day of your vengeance I will aid the Fallen. I swear in my name and in the name of all those who bear this weapon."

Arngrim rose and put his helm back on. His voice still rumbled like a storm on a distant mountain.

"*Fordæmdur.* Until the day of our vengeance."

The dark clouds overhead were suddenly lit by a burning red-orange and in the sky a great circle formed—a fiery mandala that mirrored the one I'd seen tattooed on Anna's flesh. Darkness closed in around me until all I could see was the circle and its unreadable, terrifying runes.

The sign of the enemy. Arngrim's voice echoed from everywhere at once. *The sign of his coming.*

Darkness swallowed me and I fell through the shadows of a million worlds.

* * *

My vision was so blurry I could barely see the keyboard. Outside the sun had not yet risen, but I typed away in the light of a single lamp.

I sat at my workstation in the filthy clothes from last night, desperately trying to shake off the fog of sleep that still enveloped my brain, while at the same time not forgetting the events of my dream and the images that I had seen. Tea wasn't enough—a steaming mug of coffee sat at my elbow, dark and bitter enough to melt lead.

It took me several tries before I figured out that *Fordæmdur* was spelled with an a-e ligature character, which made sense since it represented the Nordic rune **a**, or *ansuz*. In modern Icelandic, it still meant "forsaken, lost or damned" but in older applications it had deeper and more subtle meanings, including "exile, banishment, ostracism, fall from grace."

Shit.

Dawn was just lightening the eastern sky when I got a hit from a site at the University of Iceland. It was going to be a beautiful day, but as I ran a translator and read the resulting text, I didn't pay much attention.

Fordæmdur *(***fordamdur***): A group of semi-divine warriors or possibly Jötun (giants), summoned by a priest of the Aaldvög tribe of Northern Sweden, in response to an invasion by a rival tribe (called by Ófreskja by the 11th century Christian chronicler Njarl Gündarsonn, a term that translates roughly as "monster" and described variously as "trolls," "devils" or "evil ones" to add drama to an ancient tale of tribal warfare). Their name variously translates to "Damned," "Forsaken" and "Exiled." The* Fordæmdur *successfully drove out the Aaldvög's enemies, but proved to be almost as great a threat for they immediately began to slay and burn indiscriminately, forcing many tribesfolk to flee their homes.*

True to the teachings of his church, Njarl turned the legend into a morality play, pitting Christian faith against pagan ignorance. In his version of the story, it took the efforts of a foreigner—a Christian of course, possibly a Byzantine Roman—named Pastorius (Shepherd) to tame the wild Lost Ones, meeting their chieftain Arngrim in battle. After a great struggle, Pastorius subdued his foe through the strength of his faith and his belief in Christ's mercy, but spared his life in exchange for a promise to leave the Aaldvög in peace. For his part, Pastorius swore to aid the Fordæmdur *upon their so-called 'Dagur Hefnd' or 'Day of Vengeance' when the Lost's enemies came to destroy them. Njarl's chronicle does not say whether Pastorius ever kept this promise, or whether the ominously-named Day of Vengeance ever arrived.*

I gazed wearily from my window. The sun had risen and cars rushed past. Birds sang as the growing light touched the trees that lined my street. I hadn't gotten a wink of sleep.

Inside my head, I heard only the scream of engines, and the echo of Arngrim's words, still fresh from my dream.

Fordæmdur. Until the day of our vengeance.

* * *

"'Lo?" Loren's voice was thick and sluggish. "'Zis, Alex?"

"Yeah." I changed clothes clumsily, holding the phone to my ear. "I've had some major breakthroughs about Hauser Butte and the Fallen. Can you come over?"

"Uh, yeh... uh, sure... Wha' time izzit anyway?"

"It's almost 7:30. Consuela's taking care of the printers. You didn't have any plans today, did you?"

"Uhh, no... Jus' gonna, you know, game or somethin'... Whadja wanna do?"

"Yeah," I said. "I was thinking of stalking a stripper. Want to help out?"

There was a long pause and a rustling sound.

"Uh, yeah. I guesso... When you wanna...?"

"Three o'clock this afternoon. My place."

Another pause. "Uh, Alex?" Loren's voice sounded slightly more coherent and less sleep-drugged.

"Yes?"

"You did say you wanted to stalk a stripper, right?"

"That's right."

"Okay." I heard a deep, soulful intake of breath and an equally soulful release. "I was just checking."

IV

"Jesus Christ, Alex. I can't believe you went to a strip club and you didn't invite me. Some friend you are."

I swallowed a scalding mouthful of convenience-store coffee. "Well you're here now, aren't you?"

"Sitting in a car outside a strip club isn't the same thing, Alex. Jesus Christ."

That afternoon Loren had listened to my story calmly as he constructed an epic multi-layered sandwich in the kitchen—my chat with Milo, my visit to O'Bryan Square, my encounter with Bozo the Goth and his friend, my trip to Shanny's, the vision of the Fallen, and my discovery of their origin. The only part of the story that seemed to bother him was when I went to see Anna. Since then he had not let me forget what a faithless and unreliable friend I had been by not inviting him along.

"Believe me," I said for at least the tenth time, "you didn't miss much. The place is a diseased little rat-trap. And the bouncer needs a shower."

"Yeah, great. I'd have preferred to find that out for myself."

"I tell you what. When all this is over I'll take you to a strip club. How's that? It just can't be Shanny's because the bouncer would kill me."

Loren looked only partially satisfied, but let the matter drop, taking a swig of his own coffee.

"This is like some cop show or something, isn't it? Us sitting in a dark car, waiting for the suspect to come out so we can tail him and find out what he's up to. Well, what she's up to. And it's about as boring as it is on TV too."

I had to agree. At least the weather was better. Overhead the moon sailed through a cloudless sky and the streetlights gave us a good view of Shanny's, still surrounded by a crowd of cigarette-smoking attendants. We were a block and a half away, lurking well out of sight in the shadows with a view of Shanny's and the surrounding streets. Fortunately for me, neither Anna nor Todd the bouncer had seen Yngwie so I had another measure of security to keep us from being noticed.

I shifted uncomfortably. I was wearing my long leather coat—my strange patroness had dubbed it my *aegis*, or shield, and it seemed to provide some protection from supernatural enemies. Why that was I couldn't say, but the fact that an old girlfriend had bought it for me before she'd died of a drug overdose didn't hurt.

Loren spoke quietly now, his tone serious. "So how long do you think they've been here? The Fallen, I mean."

I thought about it for a moment. "At least twelve hundred years. Maybe fifteen. I couldn't find any reference to anyone called the Aaldvög or a Byzantine named Pastorius, but their armor looked like stuff from the Sutton Hoo find, which dated back to 500 AD or so."

"Jeez. And you think this guy Pastorius was the Shepherd?"

"Well, that's what the name translates to. Remember Damien's last letter to me? It listed a bunch of other potential Shepherds from different places. One of the candidates was someone named *Hirdir* who supposedly fought the *Fordæmdur*. If Pastorius is the same person then he brought them to heel and forced them to live peacefully."

"Well given the way they cut those kids apart on Hauser Butte, I don't think they're living peacefully anymore. Do you think they'll expect you to fight with them when this enemy of theirs finally shows up?"

I shrugged. "Who knows? If they're ignoring their oath, maybe they won't care. But I might not have any choice. Arngrim implied that when the enemy comes it's going to ravage earth just like it did their world. If my dream was right, there won't be much left once they've finished."

"Who's this enemy they're so hot to fight with, anyway? How do we know he's so much worse than the Fallen? They didn't seem like very nice guys."

"If my dream and what we saw in Hayes are any indication, this enemy is worse by several orders of magnitude. The Fallen murder individuals. This enemy—whoever, whatever he is— murders worlds."

We fell silent for a while before I spoke again.

"We've got to learn more. We've got to, or I'm afraid something very, very bad is going to happen."

The coffee was finished. The radio was playing crap as usual so I hooked up my MP3 player. Loren hated folk and doom metal, and I couldn't stand the techno-tribal stuff he listened to, but the Venn diagram of our musical tastes intersected at industrial metal. For the next half hour we sat, heads nodding as we listened to the likes of Ministry, Deadstar Assembly, and Power Man 5000. Midnight was approaching and with it what I hoped was the end of Anna's shift.

"Alex, heads up! Is that her?"

A slight figure walked from the building, past the smoking bikers. The imposing silhouette of Todd the bouncer walked beside her. Even wrapped in a light coat her hair and pale skin were dead giveaways.

"It's her," I said. "And that's the bouncer. Todd."

"Ah, yes. Escorting the stripper out are we, Todd? Expecting to get a little gratitude? A little something extra?" Loren was almost muttering to himself.

"Seems unlikely." I fingered the ignition key. If they went too far we'd have to follow them, but doing so in a hulking black muscle car wasn't the most subtle thing in the world. "Get ready to follow on foot if we have to."

Loren nodded and we kept watching. They stopped at a bus shelter on Interstate. There were a couple of other figures there.

"Looks like she's a fan of public transportation," Loren said. "So is our boy Todd going home with here? Nope, nope... Not looking good for Todd. She's giving him a hug... He's walking away, a look of disappointment on his ugly face... Nope, sorry, asshole. That's all you're gonna get tonight. Denied. Ha."

"Don't be too snarky," I cautioned. "I suspect being a bouncer at a strip club is one of the most thankless jobs in the world."

"Good point. Sorry, Todd."

Todd wandered back to Shanny's while Anna waited at the bus stop. In the distance, bundled in her coat, she didn't look any different from anyone else. I noted, with a sense of relief that surprised me, that she wasn't smoking but was instead sitting on the bench reading a book.

I held the wheel with sweating hands and there was a sick feeling in my stomach. I reminded myself that I really didn't know what Anna's game was. She bore the sign of the Fallen's great enemy. She'd said that it had been Jammer's idea, and that she'd broken up with him afterwards, but maybe that was a lie—a show of innocence to a man she didn't know, who asked her questions she didn't want to answer.

I felt guilty, like a jilted boyfriend following his ex around and watching her go from place to place, not knowing that someone was spying on her. I'd joked about stalking with Loren, but now that we were doing it, I felt like a complete asshole.

But so far she was our only connection to Jammer, Rafferty, and the Couch Park Family, and it was obvious that there was more to her story than she'd told me. My instincts told me that I needed to learn more, but even now I wasn't sure we were doing the right thing. So we were following her. Would we follow her all the way home? And if we did, then what? She'd already had me thrown out of her club. What were the odds that she'd happily share her secrets with me if I came knocking on her door in the middle of the night?

I felt sick, but I couldn't think of anything else to do.

"Bus coming." Loren's warning interrupted my reverie. I started Yngwie as the bus snorted to a stop and the handful of passengers, including Anna, stepped on board.

Loren grinned. "The game's afoot, Watson."

I tried to forcibly ignore my misery. "Hey, watch who you call Watson, Watson."

I pulled out onto Greeley. It was late, the street was empty and a massive, well-lit city transit bus is easy to follow. We hung back, driving slowly, giving the bus plenty of room and slowing down when it stopped for passengers. Every time it stopped, we strained to see if Anna got off.

Shaver... Skidmore... Roselawn... The bus slid through the now-quiet streets of Northeast Portland like a whale with tail lights. Most businesses were shut down and everyone sensible was home in bed, but a few hardy souls still traveled, getting on and off every few blocks.

Loren looked at street signs as we passed Ainsworth. "Dude, we're running out of Portland. Where the hell does she live?"

The answer wasn't too long in coming as the bus rumbled over an old concrete bridge spanning the sluggish waters of the Columbia Slough. Ahead was a tree-lined berm and the last bus stop before the vast golf-course and warehouse-filled wilderness along Marine Drive. The bus hissed to a stop, disgorging its single passenger.

"Home at last." Loren sounded puzzled. "But where's home?"

The bus disappeared into the darkness, and I pulled to a stop in a gravel turnaround, lights off. A lone street light illuminated Anna as she trudged along the berm.

I looked off to our right and saw a few yellow lights burning. "There's a trailer park down there. I think that's where she's headed."

"Yeah, but which trailer? We'll lose her once she gets off the road and I think she's going to notice if you follow here in this gunboat."

He was right. I uttered an annoyed grunt.

"Shit." I pushed open my door. "Come on. We'll have to follow her."

Loren put a hand on my arm. "She'll recognize you, dude. If she sees you, she'll freak completely."

I sighed. My unease and sick uncertainty returned at the thought of terrifying an innocent woman, even when I didn't know for sure that she was innocent. "I hate when you're right, Loren. You know that?"

"I know, I know." He stepped out, brandishing his cell phone. "If I need backup, I'll call."

I nodded and returned his gaze. "I'll be here."

I must have sounded worried. "Don't worry, Dude. I'll be fine. I know what I'm doing. I've seen a million cop movies."

"Is that supposed to reassure me?"

"Well, yeah." He looked suddenly dubious. "Sounds kind of stupid, doesn't it?"

"Never mind that. Just see where she goes. Get her address and get out. We'll figure out how to contact her later." I was utterly out of ideas. Maybe I'd write her a letter or something.

Loren nodded. "By your command."

Sometimes I wonder where Loren has room for anything practical, given how jammed his head is with all that geek culture crap.

I watched as he trudged down the road. Anna was at least a hundred yards ahead and hopefully wouldn't see him, or at least wouldn't be too worried about someone walking so far behind.

I couldn't stand sitting and finally got out of the car and paced, looking periodically at my cell phone to make sure it was on. In the distance, Anna's tiny figure turned down a street that cut through the berm, and Loren followed a few moments later.

A hundred different scenarios of what might happen to him flashed through my mind. We hadn't brought any weapons—no pistols, no sword, no shotguns—nothing. I'd figured that if things did go pear-shaped and someone called the police, I didn't want anything incriminating in the car. Now of course it seemed short-sighted and overly-cautious. I kicked myself mentally several times. It was something I did at least twice a day.

The phone vibrated and I jumped a foot, almost dropping it. Yes, it was Loren.

I dragged the green slider across the screen. "What?"

"We got trouble, Alex. It's Bozo the Goth and his cartoon pals. They're waiting down here in a POS pedophile van. She just walked past and... Oh, shit Alex... They're getting out and..."

I didn't wait for the rest. I was behind the wheel in an instant, kicking the engine to life and jamming it into gear, speeding out of the turnaround in a shower of gravel.

I hit the right turn onto the side road a little too fast, tires squealing, rear end slewing around, trying desperately to drag me into a skid. I steered into it. Yngwie wobbled and straightened as we barreled along a narrow downward slope.

About a hundred yards distant was a cluster of rectangular trailer homes, lit here and there by yellow porch lights. On the road ahead of me, five figures struggled near a battered panel van—Anna had fallen and was grappling with the shaggy-headed punk girl I recognized as Dreads, while the pair I'd seen at the park—Army Jacket and Bozo—were engaged with Loren. Army Jacket had grabbed him from behind in a headlock while Bozo punched at his face and body. He struggled to avoid the blows, but a few of them landed. As I watched, Bozo reached for an ankle sheath and pulled out a black-bladed combat knife.

I pounded on the horn and stomped my foot to the floor. The sudden noise and flood of light made everyone startle, and Loren took the opportunity to flip Army Jacket over his back and onto the asphalt, where he delivered a ferocious kick to the kid's face. Army Jacket grabbed his foot and yanked, dragging Loren down with him.

Bozo turned, his white face a mask of amazement, his black-outlined eyes widening, his beefy silhouette looming like a hippo in the headlights. Then he was on my hood, the knife bouncing away as he crashed into my windshield, which shattered with an alarming CRACK.

I swerved to avoid Anna and Dreads, slamming on the brakes as Bozo went tumbling ponderously off my hood, landing with a meaty thud on the pavement.

Bozo groaned, moving feebly while Loren and Army Jacket wrestled on the pavement. Dreads had a knife in one hand and held Anna by the wrist with the other, dragging her toward the van.

I kicked open Yngwie's door and leaped, grabbing Dreads' knife hand and yanking down on her thumb. I felt a satisfying snap as it dislocated. She screamed, dropping the knife and scrambling away, glaring. Anna lay on the road, sobbing but unhurt.

"Fuck you! I'll fucking kill you!" Dreads shrieked, cradling her broken hand and backing up.

I was about to go after her when something struck me from behind, throwing me forward. My head slammed loudly against the rusted side of the van, leaving a dent, sending the world into a wild dizzying spin.

Pain shot through my chest and stomach as Army Jacket kicked me with steel-toed boots. I collapsed on the ground, throwing my arms over my head for protection. He stomped a few times, then a loud voice echoed from inside the van.

"Grab the bitch and get in! Get the fuck in!"

Army Jacket stopped kicking me and turned away. Dreads held Anna with her good arm and Army Jacket unceremoniously slammed his fist into her face. She went limp and the two dragged her through the open van doors. I struggled to clear my head and get on my feet as Bozo half-walked, half-crawled inside as the van's springs groaned and protested. He spared me a final venomous stare.

"You're playin' with death, fuckface!" he snarled. Then the door slammed and they were gone, taillights speeding up the road, past the berm and away. Desperately I tried to read the license number, but failed.

Fuckface. The last refuge of the cretin, I thought. Bozo kept living down to my expectations.

I looked back at Yngwie. The hood was badly dented and his windshield was a total loss—we'd never be able to pursue.

Loren lay on the ground, moving feebly. When he looked up, I saw blood on his face.

"They got her, Alex," he groaned. "They got her. What the hell are we gonna do now?"

I shook my head. Everything hurt and I had barely slept in thirty-six hours.

"I don't know," I replied miserably. "I really don't know."

***

I called 911 from one of the few payphones still left in Portland and gave them the time, location, and particulars of the crime, including the names of all involved even though I still didn't know Anna's last name. I didn't give them my name, either—after the I-84 Killer case my relationship with them wasn't too good and these days they probably viewed me with all the enthusiasm of a serious skin rash.

We made it home without encountering Portland's finest, I stowed Yngwie in the garage and we staggered inside. I tottered on the edge of utter exhaustion and my brain was misfiring left and right, but through the haze I still had an idea of who might be able to help. With grim determination I threw myself on the couch and dialed Milo's number. To my relief, he answered on the second ring.

"Alex?" He sounded sleepy, but I didn't especially care. "What's up?"

"Emergency, dude," I replied. "Do you think you can remember the location of the house where you partied with the Couch Park assholes?"

V

The shadows of a sultry evening deepened around us as Loren drove us down Pacific Highway, a lonely road that stretches from Oregon City south to Canby. On our left was a bare cliff face, covered in mesh to prevent slides. Railroad tracks ran along the right side of the road and beyond them, screened by more trees, was the brown expanse of the Willamette River. The sun was setting behind shaggy hills on the opposite bank, and there was hardly anyone else on the road. Nevertheless, the cops in this part of the state didn't fool around, so we treated the speed limits with nearly religious reverence. I didn't want anyone seeing what was in the trunk of Loren's Taurus.

Milo hadn't been completely sure about the location of the house—just that they'd had to crawl through a gap in a chain link fence. That was all we had to go on, and neither of us wanted to think about what might be happening to Anna while we tried to find her, but neither of us had any better ideas. It took the rest of the day and we'd slept in shifts, but with the help of Google Maps satellite view we managed to narrow our choices down.

There were indeed several empty houses north of Canby surrounded by fencing—part of a development left half built then abandoned by a bankrupt developer. Once we showed him pictures, Milo agreed that he'd been to one of the houses but didn't remember which.

Loren's face was deep in gloom as he drove, lit only by the instrument panel. "Jesus Christ Alex, we don't even know she's there. This is such a longshot it's not even funny."

I didn't disagree. "Yeah, but it's the only shot we've got right now. We need to find out why the Family wanted her so bad they kidnapped her right off the street."

"You know she might be dead, Alex. Have you thought about that?"

I had but I didn't want to admit to it. "If they wanted her dead they'd have just killed her. They need her alive for some reason, and my guess it has something to do with that tattoo and her relationship with the late Mister Jammer."

"They've had her for almost a whole day, man." Loren sounded grim. "God only knows what they've done to her."

I didn't answer. It was too awful to think about. I tried to shut out memories of what Onatochee's followers had done to Mia Jordan, but they crept through anyway.

I cursed myself inwardly. All we knew right now was that Anna bore the symbol of the Fallen's unnamed great enemy and that the Family had her. That alone made it imperative that we at least try to find her. And given the powers that I'd seen Family members unleash, I was reluctant to entrust Anna's safety to the police.

Was I right? I had information about where she might be— were we complete fools for riding in alone, risking her life while ignoring professionals who did this for a living? Or would calling in the police simply put more people in danger?

I'd made a decision and I was sticking with it, but that didn't mean I was comfortable. If I ended up with Anna's blood on my hands, I wasn't sure what I would do.

On we drove into the night, the lights of Oregon City disappearing around a bend in the road, cut off by the tall cliffs on our left.

It was discomfiting. The Taurus was much smaller than Yngwie, and a hell of a lot wimpier. I felt as if we were driving down the road in a four-wheeled paper bag. I missed my Camaro.

On the plus side, our gas mileage was much better.

I looked down at my phone where a GPS app was running. "In about two miles, there'll be an access road on the left."

Loren nodded. "I'm keeping an eye out."

Fortunately for us the place was well off the beaten path—the sheriff wasn't likely to drive by if we went barging in loaded down with firearms. It had once been a filbert plantation, bought, rezoned, and bulldozed by a developer, much to the dismay of local conservationists.

The narrow road was marked "PRIVATE. NO TRESPASSING" which for us was usually an open invitation. The sun was gone, the clouds on the horizon were glowing pink, and the road in both directions was utterly empty as we turned off.

"About another half mile. Damn. I'm losing reception."

That made Loren laugh. "So some idiot built a development in a dead zone? This just gets better and better."

The road turned to dirt a few hundred yards later, and finally came to a halt at a chain link gate and a wall of razor-wire topped fencing. There were more rusty "NO TRESPASSING" signs, and the fencing was overgrown with blackberries. Loren pulled off the road, between two towering piles of the stuff, ominous in the growing darkness. Silence descended.

I took a deep breath. "Okay, let's armor up."

Loren popped the trunk and we got out. In addition to my sword, the armaments in the trunk were impressive, and some were downright illegal.

I pulled on a tactical vest with additional shoulder protection, then holstered my Glock, tucking an extra mag into the vest's pocket. I pulled my leather coat on over the entire affair—it was bulky, but given that it had saved my ass on several occasions, I was willing to risk it. I strapped the scabbarded sword to my back.

Loren lifted out his Mossberg 500 and began to load it with shells. "Shit, Alex. I haven't used this for anything but target practice. This isn't fooling around, is it?"

I glanced at the shotgun. "Hell no, it isn't."

It was an entirely legal weapon, of course. Lots of people owned one entirely legitimately. Not so for the case of flash-bang grenades that sat cozy and safe in the trunk. Technically they were Class III weapons, but the odds of getting Portland's boys in blue to approve my owning them—especially given my reputation with them—were about as good as my chances of being elected pope. As I attached a pair to my tactical vest, I reflected that I was putting both myself and Loren in serious legal jeopardy, and if we didn't find the Family it would be for nothing.

I wasn't worried about myself. I was willing to take whatever the system doled out to me, but looking at Loren, carefully attaching his own selection of grenades, I felt an all-too-familiar wave of guilt and concern, and for the thousandth time I reminded myself that he was a volunteer.

Well, technically so was I, but when you're presented with the choice of walking away and letting your home and everything you love burn, or taking up a sword and agreeing to run around like Captain Fucking Incredible, fighting evil wherever it may lurk... Well, it isn't really a choice, is it?

We finished our ensembles off with our night vision goggles. I'd looked through them so much lately I was starting to dream in green and black.

Without another word, we crept toward the fence. A quick inspection revealed clear evidence that the "temporarily" abandoned development had been visited in the form of a human-sized trench dug in the shelter of a tangle of blackberries, crushed down to form a trail and dotted here and there with cigarette butts. Not only had the place been visited, it had been visited regularly.

I held up the chain link, allowing Loren to scramble through, then he did the same for me from the other side.

We took stock of our surroundings. All around us stood the forlorn skeletons of about a score of houses in various states of completion, from bare frames to nearly-finished structures with walls, roofs, and even windows, now covered with plywood. Piles of building materials—shingles, plastic piping, lumber—lay scattered, slowly disintegrating, weathering away or lying inert, still awaiting the contractors who would probably never come back. Nearby I saw a street sign standing alone at an intersection, marking what would have been called *Oakwood Terrace.*

It all felt terribly sad. The streets were those artfully curved, winding avenues that you see throughout suburbia. They were thick with blackberries and undergrowth. The imaginary dollar signs of the great housing bubble were all over this place, and they were rotting along with the skeletal houses.

I motioned silently and we moved out, warily creeping from street to street. We stayed in cover; if the Family was here, I didn't want to risk blundering into any lookouts. Of course we *had* driven right up to the fence with our lights on—*that* wasn't likely to attract any attention, was it? I sighed. It was too late to do anything about it now.

We were crouching behind a pile of plastic piping, secured by a disintegrating wooden frame near the once and future Overlook Street when Loren tapped my shoulder and pointed, mouthing the word "Dreads."

About fifty yards away, a lone figure stood outside a mostly-completed ranch house, smoking a cigarette. At this distance, I couldn't make out features or even gender, but I could see a shaggy head of dreadlocked hair.

I nodded and pointed to my eyes, then at Dreads, then down at the ground. We crouched, motionless for long minutes watching as Dreads sucked every last molecule of nicotine out of her cigarette and finally flicked the butt away. She paused, looked up and down the street, then turned and went inside the house. We relaxed.

"No sentries," I muttered. "Well no one's ever accused them of being too smart."

"Good thing." Loren crouched, poised to move. "Lead the way."

I didn't feel terribly comfortable at the notion of being point man, but I moved as stealthily as I could to the next obstacle, a half-built garage attached to the bones of a house. I motioned for Loren to follow.

We were closer now. I peeked around the corner of the garage toward the back of the house where Dreads had gone. The windows were boarded up, just like all the others, but a thin sliver of light shone out from between boards like a shining beacon in the green-and-black dimness.

"I think they're in there," I whispered. "The light is coming from the front room. You ready?"

Loren nodded at his shotgun. "Two breaching rounds on top. I'll take the door down and you throw in the flash-bangs."

I nodded. "Okay. Time to press start."

"Fuck, Alex. We're really doing this, aren't we?" I couldn't see his expression behind the goggles, but he sounded very apprehensive.

"I'm afraid so." It had been years since we'd fought for real, and even then we'd been improvising—underequipped and afraid. We'd been determined not to be caught unprepared again and had rehearsed assaults like this a dozen times, using simulated flash-bangs loaded with CO_2, but even with all our foresight I was still scared. "Just stay calm."

"Easy for you to say." Loren checked his weapon one more time, then wrapped the strap around his forearm and prepared to shove off. "Let's go."

We made our way cautiously through overgrown back yards and half-built fences. Finally we were at the corner of the house, plastered tight against the outside wall.

Angry voices echoed from inside. Carefully I pressed my ear against the wall.

The first voice was high-pitched, slightly whiny. "I looked, man. I looked all over the fuckin' place. There's no one there. I swear."

"I know how hard you looked, Dreads." The second voice was deeper and spoke with slow, deliberate authority. "You took just enough time to finish off your cig and came right back in here. Slash says he saw headlights so you were supposed to go up to the fence and check it out."

"I did," Dreads replied lamely. "I just ran all the way."

"Bullshit. You don't understand how dangerous this fucker is. Grandfather thinks that guy is working with the Fallen, and you know what *that* means—he helped take out Boner and Possum and all the others out in Hicksville last month. And you shitheads had to go and give him a nice long look at your faces when you grabbed this bitch. Stupid fuckers. You want to give me a good reason why I don't slit your fucking throats right now?"

Another voice spoke up, this one thick and nasal, as if he was talking with his nose plugged. "Look, man... He didn't follow us. His windshield was totally smashed when he hit me. Shit, Tom... There's no way he knows where we are." There was a pause and a rustle. "I think we should just kill this bitch."

"You will leave her alive as Grandfather decreed, boy," said a fourth voice—cool, commanding and feminine. "Grandfather wants to find out how much she knows about us, and how she resisted the call. We are to wait here until the lantern gate opens. I will then leave with her and your task will be completed. Deviate from this pathway and you will be punished. Do you understand?"

A sullen chorus of "Yeah" spoke in reply.

That apparently wasn't good enough for her. She spoke again, her words sharper. "Do. You. Understand?"

"Yes, ma'am." The voices were louder now, respectful and laced with fear.

That made at least four targets—Dreads, Slash, a man whom I guessed was Father Tom, and a woman who talked like a professional dominatrix. Army Jacket was probably in there too though I hadn't heard him speak.

It also sounded as if Anna was alive, but the mysterious woman would be leaving with her very shortly. I waved for Loren to follow and we moved toward the front door.

Slash didn't think we'd be able to figure out where they were. It was the most recent in what was no doubt a very long series of bad decisions that had probably started with the mohawk.

Loren pressed the Mossberg's serrated breaching choke against the door. We exchanged a glance as I prepped a flash-bang.

I nodded.

Slug-shot exploded from Loren's shotgun, tearing a ragged hole in the door, followed an instant later by a second round for good measure. The entire deadbolt assembly went flying in pieces. The people inside would have barely realized what was happening, but we were just getting started. I spun, shattered the door with a single kick, tossed my flash-bang then hugged the opposite side of the entrance as the charge detonated.

Blinding light exploded inside the confined space of the living room, filling our ears with a near-deafening roar, dust billowing from the open portal.

I shot a glance at Loren. He was still in position a few feet back, his shotgun at the ready. I unclipped another grenade and pulled the pin.

"Fire in the hole," I said, unnecessarily, tossing it in and ducking away from the second blinding flash and deafening report.

My ears were ringing but it was nothing compared to what the people inside were feeling. Loren and I exchanged glances. "Ready?"

"Ready!"

I nodded and he was through the door. I followed and observed the carnage we'd visited inside.

I fought back the urge to cough. The air was filled with dust— the charges had knocked loose years of accumulation from the ceiling and walls. There was a scatter of old furniture—chairs and a couple of tables, covered with fast food wrappers, and miscellaneous groceries. The center of the room was bare and on the wood floor, daubed in black paint, was the same image I'd seen tattooed on Anna's back—a circle of incomprehensible runes surrounding an elaborate mandala-like pattern.

A half dozen or so bodies were sprawled all around the room, moving feebly. The blindness would last for another minute or so—the disorientation from the explosion would take longer for them to shake off. Either way, we had enough time if we moved quickly.

Dreads was the closest, lying on her back, eyes rolling up in her head, and Slash's ponderous bulk was draped across a chair nearby. He groaned piteously as I strode into the room behind Loren. Army Jacket lay in a motionless heap nearby— he'd been standing right where I'd thrown the grenade. There were a couple of girls and some others I didn't recognize, but none of them seemed inclined to give us any trouble.

A motionless figure lay on its side on an old dirty couch. With a mixture of relief and anger, I saw that it was Anna. Her wrists and ankles were secured with duct tape and she had another strip across her mouth. Her shirt was in tatters—torn open to expose the mandala pattern on her back. As I watched, I fancied I could see a faint tracery of fiery orange around it. She lay still—either drugged or knocked out by the blast—but looked otherwise unhurt.

On closer inspection I saw that she hadn't been idle during her captivity—the duct tape at her wrists and ankles was frayed as if she'd been working away at it. That was a good sign—she had clearly been conscious and clear-headed at some point, though how she planned on escaping from a room full of violence-prone thugs wasn't clear.

"Keep these assholes covered," I said. "I'll get her out of here."

From the shadows in the corner a voice rose up, as ugly as a rusty metal rasp. "Couldn't stay away could you, motherfucker?"

In the rush I hadn't noticed that Father Tom wasn't among the casualties.

Careless of me.

The blasts hadn't affected him at all, save for covering him with dust. He was even less savory-looking than the photo I'd seen—his face had grown more jaundiced, his hair thinner and grayer. His eyes were the worst—empty black sockets, staring at me like the gates of hell. In one hand he held an oversized cleaver like the one Rafferty had carried.

Beside him, silent and imperious, stood a woman of a type that would make strong men fall down on their knees and beg. She was taller than Tom and built like a swimsuit model. Her hair was like spun platinum and she regarded me with cold ice-blue eyes that impaled me like daggers. She was dressed in a severe gray business suit, complete with heels—dusty now but still looking sharp as hell—but her expression suggested that she wasn't all that interested in facilitating a staff meeting.

Loren seemed unimpressed. He leveled his shotgun at the pair. "Stay where you are, both of you." His words were calm and deadly, nothing like his normal jaunty, geek-friendly tone. "We're taking Anna and leaving."

"Are you now?" Father Tom stepped forward, raising his weapon. The woman remained motionless, watching us with an arrogant gaze. "Why don't you just go ahead and try it, boy?"

Loren squeezed the trigger, firing once, then ejected the shell and fired again. Two heavy pitbull rounds slammed into Father Tom's chest, each with six .00 pellets and a heavy one-ounce slug.

Dark rents appeared in his clothing, red with a spatter of blood. Tom didn't fall but only winced and continued to advance. With one hand, he flung aside a fallen chair and it shattered against the wall. In rising alarm, I saw a dim glow emanating from the painted mandala on the floor and felt the first stirrings of a stabbing pain in my head.

"Ow." A deep orange light grew in his empty eye sockets, like the coals of a fire. "That fucking *hurts.*"

My sword seemed to leap from the scabbard under its own volition, flaming bright silver and trailing blue sparks. I hadn't felt this much power rage through the weapon since the last fight with Onatochee.

Father Tom held his big cleaver aloft and it began to glow hot yellow-orange. "You're the fuck that killed Rafferty." There was a strange overlay to his voice, as if he were speaking through a distortion pedal or vocoder. I'd heard that sort of thing before and I didn't like it. "You and those biker cocksuckers."

"You got me, fair and square." I wasn't about to tell him that Frank Magruder had actually done the deed. "Me and my Viking friends."

Tom bared his teeth in an unnatural grimace, skinning his lips back like a desiccated corpse. Loren retreated a step, his shotgun still leveled at Tom and the woman.

"You gotta have shit for brains to throw in with those freaks." Tom's words had the edge of a feral growl now, still strangely metallic and distorted. "You know what they want. They don't care if the whole fucking world burns."

I tried to keep him talking, wildly adding two plus two and hoping that my answer made sense. "And your master's offering something better? I don't think so."

I didn't know who his master truly was, but I needed to keep him talking. We circled warily, keeping the painted mandala between us. Around us, the Family kids were beginning to stir, throwing off the effects of the two flash-bangs, and on the couch Anna moved feebly. The blonde business-suited amazon remained where she was, watching our every move intently.

"At least he'll let this world live. As long as we play ball." Tom sounded as if he thought I knew what he was talking about. "It's not so bad, really. Not once you get used to it."

In the middle of the room the circle of weird hieroglyphics glowed with the same orange color as Father Tom's eyes. A faint reddish sheen touched the mandala pattern inside the circle.

"What did they offer you, mister?" Tom continued to circle me, sword on guard, his smoldering eyes searching for an opening. "They offer you power? Said they'd make you one of them? Did they give you that sword?"

He was on the wrong track, but I let him stay there. "What do you think?"

"I think you're a fucking traitor, selling out to the first buncha faggot bikers that offered you free blowjobs, that's what I think. You got a problem with that?"

He was trying to get a rise out of me. The circle was cherry red now, with yellow-orange luminescence along the lines of the central pattern. It started to overwhelm my goggles. With a single motion, never taking my eyes from Tom, I flipped them up and saw him lit by a glow like a dying fire. Orange sparks swirled around him, a smoldering counterpart to the sword's attendant motes of shining silver-blue.

I blinked, looking away from Tom for an instant. I saw a faint tracery of orange lines or threads, as delicate as cobwebs blown on the breeze. A bundle of them extended from the center of the mandala into Tom's forehead then radiated out from him to each of the Family members scattered around the room, just as they had in Malheur County. One reached blindly toward Anna. She was conscious now, straining against her bonds. When she saw me, her eyes widened and she redoubled her efforts.

The circle grew brighter still, and the jabbing pain in my head intensified. Shit. It was Hauser Butte all over again, but I suspected Father Tom was a more dangerous opponent than Jack Rafferty; he'd already shrugged off the worst that Loren could throw at him.

The mandala's burning wheel illuminated the entire living room like a sunset. Deep inside the shining circle I saw something stir—the same mass of unclean flesh I'd glimpsed on Hauser Butte.

I reversed direction, placing myself between Tom and the couch where Anna lay. The thread that reached toward her looked almost white-hot, but it seemed somehow incomplete, flickering as if it was trying to connect to her but couldn't.

"Loren. Grab Anna and get the hell out of there. I'll hold this asshole off."

Loren shot me a quick, worried glance. He'd raised his goggles too.

I spared him a nod in response. "Go!"

Loren moved toward the couch.

Then all hell broke loose.

Dreads and Army Jacket leaped to their feet, moving clumsily like puppets as the orange threads pulsated. Army Jacket's face was bruised from Loren's attentions, and Dreads' hand was splinted where I'd dislocated her thumb.

Slash looked like he'd been hit by a car, which made sense since he had. He was even more sluggish than the others, as if his physical bulk simply made it harder to manipulate him. Three others moved—two tough-looking girls and a skinny guy with duct-taped glasses—rising painfully to their knees and crawling towards us. None of them made a sound.

Dreads limped toward the couch. Her battered face was contorted as if each step was agony, and smoldering sparks flashed down the thread that connected her head to Father Tom. For his part, Father Tom's thin mouth turned up in a slight smile.

Loren snapped his shotgun down, aiming at Dreads.

"Don't shoot her!" Through a haze of pain I forced my feet to move, stepping toward Tom. Burning needles stabbed into my head. I raised the sword, gathering myself to swing at Dread's fiery cord, but the pain suddenly redoubled, hitting me like a blow, even worse than the kids' attack on the butte.

Behind Tom the blonde woman had raising her arms and was shouting. Her eyes burned with the same angry fire as Tom's and her voice thundered through the room like a great, dissonant orchestra.

Ati Me Peta Babka!

As the words rumbled and growled inside my head, I recognized them. They were proto-Sumerian and I had uttered them myself during the ritual to summon the goddess She Who Watches.

They meant "Gatekeeper, open the way for me."

"*No!*" I shouted, and threw myself toward the woman, but the words continued.

Zi Dingir Girru Kanpa! Mimma-Lemnu! Usella Mituti Ikkalu Baltuti!

I didn't recognize those words, but they didn't sound very friendly. Her eyes pulsated like burning hearts, my pain growing and contracting along with them. I stumbled, screaming. The mandala on the floor was a raging inferno now, its characters blurred together and unrecognizable. Something moved there, closer now, clawing its way out of the burning circle.

Dreads blundered into Loren, pushing him back, but Loren swung the shotgun, slamming its metal stock under Dreads' chin, snapping her head back, sending her to the floor. Then Army Jacket advanced, moving with greater speed and deliberation, followed by Slash and the other Family kids, all trailing pulsing orange threads.

I forced my attention back toward the woman, but Tom now stood between us. His great cleaver-sword burned angry white-orange, heat radiating out and singing my face. I advanced, pain lancing through my head. I fought to ignore it.

From the flaming mandala I heard a voice echoing inside my head...

Who are you? It was a commanding voice—calm, forceful, commanding. *What do you want?*

It wasn't Tom—he stood before me, smirking—and it wasn't the woman; she was still shouting the Sumerian invocation. The voice in my head throbbed, pounding on me like a sledge hammer, trying to force me to fall, to drop the sword, to answer its insistent demands.

Give it up, whoever you are. Tell me who you are, what you are. Take the mark and you'll live and be powerful. Be one of us and be blessed by wisdom. Know the truth.

Confused images flashed through my brain. I could only grasp a few of them, as if I were listening to someone speaking in a language I only partly understood. I saw a scene in the desert—men and women gathered around a sandstone altar, bowing before the statue of a multi-armed creature with an elongated head and three strange triangular eyes. I saw men in bronze helmets and crude armor crafted of animal skins struggling on the battlefield with spears and clubs. I saw rough cart-like chariots pulled by wild horses, and kings in gold crowns, clad in robes of blue and red. And I saw blood—cities burning, long ships lining beaches as armored warriors dragged screaming men, women, and children away by their hair. I saw bearded warriors kicking down doors, cutting men to pieces with longswords, throwing themselves on the women, laughing...

And there amid the wreckage was Arngrim, clad in mail to his knees, a bloody axe in one hand, his dragon-crested helm crouched on his head. He shouted to his men as they stabbed and rent and burned and killed and raped...

Suddenly it was years later and I beheld a room full of black men and women, simply dressed and unassuming, standing before a statue of the same multi-armed, three-eyed creature. Each in turn stepped up to the statue and placed an object at its foot—money, food, small carvings...

Without warning the door flew open, and a band of white men in jungle fatigues burst in, indiscriminately firing submachine guns and hacking with machetes, mercilessly cutting down the worshipers, then slitting the throats of the handful that survived.

Arngrim stood in the doorway. Now he wore a cap, but on his shoulder was a patch bearing the ubiquitous dragon embroidered in black.

See your Fallen? See what they've done? They don't care for this world—it's nothing but a refuge for them, a place where they gather strength and await the reckoning when the Master comes and brings justice. He'll show the way to all of us, and the Fallen will be vanquished. Those with the mark will be spared and know wisdom. Join us, and know the truth.

The words stirred up anger inside me. The voice was smooth, self-assured, arrogant—it made me think of a smarmy politician or the talking heads on cable news, a rich kid telling a poor person how to live, or a religious fanatic saying that he knows what God wants. They echoed a thousand other voices I'd heard all my life, and even though the words were simple and uncomplicated, their tone was all too familiar.

I was not with the Fallen. They thought I was, but I saw the Fallen for what they were, and they were as fell and evil as the Family. Anger rose...

In the past rage had driven me, giving strength to my movements. Now it grew again—anger at the Family, at Father Tom, at the Fallen, at the voice echoing inside my head—anger fired by the knowledge that I was dealing with arrogant fools who had given up their humanity in exchange for some alien creature's promise, and now wanted me and the people I loved to do the same.

Beside me, Loren backed up before Bozo the Goth's increasingly confident advances. Behind him, the other Family members advanced as well.

"*Aleeex!* We gotta do something! Fast!"

The pain in my head threatened to overwhelm me completely, but the anger in my chest gave me one last act. There was no time to shout a warning. Only an instant left before the incessant pressure of Father Tom and the thing in the circle finally crushed me...

I whirled, dragging against the chains of agony that held me and swung the sword, slicing through the burning threads that emerged from the circle.

I didn't feel anything, but the effect on the Family kids was instantaneous. As one they convulsed as if they were being electrocuted, faces screwed up into tight grimaces, then fell, twitching and shaking to the floor. The thread that had been reaching for Anna vanished into the air.

The blonde woman gasped, clutching her head, then screamed and stumbled backwards, unsteady on her heels, and fell against the wall.

The circle had transformed into a tangled jumble of random kaleidoscopic light. The painted glyphs burst into flames, blurring together into a ring of fire. The voice and the pressure in my head were gone, along with the fiery threads, blown away as if by the winds of a cyclone. The kids were all down, groaning or moving feebly, and none of them seemed to have any inclination to come at us again.

I coughed and spat. The air was full of dust and the burning symbols lit the room with flickering yellow. "Loren, get Anna out of here."

"Right, boss." Loren crouched beside the couch. Anna had already gotten her hands mostly free and was busy tearing the tape off her mouth as Loren set down his weapon and used his Leatherman to slice her ankles free.

"Can you walk?" he asked. She nodded and he started to help her rise, scooping up the shotgun with his other hand. She was wobbly after a day in captivity but managed to get unsteadily on her feet.

Something moved in the wavering shadows.

"Not so fast, asshole."

Father Tom stood between us and the door. Cutting the threads hadn't hurt him—the fire in his eyes still raged and his weapon glowed red-hot. Anna stumbled against Loren and he moved to support her. I stepped in front of Tom, sword on guard.

"Who the fuck are you?" he demanded, feet apart, his own burning weapon raised. "Whoever you are, you are fucking with the wrong people."

I glared and spoke slowly. "I'm *Nomeus*. Shepherd. *Panigara*. Guardian of the Boundary Stone. Tell your friends. They'll know who I am."

Tom's face registered something that might have been shock or even fear while beside him the blonde woman dragged herself back on her feet, eyes fixed on me with a look of utter hatred.

"Panigara!" The word burst from her, metallic and distorted. *"Edin na zu!"*

I stood my ground. All we had to do now was get the hell out. I'd settle with these bastards later.

For an instant Tom seemed to waver, his gaze darting back towards the door, as if weighing his chances of success if he fled. Then his face hardened.

"I don't care what the fuck you're called. You're just another stupid asshole who doesn't know his place. You had your chance, now you're gonna get fucked up."

Behind him the woman shouted again and once more the words cut through my brain like a burning knife.

"Amelnakru! Lilitu! Lilitu! Mimma-Lemnu wardum daku!"

In the center of the circle the blurred colors drew together, coalescing into a massive shape, pressing out like toothpaste from a tube. It unfolded into a shaggy form the size of a bear with wet, matted fur and the face of a wolf. Its jaws were huge, far out of proportion to its face bristling with a double-row of slimy brown teeth. Three yellow eyes glared at me, elongated and strange like the eyes of the statue in my vision. From its shoulders rose a pair of leathery wings and from its back a segmented tail ending in a needle-sharp scorpion's stinger.

Anna shrieked at the sight and Loren was frozen in mute horror, his eyes wide with fear, staring at the horror that dragged its way from the burning circle.

The beast ignored them and strode deliberately toward me. I'd seen its like before, in my first dream of the Fallen. They had flown with the army of burning demons, driving the Fallen from their world... But I had seen hundreds, and this was only one.

It seemed more than enough for me right now.

The floor was completely aflame now, orange tongues licking eagerly across it. Without preamble the wolf-thing gathered itself and leaped, slavering jaws split wide, teeth bristling like rusted barbed wire. Fortunately it was massive and moved like a freight train, telegraphing where it was going. I scrambled out of the way and its great black paws crashed into the floor, cracking floorboards and sending up more dust.

The living room was big, but this monstrosity was huge and couldn't maneuver without knocking a couple of walls down. I saw my opening and rushed at it, stabbing at its flank just behind its ponderous hind leg. With a flash of blue, the sword sliced cleanly, stabbing through one side and out the other.

Uttering a ferocious howl of pain and anger the thing twisted, its wings and stinger brushing the ceiling, its body blundering into the wall. I tried to pull the sword free but realized with horror that it was stuck. The wolf-thing slammed against the wall again, and the hilt was ripped from my grasp.

Then Father Tom was on me, swinging his cleaver. I grabbed a fallen chair and blocked his blow. The chair disintegrated into kindling, but it sent Tom off balance and he stumbled, falling to his knees. I charged, driving an elbow into the back of his head, kicking away the cleaver. It tumbled out of his hand and clanged to the floor near the entrance to the kitchen, a bare room with the skeletons of cabinetry and bare wires for appliances.

There was a shout from the other side of the room. The wolf-thing turned away from me and advanced on Loren who backed away, the shotgun unsteady in both hands. He unleashed his last pitbull rounds into the thing's face. Flesh was torn off, bone chipped, and blood splattered. It yelped and fell back, wounded but still alive and angry, my sword projecting from its side.

The stinger waved ominously, seeking a target. Loren had fallen to his knees and stared upward as if transfixed while

Anna crouched behind him, limbs shaking, struggling to stand, fighting a day of weakness and deprivation.

I only had an instant. Even without the sword, my perception of time seemed to slow, and as the stinger descended, aimed straight for Loren's chest, I moved, sprinting forward. It was half way through its arc when my fingers made contact with the sword's grip, sticking obscenely from the wolf-creature's hide.

Energy raced up my arm, as intense as an electric shock. I yanked the sword with all my strength and this time it came free, cutting through the thing's flesh as I did so, and a gush of dark fluids burst from the wound. The stinger shuddered and stopped mid-strike.

It turned back toward me, yowling, its eyes blazing with hatred, and now the stinger came down on me, striking my shoulder but glancing off the black leather. Blindingly fast, it whipped back and thrust downward again. I retreated, but fell against the prostrate form of Dreads and tumbled backwards. The stinger descended, spearing Dreads in the belly. She convulsed, face contorted, and a strangled cry of agony escaped her lips. Then the stinger drew back again, dripping dark venom. Dreads thrashed, her cries fading, then lay still, her sickly pale flesh discoloring to ugly blue-black.

I charged forward, drawing the sword back and swinging it down two-handed, impacting on the beast's shaggy neck.

It was like cutting through a sack full of garbage. Its skin split, bones fractured and with a rush of foul-smelling gore the scorpion-wolf was on the ground in two pieces, its jaws snapping, tail lashing and striking out at random. As I watched, its outlines began to blur and disintegrate—like other alien creatures its material form couldn't persist in our world after its death.

A piercing, ululating scream echoed from behind me and I whirled. The blonde woman was in motion, racing at me. As she came she changed, flames swirling around her—her clothing burned away, her model's face melted into a grinning skull-visage, her silver-blonde hair burst into flames and in her hands appeared a massive flame-bladed scythe. Tom was only a step or two behind her, raising his cleaver and bellowing incoherently.

The woman was naked by the time she reached me, and at least a foot taller. Her head was now nothing but a skull with flaming eye sockets. I scrambled aside, trying to keep her between me and Tom. The scythe slashed through the air, trailing fire and I barely managed to parry it, sending out a shower of red and silver sparks.

Then Tom swung his cleaver. I disengaged my blade, rolling away as his weapon smashed into the floor, splintering wood. As he struggled to pull it free I whirled and swung wildly, slicing his thigh, spitting more sparks.

The fire in Tom's eyes died and he shrieked, releasing his grip on the cleaver and falling to the floor, clutching his leg where I'd struck it. Blood gushed through his fingers.

I didn't spare him a moment but struck back at the woman. Our weapons clashed together in a renewed explosion of orange and silver-blue. I pressed forward and she gave ground. Smoke billowed through the air—the center of the room was a pillar of flames, burning up into the ceiling.

Loren was on his feet, helping Anna to stand, staring at the space where the scorpion-wolf had been.

"Get going!" I shouted. "I'll be okay!"

The woman came on again, but I dodged and the scythe blade passed through empty air, crashing into the wall, shattering sheetrock and triggering a new slide of debris from the ceiling. I backed away, sword on guard. She didn't follow but stood her ground, empty eye sockets staring, her skull wreathed in flames. On the floor, Father Tom writhed and moaned in pain.

The Couch Park kids were scattered all around me. They were bad—delinquents, thugs, probably killers, but I wasn't an executioner and I didn't have the right to let helpless people die, however bad they were. Dreads was curled in a lifeless, motionless ball. It was probably too late for her.

"And get them out of here too, Loren!" I motioned with my free hand. "I'll deal with this one!"

Loren threw me one last troubled glance, then turned, helping Anna toward the door.

"They're gone now." I glared at the skull-faced creature. "Your pet's dead and you've lost your prisoner. The Master won't approve."

She didn't reply but rushed at me again, striking high, then low, then sidestepping and trying to take me in the flank. I deflected every blow, though they shivered through my arm like electrical shocks. I swung back, but she moved with fearsome speed and grace, dancing out of the way.

Then Loren was back, dodging through flames. He grabbed one of the boys around the shoulders and began to drag him out.

I bore down on the demon-woman, hitting wildly, my blade clanging against hers. The air was filled with smoke as flames began to consume the walls and ceilings. She returned every one of my blows and did not retreat.

Behind us Loren struggled with Slash's girthy bulk. The entire living room was ablaze, flames licking the ceiling, a rush of hot air burning my lungs. I prepared to meet another onslaught from the skull-creature.

When she finally moved, it wasn't in the direction I expected. She pivoted and my blow caught her on the shoulder, hacking at her flawless pale skin and eliciting an angry distorted scream, but she didn't counterattack. Instead the scythe vanished into a puff of angry orange spiderwebs as she seized Father Tom by his injured leg and dragged him with superhuman strength toward the pillar of fire where the summoning circle had been. Tom screamed, but she ignored him.

Above us a huge piece of the ceiling collapsed, bringing down plaster and burning wood, forcing me back and away from her as she bore her burden directly into the flames.

Mimma-Lemnu! Harani barag!

Her final words pounded in my head, and then they vanished in a renewed burst of heat and fire. I stumbled away as the rest of the ceiling collapsed, dodging more burning debris and stumbling out the door into the blessed coolness of the night air.

Loren sat with Anna, watching the house burn. The other family kids lay about, variously groaning or shivering pitifully.

"You get 'em all?" I asked.

Loren nodded. His adrenaline high was beginning to fade, and now he looked shaken and slightly sick. "All but Dreads. She was dead when I got to her." He waved a hand at Slash, lying nearby, aspirating loudly like a beached whale. "That fucker almost gave me a hernia, but yeah. I got the rest of 'em out. Damn. Never thought I'd be saving guys like that asshole. What do you bet he never even thanks me?"

The burning framework of the house collapsed in a tower of sparks and a wall of hot air washed over us like an ocean wave.

I knelt beside them and looked at Anna. She was bruised and exhausted but didn't seem injured otherwise.

"You're okay now," I said. "We'll get you out of here. It's me, Alex. Remember?"

There was a brief flicker of fear in her eyes then the sudden realization of where she was.

"Oh yeah," she said, her voice weak but still retaining a spark of sarcasm. "Alex. How could I possibly forget?"

VII

I felt as if we were driving home through absolute darkness, lit only by the Taurus' headlamps. The occasional point of light across the river seemed tiny and lost in a featureless sea of black and overhead even the stars seemed muted.

"What day is it?" Anna's voice was groggy, but she seemed relatively unhurt, lying on the back seat of the Taurus, wrapped in my coat.

"Saturday, June 14th," I said. "They just got you last night."

"Well I'm glad to know that Friday the 13th's reputation remains intact," she said, showing a hell of a lot more humor than I would have under the same circumstances. "How did you find me?"

"Luck, mostly," Loren said. "Alex knows someone who knows the Couch Park Family and he told us about the house."

"Good thing they're so stupid," I said. "There was no guarantee that you'd be there but it was the only lead we had."

She sat up, frowning, holding the coat around her shoulders. "And what's your interest in me? Why did you show up at Shanny's and spout all that bullshit?"

I sighed. "It's a long story. I'm really sorry I freaked you out. I'm not always the most diplomatic guy in the world."

She forced a smile, but it looked like it hurt. "Well, I could have handled it myself, but for what it's worth, thanks for rescuing me."

Loren waved a hand. "Hey, distressed damsels are our meat and potatoes."

She gave him a sour look. "What are you guys? Detectives or something?"

"Or something," I replied. "We specialize."

"You specialize." Her face was weary and haggard, but she laughed. "In what? Giant wolves and skull-monsters? Stuff that you need grenades and a sword to put down?"

"Sometimes." She'd been awake for the show, if a bit groggy—she'd seen the scorpion-wolf and the scythe-bearer and what we'd done to them, but I was still surprised at her matter-of-factness. "You may have noticed the Couch Park people have some..." I paused. "Some *assets* that the cops aren't equipped to handle?"

"I thought they were just garden variety sickos. At least until Wayne started babbling about his demon god and shit."

I turned, staring so intensely that her eyes widened in surprise. "Wayne? You mean Jammer?"

"Yeah, him." There was no affection in her voice, only contempt. "He was the guy who persuaded me to get the tattoo."

"And he had one just like it?"

"Yeah. Like I said, he tried to tell me some bullshit about it being romantic or something." She looked suddenly worried. "He wasn't there, was he? Have you seen him? Do you know where he is?"

I drew a deep breath. No sense hiding anything from her now. "Sorry, Anna. He's dead. He and a bunch of other Family members were killed out in Eastern Oregon."

She stared, open-mouthed. "Dead? What the fuck happened?" Now she looked scared again. "Jesus. Did you...?"

I shook my head emphatically. "No, we didn't do it. But you probably don't want to meet the guys who did."

"Oh, fuck." She didn't seem terribly sad at news of Jammer's demise, but her tone was still fearful. "Who did it? Was it some gang war or something?"

"Maybe. Did Jammer or his friends ever talk about a bunch of bikers called the Fallen?"

"The Fallen?" Naked terror flashed in her eyes. She covered her mouth with her hand. "Oh my God. Oh my God."

Alarm bells rang in my head. "Anna, who are the Fallen? How do you know...?"

I broke off abruptly. The pain was back, a hot needle stabbing through my brain.

Loren shouted. "Alex! Look!"

On the road ahead a pair of headlights shone in the darkness. At first it looked like an oncoming car, but then they split apart, racing ahead on either side of us.

Something flashed in the rear window. I looked back in sudden alarm. Two more lights appeared behind us, joined a moment later by two more. In the distance I heard the whine of motorcycle engines. Behind me, Anna cried out in wordless terror.

"Loren! We've got company at six o'clock!"

"I noticed!" Loren tromped his foot to the floor—it didn't have quite the same effect as it did on Yngwie, but we took off at a fair clip. The lights behind dropped back, but the ones ahead bore down even faster, coming at us from either side.

"I'm gonna try to go between!" Loren growled through gritted teeth, fingers tight on the wheel. "Hang on..."

In the instant before we rushed past the two riders ahead I had a glimpse of them—the same grim, handsome faces I'd seen on Hauser Butte, eyes masked by goggles, chests bare save for leather vests. A blurred flash revealed their true appearance— the crimson demon-things mounted on snorting black beasts... Each one guided his mount with one hand, and in the other...

In the other he gripped a brutal black metal weapon, and we were about to drive straight between them, right through the blades of the mincing machine...

"Loren! Look out! They're—"

I was too late. The Fallen riders swung their weapons as they roared past. There was a bang and a shriek of metal. The headlights exploded, fenders shredded apart, tires disintegrated. As the blades sliced through the Taurus' flanks, our passenger windows burst into thousands of fragments and the entire car lurched sideways, wheels digging into the pavement, angry sparks showering as we skidded.

"SHIT!" Loren desperately fought the wheel as it wrenched itself out of his hands, jumping first one way then the other. Then with a screech the entire car rolled, metal crunching, glass breaking. The world outside spun, gravity pressed us down into our seats one moment, trying to tear us loose the next.

For what seemed like hours we tumbled; in reality it was only a few seconds before we finally came to rest, tilted down, half on the road and half in the railroad cut. Loren's car was reduced to a mass of tortured metal, leaking fluids and steaming. My head pounded, and I'd taken a beating, but I didn't seem to have broken anything.

"Are you all right?" I demanded. "Loren? Anna?"

"I'm okay..." Loren grunted, kicking at his door. It resisted for a moment, then flew open. "Okay being a relative term."

"I think..." Anna's voice sounded small and lost, but she moved well enough as Loren helped her to climb over the seat and out his door. "I don't think I'm hurt."

That was something anyway. My door was jammed shut and I had to scramble through the broken window, under the crumpled roof and out onto the road. Behind us the two riders were turning and getting ready to come back. Beyond them were more headlights than I wanted to count.

I dashed for the trunk. It was as crumpled as the rest of the car. I tried to focus, to think, but my mind felt fogged, sluggish in the aftermath of the fight at the house and the crash. "Can you get this open?"

Loren looked numb, as if trying to shake off the same enervation that I felt, then ran back toward the driver's seat and pulled the trunk release. To my relief, it actually clicked and the tortured lid popped open an inch.

We wrenched it free with effort. Our equipment was jumbled but intact, and I still had my Glock. I unsheathed the sword and strode back toward the road. I felt the energy—the power that pulsed through the weapon in the presence of otherworldly threats, cutting through fatigue and the fog in my brain. My back hurt and my knee protested—I'd probably sprained it, but if that was the worst thing that had happened we were lucky. I doubted that the Fallen would let us off with just a few bruises.

"You two stay back," I shouted. "I'll deal with this."

"Like hell, Alex!" Loren looked at the Mossberg in disgust. "Crap. I used the last of the ammo on that scorpion-wolf thing."

I handed him my Glock. "Come on, then!"

Anna crouched against the ruins of the car. Her eyes were wide with fear and something even deeper and more profound, as if she was a little girl whose childhood monsters had come to life. I didn't want to think about it.

I scrambled out of the cut and onto the road where I stood, sword on guard. Loren knelt down in firing stance slightly behind me, taking aim at the oncoming headlights.

The sound of engines sliced through the night, mid-way between somewhere and nowhere. The trees were dark, the cliff face vanished overhead, and the moon shone down serenely, as if nothing that happened here could ever affect her.

Two riders were coming, swords out, once more splitting up so that they would be able to attack us from both sides the same way they'd crippled the car. I wasn't going to wait around.

"If I miss, blast 'em," I shouted as I started to run forward, boots pounding on the asphalt. They came on even faster— shiny machine-beasts, handsome blonde and bearded-crimson fanged animal faces... In an instant I'd be in between them and they'd cut me in half.

I braced myself, feeling the energy streaming through me, the power that the sword channeled, the strength granted me by a being who had appeared as a graceful winged woman, but who was from a different place, a place as strange as that which the Fallen had fled...

Time slowed to a crawl. Even though there was only an eyeblink instant before they were on me, I felt unhurried, deliberate. I threw myself to the left, faster and more nimbly than humanly possible, rolling across the pavement so that the nearest cycle passed by inches to my right. The sword flashed silver-blue, cutting through the cycle's front wheel. The tire burst and the wheel disintegrated into a shower of chrome fragments.

Then I was on my feet again, crouched, sword poised.

A scream rent the air—part metal, part animal. The wounded machine tumbled, careening into the second cycle and they both burst apart, wheels spinning through the air, chrome and steel crumpling and shattering, the two riders flung helplessly, crashing to the asphalt and bouncing like rag dolls.

The riders rolled to a stop amid the carnage that I perceived as chunks of both metal and bloody black flesh. Had they been human they'd have been pulverized, but not the Fallen. They lay, sorely injured and groaning, but still very much alive.

A chorus of engines roared behind me. I turned to confront a body of riders filling the road in a double column that stretched back at least a dozen deep. They all seemed like sons of the same father—northern European, blonde, blue-eyed, with long lustrous hair and chiseled features, clad in a variety of leather and denim outfits, their vests bearing savage emblems from a hundred nations, their metal mounts screaming with barely-restrained barbarity.

Arngrim led the way, the dragon sigil resting against his bronzed chest. His vest bore other insignia—a German iron cross, a wolf's head, a pair of crossed swords, a grotesque Samurai mask and others.

He drew near, raising a hand and the column came to an instant halt. He continued to roll forward until he stopped about ten feet from me. He raised his goggles, regarding me coolly.

I met his gaze. "Arngrim?"

He nodded politely. "*Hirdir.*" His voice rumbled like distant thunder. "No man has held that sword in centuries. You wield it well, my friend."

I didn't lower my guard. "I'm not your friend, Arngrim. Your friends just tried to kill me."

"You have broken faith with us, Shepherd." He raised a gloved hand and pointed behind me. "You give aid to the servants of the enemy."

I looked back. Anna stood on the edge of the railroad cut, trembling and gazing at Arngrim with undisguised horror.

"She bears his mark," Arngrim said.

I shifted my grip on the sword. "It was applied against her will and without her knowledge of what it was, *Fordæmdur.* She's not a servant of your enemy. She's under our protection now."

Arngrim and the assembled Fallen behind him were unmoved. Their stern collective gaze rested on Anna, and she cried out. Loren moved, stepping protectively beside her, his weapon still trained on Arngrim.

"No mercy for the servants of the enemy," Arngrim said. "She bears the mark. She is the enemy's creature. Give her to us or be named oathbreaker and enemy of the Fallen."

I felt a touch of fear myself. Even with the sword, I could never hope to stand against the entire clan of Fallen. And Loren would probably have no better luck with my Glock than he'd had with his shotgun against Father Tom.

"She isn't with them. We rescued her from a house full of your enemies, back down the road in Canby."

Arngrim smiled. It wasn't a very happy smile. "We know." He whistled. "Gunnar! Show him!"

A rider rolled forward from the main body. I recognized him as the hammer-wielder from Hauser Butte—the one with the spiral triskelion emblem. He turned and reached down to pluck something big and bulky from his saddlebags.

Behind me Anna screamed and Loren swore.

Gunnar brandished his burden so that we could see it. Slash's head hung from his fist, mouth distended, black tongue bulging out from between his lips, his eyes rolled up in their sockets. Blood still leaked from his severed neck. Apparently the Fallen didn't always leave their foes as desiccated scraps of skin and bone.

"We found the enemy's slaves where you left them, Shepherd." Arngrim made a disgusted sound. "You are weak, Shepherd. You show mercy to an enemy who does not understand mercy. You leave them alive to carry out their master's dictates. We finished your task, as you should have." He turned his harsh gaze back on Anna, who now knelt on the road, weeping. Loren crouched beside her, his arm around her shoulders.

"Jesus Christ, you assholes!" he snarled angrily. "Can't you see she had nothing to do with any of that shit? It wasn't even her fault!"

"You swear by your God." Arngrim didn't seem impressed. "Once an oath such as yours had meaning. Now, it is nothing. The old ways are gone, and soon you will have no defense against the enemy. Once, a man wielded that sword—a noble man with noble intentions. He swore in the name of all who came after him that on our *Dagur Hefnd,* the one who bore the sword would stand with the Fallen and face the enemy." He lowered the kickstand and dismounted, walking toward me with measured strides. I didn't lower the sword.

He went on, his voice low threatening. "For fourteen centuries we kept faith, Shepherd. Now the enemy returns. His agents prepare the way."

Our eyes met and then we were alone together, standing in a featureless void.

Arngrim's voice echoed. *We are linked by fate and blood, you and I. See our story, Hirdir. See what the Fallen have become.*

The void melted, shifting into an arid, barren landscape. Arngrim rode there, mounted on a jet-black, caparisoned warhorse, his leather riding gear transformed into blood-stained mail. At the head of the Fallen he rode, and all around him men shouted "Saint George! Saint George!" as they fell upon a crowd of dismounted Saracens frantically trying to reload their crossbows. The Fallen swung swords and maces, stabbed with lances, and enemies fell before them in a bloody tangle...

The scene blurred and vanished, but Arngrim's stern visage remained, now dirty and covered in stubble. He glared from beneath a gray cavalry hat as he swung a saber from horseback, cutting down a fleeing boy. The other Fallen rode about nearby, all clad in gray uniforms, riding down screaming women and crying children, stabbing with swords and shooting with pistols. The surrounding buildings were aflame and the sound of screams rent the air. In the distance through billowing smoke, I saw a rider bearing a Confederate banner. A great structure nearby collapsed in ruin, but before it fell I glimpsed the words "Titan Millinery, Lawrence, Kansas."

Again the landscape and carnage blurred into darkness, then refocused on Arngrim's face. Now he was clean-shaven, clad in a black uniform. Perched on his head was a black cap that bore a silver *totenkopf*—a skull and crossbones. His horse was now a rumbling Tiger tank, its metal flesh a mottled green and tan. Spouting black smoke he raced across a grassy plain as the main gun spat flames. Ahead of him, a dusty green tank with Cyrillic lettering on its turret exploded. A moment later a dozen more Russian tanks rolled through the smoke, guns firing. The shells landed all around Arngrim's Tiger, dirt cratering, the din of battle filling the air...

The scene faded once more and Arngrim stood in the road before me, bare chested and forbidding.

"No man has wielded the Shepherd's sword for generations," he intoned. "Our oath died with Pastorius, and when he passed we took up swords again. For all those days have we wandered, we the Lost, we the Damned. We bore swords, we bore guns, we rode horses, we rode machines. We fought and slew, we reveled in slaughter and the blood of the innocent, yet even so we kept faith and awaited the Shepherd's return. Yet long did we watch for the agents of the enemy. Long have we waited, long have we watched, long have we slain the agents of the enemy wherever we found them. Now at last the gates are opening and the great enemy stirs."

Behind Arngrim the Fallen muttered and nodded.

"The hour draws nigh, Shepherd. The enemy comes. Then shall rise flames, then shall fall cities, then shall come darkness to this world, and then shall the *Fordæmdur* take their vengeance. And then shall you fulfill your oath, to stand and die beside the *Fordæmdur.* Stand with us, Shepherd, or you too shall be our enemy."

Arngrim turned his face toward the sky and screamed with raised fists. In the scream I heard echoes from a millennium of carnage, ruin, and murder, and in those echoes a mad lust for blood and vengeance. As one, the assembled Fallen joined in the shriek, and the earth seemed to shake at its sound.

I staggered back, but kept my grip on the sword. As the echoes of the scream faded, I raised it up once more.

"You call on me to keep another man's oath," I said. "To fight your enemy when he comes. And if this world is destroyed in the process, then too bad? Is that what you're saying?"

Arngrim smiled darkly. "Your world is doomed either way, Shepherd. The enemy speaks sweet words to his slaves, telling them that they will be powerful and that all their desires will be fulfilled. Take the mark, he says, and you will be the rulers of my new domain. He is the lord of deceit, this enemy—his words are false, but in the ears of the foolish and greedy they ring with truth. When he comes he brings fire, he brings water, he brings ice and hunger and despair. His servants will not receive the power they were promised... In the end they will be happy to be granted the surcease of oblivion."

I didn't answer. My head was throbbing and spinning with a thousand different thoughts.

"Give us the woman, Shepherd. Give her to us and stand with us on the Day of Vengeance. Keep your faith, *Hirdir.* Fulfill the promise given in your name."

Despite the pain in my head, the outrage that I'd felt at the house when Grandfather had talked to me returned. I'd seen what these creatures had done. I knew what they were.

"No." I stared at Arngrim as intensely as I could manage. "I'm not bound by a promise made by another almost a millennium and a half ago. You yourself said your oath died with Pastorius. I will not give you the woman, and I will not help you if it means destroying my own world. If you want the woman, you're going to have to go through me."

"And me." Loren's aim didn't waver, centered squarely on Arngrim. "This might not do much to you, asshole, but I'll bet it stings like hell."

Arngrim hesitated, and for the first time I saw doubt in his eyes. Behind him the Fallen exchanged worried glances, shook their heads, argued angrily.

There hadn't been a Shepherd since Pastorius, and his death had released the Fallen from their oath. They were warriors, and for almost a millennium and a half they had made their living the only way they knew—by slaughter. But now at last another bore the sword—the symbol of the only human who had ever defeated them, and the only human they truly feared and respected—and he was calling bullshit.

Arngrim's contemptuous glance fell on Anna.

"You want the whore, Shepherd?" he spat. "Keep the whore. Keep your whole filthy world and your entire pathetic race."

He turned on his heel, motioning at the riders behind him. "Gunnar! Kodran! Go help those fools!"

Two riders dismounted and hastened forward, carrying the injured Fallen from the wreckage of their mounts.

Arngrim sat astride his bike, glaring at me. "Out of the respect that I once felt for your predecessor, I'll not fight you, *Hirdir.* You can go your way in peace. None of this will mean anything when the enemy comes and this world burns. On that day you will either stand with us or against us." He kicked the starter and his engine roared to life. He gunned it and it screamed with the metal voice of a bound demon. "The decision will be yours, Shepherd. And either way your world's fate is the same."

He turned the cycle, and the others followed, moving in practiced unison, turning their leather-clad backs to us, showing their inverted angel wings sigil. Moments later they had vanished into the night, thirty or more tail lights dwindling like a vast red-lit snake. Soon even the sound of their engines was gone, replaced by the soft rush of the river a few yards away.

My shoulders slumped. I wanted to collapse on the road and just fall asleep. I didn't even care if I got run over by an 18-wheeler. But I force myself to move, turning to Loren and Anna.

Her head was down and her shoulders heaved. Sobs echoed through the renewed stillness. Loren had his arm around her and was stroking her hair gently.

"They're gone," I said softly. "Don't worry. I won't let them hurt you."

She looked up, her tear-streaked face distraught.

"You can't do anything," she said, sobbing. "You can't help me."

I frowned. "What are you talking about? You know who those bastards are?"

She nodded. "I've seen them before."

"Shit." We helped her to her feet. "You've seen them? When? Where?"

"When I was a little girl in Arizona. I saw them on the highway." She glanced down the highway. The Fallen were gone, but the memory of their savage faces and ugly weapons remained. "I knew they'd come back for me someday. And there was nothing I could do to stop it."

* * *

The eastern sky was pale with oncoming dawn when we stepped out of a cab and climbed up the steps to my front door. The wreckage of Loren's car was gone—I'd called a friend who ran a wrecking yard in Oregon City and he had dragged it away. It would soon be just another piece of scrap, permanently hidden from the police and other unwanted observers.

The events of the last several hours tumbled and whirled in my mind, disparate and unrelated, like clothes in a dryer. I just wanted to go to bed, let sleep erase my weariness and wring the soreness out of my muscles.

Beowulf greeted us with unrestrained joy and relief, and his expression suggested annoyance that we hadn't brought him with us. He treated Anna like an old and familiar friend, escorting her to the spare bedroom and lying on the floor beside the bed as she crawled under the covers. Loren crashed on the couch and was instantly asleep. As for myself, I drew the blackout curtains and collapsed on my bed.

I dreamed again—vague images of the Fallen as they rode down a long, straight highway, past the thick trunks of ancient trees like the columns of an old cathedral. Arngrim led them, but his expression was different than I'd seen before—distant, distracted, and almost sorrowful

He looked up as he rode, as if he realized that I was watching him. He glared at me angrily for a moment, then returned his attention to the road, his sad expression returning.

Into the growing light of morning, the Fallen rode, and now there was something different about them, something I couldn't quite identify.

Even though the picture was still incomplete, we knew more than we'd known yesterday. The pieces were in place and the game was unfolding, but where it was going and who would make the next move I couldn't say.

The metal and flesh ranks of the Fallen rode away eastward, into the rising sun. Soon they had vanished, and I sank at last into a deep and dreamless slumber.

VIII

"I met Wayne when I first moved up here, three years ago." As Beowulf sat at her feet, hoping for something to drop off the table, Anna eagerly slathered her pancakes with syrup. She had bounced back from her ordeal with amazing resilience and apparently gained a healthy appetite in the process.

"You mean that little creep Jammer?" Loren bustled in from the kitchen, delivering a platterful of scrambled eggs. Truth be told, he was a hell of a lot better at being a short-order cook than he was at being an editor. I chose not to tell him that, however.

"Yeah," Anna said. "But back then he was just Wayne."

"Frankly I was wondering about that," I said. "How a... Uh... A sweet, innocent girl like you...?"

"Ended up dating meth-dealing scum like Jammer?" she finished for me. "All I can say is that he was nicer then. He was only seventeen. A sweet kid working night shift at Plaid Pantry and washing dishes at Denny's. And me? I was nineteen and fresh off the bus from Arizona."

"Just a couple of lost souls, huh?" Loren said. "Two young kids with nothing but a dream and their love to keep them warm?"

She cast me an exasperated look. "Is he always such a smartass?"

"No," I replied. "He's usually worse. Just give him time to recover from his injuries."

Outside it was an early summer day in Portland. The dining room window was open and the air smelled of fresh earth, leaves and cut grass. It was a stark and depressing contrast to the images I'd seen of Arngrim's world and of the burning doom that his unnamed enemy had brought there.

"He changed," Anna continued sadly. "Started hanging out with the Couch Park Family, said everyone had to call him 'Jammer,' kept going on about what a great guy Father Tom was. I met them a few times, but I didn't like them at all. They gave me the creeps."

"Why'd you stay with him?" I asked.

She looked down. "I didn't. Not exactly. Oh, I still slept with him, and I still let him say he was my boyfriend, but well... You know, after a while you realize that life's a choice between making your own decisions and letting other people make them for you. I decided to make my own. Working fast food and trying to put myself through college wasn't going as well as I'd wanted, so I started getting tattoos and decided to take my clothes off for money."

"How'd Jammer feel about that?"

"He didn't like it, but by that time I didn't really care what he thought. I was still hoping that we could make it work, but I think in my heart of hearts I knew it was over."

"What classes were you taking?" Loren asked, bringing out a plate of bacon. I had to admit it. The man was a breakfast cooking machine.

"Biology," she replied. "I don't mind dancing, but my real goal is to become a veterinarian, 'cause I love children. And yes, I stole that joke from *Earth Girls are Easy*."

That got a double take from me and an approving gaze from Loren.

"Anyone ever tell you you're cool?" he asked. There was a hint of real affection in his voice. She seemed to have that effect on people.

"All the time when I'm dancing," Anna replied. "Otherwise, not so much."

I tried to get the discussion back on track. "So how did you get the tattoo?"

She stopped short, suddenly serious. "Oh, yeah. That thing. The reason I had Todd throw you out in the street. Sorry about that."

"No offense taken," I said. "You were scared."

"Not as scared as I am now." She contemplated a piece of bacon and finally took a bite. She didn't seem scared, but I knew appearances could be deceiving. "Jammer just showed up with his. Just poof—one day nothing and the next day a back piece that should have cost hundreds of dollars. No preliminaries. No multiple visits. No outlines. No scabs. Just a permanent, fully healed tattoo. Just like magic."

"It probably *was* magic," I said, feeling suddenly chilled despite the beautiful day outside and the beautiful woman at my breakfast table. "My guess is that all the Couch Park kids had one."

She nodded. "I found that out later. He showed it to me and told me he had a friend who had some new technique for doing tats with no pain and no healing time. He told me he loved me, and that he knew things weren't great between us. He started crying. He'd met people who had changed his life, made things better. He begged me, Alex. Said that if I got the same tattoo I'd understand everything and we'd be together forever. Just like it used to be."

Loren's head appeared in the kitchen doorway. "You didn't believe that bullshit, did you?"

She shook her head. "Oh hell, no. It scared the hell out of me, but it was just a tattoo. I told myself what was the harm in indulging him a little? Go see his friend and see how they could make these magic tattoos that didn't scab up or need to heal. That they could make in just one day. Even if I didn't get his stupid little magic circle, maybe I could get something else— angel's wings or something."

"So you went with him?" Loren was aghast. "Jesus Christ. I'd have hopped the first bus back to Arizona."

"Oh right." Anna snorted. "You've obviously never met my mother, have you? Even a cult of devil worshippers is better than her. Anyway, yeah. I was stupid. I went with him."

"Where did you go?" I asked. We were definitely getting warm.

She spoke quietly, as if fearful of revealing a secret. "You ever hear of the Pilgrim Foundation?"

Loren and I exchanged alarmed glances.

"Yeah," I said. "We've heard of them."

"Jammer said they were helping out all the Couch Park kids. That they were making a real difference, showing them how much better life could be. Shit like that. They're renovating an old building downtown off West Burnside and Jammer took me there in the middle of the night. He had a key and knew the security combo and everything. We met up with this woman, I think her name was Bethany." She paused, looking at me warily. "Remember her from last night? Blonde and built like a Playboy playmate?"

Now she really had my attention. "Turns into a demon with a scythe when she's stressed out?"

Anna nodded. "The same. They kept me drugged up most of the day so I don't remember much about the house. But I remember her. When she said jump, Dreads and that fat fuck Slash asked how high."

"How about Father Tom?" I asked. "Did he take orders from her too?"

"Yeah, but he didn't seem as scared of her as the others. They kept talking about someone called Grandfather, and I think she was his right-hand bitch. I can't remember much else. It was like seeing them through a fog. Assholes."

I didn't reply but let her continue.

"So we met Bethany—before she pulled all that demon shit of course—she led us into an office, brought us some Cokes, and started to tell me all about what the Pilgrim Foundation was doing for today's homeless youth and what a great asset

Wayne and his little friends were proving, et cetera, et cetera. I was wondering what all this shit had to do with me getting a tattoo, and then..."

She faltered and I saw tears in her eyes.

"Then what?" Loren stepped in from the kitchen, setting a coffee pot down on a trivet, then stopped when he saw her.

"Then..." Her voice was on the edge of breaking. "Then, nothing. Then I don't remember shit. That bitch must have put Roofies in my Coke or something because then next thing I knew I was in another room with brick walls and I was lying face-down on a table so I could barely see anything. I tried to move but I couldn't—they had me strapped down to the fucking table."

"Oh God," Loren looked horrified. "Who was there? Jammer? Bethany?"

"Yeah, both of them," Anna replied. "And some others too. Five, six, maybe more. I just saw legs and shoes. And voices. Two male, two female at least. They were... They were chanting. Chanting the same thing over and over again."

She paused for a long time in silence broken only by the buzz of a distant lawnmower.

"*Mimma-Lemnu,*" she said softly. "*Mimma-lemnu. Mimma-lemnu.*"

Cold fingers touched my scalp. I'd heard the name before.

Loren sat down hard. "Last night, Alex. Isn't that what—"

"Yeah," I said. "Yeah it was."

Bethany's words echoed in my mind.

Zi Dingir Girru Kanpa! Mimma-Lemnu! Usella Mituti Ikkalu Baltuti!

But that wasn't the first time I'd heard the words. More distant memory stirred. I stood and headed upstairs, heedless of Loren and Anna's confused questions.

In my office I yanked open a filing cabinet and pulled out a thick sheaf of papers, then returned downstairs, flipping frantically through them.

"Here it is," I said, pulling out several sheets stapled together, carefully and respectfully preserved, as if it was a holy relic.

To me it was—a part of Damien Smith's last letter to me, where he revealed his research into the Shepherd and She Who Watches, and proved that the story had been repeated in dozens of cultures over thousands of years.

I read in a halting voice, hearing echoes of my friend with every syllable. "'In some very old Sumerian tales, Panigara, Lord of the Frontier-Stone was a warrior given sacred duty by the goddess Belet-Ili to guard the world against incursion by evil spirits and monsters such as the red-skinned *Kussariku* and the demon-lord...' " My voice broke. I swallowed hard and continued. "'The demon-lord Mimma-Lemnu.'"

"Demon lord?" Loren groaned. "Please. Not another one."

"There's more," I said. The first time I'd just scanned the highlights. Now I read the details. " 'Mimma-Lemnu, whose name means "All That is Evil" led the Demons of Darkness against Belet-Ili's champions and the legions of Marduk and Nabu, the Lords of Sunlight. Among his retinue were the nobles of hell— Nergal, Ereshkigal, Idimma-Xul the Annihilator, dragons, behemoths, the *ghul* who are eaters of corpses, the Seven *Sebitti*, the *lilitu* who ride the desert wind on leathern wings and sting like scorpions, and the *Shu-hadaku'idim*—demon-women who bear burning scythes and harvest the souls of the innocent.' "

"*Lilitu,* " Loren muttered. "That scorpion-wolf thing. And demon-women with scythes. Bethany the blonde amazon?"

I nodded. "And don't forget the *Kussariku*. Red-skinned demons. The Fallen?"

Things were finally starting to make sense. "*Kussariku. Fordæmdur.* Fallen. Demons, but enemies of Mimma-Lemnu? He conquered their world so they fled to earth. I dreamed it. I had a vision of them fleeing their world, escaping from the flames, and transforming themselves into humans. But Mimma-Lemnu has worshippers here too. The Fallen have been fighting them for centuries. The Pilgrim Foundation must be a front for Mimma-Lemnu's cult."

I looked toward Anna. She still looked scared, but there was a hint of steely determination behind her expression. "What happened after you heard the chanting? Did they put the tattoo on you then?"

She shrugged. "I passed out. When I came back it was hours later and I was just wandering around downtown. When I finally got home I looked at my back." She tilted her head. "There it was. Just like Jammer's. Complete. Painless. No scabs, no healing."

"They must use the tattoos to communicate and control the cultists," I said. "I saw thin orange threads extending from those kids into that gate last night. When I cut them with the sword they all fell over."

"Well it didn't work on me," Anna said, angrily. "I was still drugged out. I fell asleep and I dreamed... Hell, I dreamed that this guy was talking to me. Middle-aged, good looking. In a suit and everything. He looked really happy to see me, as if he was expecting me to throw my arms around him and give him a big hug. He said to call him Grandfather and welcomed me to the family. I told him to go fuck himself. He seemed surprised. I didn't dream about him again."

"They were trying to control you," I said. "They put the tattoo on and were trying to control you like they controlled those kids last night. But you resisted. That's why they wanted you. They wanted to find out how you resisted, and how much you knew about them. Then Loren and I—the guys who helped kill Rafferty and mess up their schemes in Hayes—showed up and pretty much confirmed their suspicions."

"I moved out the next morning. I found that shitty trailer in North Portland and as soon as I got enough money I was going to move as far away from Jammer and the Family and the fucking Pilgrim Foundation as I could."

"Moving away doesn't help," Loren said. He was staring at his smart phone, tapping in characters. "I've tried."

"What the hell are you doing, Loren?" I asked. "I swear to God, you'd better not be playing Flappy Bird."

"Shut up. I got our chief suspect right here."

He held up his phone, revealing a headshot of a handsome man in his early fifties. He was sharply dressed and smiling, a politician and philanthropist in equal measure. His jaw was firm, his hair a tasteful blend of gray and black, and the image inspired both respect and confidence.

"Is this the guy you saw in your dream, Anna? The one who wanted you to call him Grandfather?"

Anna's eyes widened and she grew even paler.

"Yeah. That's him."

Loren smiled grimly. "Roger Dandridge. Founder and Chief Executive Officer of the Pilgrim Foundation."

* * *

It was obvious that Anna had to stay with us. Father Tom and his skull-faced girlfriend had escaped last night's ruckus and knew where she lived. Both circumstances and simple decency dictated that she was now my responsibility, so after breakfast I rented a van and drove through the late morning sunshine to her trailer, intent on grabbing only the most important possessions and getting her back to Smith House as quickly and unobtrusively as possible.

She seemed more sober now—reflective and thoughtful. After riding along in silence for a time she looked me up and down and frowned, as if trying to figure out a difficult math problem.

"You want to ask me who the hell I am," I suggested. "Who Loren is. Where I got the sword, how we knew you were in trouble."

She gazed down toward the floorboards. "Something like that, yeah."

I tried to smile reassuringly. "Well we have a few minutes. I can give it a try."

And I did. God knows I'm a lousy storyteller, and it was hard enough to explain things that even I didn't fully understand yet, but I tried. It was the same story we'd given Frank, but with a few more details. I told her about Damien, about the paper, about Michael O'Regan and Onatochee. I told her about She Who

139

Watches, about the sword and the legends of the Shepherd. I even told her about falling for Trish and how she'd betrayed us.

The only thing I didn't tell her was that Trish had died on my blade, a monster bearing the last remnants of a demon.

When I finished, she continued to sit, still looking thoughtful. Then she nodded.

"Well that explains a lot."

I stared at her, incredulously. "You believe me?"

"Oh yeah," she said, then pointed toward the windshield. "Truck."

With a start I focused on the road and slammed on the brakes, coming to rest a few inches away from the chrome bumper of a big F-150 at a four-way stop.

"Nice driving," she said. "Now keep your eyes on the road, big guy."

"Jesus." The truck pulled away and I followed, hands shaking.

"I believe you, Alex," she assured me. "Remember all the shit I've seen over the past few days." Her face clouded and her bright expression faded. "And what I saw when I was a little girl."

"My God," I said, recalling what she'd told me the night before. "The Fallen. You'd seen them before."

"Yeah. It's been so long that I almost convinced myself it didn't really happen." She gazed out the window at the rich greens of summer and spoke almost wistfully. "I've had dreams like you—the one where you saw the Fallen escaping from their world. They scared the hell out of me. I saw it all—the fire, the volcanoes, the rivers of lava. I saw dragons and wolves and flying things. And I dreamed about the Fallen, racing down the highway. Mom said it was from watching too much television and getting my head filled with secular nonsense at school. She even complained to the school."

"What about your dad?"

Anna's melancholy expression deepened. "My dad left when I was five. Mom told me he was dead. She said he was a no-good drunk and we were well rid of him. I don't remember much about him—just some vague memories of playing on the

beach in Seaside and having breakfast at the Pig-n-Pancake."
She sighed. "I always wondered what he was really like. I used to
pretend that he was a spy or a mercenary and he'd died in some
kind of secret mission to Iran or China or something. It was
bullshit of course, but I always thought Mom was lying about
him. That he'd left to get away from her, that he still loved me."

"You never tried to find him? Find out what really happened
to him?"

"Nope. I guess I didn't want to know. Not really. Anyway,
when Mom complained to the school they had a counselor talk
to me. He recommended that I play outside more, make more
friends, watch Barney the Dinosaur instead of *Law and Order*."
She snorted. "And it worked. At least I never talked to them
about it again."

"You still had the dreams?"

"Not as often, but yeah. But then something else happened.
I think I was seven or eight. I was playing on the front porch
of our house in Arizona. It was summer. It must have been a
hundred and ten degrees out, but I was a kid and I didn't notice.
I had all my dolls and action figures laid out." She rubbed at the
dashboard absently as if trying to erase a stain only she could
see. "I saw them, Alex. Riding down the road. Twenty, thirty
of them. They looked like blonde men riding motorcycles,
but when I blinked I saw something else. Monsters. Red devils
riding on big ugly things with metal skin. They just rode by and
disappeared. I never told mom. And after that I never dreamed
about them again. I never really thought about it that much. I
guess I just assumed that seeing them on the road that time was
another dream, but... But I know it wasn't. It was real."

"God damn it." My fingers tightened on the steering wheel.
"You've been a part of this all along."

"Sure sounds like it, doesn't it?"

"You've seen the Fallen. You resisted Grandfather and the
Family's psychic attacks." I frowned at the road. We were just
driving onto the bridge over Columbia Slough, and the grassy
berm above her trailer park was up ahead. "What the hell is
your connection? Why the hell are you so important?"

She bit her lip and looked away, suddenly distraught. Now I felt bad.

"Damned if I know, Alex," she said softly. "If you find out, be sure and let me know, okay?"

***

I cased the trailer park as well as possible, assuring myself that there were no obvious concentrations of cultists or demon bikers. It was a run-down, filthy place with little cheer or joy, and I was glad to help her get out.

"What are your employment prospects?" I asked as she unlocked the door. "Will Shanny's get upset if you quit?"

She shrugged. "Quitting in this business consists of just not showing up for work. There's lots of alternates to fill in at the last minute, and there's lots of other places I can audition at. I had a regular who said he ran a bikini coffee stand and told me I can come to work for him any time."

That didn't exactly sound like a job with lots of advancement potential. I frowned, following her into the living room. She turned on the light revealing an untidy maze of cardboard boxes, milk crates, plastic garbage bags, and loose piles of magazines and DVDs. Her threadbare couch was almost invisible under a pile of clothing—mundane outfits and one end, stripper wear at the other. And, I noted with satisfaction, there were unsteady-looking towers of books everywhere.

"Have you ever considered more, well, *conventional* employment?"

She rolled her eyes. "You're serious, right?"

"I'm always serious. Too serious. That's what Loren says anyway."

She began throwing clothes and books indiscriminately into boxes. Among the books I noted history and biology texts, volumes of philosophy and a large number of Charlaine Harris and Laurel K. Hamilton novels, along with Tolkien, Frank Herbert, Thomas Pynchon, and HP Lovecraft.

She contemplated a worn pair of red vinyl platform shoes. "I'm half-way to a degree in veterinary medicine. Unfortunately I'm in debt up to my eyeballs and school takes so much time I never could get a *real* job. That's why I started dancing, and finally when the stress got to be too much my GPA fell off a cliff and I wasn't able to stay in school. I don't have experience other than waiting tables and taking my clothes off, so who would hire me?"

She made a helpless gesture, encompassing the tiny confines of the trailer. "I mean, thanks for helping me get out of here, Alex, and thanks for the offer of protection, but I can't live off you forever. Once I get back to the working world I'm going to be in the same place I was before—scraping by and hoping I'll make enough dancing to pay rent and buy food while wondering whether the Couch Park Family or the Fallen are going to find me first and what they're going to do to me."

"Hm." Wheels were turning in my head. Anna was important for reasons I hadn't yet determined and besides I liked her. I'd be damned if I was about to turn her over to the tender mercies of either Arngrim or the Family and the Pilgrim Foundation.

"Uh, Anna, don't take this wrong, but..."

She stopped packing and looked up, weary amusement in her pale blue eyes.

"Let me guess. You're really attracted to me, right?"

The comment was so jarring that I almost took a step back. "Uh, no. I mean, yes." I struggled to keep from babbling. "Yes, I am, but that isn't what I... I mean, I wanted to ask..."

"Spit it out, Alex. I'm just fucking with you."

"Anna." I forced myself to speak calmly and professionally. "How's your typing?"

***

Where do you go when it feels as if you've opened every door and explored every hallway? Who do you talk to when your enemies want you dead and your friends don't know any more than you do? How do you find answers if you only barely understand the questions?

Alone in my office as night crept through the world outside, I stared into my monitor. In my mind, I saw flames and monsters—demons mounted on snorting black metal beasts, naked shrieking women with scythes, warriors in rusted armor, flying wolves with scorpion tails. And I saw the little girl on Hauser Butte, bound and helpless. I saw Anna as she twirled and danced, and Loren as he hugged Beowulf.

I cared about them all. What would happen when those visions united and became one? Would we survive the flames?

The Fallen had. But they'd had the option to flee to another world, buying a few hundred years' respite until at last the Day of Vengeance came and they could either perish or triumph. But we were humans. We couldn't flee. This was our world. Sad and troubled as it was, it was also green and blue and beautiful.

I wouldn't let it die without a fight. I wouldn't let the flames take my friends without at least standing in their way. And if I had to fight all of them—Fallen, Foundation, Family and their demonic god's burning legions—well, so be it. I'd taken the job with my eyes open.

Where do you begin when there's no end in sight? How do you fight when you're lost in shadow?

I drew a deep breath and thought of Damien, and what he would advise.

Light a candle. Stand in the doorway. Tell the monsters that you won't give in without a fight.

On the screen in front of me was the home page of the Pilgrim Foundation, and a large, prominent picture of Roger Dandridge with the caption *Our Founder.*

"Looks like we have a few things to discuss, just you and me," I muttered.

I stared into the photo. There was nothing overtly evil there, nothing but a tanned, good-looking man with a friendly smile and kind eyes.

"Right, Grandfather?"

PART THREE

I AM MADNESS

"Hey, Alex." Loren gestured at his computer screen. "I think I've found the smoking gun."

I rolled my chair to his desk and looked. "In the *Oregonian* archives?" I asked. "It can't be that easy."

"You wouldn't think, would you? Look who's in the picture, though."

The *Oregonian* story was headlined "Pilgrim Foundation Center Opens Its Arms" and was about the new headquarters' grand opening and some words from its director, Bethany Jones.

"Holy shit," I said. "It's her."

The accompanying photo showed Bethany—in her tall, blonde and impeccably dressed form rather than as a naked burning-skulled demon of course—speaking to a crowd gathered outside the new center.

I scanned the article. It was a harmless puff-piece filled with boilerplate about the foundation and its valuable mission, as well as its founder.

The privileged son of the wealthy Dandridge family, Roger has shunned the normal trappings of wealth and power, preferring instead to use his resources to improve the lot of the less fortunate. Founded in 2002, the Pilgrim Foundation has become one of the most successful charities in the Seattle area, maintaining a network of 20 homeless shelters, counseling centers, food banks and youth activity facilities, aiding homeless and at-risk youth and reuniting families across the state. A press release from Roger Dandridge stated that he "looks forward to expanding our operation into Oregon and working closely with local officials."

Flanking Jones was our illustrious mayor and a city councilman, the chief of police and several other individuals in suits whom I didn't recognize. Among the crowd were a number of the new center's would-be clients—homeless men and women, street kids and others. Loren had thoughtfully drawn boxes around three of their faces.

"And those guys in the crowd—do they look familiar?" he asked.

I squinted. The focus was on Bethany and the other speakers, so the faces were blurry.

"Can you enhance this?"

Loren's face hardened and his tone grew grave. "Well, I'll need to generate a random encryption algorithm and rotate the image two-hundred and seventy degrees along the horizontal axis while using bitmap graphic resolution i/o." He looked back at me with an exasperated expression. "No, I cannot *enhance* it, you dipshit."

"What? You mean you can't just zoom in on Bethany Jones' cornea and get a reflection of who she was looking at?" It was a game we played after watching too many *CSI* reruns. "Just tell me who they're supposed to be and I'll be happy."

Loren jabbed a finger at each in turn. "Jack Rafferty, Father Tom, and Boner Hamilton, one of the kids from Hauser Butte. What did Damien used to say? One's a coincidence, two's a conspiracy, and three's a movement?"

"Something like that." Now that he'd identified them, it was obvious, even with the poor image quality. I contemplated the picture, imagining the delicate smoldering orange threads that stretched from Boner to Jack Rafferty to Father Tom to... Where? My guess was that each of the three bore one of those circular tattoos as well. Had I seen one on Jack Rafferty, under all the blood and filth? I didn't remember.

My next guess was that they stretched to Roger Dandridge, holed up in his steel-and-glass fastness in Seattle, overseeing his foundation, caring for the homeless, giving interviews and preparing the way for Mimma-Lemnu and his friends.

I didn't need any further convincing. "I think your theory is correct. The Foundation gathers the money and the power, then uses people like Father Tom to do its dirty work."

"And of course no one suspects Mister Rich and Handsome Roger Douchebag since he's just the greatest and coolest thing since sliced bread."

Loren had developed a chip on his shoulder regarding the Dandridge, something that he tended to do when other people got too much attention, but given my suspicions about Dandridge's true goals, I didn't blame him.

Dandridge was handsome, he was charming and rich, he dressed as if he'd stepped off the pages of GQ, he was humble, and—hey, ladies—he was single. A fifty-four-year-old single man was bound to attract gossip, even in the northwest, but Dandridge's seemingly-selfless devotion to the cause of at-risk youth equipped him with a coat of shining white Teflon. Profiles of the man were inevitably gushing, uncritical puff pieces with no real facts to speak of.

On the desk was a copy of an article from the Seattle *Post Intelligencer*. I picked it up and read out loud.

Philanthropist Roger Dandridge, CEO of the charitable Pilgrim Foundation was the guest of honor at a black-tie banquet last night. At an event sponsored by the City of Seattle, guests paid $1000 per plate to hear Dandridge speak about the importance of drug and sex awareness for youth, and to discuss the growing dangers of the child sex trade.

"When society fails these kids, it's up to those of us with resources and a willingness to help to step in," he said. "Myself, I'm a very lucky guy. I didn't have to work for my livelihood. I was never a victim of child abuse. I was the fortunate son of two very devoted parents who didn't let their wealth interfere with their love of family. Every day I see kids who don't have the chances I had, who don't have success and easy living handed to them on a platter, and I remind myself that everything I needed was given to me—love, food, shelter, money. Every time I drive

down the street and see people with hand-lettered cardboard signs asking for help, I remind myself that I've always had it easy. And every time I read about another family tragedy—abused or murdered children, alcohol and drug abuse, absentee parents and latchkey kids—I remind myself that I have an obligation to share what's mine and to hold out a helping hand to those kids who weren't as lucky as me.'"

I couldn't tell whether what he said was sincere or simply guilty billionaire smarm but actions spoke louder than words, and Dandridge was also a man of action. Millions flowed from his coffers—both personal wealth and money raised from the elite of the Pacific Northwest. Roger Dandridge was from old money, and knew how to talk to the rich and the powerful.

Unfortunately for Dandridge's inspiring tale of wealth and privilege turned to the betterment of humanity, we'd found very little about his supposedly wealthy and powerful family. The Dandridges had been active in shipping and transportation until the 1950s. They had supposedly made a fortune during the Second World War, but the entire company had been divided up and sold by 1960, when Roger was still a young boy. His youth and young adulthood were one big long blur—the adoring bios all implied that he'd been some kind of globe-trotting playboy, obsessed with partying and womanizing, until he invented an armored suit and began to fight crime.

At this point in our research, I pointed out to Loren that he was getting Roger Dandridge confused with Tony Stark. In reality, Dandridge was a huge cypher until the early 2000s when he created the Pilgrim Foundation. After that, if you lived in Seattle and made more than 500 grand a year, you simply couldn't avoid him. He knew the ins and outs of rich society in the Northwest, and when it came to asking others to share the wealth he was extremely persistent. Most influential Seattleites simply wrote him a check every year just to shut him up.

His galas, fundraisers, and public events were legendary, from Formula I races to air shows to marathons and of course wealthy bachelor auctions. Roger himself served as women's dates several times, raking in thousands, but apparently nothing came of it and he remained stubbornly single. He'd authored two books about social problems, both full of platitudes and anecdotes, both brimming full of hope, tinged with a hint of recrimination for affluent folks who didn't want to help their less fortunate brethren. Copies were available for free at every Pilgrim Foundation center, and for $100 you could get one with an autograph. For $500 he'd even personalize it. I wondered what he'd write if I asked for one.

To my biggest fan, Alex. Thanks for wrecking my plans for world domination! See you in hell—Roger Dandridge.

It was all a little too nice and tidy for me, and the presence of known criminals at the Portland opening didn't help matters.

"The evidence is starting to shade into the overwhelming category," I admitted, rotating my chair and looking back at our corkboard, now bristling with pictures and articles about the Foundation and its leader. "I'm still not quite ready to go place Roger Dandridge under citizen's arrest for Conspiracy to Summon a Hostile Deity, though. The paperwork alone would be a bitch."

"So what do we do then? Make rude gestures from a distance?"

I stood up and walked over to the corkboard. There was a very nice headshot of Dandridge from the jacket of his book *Finding the Way* right in the middle. He rested his head on his fist and gazed mildly into the camera with a pair of pale blue eyes and only the merest suggestion of crow's feet. Likewise his hair was only faintly touched by age—dark and perfectly coiffed with a slight frosting of gray, just enough to make him seem paternal without looking decrepit.

"No," I said. "If he's really behind all of this, he's way too canny to respond to random provocation. We need to do something that'll get us noticed."

***

Beethoven dieseled loudly as Loren pulled to a stop on Northwest Hoyt. He swore as he set the hand brake.

"God damn, Alex, I love this van, but that engine just won't stay fucking tuned."

"It's what we get for buying a VW van with a sports car engine," I replied, jumping down from the passenger seat and slamming the door. "I warned you, didn't I?"

Loren's new vehicle was a 1978 Westphalia van with a camper top, ice box, and fold-out bed in back. To all appearances it looked like an ordinary white hippie van of the sort one used to see at Grateful Dead shows before all the counterculture types started driving Priuses. Its power plant was unusual, however—a pancake Porsche engine with twin Delorto competition carbs that provided impressive acceleration and a top speed of over 100 mph. During our test drive, we'd roared past other cars while racing up Mount Tabor, much to their drivers' shock and disbelief.

I'd assuaged my guilty feelings about Loren's wrecked Taurus by paying for most of it, though Loren had sprung for all the repairs and tweaks it needed.

The name was Loren's idea. When he'd announced that he'd dubbed it "Beethoven" I had looked at him strangely.

"It's a camper van," he explained. When I still didn't show any comprehension he'd continued, "Camper Van Beethoven. Get it?"

"I don't, Loren. Enlighten me."

"They were a band. Back in the 80s. Haven't you ever heard them? "Take the Skinheads Bowling"?"

I couldn't say that I'd had the pleasure, but it was his van so the name stood. Besides, once I got used to it I thought Beethoven was a pretty nifty name.

The streets were empty. Wednesday morning at 1:00 a.m. wasn't exactly prime club time. This section of northwest was imaginatively dubbed "Old Town" and had once been the location of Portland's skid road—some claimed that the term itself originated here, but I always suspected that Seattle had a better claim. Today it was crowded with Chinese restaurants, dance clubs and bars, where trendy night-time denizens rubbed shoulders with the homeless.

It was warm, most of the homeless were sleeping in the Park Blocks, and the clubbers had gone home. The new Portland headquarters of the Pilgrim Foundation was two blocks away, between a delicatessen and an art gallery. On the pavement out front was a sidewalk skylight with a grid of thick purple glass panes, some broken, others patched with cement. It had been built along with the main building back in 1908, which suggested that it, like so many buildings in the area, had extra rooms and storage below street level.

We were dressed casually, and both slung backpacks—I didn't think that the Ninja assault warrior look we'd had when we went to Canby would go over very well if a zealous cop happened to be cruising by. I handled my pack gingerly, even though I knew its contents weren't dangerous. Not yet, anyway.

The sword was another matter. I carried it with as much discretion as I could manage, tucked between my arm and body so a casual observer wouldn't notice it.

A narrow alley ran between the art gallery and the next building, a big retro arcade game center. Sparing one quick glance up and down the street, we ducked into the alley, taking shelter behind a dumpster that smelled of grease and moldy bread. Crouching, I looked up. Nope, Google Street View had not failed me—the black skeleton of a fire escape rose above us, along the side of the Foundation's building.

I nodded to Loren. "Okay, Tex. Do your stuff."

He busied himself with his backpack for a moment, pulling out a nylon rope and four-talon grappling hook muffled with cloth. Paying out some line, he judged the distance to the counterweighted stair section and gently tossed it upward. It was only a few feet above our heads and caught easily. With a tug, Loren pulled it down. It resisted for a moment, then an ancient spring gave up the ghost with a metallic ping and the stair section slid downward.

The street was still empty, and no lights came on. The suites above the art gallery were only partly-occupied by businesses and all of them were closed at night. Since the Foundation's offices were almost certainly protected by a security system, I hoped that we'd be safer coming in from above.

I sheathed the sword under my backpack. It would be clumsy but I needed both hands. Loren was up the stairs like a monkey and I followed, pulling them up behind us. We wore sneakers and our feet made dull metallic sounds as we climbed. In a few moments we were at the top platform, the alley yawning like a canyon below us.

The streetlights were far below. The moon was bright—we'd decided against night vision goggles to avoid attracting attention.

Loren glanced up then looked back at me. "This is the hard part, I guess."

I nodded. Above us was a decorative façade that we'd have to get past if we hoped to make it to the roof. It extended about ten feet, just enough for one of us to boost the other. The only question was who would boost and who would go up.

"Rochambeau you for it," I said, extending a fist.

Loren shrugged and held out his own fist.

"Ready?" he said. "One... Two... Three..."

I subscribed to the theory that everyone always does scissors the first time. Unfortunately Loren had studied the same theories as I had, and the first two times we tied with a rock, then the third decided to use strategy and tied with scissors. Finally I won with paper.

"Well fought, sir," I said. "Now help me tie off and give me a shove."

We looped some of the rope around the railing and then around my waist. Loren laced his fingers together and nodded.

"Ready when you are."

I set my foot in his stirrup and scrambled up, my fingers reaching around the façade, kicking off with a strong push from below. I grabbed the edge of the roof and with an effort pulled myself over, rolling onto the tar-covered surface. After a moment to catch my breath I pulled Loren up after me with help from the rope.

We sat panting on the roof for several minutes before I finally took stock of our surroundings.

The sky was clear and the moon illuminated the black tarred expanse. A few yards ahead of us, projecting up like the peaked roof of a house, was a skylight. Dandridge had purchased the office outright, including all three floors above it, floors that were currently unoccupied and being renovated by the Foundation. If we were lucky they hadn't bothered to rig the skylight with an alarm, and we could use it to get inside.

Loren knelt beside it. The panes were hinged at the top and made from dirty, wire-reinforced glass, cracked here and there but intact. He pressed his fingers against the lower edge of the glass and lifted.

"No dice, Alex. It's tight as a drum."

I knelt beside Loren and added my strength to the effort, but the panels had been neglected for decades and were welded shut with countless layers of dirt and paint.

"Damnation." I opened my backpack and pulled out a small crowbar. "Try this."

Loren pressed the crowbar against the panels, levering it up.

"I think..." He grunted, leaning down on the bar. "I think it's..."

I braced against the panel, knees bent, pulling upward. It began to move, slowly at first, old paint splitting and ripping apart, then finally popping fully open.

I fished a Maglight from my pack and flashed it into the space below, revealing a dusty hallway, fresh sheetrock, sawhorses, power tools... Just the sort of thing I'd have expected.

I reached into my pack and pulled out a ski mask. I handed it to Loren.

"You ready?"

"As ready as I'm gonna be."

I pulled on my mask and began to climb down.

* * *

The upper floors didn't contain anything of note besides tools, spools of wire, piles of lumber, and more sheetrock. That wasn't much of a surprise.

A quick scan of the ground floor didn't reveal any cameras—at least none that we could see. If they had any hidden devices I hoped the ski masks would at least give us some anonymity. The item strapped to my back would clearly identify me as the Foundation's sword-wielding nemesis from Canby and Hauser Butte, but I hoped that they still didn't know exactly who I was.

The main office was a pleasant enough place, with stylish white walls combined with old rough brick, decorated with original art. I was tempted to rifle through their filing cabinets and see if we could hack into their workstations, but my instincts told me we wouldn't find anything useful.

No, what we wanted wasn't above ground anyway. My guess was that the secret ritual room where they'd taken Anna was somewhere below, probably under that ancient sidewalk skylight.

We spent the next few minutes searching. There were several meeting rooms, a break room with a sink, fridge and microwave, and a couple of locked offices, which opened easily to my burglar tools. Nothing there either—the expected executive desks, fancy workstations, cabinets and bookshelves, and no obvious exits.

In the back was a small cube farm, with six low-walled enclosures. It looked like this was where the clerical help and phone solicitors sat. The last one was different—the computer was covered with post-its, the shelves were crowded with Star Wars and Simpsons action figures, and the walls papered with Dilbert cartoons and demotivational posters.

"Who the hell sits here?" I asked, looking at the action figures with a combination of distaste and envy.

Loren looked at one of the posters. It portrayed a cat in a cardboard box with the caption *I iz in ur quantum box. Maybe.*

"That should be obvious," he said. "It's the IT guy."

So far we'd come up empty. I was beginning to wonder whether we should start tapping walls and pulling on random books in the hope of triggering a secret panel when Loren whispered urgently from beside a narrow door.

"Check it out! High security lock."

I looked. The door was keyless with only an electronic number pad beside it. Above it a red light shone.

Loren pressed his ear against the door. "I hear humming. They've got a nice network, but we haven't seen any servers yet. You think they're back here?"

I nodded. "Yeah, probably. And maybe the way down below too. So how do we get in?"

"Hm. Wait here." Loren stepped away from the door and returned a moment later with a handful of yellow sticky notes.

"The IT guy?" I asked.

"Yup." He started sticking the notes to the door. It looked as if he'd taken anything with a number on it. "The dorks who manage other people's security are the worst at keeping it."

I agreed. "Yeah, doctors make the worst patients, don't they?"

Loren's guess that our action-figure collecting friend had written down the latest security code proved correct on the sixth sticky. The red light turned green and the door clicked.

I held out my hand. "Good work."

Loren shook it. "Sometimes it pays to be a geek."

Sure enough the narrow room contained a rack with three softly-humming servers, a punchdown board, and the usual tangle of cables that only the IT guy fully understood. I ignored all of it—this wasn't our goal and I suspected that nothing beyond data about the Foundation's charities would be on them. I was more interested in the plain, hollow-core door at the back of the room. It was conventionally locked, but that wasn't much of a barrier to me anymore. A few moments with my picks and the lock clicked open.

Loren stood behind me with a flashlight as I drew the sword and placed my hand on the doorknob. The room was too narrow for us to stand abreast. Anything that came up the stairs would be on me first.

Fortunately, the only thing that rushed out when I opened the door was a gust of cool, earth-scented air. Loren's light illuminated rough brick walls and rickety stairs going down. Dim light shone from below.

I looked back. "Turn off your flash. I think there's enough light down there."

Loren complied and I set my foot on the first stair. It looked old—very old. It was possible, I reflected, that this stair was already here when the building was first raised in 1908. Slowly, making as little noise as possible, we descended.

A single bulb hung from the ceiling of the basement, and faint light filtered in through the skylight from the street above. I hadn't really been expecting this to be our tattoo parlor-cum-Mimma-Lemnu temple but even so I was disappointed. The space was crammed with more building supplies, stacks of printer paper and toner, boxes of staples and paperclips and spools of wire. After a few minutes of poking around I was ready to give up.

"I'm beginning to think that we broke the law for nothing," I said, sitting down dejectedly on the lowest step. "Maybe they didn't do the ritual on Anna here. Maybe they drugged her and took her somewhere else. Any thoughts?"

Loren looked like he was about to reply, then something on the floor caught his eye.

He pointed at the corner. "Alex! Look here."

The floor was cracked, and dirty footprints led to and from the piles of supplies. Two empty bookshelves stood in the corner and in the dirt beside them, drag marks that suggested they had been pulled out of the way and put back several times.

"Crude," I said. "Very crude. Help me."

We shoved the book cases aside, revealing a riveted metal trap door in the floor with a rusted iron ring in the center.

Loren smiled coolly. "Looks like I rolled a twenty on my search check, huh?"

"Loren, you really need to stop talking like that. People will think you're a gamer or something." I kneeled beside the door and tested the ring. It was heavy and rusty but it moved freely. "But yeah, you sure as hell did."

With help from my prybar, we opened the door, and a gust of even cooler, moist air swept up. A metal ladder extended down into dimly-lit shadows. It felt solid.

I went first. The opening was just wide enough to let me and the sword pass. Step by step I descended. There was no sound from below, only the heavy stillness of brick and earth.

A moment later, we stood in a narrow brick passageway. The stones had been laid in carelessly uneven profusion, mortar oozing from between them. Overhead a string of white Christmas tree lights ran along the wood-beamed ceiling, providing just enough illumination to move without hitting a wall. The floor was packed dirt, covered here and there by pieces of worn plywood.

Loren knelt down and drew his Glock. "Where the hell are we, Alex?"

"I think these are Shanghai tunnels." I pressed my fingers against the rough brick. "They were built back in the 1800s to move cargo from the waterfront to downtown. They also used to kidnap people and take them through these tunnels to put them on ships as forced labor. Slaves and Chinese prostitutes too. At least that's what they tell the tourists, but I think it's just so they can charge more for tours." I looked left and right. To the right was a tumble of old stones and rubble. To the left were several openings in the corridor. "This might be a section no one knows about. Come on."

I drew the sword and led the way. We inched along the tunnel, staying close to the wall. I still didn't hear anything. Was the Foundation so careless as to leave this place completely unguarded?

The first opening was a small chamber, apparently someone's sleeping quarters. There was a bedroll, pillows, bottled water, and some bags of snacks. It was all neatly arranged, and the space was swept as clean as possible.

Loren opened a can of nuts and took some, talking with his mouth full. "Looks like someone's crash pad."

I looked around the corner and into the next chamber.

"Eureka."

It was a larger room, with the same rough brick walls, but had a well-built arch at the entrance. The floor was painted with the now-familiar circle of runes, and in the center was a padded table with attached leather ankle and wrist restraints.

Loren pointed. "Shit. There's the tattoo equipment."

On a table beside the bench was an open case with bottles of ink, tattoo guns, and needles all neatly arranged. There was a floodlight on a stand beside the table. I caught a whiff of alcohol as I stepped closer. At least they kept everything sterile.

The walls were painted with more of the alien letters and there were folding chairs set up along the walls. At the far end of the room, just outside the circle, was a long table, set with candlesticks, a large mortar and pestle, and glass jars filled with powders and crystals. In the middle of the table was a book stand, and on it a heavy leather-bound volume. There was no blood or gore, but it still looked familiar.

"Shit," I muttered. "Where have we seen this before?"

"Jack Rafferty's garage?" Loren looked down at the circle, then at me. "Remember what happened when you messed with that?"

"Yeah, I remember." I felt no foreboding as I looked at the painted circle, but I wanted to play it safe nevertheless. "I think we should stay out of the circle for now."

Loren didn't look as if he needed any convincing.

We stepped gingerly around the circle, toward the table with its ritual implements. The book lay open on its stand. Compared to the filthy volumes I'd seen at Rafferty's, this one looked as if it had just come out of the box from Amazon. Its pages were covered with more of the weird letters, written in a neat, compact hand. I reached for it.

"Alex!" Loren's voice cut through the silence. "You sure you want to do that?"

"No," I admitted. "But my Spidey senses aren't picking up anything threatening in here, and there aren't any dead bodies around to create one of those necromantic guardians."

"Not that we can see, anyway."

"Good point." I looked back at the book. Taking it out of here would probably piss the Foundation off royally. And that's exactly what I wanted to do. "But that's a chance I'm willing to take."

With that I flipped the book shut and lifted it off the stand.

Nothing happened. Loren heaved a huge sigh of relief.

I hefted the volume. "Heavy."

"Yeah. Heavy with evil." Loren looked at me as if I'd just eaten a spider. "Okay, you've had your fun. Shall we do the deed and get out of here?"

I was about to reply when the lights flickered and a hollow whooshing sound echoed through the chamber.

"Oh shit." Loren's voice overflowed with resignation. "I knew it."

I held up my hand. "Sh! It came from outside. Come on." I edged cautiously toward the archway. Outside the dim light of the brick corridor was further enhanced by a swimming, irregular red illumination. I set the book on the floor just inside the arch and drew the sword.

Loren crouched behind me, Glock drawn.

I touched a finger to my lips and pointed down the corridor. Loren nodded and we moved out, hugging the walls, moving toward the source of the red light.

There was another arched opening a few yards down the passageway. Shifting light danced on the brick wall opposite.

We pressed ourselves against the bricks just outside the second arch. From inside the chamber I heard faint voices, though I couldn't quite make out what they were saying.

Slowly, trying my best to become part of the wall, my cheek against the rough brick and sloppy mortar, I made room for Loren and we peeked around the corner.

The room was round, made of the same half-assed brickwork as the rest of the place. The red light came from a cylindrical object resting on a brick pedestal in the center of the floor. It looked like an old-fashioned lantern, with a ring-shaped grip on top and several hinged doors, three of which were open.

The light shone through the open panels, each illuminating a rectangular section of the wall that looked like...

Yes. They looked like doorways, filled with swirling orange flames.

Two figures stood facing the rightmost doorway, their backs to me. The first was a burly man with close-cropped hair, clad in a camouflage coverall, a pistol holstered on his web belt while his companion had Couch Park Family written all over him. He had long, greasy hair and wore a dirty *bundeswehr* tank top. I glimpsed an elaborate gothic letter "A" tattooed on his left shoulder, and under the tank top I saw the edges of the Foundation mandala pattern peeking up above the white fabric.

As I watched, the doorway flickered briefly a landscape appeared—arid, rocky, and moonlit. I glimpsed it only briefly, but I recognized the slopes of Hauser Butte. A third figure appeared in the doorway and stepped into the room. Behind him the scene vanished, replaced by the swirling flames.

It was Father Tom, haggard and wasted-looking, limping along on the leg I had almost severed not two nights ago...

No... It wasn't his leg. Now he had something that looked more like the haunch of a big tawny-pelted lion. He moved clumsily, unfamiliar with his new equipment.

In my hand the sword began to grow warm, and the urge to charge in swinging grew along with it. I held it in check, forcing myself not to move unless they came towards us.

"How long we gotta wait here?" demanded Mister A. His tone was petulant, but strangely distorted, probably by the arcane forces that were flowing from the lantern and the open doorways. "This place gives me the creeps."

"'Til I say so, dipshit." My little chat with Father Tom hadn't mellowed him one tiny bit. He glared at the kid with undisguised hostility. "Grandfather says we wait for her here, so just shut the fuck up and wait."

In the chamber the center doorway began to pulsate and flicker. Beyond it I saw tan-colored rocks and ancient worn stonework, a corridor filled with tumbled masonry.

The sword grew hotter in my grip and the heat was spreading to my chest and neck. I felt growing pressure like the rush of air that precedes a subway train. My head began to throb.

Something was coming through the doorway and it wasn't very nice.

The opening itself squirmed and writhed, expanding to allow a shadowy form to slip through, coalescing inside the chamber. As it unfolded into a tall, looming shape, the kid let out a cry of fear.

"Shut up." Tom spat.

The shadow expanded further, forcing the trio to step back. At last it gained substance, growing dark and solid before my eyes.

It was about eight feet tall and had to crouch to fit inside the room. Its body was roughly human—pale and hairless with a pair of sagging breasts that hung from its chest. Its face was more canine than human, with a short muzzle, pointed ears and black, pupilless eyes. Her arms hung down below her knees, big and muscular with curved black talons and her twisted jacklegs ended in clawed feet.

The urge to attack grew almost unbearable, but so did my own fear and caution. I felt power radiate from her, shivering through the sword and into my arm, but it was different from creatures like Onatochee and his minions. It was heavier, more mundane, grounded.

I began to suspect that she wasn't one of Michael O'Regan's extradimensional entities. She was a real, terrestrial creature, born and bred in the hidden shadows of our reality. Whether I could face her alone with the sword was uncertain, but with three human accomplices something told me I'd be at a disadvantage, even with Loren on my side. I struggled to keep my breath even, battling against the compulsion to throw myself into the room, sword swinging.

"Hail Idimma-Xul, Queen with Seven Names, Mistress of the *Ghul*, Daughter of Mordiggian," Father Tom intoned with more subtlety than I'd given him credit for. "We serve the high priest Grandfather Azat Parzillu and are your servants and guides in this world."

The creature grunted. "Very well." Its voice was guttural and ugly, but definitely female. "My people have heard his call and stir in their fastnesses beneath your cities and your lich-fields. We heed the coming of the Lord of Doorways. Guide us to the high priest, o slave."

Tom stepped toward the leftmost doorway. "Follow us, Great Queen."

Idimma-Xul started to follow, stepping almost delicately, then paused abruptly, her nostrils flaring, sniffing. The weight of her presence seemed to redouble, turning my limbs to lead despite the sword's roaring exhortations to attack, leaving me still and paralyzed. If she saw us, I wasn't sure I could even move to defend myself.

"Wait," she rumbled. "I sense..."

Father Tom spoke impatiently. "Come on, quickly, Great Queen. Before the flame goes out." I noticed idly that he hadn't called her dipshit.

She growled with a deep lupine sound, then turned and followed. Father Tom ducked through the portal, then Idimma-Xul followed. It expanded as she approached, growing into a great shimmering oval to admit her. The landscape beyond was a forested slope, and in the distance I thought I could see yellow lights burning. Then her bulk filled the opening and she stepped through into the forest.

The camouflaged merc followed and the kid took up the rear, though he moved with extreme reluctance. The red-orange luminance surrounded him and he began to fade away.

With Idimma-Xul's departure, the paralysis left my limbs and I moved instinctively, setting down the sword and darting into the room toward the pedestal. I seized the lantern, slamming its doors shut as I did so.

From the left hand opening, I had one final glance at the kid, turning and seeing me, eyes widening with panic. Then the lamp was extinguished and the three portals vanished, plunging the chamber back into gloom lit only by the feeble Christmas lights. From the closed left portal, I heard a brief shout of warning, cut off along with the light.

Then Loren was beside me, waving his pistol left and right, searching for a threat.

"What hell *was* that thing, Alex?" He saw the lantern in my hand. "And what the hell is *that?*"

I looked at the blank wall where the last portal had vanished. "I suspect it's something very valuable to the Foundation." I picked up the sword. "Come on. Let's set the charges and get the hell out of here."

* * *

A few ounces of C4 explosive can cause significant damage. The charges we carried in our packs were small yet powerful, but until we set them with electric detonators they were completely inert. We left one in the circular chamber and the other in the tattoo parlor. I stopped to collect the leather-bound book before we left.

"We need to be out of here in ten minutes," Loren cautioned. "I sure as hell hope those charges don't bring the whole block down."

"I don't think they're quite big enough for that," I replied as we made for the ladder. "All they should do is cave this place in. At least I hope that's all they do. I don't think I want the FBI involved just yet."

We clambered up the ladder and raced through the server room, past reception and up the stairs to the unfinished floors. Loren boosted me through the open skylight and I dropped a rope down to pull him up. By the time we jumped from the fire escape, stripping off our ski masks and trying to look casual, we had three minutes left.

I tried to walk slowly from the alley, burdened with both the sword and the lantern. Loren carried the book under one arm as we made our way back to Hoyt Street where we'd parked Beethoven. Half way there, I heard a single muffled "whoomp" and a slight tremor rumbling up through the sidewalk, followed a few moments later by a second. Dust rose up from the metal doors of a street elevator nearby, but no buildings tottered or collapsed. Nevertheless I felt a growing sense of unease at the thought of what we'd done.

We didn't speak until we were in the van, driving over the Broadway Bridge, its grating whining beneath our tires.

"Idimma-Xul," Loren muttered as he downshifted at a red light. "She was one of those *ghul* things. Eaters of the dead. *Ghul.* Ghoul?"

I nodded. "And I don't think she's a demon or anything like that. I didn't feel the right sensations through the sword. I think she's from our reality."

"Did you feel it when she looked toward us? It felt like I was frozen in place. Paralyzed."

"Yeah, I felt it too. The sword didn't provide any protection."

"She said her people were stirring. That means there's more like her." Loren nervously scanned the streets nearby. "God. An army of those things. And they must use that lantern to move between thin places."

"That's my guess, yeah." The lantern rested in my lap. It was cold now, an inert brass cylinder.

"Well, I guess you succeeded in pissing those assholes off." Loren waited for the light, then we started up with a lurch. "What happens now?"

Outside the world was dark except for street lights. I looked at my watch. It was after three.

"That," I said, leaning back in the seat and trying to relax as we bumped and rattled over a section of old paving stones, "is up to the Pilgrim Foundation."

Despite what looked like success—the destruction of the Foundation's underground one-stop ritual-teleportation shop, I felt anything but satisfied. Had I made a mistake? Would this force the Foundation out into the open, or just enrage them to the point that they'd want to retaliate? My unease was still there, the empty realization that I'd done everything I could and now the next move was up to them.

Suddenly I was very worried.

III

Days went by. I watched the Fourth of July fireworks from Waterfront Park along with the *Ranger* staff, we brought out our "Declare Your Food Cart Independence" issue (Loren had insisted on taking part in all of the taste tests), and I received a postcard from our friend Kay, who had survived the final battle with Onatochee, telling me that she was engaged and working as an ER nurse in Michigan. I wondered whether she had really moved on from the horrors of the past, or whether she'd be nervously glancing over her shoulder for the rest of her life, wondering what was real and what wasn't.

Anna threw herself into work as the office gofer and Girl Friday. No one on the staff objected or even thought it was unusual that a new alternative culture woman in her early twenties was working here—we'd seen a steady parade of them over the years, and Anna was no different.

Consuela darted a few suspicious glances when Anna and I spoke quietly but said nothing. I could see the wheels turning in her head and decided she thought Anna was the boss' new girlfriend or something. Then Anna threw Consuela a curve ball, flirting with both her and Loren in front of everybody.

Our plan was to get her an apartment, but none of us really took the initiative. She seemed to like staying at Smith House, helping us with research, learning more about our lives, hanging out with me, Loren, Beowulf or all three, watching movies, fixing dinner, playing video games or showing off her skills on my Roland keyboard in the basement. For a couple of weeks things felt almost normal.

I knew it wouldn't last. The Family had kidnapped Anna for a reason, and a bunch of their people had died when we took her back. We'd wounded Father Tom, discovered Bethany Jones' true nature and—probably worst of all—stolen artifacts and blown up their ritual space so that it could never be used again. Any one of those things seemed sufficient to earn the Family and the Foundation's undying enmity and we'd done all of them.

Our research continued but didn't add much to our knowledge. The book was just another jumble of unreadable characters, some of which matched those on Anna's tattoo. The lantern was clearly ancient, and it resembled a design from an excavation in the Sumerian city of Kissura. The sword came faintly alive in its presence, suggesting some kind of extradimensional element to its design, but it had no decoration or indication of its function, and I had no clue as to how to make it open mystical portals to other locations.

Mister A from the shanghai tunnels turned out to be one Andrew John Garibaldi, or "AJ", an especially vile member of the Couch Park gang. Anna told us that he was a would-be alpha male who expressed nothing but contempt for women but constantly tried to get them into bed. She suspected him of trying to drug her at a party, but she'd managed to avoid his attentions and persuaded Jammer to take her home. From her description, I was sorry that the Ghoul-Queen hadn't eaten him right there in front of us.

I had better luck investigating her majesty. Idimma-Xul—aka "The Annihilator"—was a Sumerian demigoddess with a penchant for hanging out in crypts and burial mounds. She was known for spreading sickness and devouring babies, but if propitiated correctly she could be called upon to inflict pain and disease on one's enemies.

Unfortunately for us, we were probably counted among the Foundation's enemies now.

We tried not to think about it too much. For her part Anna was friendly and outgoing, learning the office routine and making friends with the other employees. Our conversations as I drove her home had been polite but not terribly deep.

She'd moved to Arizona with her mom soon after her father's departure, whose footsteps Anna followed in a few years later, disgusted with mom's anti-immigrant, Tea Party political leanings. A return to Oregon seemed like a natural decision, though as she'd discussed with me her college career had run aground and circumstances left her with a choice between starvation, low-wage work, and taking her clothes off for money.

In the end, the choice had been relatively easy.

"I make money, I get attention, I work three or four nights a week and guys like Todd take care of the assholes. No offense meant."

"None taken." I shifted Yngwie into gear, powered around the cloverleaf and onto the Hawthorne Bridge. "I respect you making an informed choice, but doesn't it get to be a little much, grinding on night after night and getting treated like... well..."

"Like an object? That's the term, isn't it?" She smiled, and it reminded me of the first time I'd seen her and she'd been a ray of light in the gloomy club. "Yeah, some guys are jerks. Some guys should be chained up in the cellar and only let out for exercise. A drunk guy asking me how much I charge by the hour, someone who thinks nudity equals consent... Shit, that'll ruin my whole evening."

I frowned. "I hope I wasn't..."

"Oh, shut up. I didn't mean you. You were nice. Why do you think I sat in your lap?" She settled back in her bucket seat, looking thoughtful behind her ugly glasses. "The fact is I like having guys look at me the way you did. If I didn't, I'd probably still be at a counter asking if you want fries with that."

"Is that the only reason? Kind of like... You know... Enjoying being looked at?"

"Exhibitionism, it's called." She nodded. "Yeah, there's an element of that. But there's other reasons too. A lot of guys go to strip clubs because they can't talk to girls. The only way they can see a friendly naked girl is to pay her. I always try to be nice to guys like that. Talk to them like they're human beings and not customers. Tell them I like to play video games, I read science fiction, I play the piano, that they can talk to me, and I won't shoot them down just for looking at me. And I tell myself that maybe if a guy figures out that he can talk to a cute stripper with tattoos, he can go talk to that girl he likes in chem class or that barista at the coffee shop that he has a crush on and not come across like a creepy stalker or some kind of dudebro looking to get laid. I like to think I'm teaching them to be nice."

She laughed, shaking her head. "Maybe I'm deluding myself. Maybe it's all just exploitation. When some fuckwad comes in and waves a twenty at me and expects a blowjob, I'm ready to believe it too. But there are other times too. When I feel like I'm making someone feel good, well, that makes it a little easier to put up with. Of course I can have a thousand polite customers, then one asshole will come along and ruin everything."

I swallowed. My throat was dry for some reason. The colorful environs of Hawthorne Boulevard closed in around us. It was the closest thing Portland had to Soho in New York, but it was much, much more ironic. On the crosswalk in front of us, a woman in a motley jester's hat walked an invisible dog, followed by a bagpipe-playing highlander on a unicycle.

Paranoia was becoming routine for me, and I scanned the street as we pulled up to Smith House. No dangerous-looking street kids? Check. No handsome blonde bikers? Check. No demons?

I looked again more carefully. Nope, no demons.

"Okay," I said. "Looks like the coast is still clear."

She didn't move. "You guys really are worried about me, aren't you?"

"Yeah, we are. Loren and I have had problems with our associates in the past, and we don't want to repeat our previous mistakes, so we've become a little over-protective."

"You worry too much." She looked toward the front porch, then back at me. "Alex, listen. You've been great. You've really helped out a lot, but I don't want you to worry about me. I'll be fine."

I forced a grim smile. "Let me be the judge of that, young lady. I feel as if I got you into this situation, now it's my responsibility to keep you out of any further trouble."

She rolled her eyes. "Alex, I..." She paused and took a breath. "Alex, let me take you out for a drink. I feel like I owe you that much."

I frowned. "A drink? It's still light out."

"What the hell does that have to do with anything? Come on. Drive me over to the Space Room. You need to try the Purple Alien." Behind her glasses, her eyes gleamed mischievously. "This time you can consider it a date."

I tried to think of a way to protest. No woman had ever invited *me* out before. I faltered.

"Okay, sure." I shifted Yngwie into reverse.

What choice did I have?

* * *

The Space Room was the kind of place that would have looked futuristic in 1962. Now it was all very retro, with blacklight paintings of Portland on the walls and tiny lights twinkling like stars from the ceiling. We sat at a table with a plexiglass top covering pictures from science fiction movies and books. In the other half of the bar, a rowdy group of locals with tattoos and punk rock fashion played trivia. Through the window we could see across the street to the Bar of the Gods and the Mt. Tabor Theater, surrounded by milling crowds of hipsters. If the barmaid had been wearing one of those Jetsons rings-of-Saturn type dresses, it would have been perfect, but much to my regret she was dressed mundanely and looked overworked.

I took a sip of my drink. "You're right. Best Purple Alien I've ever had."

Anna nursed a happy red drink called a Liz-a-Licious. She pulled out the cherry. "The guys at the clubs are always asking me to tie a knot in the stem with my tongue. I finally learned how. If it's long enough I can tie a cloverleaf."

"Wow."

She sighed. "Yeah, too bad it's not on the list of qualifications to be a veterinarian."

"I thought you liked dancing."

"Yeah I do. I also like working at *the Ranger*, but that doesn't mean it's what I want to do for the rest of my life." She shook her head. "I'm just another one of those faceless women who have to put their dreams aside and hang on by their fingernails."

I felt a wave of sympathy. Maybe it was the booze. "I hear you. And it's not just faceless women, either. We're all faceless men and women, and fate doesn't give a good god damn what happens to us."

She looked away. "As flies to wanton boys are we to the gods. They kill us for their sport."

That stopped me cold. "What did you just say?"

Anna looked back at me and her gaze was fierce. It didn't seem directed at me, but her words had an edge of bitterness nonetheless. "Surprised? Christ, Alex, that's the story of my life. I have to prove to everyone that I'm a worthwhile human being. I have to tell Loren that I like playing video games. I have to persuade the nerdy guys that I can use a computer. I have to show Consuela how hip I am by flirting with her. Shit. I even have to quote Shakespeare to you to convince you I'm not just a stupid stripper."

Slightly ashamed, I focused on a picture of a Babylon 5 Starfury, slightly faded despite the plexiglass cover. "Anna, I never thought you were stupid."

"Yeah, but I'll bet when you saw me your first thought wasn't, Boy, I'll bet she's intelligent."

I groaned. "That's not fair, Anna. You were dressed in vinyl hot pants and spike heels, not a lab coat. Besides, we're humans. Mammals. With instincts. Instincts that say, hey, that other human looks like a good breeder and not, hey, that other human looks like a Rhodes Scholar. At least we're sophisticated enough to try to set aside our instincts and consider each other as something other than potential mates. And some of us are sophisticated enough not to act like assholes just because a woman's trying to make a living."

She smiled at that. "Yeah, you're right. I can't expect guys to consider my intellectual prowess when they're watching me undress. Not right away at any rate." She sipped her drink through two tiny straws. "God damn it. This afternoon I was telling you how much I liked dancing, now I'm talking about how much it sucks. I'm really not schizophrenic, Alex. Please believe me."

"I believe you. I've heard much worse." I paused, overwhelmed by a sudden sense of foreboding. "You aren't into alternative religions and spiritual practices, are you?"

She snorted. "Hell, no. After all of Mom's fundamentalist bullshit, I steer as far clear of religion as possible. None of that New Age stuff either, thank you very much."

I felt a warm sense of relief at that. I wasn't too keen on having history repeat itself.

"That's really why I wanted to talk to you, Alex." She was serious now, though her drink had taken some of her edge off. "You and Loren have been great, but I can take care of myself. I don't want you thinking of me as a helpless little damsel in need of rescue. I'd rather you thought of me... Well... As an equal."

"Oh, you're more than that, Anna. My fragile male ego may not be able to take it, but I think you're a lot smarter than me. I did really poorly in my bio classes. Fortunately you don't need them to be a journalist."

"That's not what I'm talking about, Alex." She was as intense and serious as I'd ever seen her. "It's what happened in Canby. It's about you. And Loren. And the Fallen and the Family and a big ass sword that looks like it belongs in a Final Fantasy game. It's about the fact that I'm involved in this whether you want me to be or not."

I let my shoulders slump.

"Anna, you've seen how serious all this can be," I said softly. "People get killed. Friends get killed. Friends and..." I faltered and felt tears sting my eyes. "Friends and lovers. People I cared about. I'm worried enough about Loren and Beowulf, and I sure as hell don't want to lose someone else that I..."

I stopped again and looked down at the table, into the eyes of Bossk the Bounty Hunter from *Star Wars*. "Someone else that I care about."

A knowing look crept into her expression. "Your girlfriend. What was her name? Trish?"

I nodded, dreading what was coming next.

"What happened to her? Is she...?"

I sighed. "She didn't make it. She's gone like all the others. All the others I..." I stopped, fighting tears. "All the others I loved."

Anna fell silent, and I was relieved that she let the matter drop.

I wanted to tell her. God knows—I'd *have* to one day, but at that moment I couldn't. I'd killed someone I loved, and I couldn't bring myself to admit it. Especially to someone I was starting to...

Starting to what? Starting to fall in love with? God, I couldn't even say the words. I felt an overwhelming wave of self-loathing and misery.

I'd told Loren about Trish, and he'd understood. He'd stood with me through the entire ordeal and he knew what had happened, the threat that Trish represented. He knew that the creature I'd confronted wasn't Trish anymore, and that what I'd done was necessary. But I couldn't say the words to Anna. Not now. Not yet. Uncomfortably I pushed the entire matter to the back of my mind.

"I care about you, Anna," I said at last, quietly and lamely. "I don't want you to get hurt."

She gave me a thin smile. "You care about me? My God, what a shock. You got yourself humiliated in dive bar, you fought your way through the Couch Park Family, and faced down a gang of demon bikers. No one's ever done anything like what you and Loren did for me. So yeah, I guess you care about me, huh?"

I must have looked miserable because she reached out and touched my shoulder. "And I care about you too, Alex."

That helped. A little bit, anyway. Then I met her gaze and for an instant saw another pair of eyes, deep and violet, gazing at me across a gulf of months and years and what felt like a million miles.

What had happened to Trish was much worse than I was admitting, and I truly *didn't* want that to happen to Anna. Yet, she seemed different somehow. Stronger? No, Trish had been strong. There was something else going on here, something that lurked behind Anna's mild pale-blue gaze.

The ghoul-queen we'd glimpsed at the Pilgrim Foundation building had been anchored in our world, a terrestrial monster who served an extradimensional god or demon. I'd felt it, and known that the sword's powers would be limited. Now I felt something different—as if Anna, seemingly a child of our reality, held a spark of that same otherness that blazed in the silver-blue eyes of She Who Watches.

Anna finished off her Liz-a-Licious and ordered another. My Purple Alien was nesting warmly inside me, but I was driving. I ordered a diet Zap. None of the carbs, but with extra caffeine to make up for it.

Things were a little less serious after that, possibly owing to the goofiness of our surroundings and the fact that Anna had downed a couple of red bubblies. We just talked, and I let the words flow out of me with no regard to time or space.

It was well past eleven when I drove us back to Smith House. The three hours since my Purple Alien had sobered me up, but Anna was definitely in a very relaxed state.

"You know what I'm feeling right now?" She tilted her head back and stretched. It did amazing things to her body. "I'm feeling relieved. That I'm finally able to talk to someone who's had a weirder life than me."

"Happy to oblige." I grunted, feeling glad and sad at the same time. "I'm relieved that I can talk to someone about demons and magic swords and ancient goddesses and not have her decide I'm utterly insane."

Unspoken in the warm good feeling of the moment was my realization that here, too was someone I'd shared my own secrets with, who knew the shameful things of my past, and chose to be my friend anyway.

And with it was the sick fact that I hadn't told her the worst thing, for fear that she truly would run screaming in fear.

How the hell could I ever tell her and expect her to truly understand what I'd done?

As I was busy trying to put my mixture of joy and sadness into words, she reached over and stroked my ear.

"You look so serious," she said. "You're cute when you're trying to look serious."

I stabbed my finger into the garage door opener with more force than necessary and guided Yngwie inside.

I looked at her as the engine rumbled to a halt. "Yes, I'm trying to look serious, and trying to explain to you how important..." I faltered, feeling something wet against my ear. " How important it is... That someone... That someone thinks my life story... That it actually makes sense... *and now you're nibbling on my ear.* Stop that!"

She withdrew but still regarded me with an impish expression.

"Okay, Mister Shepherd, wielder of the sword of justice, want to guide a slightly drunk girl inside?"

I sighed. "Sure. Just watch your step, okay?"

She was tipsy, though perhaps not as much as she wanted me to think she was. As I guided her from the car toward the back door, the nagging fear I'd felt for weeks returned, lurking unpleasantly in the back of my mind. It was closer now.

I managed to get the door open despite being burdened by Anna's semi-recumbent form. She slumped against me melodramatically as I turned on the living room light. I tried to hold her up, but she twisted in my arms, turning to face me. She felt warm. My heart was racing, but it wasn't all that unpleasant.

"Okay, you got me," she breathed, stroking my hair with one hand. "I'm helpless in your arms."

"Anna, I don't..."

She didn't let me finish, but grabbed the back of my head and yanked me down, her lips urgently pressed against mine. She tasted like Strawberries.

My mind was going in one direction and my body in the other. I didn't put up any resistance, and a moment later I was lying on the couch and she was astride me, pulling off her shirt and tossing it aside. She wasn't wearing a bra—her nipple piercings gleamed in the suffuse light from overhead.

"Oh, yes." She smiled, riding forward and backward against me. "Just like at Shanny's. You're a very good boy."

I had to talk through gritted teeth. My inner conflict had turned into a raging battle, with my mind demanding caution and my body screaming at the mind to shut the fuck up and pay attention to the enthusiastic, pretty woman.

"Anna, I don't know if I... I mean, you've been drinking and... I don't want to take advantage... Are you sure... You're consenting...?"

She lay down on me, pressing me down into the couch, her hands on my shoulders.

"Alex, I'm practically tearing your clothes off," she said in a calm and entirely sober tone. "Is that consent enough for you?"

My mind surrendered at that point.

* * *

I didn't let her do *all* the work—by the time I managed to nail shut the coffin of my moral ambiguity and we got out of our more restrictive clothing I was on top and playing with those intriguing nipple piercings. She responded, her body tensing, a groan rising in her throat.

"Too hard?" I whispered.

"*Fuck* no." She grabbed a handful of my hair and pulled. "Do it harder."

I obliged, biting and toying for a while before kissing my way down her stomach, tracing the outline of the tattoo that surrounded her navel, then kissing along the wings of her blue peacocks and down to the softness between her thighs.

"Ah." Her breath came faster. "Atta boy. You know what I like."

Despite my fears that I was taking advantage of Anna's intoxication, she was sober enough when she rolled on top of me and returned the favor, tasting me with lips and tongue, then springing up and bounding toward the bathroom.

"Hold that thought, guy," she yelled over her shoulder. "I need to go get supplies."

She returned with a condom. Thank goodness she'd lived here long enough to know where to look. In a moment, she was astride me, head back, snarling and crying out ferociously, teeth bared. We climaxed within a few moments of each other and finally lay together, panting, her skin hot and sweaty against mine.

"God damn." Her voice was a soft whisper in my ear. "It's been way too long."

The warm afterglow of energetic sex washed over me as I gazed down along the soft contours of her back, from the gentle hills of her hips to the soft valley of her back, framed by twin blue peacock tails. My gaze traveled up toward the mandala, and the strange unreadable letters that could have bound her to...

I froze mentally, a whispered endearment dying stillborn on my tongue.

"What's wrong, honey?" she asked, her voice suddenly taut with concern.

The outer ring of her mandala was flickering with faint orange flames. As I watched in rapt, dread fascination the center came alive too, but this was with the gleaming fire of a familiar color.

For long minutes, burning-orange and cool silver-blue flickered and chased each other round and round like a yin-yang symbol matching gentle comfort and love against the flames of conquest and utter destruction.

IV

"So she's seen the Fallen, she can resist this Grandfather asshole and she might even be connected to She Who Watches. You think that's why the Foundation wants her so bad? You think they want to use her somehow?"

Loren stared blearily into his steaming coffee cup as I made scrambled eggs. He'd come over on the way to work after my urgent call. Anna sat beside him, and was even more haggard owing to only a couple hours of sleep.

"It seems likely," I said. Under Beowulf's watchful eye, I dished up eggs and bacon and brought them to the table. I looked across the table at Anna. "I'm betting you have powers that we don't know about yet. Powers they can exploit. You may be just the sort that they want on their side."

"Or maybe they just want me dead." Anna spoke quietly, her eyes downcast. She ate with all the enthusiasm of a condemned prisoner at his last meal. "Everything I can do hurts the Foundation somehow."

"That's unlikely," I said. "Bethany said that Grandfather had ordered you to be left unharmed. No, I still think you've got something that they want."

"Yeah, but what is it?" Loren was shoveling down eggs like a starving man. "Maybe she's got some kind of link to the Fallen and can tell Dandridge where they are so he and his goons can go wipe them out once and for all."

Anna shook her head slowly. "Jesus. What kind of a connection would I have to those freaks? Why did I dream about them when I was a kid and not now?"

I set down my plate and seated myself. "I'm sure Roger Dandridge knows, but he's not telling. It must be something important since he was willing to kill to get it."

"You really know how to cheer a girl up, Alex." Anna sighed dejectedly and continued to pick at her eggs. "Do you do this to all the girls you sleep with?"

Loren looked as if she'd just thrown cold water in his face. His fork froze midway to his mouth and he stared at me, eyes disintegrating into something between anger and disappointment. When his fork clattered to the plate it was as loud as a rifle shot.

Beowulf whined uncertainly and took shelter behind Loren's legs.

I suddenly felt as if I'd just shot Loren's mom. "Loren, I..."

"You did, didn't you?" His voice was flat, emotionless. He looked at Anna, who continued staring at her eggs. "God damn it."

Anna sounded even tinier still. "I'm sorry, Loren. I didn't..."

"Don't bother." He stood abruptly, pushing his chair back and slapping his coffee cup across the table, spilling violently and splattering across the floor. He turned and stalked toward the door. "I gotta go. You guys probably want to be alone anyway."

By the time I'd stood up and called after him, he was already to the door. Sparing me a single, contemptuous glance, Beowulf trotted along after him.

"Loren!"

Anna waved a hand. She looked weary but resigned—she'd probably spent most of her life dealing with males and their erratic behavior, and now probably wasn't any different.

"You wait. I'll talk to him."

I watched as she hurried after Loren and the dog, then I discreetly stepped up to the window and peered out. Anna overtook Loren as he was opening Beethoven's door and spoke to him earnestly for a few moments. I wondered what she was saying.

It must have worked, because his angry expression softened. She spoke for a few more moments, then was silent, as if waiting for him to reply. At first he looked a little nonplussed, then he nodded his head and said something. She hugged him and he opened the van door, let Beowulf leap in, and got inside. As she walked up the steps toward the house, the door slammed and Loren pulled away. I watched as his car turned a corner and vanished.

Anna came back into the dining room, looking serious.

I didn't look at her, but continued to stare out the window after Loren. "So what did you tell him? That you were drunk and didn't mean it, and it was just a one-time only thing? That you're really not that into me?"

I must have sounded a tiny bit petulant.

"Alex, it's not as if I haven't had enough shit come down in the last couple of days, now you two boys have to start fighting over me."

She'd called us "boys." And she was right.

I felt like an even bigger heel than before. I could feel the fight draining out of me. "You know he really likes you. He's told me."

"Yeah, I know. It was pretty obvious, actually." She sat down at the table and put her face in her hands. "I told him that I really liked you."

"Oh." I sat down beside her. "I see. He seemed to take it okay."

She sighed. "Alex, I told him that I really liked him too."

I didn't reply for a few moments as I desperately tried to read between the lines to figure out what she was really telling me. When I finally did, I said the only thing I could think of.

"Oh."

* * *

The office appeared to be running perfectly on its own, without the need for an editor-in-chief and his Girl Friday. Anna braved the main door while I slipped in discreetly through the side and crept into my office, hoping to avoid Loren as long as possible.

In that endeavor I failed miserably, for barely had I seated myself and turned on my workstation than I heard a soft knock at the door.

"Come in."

Loren's head appeared, looking only slightly less enthusiastic than usual.

"Alex, you need to—"

I cut him off. "Loren, I know we need to talk. I'm really sorry about what happened and..."

"No, Alex." He stepped in, holding out an envelope. His tone suggested that something more important had intervened in our personal misunderstanding. "This arrived with the mail. You need to look at it."

I accepted the envelope gravely and unfolded the note inside. It was printed on Pilgrim Foundation letterhead. My heart tried to climb up my throat. I read with growing alarm.

You and a guest are cordially invited to attend a fundraising dinner hosted by Pilgrim Foundation founder and CEO Roger Dandridge on Friday July 11, 8 pm at the Miller Event Center. Mister Dandridge will give a talk regarding the future of the Foundation in the Portland area, and will be available for interviews afterwards.

I looked at the envelope. The printed address label read "Editor-in-Chief, *the Ranger.*"

"Crap," I muttered. "Not my name. Just my title."

Loren eased himself into a chair "You think it's just a mass mailing to local reporters? Or do you think they know who you are?"

"Oh, they know who I am all right." I threw the letter down on my desk. "They're playing with us. They sent it to confuse us, make us ask the same questions you're asking, make us wonder whether they really know or not."

Loren looked down at the letter. "Assholes."

"I can't really blame them for being pissed. We beat up their chief errand boy and girl and killed their pet scorpion-wolf, then we blew up their underground tattoo parlor, and stole their magic lantern. I'm surprised they didn't send us a letter bomb."

Loren glanced nervously toward the door. "If they know about you, then they'll know about Anna. They'll know she's working here."

"Maybe." If the Foundation had figured out who I was, they knew where I lived, and if they had been watching me, or watching my house...

I looked back at the invitation. "No. I think I know what this is. It's a truce. An invitation to a peace conference. It's at a big banquet so I know they won't try anything fishy."

Loren looked skeptical. "Are you sure? These are the guys who use Father Tom and his family to do their dirty work."

"No, I'm not sure. I'm never sure about anything, but I think they're offering us a cease-fire. They tried using muscle and it didn't work so now they're proposing a diplomatic solution in a safe, neutral location."

"So what should we do?"

"I guess..." I leaned forward and opened my calendar. "I guess all three of us should go to that banquet on Friday."

"But it just says you and a guest."

I snorted. "It won't kill them to put out another place setting."

"What if they don't know, Alex? What if they're just trying to flush you out? You're talking about showing up and handing Anna to them on a platter."

He had a point. "The alternative is not going at all. Or leaving her behind while I go party with Dandridge. If this *is* a safe-conduct offer I'd rather she was at the banquet than here. Maybe we should ask Anna. She's going to be the one in the line of fire. If she wants to hole up while I go to the banquet then you should stay with her and make sure no scorpion wolves show up."

That didn't seem to sit any better with Loren, but I could tell that he too was weighing the options in his head and discovering that he didn't like any of them. "Jesus, I hope you know what you're doing, Alex."

I drummed my fingers nervously. "So do I, Loren. So do I."

* * *

It was after 5:30 by the time we got back home. It was a hot afternoon and the heat pump was working overtime, keeping the office reasonably temperate as the street outside baked. Beowulf seemed to sense our tension and chose to remain downstairs, asleep on the couch, probably dreaming about eating demons.

I turned my chair away from my monitor. "It looks completely legitimate. It's in the paper, the mayor will be there, and so will at least one city councilman and the chief of police. Half of Portland's glitterati are invited and they'll probably be sneaking the other half in through a side door. They're going to be taping it for the TV news and they've also invited reporters from both the *Oregonian* and *Willamette Week.*"

Anna made a face. "And the editor of a free newspaper that they give away in bars."

"I realize that too," I admitted. "It hasn't escaped my notice that we usually only get invitations to the Safari Room's wet t-shirt contest. The foundation's motivations are about as obvious as they can get without them sending a guy to the office shouting 'Hey, St. John! We know all about you! Show up at our banquet!'"

"What do you think they'll do if we all show up?" Loren asked. He'd been dubious about my plan since the start, and I didn't entirely blame him. "They could tell one of us to get lost."

"If they insist, then you guys can get out and I'll go to the banquet alone. I still don't think they'll try anything in a crowded building downtown with half the journalists and politicians in town." I felt uneasy as I spoke, but Dandridge and company had left us with an ugly array of bad choices.

I turned toward Anna. "Since you may be the one who's in the most danger right now, I guess it's up to you. Do you want to go to this shindig and see the enemy face-to-face?"

She'd recovered some of her self-confidence and looked serious behind her black glasses. "Well as we seem to have several enemies, I guess it would be sensible to get to know them better. I'm not sure which one sounds worse right now—the demon-worshippers or the demon-bikers, since I suspect they both want me dead or worse."

"We still don't know that," I said. "The Fallen probably don't give a damn about you anymore, and as for Dandridge—well, at least they seem to want to keep you alive."

It didn't reassure her. "Yeah, but alive for what?"

It was the same question we'd been asking for weeks.

"Either way you're our responsibility." Loren put a hand on her shoulder and she covered it with her own. To my own surprise I didn't mind that much. "If it was up to me you'd be on a plane to London, but that probably wouldn't help. I wish there was some other way, but I have to agree with Alex—he needs to go to that banquet, and if he goes, we should go too."

I made a frustrated sound. "Yeah, it's sure looking that way." I turned back to the monitor and opened Google. "You know the name of a good tuxedo rental shop?"

* * *

Loren suggested beer, pizza, and an episode of *Mystery Science Theater 3000,* which despite my dislike of sophomoric humor, I couldn't object to. After about a half hour and three beers, the damned thing actually started to get funny.

By the time we'd finished the episode I was feeling considerably fewer qualms about the whole situation, but alcohol is good for soothing deeper concerns. I sprawled in the wing back chair while Loren and Anna sat on the couch. The coffee table was littered with a dozen different ale and beer bottles. Beowulf snoozed comfortably between them.

I gestured at Anna with a bottle of Full Sail Ale.

"You're bad," I said. "You want to have your cake and eat it too. You lead us both on, you drink too much, and then you seduce me, you sly little vixen." I tried to look at her sternly, but it only made her giggle. "If it had been Loren driving you home, you'd have gone for him, wouldn't you?"

She shrugged. "I dunno. Maybe. Maybe I'd have taken him out for a Purple Alien and not you. Once the Purple Alien strikes, all bets are off."

"You didn't have a Purple Alien. I did."

"Oh yeah. I had that strawberry thing, didn't I?"

"Aw jeez." Loren crunched himself into one end of the couch, looking miserable. "You take him out for Purple Aliens, you tell him your secrets, you take him to bed. Jeez. I never get the girl. It's just me and Beowulf, all alone."

At the mention of his name, Beowulf looked up blearily, then sighed and settled back to sleep.

Anna poked Loren with her finger. "Mr. Hodges, you are wallowing in self-pity. *I*, on the other hand, am the truly forsaken and pitiable person here, since *I* have the unfortunate privilege of having crushes on two very nice gentlemen and don't want to break either of their hearts."

She turned her slightly unfocused gaze on me. "Unfortunately I happened to have a moment of weakness with *one* of them, and now I appear to have irrevocably fucked everything up royally. Damn and blast it all to hell, don't you know? I'd have been better off just avoiding both of you and becoming a professionish... I mean *professional*... colleague and fellow demon-fighter, given my sterling resume regarding the observation of demon-biker-Vikings. Hell, maybe I should have gone to bed with the demon-biker-Vikings." She looked away, suddenly and melodramatically contrite. "Oh, damn. They'd probably be even worse for me than the two of you. Those horns, those weapons... And God only knows *what* their genitals look like..." She snorted. "Oh, God, I'm losing it, aren't I?"

I spoke to Loren. "Anna's a lightweight, isn't she? Not like the two of us. We can hold our liquor, can't we?"

"Fuck that." Anna rolled her eyes. "One Purple Alien and you're putty in my hands."

"I feel so cheap now."

"This is just what I'm talking about," Loren said. "You buy Alex a Purple Alien, but Loren... Hell, what does he get? He gets to give you a ride home."

Anna turned an adoring gaze toward Loren. "I'll buy you a Purple Alien, Loren. You just need to ask."

Loren's taciturn expression softened, like it had the time she'd told him about playing Modern Warfare. Damn, she was good. Through a fuzzy haze, I reflected that being a stripper wasn't just about taking off clothing, it was about pretended intimacy—body language, eye contact, a friendly wink. Anna was especially good at it.

The only problem, I realized sadly, was that if she was so convincing, there would always be the question whether she really meant it.

"So you'll get me drunk and seduce me?" It sounded like one of those things you say hoping that someone will say "yes" but ready to claim that it was all a joke if she says "no."

"Sure." Now Anna looked back at me, and her expression wasn't entirely playful. "As long as Alex doesn't get all psycho and possessive. You wouldn't do that, would you, Alex? I still like you too."

Was I being manipulated? Was I falling for a wink and a smile and a promise of intimacy that was never to be fulfilled?

No. I couldn't think like that. She was no different than anyone else. Everyone acts sometimes, everyone pretends, everyone puts up a front. It would have been no different if she was an actress or a school teacher. Once more, I'd have to trust my instincts.

And of course, *they'd* never steered me wrong, had they?

"No, I won't get all psycho and possessive. Given the recent dearth of women in my own life, I'm willing to share."

Anna grinned. "My, my aren't we a civilized bunch?"

I leaned back in my chair and closed my eyes. "No. We're just drunk."

V

After looking at SUV limo rental fees, we'd elected not to rent tuxes. Loren had a serviceable pinstripe and I had a black double-breasted that I hadn't worn since college. To my infinite relief, it still fit. Though outnumbered by her collection of fishnets and easily-removable halters, Anna assured us that she had a decent selection of dressy wear.

As she came downstairs, I had to say that I agreed. She was in a bright red sun dress with white polka dots and a small white coat. In her hand she clutched a tiny white purse. It wasn't exactly grand ball formal wear, but this was Portland and I suspected that half of the crowd would be wearing jeans and polo shirts.

"Hi." She smiled brightly, but I could tell it was the same artificial smile she used when she was dancing. There was an undercurrent of fear in her voice that she couldn't quite hide. "Ready to go face the dragon?"

"You bet." Loren didn't sound much better, but when he offered his arm, it was steady.

She took her place between us and we went down the front steps arm-in-arm.

"My guys." The fear was still there, but I could swear there was sincere happiness too. "I always wanted to be able to do this."

I returned her smile, but I was as uneasy as they were.

The SUV was at the curb out front and Milo was leaning against it, smoking a cigarette. He wore a chauffeur's cap atop his scruffy head and his tattoos were hidden under a black suit, leaving him looking like a slightly disreputable but perfectly normal hired driver. It had taken an extra fifty dollar "service fee" to persuade the rental company to let us use our own driver. This evening was getting expensive.

Milo flicked his cigarette away, looking us up and down contemptuously. "Jesus H. Christ, what the fuck is this, Crimson? You gonna have a three way in back while I drive or something?"

I opened the door and Loren climbed in.

"It's Anna," she said, seating herself between us. "And no. There really isn't enough time for a three way and Alex doesn't want to lose the cleaning deposit."

Milo rubbed a finger under his collar. "This goddamned monkey suit scratches."

"Well I bought it and I'm paying you a hundred dollars to wear it and like it," I grumbled. "So pipe down and think about what you'll do with the money."

"Yeah, yeah." Milo slid in behind the wheel and started the engine. "Where to, boss?"

"Miller Center, and don't spare the horses."

"Aye, guv'na." Milo's cockney was truly awful.

I settled back, trying to breathe normally. Loren was busy with the TV and Anna was inspecting the wet bar.

Every one of my misgivings about what we were doing returned full force as we drove, traffic and pedestrians hurrying past, visible through the dark tinted windows. I should have left Loren and Anna laagered up in the basement with weapons and a couple of game controllers. I should have left Anna someplace safe and gone with just Loren. Or left Loren and gone with Anna. I shouldn't have gone at all.

Dandridge had definitely thrown me a curve ball. I had expected him to come after me in a far less subtle way, maybe with more gang-bangers or otherworldly monsters. I had been ready for that.

In retrospect I had been a huge and unforgivably careless fool. Anna had been his target all along, and forcing Dandridge's hand had put her in danger.

And now I was riding with her in the back of a rented SUV limo to go meet Dandridge himself. And we were alone, unarmed, vulnerable.

Stupid. Stupid.

But too late to turn back.

"Miller Center ahead," Milo reported. "Looks like they're expecting us."

A line of fancy cars stood at the entrance to a parking garage and a security guard was distributing tickets. We took our place in line and slowly inched forward.

I looked back and forth between Loren and Anna. His enthusiasm for the TV had evaporated and he looked slightly ill. She sat quietly and was keeping her emotions to herself with practiced ease, but the fear was still there, hiding behind her glasses, deep in her eyes.

"You guys ready?"

"As ready as I'll ever be," Loren said. "I hope the food is good."

Milo snagged a ticket and guided us into the cool depths of the garage.

"This still looks legit." I stretched and yawned. I do that when I'm nervous. "It's obvious they're doing a serious event. They're not going to try to pull anything here. Hey Milo, park us as close to the exit as you can."

"Doin' my best, boss."

We weren't as close as I would have liked, but we did park in the middle of a cluster of other chauffeured vehicles, their drivers sitting idly, reading or listening to music.

I clambered out, helping Anna along. Milo stood near the front of the vehicle. He fit right in with the others despite his scruffiness. It seemed pretty safe.

I patted Milo on the back. "Anyone touches the car, hit 'em with a tire iron. My phone's on vibrate, so you can text me if any weirdness comes down."

Milo nodded and pulled a pack of cigs out of his pocket. "I'll be here, boss. Not goin' anywhere."

"Hey, you!" A voice echoed. A security guard with a belligerent expression stabbed a finger at Milo. "No smoking!"

Milo rolled his eyes. "Fuck. Okay, don't take too long, Alex or I'm gonna have a nic fit and punch someone."

"You need to cut down," I called back over my shoulder as we walked toward the elevators. "Those things'll stunt your growth."

"Tell me about it," Milo muttered.

* * *

The friendly woman at the door of the banquet hall didn't bat an eye when I told her I had two guests instead of one. We were duly issued our "Hello! My name is..." badges and ushered to a table, where a waiter was hastily setting another place and cramming in another chair.

Our table mates included a couple of execs from Nike Corporation and a wealthy couple whose name I didn't catch. I kept quiet, Loren was his usual nerdy self, chatting about computer games with one of the Nike guys, and Anna was a living, breathing mass of charm in a cute, redheaded body.

The room was brightly lit, the tables crowded with men and women in a bewildering variety of clothing from casual to formal. Waiters brought water and coffee, and the air was filled with the babble of hushed conversation. At the front of the room was a platform with a lectern. I could see the mayor and several other local luminaries seated at the tables flanking it. Roger Dandridge wasn't in evidence yet and I didn't see Bethany Jones either. The mundanity of the situation made me slightly less ill-at-ease.

But I was still nervous.

Dinner came first, but I'd eaten beforehand and contented myself with water from a carafe that the others shared. Loren and Anna weren't as cautious—he had the baked salmon and she went for the tri-tip. When they didn't suddenly clutch their throats and fall to the floor, convulsing, I felt a touch of regret at settling for a double cheeseburger.

I was being paranoid. The food was prepared by the conference center staff before the event had even started. The Foundation was smart. It would look bad for three of their guests to drop dead at a fundraising event. Besides, if they had wanted us dead there were less complicated ways of doing it.

No, this had to be what I'd thought—a temporary truce in a safe location.

I speared a piece of Loren's salmon in spite of his annoyed protests.

"Pretty good," I said, chewing and washing it down with some of Anna's pinot noir.

"Hey, get your own, junior," she said, grabbing the glass back.

I was busy trying to come up with a retort when the lights went down and a spot illuminated the lectern.

It was the signal for a hush and quiet applause as the mayor rose and stepped up to the lectern.

"Good evening, everyone, and welcome to the Pilgrim Foundation fundraiser banquet." He scanned the room and nodded, smiling. "It's good to see all of you here tonight—prominent citizens, city officials, members of the press. We've all heard about the Foundation's good works by now. In fact many of you are probably sick of hearing about them." This garnered some polite laughter. "But now comes our first opportunity to actually meet Roger Dandridge, founder and CEO of the Pilgrim Foundation, and hear in his own words about the Foundation's future plans. So without further delay, I'd like to introduce our host for the evening, the honorable Roger Dandridge."

To a thunderous round of applause, the man himself emerged from a side door, stepping briskly onto the platform. He was everything I had expected, from his neat graying hair to his handsome but fatherly face and gentle blue eyes to his impeccably tailored suit and tanned, healthy physique. He moved like a twenty-year old, waving, smiling brightly, moving to the lectern and waiting patiently for the audience's exultation to subside.

"Thank you. Thank you." His voice was rich and vibrant but also soft and reassuring. "Thank you so much."

At last the applause dwindled and he began to speak. "You know, it's always a pleasure to see this kind of a turnout for our fundraisers because I know that you're not here to listen to a boring guy like me speak. You're here because you care. Because you believe in what the Pilgrim Foundation represents. You believe in a world where young people can live their lives without the threat of drugs, abuse, violence, and sex trafficking. And for that I and the entire Pilgrim Foundation thank you."

Another wave of applause followed and after it too died down, Dandridge continued with his address.

It was a fine speech, and kept us all in rapt attention for the next hour. It was a story that I was already familiar with—child of privilege, spoiled playboy, death of parents made him realize the value of life, opened his eyes, saw the sadness and crime around him, yadda yadda yadda. Once he'd finished with his life story, as generic and hard to verify as it was, Dandridge moved on to the story of the Foundation and its works.

As for the future, well the future was limitless, and the Foundation was planning to help at-risk youth across the country from its west coast base. From there, the world was their oyster, filled with new and greater challenges. Roger Dandridge envisioned a world-wide empire of hope, bringing safety and salvation to children and young people everywhere. It was a beautiful vision, certainly.

The audience agreed, giving Roger a prolonged standing ovation despite his modest attempts to keep them quiet.

At length it was over, and Roger concluded with a brief afterword.

"I'd like to thank all of you for attending tonight. I invite you to stay and chat, linger over your wine, and enjoy the remainder of the evening. I'll be available for interviews or just to get acquainted for the next couple of hours, so if you'd like some one-on-one time, please let one of our staffers know and we'll see what we can arrange. Thank you."

Then Roger stepped down from the podium and departed through the side door, and the room dissolved into a dim roar of conversation. Our table mates had stepped away, talking to other acquaintances, leaving the three of us by ourselves.

Loren looked perplexed. "That was it?"

Anna frowned. "I guess so. What was the point of all that?"

I was about to add my own speculations when my phone buzzed. I looked down at it and didn't recognize the number. I answered.

"Hello?"

The voice on the other end was familiar. I'd just been listening to it for almost an hour.

"Mister St. John." He pronounced it correctly. "This is Roger Dandridge. I want to thank you for your attendance tonight."

"I appreciate that, Mister Dandridge," I replied to the startled stares of my companions. I didn't bother to wonder how he'd gotten my number. "But you've thanked us already."

A polite chuckle. "Well, I'd like to extend an invitation to you for a brief meeting, Mr. St. John. I'm in one of the upstairs conference rooms. They're all named after trees. I think this one is the Cedar."

"Not that I don't appreciate the offer, Mister Dandridge, but I think it might be best if..."

"You have my word that neither you nor your companions will be harmed in any way or prevented from leaving once we're done. But you're a smart man, Mister St. John. I'm sure you've already figured that out or you wouldn't be here. I just wish to chat with you for a short time then you'll be free to go."

"So this *is* a truce?"

"A truce requires the parties to be at war, Mister St. John. There is no need for us to be at war. I'll only take a few minutes of your time, but I think you'll find it very enlightening."

"Dandridge, I'm not certain I can trust..."

"I again assure you that no harm will come to you or your friends. And unlike certain of our mutual acquaintances, I can be counted on to keep my promises. Cedar conference room in five minutes. What do you say, Mister St. John?"

I hesitated for a moment, then replied. "Call me Alex."

VI

The second floor was quiet and empty, almost disturbingly so. My footsteps were muffled by fashionable tan and brown carpeting as I followed the signs toward the Cedar room. The wall beside the door was glass, but the blinds were drawn, cutting off my view of the interior.

The handle was cool against my fingers as I stood, debating whether to take the final step and go inside. At last my grip tightened, I pressed down the handle and stepped through.

He was there, alone as promised, big as life, complete with the same perfect hair, tailored suit, piercing blue eyes and easygoing manner that I'd seen before. As I entered he rose, extending his hand warmly.

"Alex! It's great to finally meet you."

I shook his hand and took a proffered seat beside him. There was enough space to seat at least a dozen, but we were alone. An iPad, a silver pitcher, and a pair of coffee cups sat on the table in front of Dandridge, along with a small ceramic container of sugar and creamer packets.

"I can't necessarily say it's a pleasure for me," I said, "though I'll admit you've certainly been hospitable."

He grinned. "A well-prepared dinner, entertaining speech and not a single attempt on your life. That's how we do it at the Pilgrim Foundation."

"I didn't eat. I was being cautious."

He sniffed and waved a hand. "What possible benefit would there be in poisoning you and your friends? I'm sure you've already realized that of course."

"As I said, cautious."

"Caution is an admirable quality." He poured himself some coffee and stirred in sugar and creamer. "Would you like some? I can have tea brought if you prefer."

I shook my head. "No thanks."

"Still being cautious, I see. I'm drinking the same coffee as you are."

"No. I'm trying to cut down. I want to know what you have to say and why you wanted to see me."

"Straight to business. Another positive. Well, the fact is that I just wanted to meet you, Alex." He blew on his coffee and took a sip, then looked at me indulgently. "You've caused quite a stir in my organization recently. You had a role, directly or indirectly, in the loss or injury of several associates. You've destroyed my property and stolen some fairly important items. Nothing we can't live without of course, but troublesome nonetheless. You also appear to have appointed yourself knight-errant and caused all sorts of mayhem on behalf of Annabelle Lee Moore, aka Crimson."

Dandridge set down his coffee and picked up his iPad, unlocked the screen, then turned it to show me a photo of the Fallen riding down a desert highway. It had been taken from a long way off, but I recognized Arngrim in the lead with Gunnar close behind.

"And by all appearances you've declared common cause with an extremely dangerous and unpredictable bunch of criminals, whom I'm sure you know are responsible for numerous atrocities over a very long period of time."

I accepted the tablet and looked at the picture.

"So what if I am? I generally consider the enemy of my enemy to be my friend." I'd been dubious when Loren had used the same phrase on the way to Canby, but right now I wasn't going to tip my hand.

Dandridge looked hurt. "You consider us your enemy, Alex?"

It was such an outrageous question that I took a moment to respond.

"Well, Roger, I'd say that murder, kidnapping, child sacrifice, and consorting with hostile extradimensional entities certainly puts you in the unfriendly category."

Now Dandridge cast me a warm politician's smile. "Ah yes. Some of my subordinates can get overly enthusiastic in their duties. Rest assured that isn't our normal approach to things."

His matter-of-fact tone irritated me. "Overly enthusiastic subordinates? You associate with people like Jack Rafferty and the Couch Park Family. Don't treat me like an idiot, Roger. I know murderers and thugs when I see them."

"Do you now?" Roger nodded at the photo of the Fallen riders. "Arngrim and his friends have committed acts that make Jack Rafferty and Father Tom look like preschool teachers. Believe me, I've been watching them for their entire tenure here."

I fixed him with a skeptical stare. "You have? I doubt it. You're what? Fifty-four?"

"Oh, you flatter me, Alex. I'm a great deal older than I look." Oh crap. "How much older?"

Our eyes locked and Dandridge's voice dropped to a grim monotone, ominous and threatening for the first time. "I think you know, Alex. You've seen visions. Visions of ancient warriors, of battles, of kings and priests. Visions of the *ùĝ saĝ gíg-ga,* the Black-Haired Ones. Of Bad-Tibira and Eridu and Akkad. Of the wars of the Lugal Kings and of Sargon of Akkad, when they brought their new gods and crushed the old ways and drove us from our temples. When they called our god All That is Evil. History is written by the victors, Alex. You wouldn't expect them to say that Mimma-Lemnu means Lord of Peace and Justice, would you? Yet, that is what we called Him when He ruled over us."

"And now you—"

His gaze held me. "Shut up, Alex. You've babbled enough ignorance for one evening. You're the *Panigara*—I know that.

The Guardian of the Frontier Stone. *Nomeus*. The Shepherd. Let me tell you something about your friends, the Fallen, the *Kussariku*. You've seen these things because of your ties to the Fallen, because of that idiotic oath that your predecessor swore almost fifteen hundred years ago, the oath that the *Kussariku* conveniently ignored. They were once guardians too, Alex, guardians of their world. It was a paradise, Alex, and our master, the one you call Mimma-Lemnu, sought to take it for his own."

"World conquest? That doesn't seem terribly benevolent to me."

"Mimma-Lemnu brings order. He brings peace. He brings law. Look at the news, Alex. You're an unusual man for this world and these times—you still read and you still write. You see what a cesspool this world is becoming. War, violence, religious fanaticism, tribalism, division, race hatred, ethnic cleansing, terrorism running wild... This world needs order, it needs law. And with order and law come peace. Mimma-Lemnu offers that. Yes, there's a price, but if I've learned anything over the past few millennia it's that the reward for our sacrifice is well worth the cost."

"Trading security for freedom? It's been tried before, Roger."

"No, it hasn't. Not the way we offer it. We offered peace to the *Kussariku*'s world, and they accepted. They were the ones who made the sacrifices and performed the rituals that would allow Mimma-Lemnu and his armies access to their world. They let him come, let him conquer, welcomed him in fact. But they are born killers—barbarians, warriors, thugs. When they realized that the world Mimma-Lemnu offered had no place for violence and bloodshed, they rebelled. They tried to drive him out."

I didn't reply, but my gaze wandered back to the tablet and the picture of the Fallen. Behind their grim blonde visages, I saw savage crimson beasts and I knew that Dandridge was telling me the truth. Or at least his own version of it.

"In your vision you saw a world of fire and rock and devastation, Alex. I know. I've seen it too. It wasn't Mimma-Lemnu who burned that world, it was the Fallen. The *Kussariku*.

They were willing to sacrifice their entire world to defeat Mimma-Lemnu, and when they failed they fled. Fled to your world, where they raised havoc and unleashed torrents of blood despite their oath. Now they're willing to do the same thing to this world that they did to theirs."

Dandridge's voice had softened now and he sat there, his hands clasped meekly on the table in front of him.

"Our work, and the work of millennia, has been to open the way for Mimma-Lemnu and his servants. This world is valuable, Alex. It's a nexus, a meeting place of many different realities. You already knew that—I've read your column. Yes, now I know that you write under a pseudonym and that you incorporate your own occult knowledge into that column. And I know that you and your friend Loren Hodges have had some contact with the other places. Rest assured it's only going to get worse, Alex. The doorways are opening, they're yawning wide, and things live on the other side that are beyond your imagination. Hell, Alex... There are things in your own world that you know nothing about—things that are just as dangerous and frightening. Mimma-Lemnu offers protection from those things. He offers a world without violence, without the pain of human folly. All he asks in return is faith."

"And the occasional sacrificial victim?"

He shook his head distastefully. "Bad things are sometimes necessary, Alex. It doesn't mean that I enjoy doing them, but after so many centuries I've gained a certain amount of perspective.

And I think that's something you well understand. We've gone to a great deal of trouble to learn about you. I know about your childhood, your schools, your promising journalism career cut short by the tragic death of your girlfriend—dead of an overdose shortly before her dealer ended up permanently disabled by individuals unknown. My compliments on a job well done, by the way. You'd have done this organization proud."

That he knew about Michelle and her damned dealer didn't surprise me. What did surprise me was that he wasn't using it as leverage to get me to cooperate. No, far from it. He was praising me for it.

I looked away. "I'm not proud of the things I've done, Dandridge. If you're saying that my mistakes mean we think the same way, you're wrong. You and anyone else who thinks that the end justifies the means."

"That's not what I believe, Alex. Bringing the greatest good to the greatest number is a tired, worn-out cliché, but at its heart it's what we believe. You think I'm a hypocrite? Running a charity and writing books about at-risk youth while secretly fronting a demon-worshipping cult? You couldn't be more wrong, Alex. I believe every word I say. Five thousand years hasn't hardened me to the plight of humanity. It's made me even more aware of the pain and suffering in the world, and even more determined to end it. We bring order. We bring peace. And all the Fallen offer is more blood."

Silence welled up between us. I felt exhausted even though Dandridge had done most of the talking.

"So is this the part where you offer me a place in your organization?" I asked. "Then I turn you down, you say something like 'That was very foolish, Mister Bond' and try to feed me to the alligators?"

Dandridge's smile returned and I actually believed it was genuine. "I *love* those movies, Alex. Especially the early ones with Sean Connery. But no, let's just skip that part, shall we? Besides, there aren't any alligators handy." He poured himself more coffee. "Sorry to have gone on like that, Alex. I'm sure you understand how passionate one can get for a cause. The fact is that I do indeed want your help. I've asked you here to see if I can show you good reasons for aiding us, or at least not impeding our activities. You don't even have to join. You certainly don't need to get the tattoo—that's for my more... well, *free-spirited* associates. And if you have any idea of exactly where the Fallen are, I'd like to know that too. Mind you, I'm not demanding, I'm not insisting. I'm just asking you. Nicely. Man to man."

With a start, I realized that I wasn't rejecting Dandridge's offer out of hand. "And in return? What about my friends?"

He spread both hands out in an all-inclusive gesture. "Mister Hodges and his dog? He's no threat to us. He can live his life any way he chooses. Miss Moore? She might have had her uses, and I would certainly like to know exactly how she managed to resist the arcane power of that little mark we put on her, but I'm willing to let her be in exchange for your cooperation."

"Right." I drew a deep breath. "So I just leave you guys alone? Don't do anything else?"

"And of course return the property you've stolen. As with Miss Moore, it's nothing we can't do without, but we do find those items of some utility. It seems only fair, Alex."

I nodded. "Can I have some time to think about it?"

"Of course. Take all the time you need. Just don't do anything... rash... in the meantime."

"And if I refuse?"

A little of his previous threatening tone returned and Dandridge's eyes darkened.

"That is probably best left unmentioned, Alex. Suffice to say, you do not want to make enemies of me and the Foundation. At this point we are friends, or at least warily neutral toward each other. For your own sake I ask you not to make me regret approaching you in this manner."

"Okay." I stood but didn't hold out my hand. "Who should I talk to if I agree?"

"Oh, Miss Jones at the center should be fine. You left quite an impression on her, by the way. I think she'd very much like to meet you again, under less confrontational circumstances."

I suppressed a shudder. "It's good to want things."

Another polite smile. "As you will. She'll relay your decision to me." He rose, but didn't offer his hand either. "Thank you for meeting with me under these circumstances, Alex. It's been a trying few weeks for both of us."

"Indeed it has."

I turned and walked out, closing the door behind me.

The banquet hall was still crowded, full of milling groups of people, and other diners sitting at tables conversing quietly. Up at the main table the mayor and chief of police were chatting with supporters.

Loren and Anna were still at the table, and they both looked relieved as I approached them.

When he saw me, Loren stood. "God damn. We were starting to get worried."

"How'd it go?" Anna asked.

I waved for them to follow and strode toward the exit.

"Let's get the hell out of here," I said. "I need a shower."

* * *

"It was the usual bullshit," I said as Milo pulled away from the conference center. I'd raised the privacy glass so he couldn't hear us.

As I spoke, I realized just how angry Dandridge had made me. "Hand the keys over to Mimma-Lemnu and he'll take care of everything. No more wars, no more hate, no more pain, rainbows and unicorns and happy bunnies everywhere. All we have to do is give up our freedom and submit. Mimma-Lemnu knows best. Submit to the wisdom of a supreme being and everything's just ginger-peachy." I made a fist and pounded on the seat. "Of course a little human sacrifice and a little torture and murder—that's unavoidable. The price we pay for a shining tomorrow. Jesus Christ. What a fucking hypocrite."

"You think he was lying?" Anna asked. "Prettying it up so you'd go along?"

"No. That's the worst part of it. I think he really believed it. Dandridge believes in spiritual totalitarianism. Serve Mimma-Lemnu and all will be well. And if you don't... well, I'm sure there'll be constructive work for you in the growing field of medical experimentation or slave labor."

I pounded my seat again. The arrogance of the man. The sheer, unadulterated, smarmy self-assured *arrogance...*

Summoning me to his presence, meeting me alone, absolutely certain of his superiority, knowing that he was presenting me with an offer I couldn't refuse.

Well, he'd miscalculated.

"I bought us some time," I said. "He may already suspect my answer's going to be no, but unless we do anything to provoke him they'll leave us alone for a while."

"And after that?" Loren didn't seem interested in the TV anymore.

I didn't answer immediately, looking through the window as the lights of the South Waterfront glided by.

"After that," I said at last, "it's war."

We drove on in silence for a while.

"I don't think we can fight those guys alone, Alex." Loren's voice was low and serious. "You saw what kind of resources they have. The guy's a fucking billionaire and God only knows what he's got stashed away. They summon demons, they hire mercenaries... Shit, Alex, I'm feeling seriously out of my league."

Anna didn't say anything, but her eyes spoke assent.

"Maybe you were right about enemy of my enemy," I said. We were on the bridge now, headed for our neighborhood. "I don't like the Fallen, but they keep looking better than the alternative."

Loren rolled his eyes. "Great. We don't even know where they are. You managed to shame them into leaving."

"I've seen them. I dreamed about them a couple of times. Maybe I can contact them that way." I looked at Anna. "Maybe you could try too. Dandridge and the Foundation wanted you for something—maybe it really is because of your connection to the Fallen."

She shrugged. "I haven't dreamed about them or any of that other shit since I was a kid. I guess I can try, though." She smiled. "What do you want me to tell them?"

I thought about it. "Tell them *Hirdir*, the Shepherd needs their help. He's seen the face of the enemy and he'll honor his oath to them. See if you can find out how we can reach them, or if they can find us. Tell them it's urgent."

I looked out the window again. Milo was just pulling up to my house.

"Tell them that. I'll tell them the same thing. And hope to God that they listen."

* * *

It was a rough, restless night. I set the alarms, turned on the cameras, made sure that Beowulf was in the living room, left a couple of shotguns and my sword handy, and went to bed. Loren and Anna crashed downstairs. This was starting to become a familiar routine.

You know how it is when you know you need to sleep, and you keep waking up every few minutes, reminding yourself that you need to sleep, but never get more than slightly drowsy? Then you find yourself staring at the ceiling at about 3:00 a.m. contemplating how small you are in comparison to the universe, and how little time the eighty or so years you get on the planet really is in comparison to eternity?

It was kind of like that.

I didn't really sleep, I didn't dream, and I certainly didn't dream about the Fallen.

God damn.

I was up at 5:30, randomly searching printouts and scanning the results of searches in my workroom. Nothing. No sign of the Fallen. No more information about the Pilgrim Foundation or Roger Dandridge. Nothing on the hieroglyphics in the books we'd taken, nothing on the magic teleportation lantern, nothing on the mandala shape.

Nothing, nothing, nothing.

I got dressed and gingerly stepped downstairs. Loren wasn't on the couch, but the door to the guest room was ajar. I peeked in discreetly.

Beowulf slept happily on the floor and didn't stir. On the bed, in the dim light of early morning, I saw two forms, lying close together, breathing quietly. Loren's arm was around Anna and she rested her head on his shoulder. They both looked very comfortable.

I stepped back and stood in the living room for a while, contemplating the wingback and the coffee table.

After everything that had happened over the past weeks, I couldn't sort my real feelings out from the spinning vortex of dread, uncertainty, anger and helplessness that churned inside me. We'd talked about it, I'd said I didn't have a problem with it, that I didn't think that one night with Anna meant I was her one and only, that I was open-minded, that I didn't make demands...

Of course we'd all been drunk, and the banquet lay on the horizon. The prospect of dining with one's sworn enemies tends to overwhelm less pressing matters. I'd shoved my relationship with both Anna and Loren to the back of my mind.

And now, even though the clock was ticking and open war with the Pilgrim Foundation seemed all but certain, here it was again, big as life.

I rubbed my eyes. I was hungry and punchy, I couldn't think straight, and I had a real job to get to.

We had to get away. We'd have to go someplace else with breathing room, where we could plan and think, and maybe even find the Fallen. As distasteful as it was for me, they seemed like our only hope of standing up to the Foundation.

We'd load up the cars—Yngwie and Beethoven. I'd go to the office and tell Consuela that there was an emergency and that we'd be gone for a few days. The next two weeks' issues were planned and almost all written, and with her at the helm my staff would be able to throw something together that we could get onto the streets and keep the advertisers happy.

It wasn't much of a plan, I realized. But it was the best I could manage.

I glanced at the guest room. Loren stirred and opened his eyes.

"Alex?" he mumbled sleepily. Then he looked at Anna, as if seeing her for the first time, still sleeping peacefully beside him. "Alex, uh..."

"Don't worry about it." I'd sort my feelings out later—there were more important things right now. "You guys get breakfast, pack up Beethoven. Food, weapons, camping gear—anything you think we'll need. I'm going downtown for a couple of hours, but be ready to leave by noon. We're getting out of town for a few days."

Loren looked bleary and confused for a moment, then nodded.

"Okay, boss."

"I'll see you in a few hours."

I stepped to the door, put the alarm on standby for thirty seconds, and stepped outside.

The morning was cool—it was deceptive, since the weatherman had predicted ninety degree heat. But for now it was fine, the cool fresh air filling my lungs and waking me up.

I got into Yngwie and drove to a Denny's for breakfast.

It would be okay, I kept telling myself. It was going to be okay.

* * *

It was a little after 7:00 when I left Yngwie at the parking garage and walked toward the office. I was early, but I could use the time to get paperwork and articles laid out with Consuela. The streets were mostly empty save for the occasional bus and earlybird like me. The Pioneer Building was just ahead.

Plans for the next two weeks cycled through my head over and over, both for what I would do with Loren and Anna, and what I'd need to leave behind for Consuela. I was so sufficiently lost in thought that I didn't hear the soft growl of a motor pulling up behind me until it was too late.

The big vehicle rolled along beside me, pulling almost to a stop. The motion of the front door opening caught my eye, and I saw that it was an imposing black SUV with dark tinted windows. A man stepped from the passenger seat—a man I recognized.

All thoughts of the morning's work drained away.

It was the buzz-cut guy from the shanghai tunnels.

Instincts screamed at me, some urging me to flee, others to fight. For two long seconds I stood, lost in indecision. Then I felt an arm snake around my throat from behind, cold metal pressed against my neck, and a massive jolt of electricity shooting through me, seizing my limbs in a deathgrip, sending me tumbling forward into the first man's grasp.

Shadows closed in as I dimly felt myself being thrust through the open door of the SUV. Then the door closed with a final, ugly thud and a stabbing pain shot through my shoulder. I saw a hand and a hypodermic that thrust roughly through my shirt. The needle stabbed into my flesh, icy cold spreading, overwhelming me, dragging me down into shadow.

I faded in and out of consciousness, vaguely aware that I was inside the SUV, and that we were driving somewhere. Once I stirred and mumbled, and was rewarded with another dose of sedatives.

Confused images swam through my head—this wasn't natural slumber, it was unconsciousness created by brute force, with ugly chemicals swirling in my veins. I saw Dandridge addressing a board meeting attended by men and women in sharp suits. Then I saw him tending a smoldering fire beside a small version of the strange four-armed, three-eyed statue. He was dressed in tattered robes that might once have been royal blue and gold, but were now torn and filthy. A few others sat nearby, similarly disheveled.

And I realized that the man tending the fire was broad-chested and black-haired, with a thick beard. He looked nothing like Roger Dandridge.

Yet I knew it was him.

Random shapes and mindless chaos overwhelmed the image and I was lost for a while.

I began to feel the stirrings of consciousness. Gravel crunched beneath our tires. We slowed and I heard voices and the squeak of metal, as if a door or gate was opening.

As we drove along a winding road, I slipped under again and glimpsed one last image.

A craggy mountain peak rose into the ice-blue sky and white snow covered the ground. Near the summit rose a statue, the carved image of a graceful nude woman, arms raised, wings spread out from her back. And on a small patch of ground that was free of snow at the foot of the statue, knelt a figure, clad in black leather pants and vest, head bowed...

Arngrim.

As I watched, his figure shifted, and he became the red-skinned demon warrior—*Kussariku*. Then even that image blurred and he became something else, something pale and silvery, the sculpted image that was the male mirror of the statue... Fine muscled, flaxen-haired, winged, almost painfully beautiful.

He was praying.

Praying to the image of the entity that I called She Who Watches.

A rough voice echoed inside my head.

"He's coming out again."

"Shit. Tough bastard. Want me to give him another dose?"

"No. We're almost there. We can carry him in. Grandfather wants to see him right away."

I struggled against the fading darkness, but it was still strong. I felt myself lifted, thrown over someone's shoulder, carried unceremoniously out of the car. It was late afternoon, and there was sunlight shining through trees. I saw the blurred, indistinct image of a vast, luxurious-looking house, then I slipped away again, almost grateful to fall back into drugged slumber.

A painful throbbing in my head and an aching in my extremities awoke me a few minutes later. I tried to move my arms, to rub my forehead, to wipe the crusted filth from my eyes, but I couldn't.

With an effort I wrenched my eyes open and was almost blinded by painful white light. I convulsed and cried out, straining to move but realizing that I was held fast on a wheeled gurney and there was a needle in my arm, attached to a drip-bottle.

A soft hand touched my forehead.

"Easy there, Cowboy." The voice was soft and feminine. "You've had a rough day."

I tried to formulate a suitably smartass rejoinder, but my head hurt too much. I opened my eyes half way, cautious of the glare.

It wasn't so bad this time. Bethany Jones stood beside my bed, as statuesque as ever, her platinum hair carefully piled atop her head. She wore a close-fitting white jumpsuit that hugged her curves greedily. On her shoulder was an embroidered patch portraying a stylized man in robes, walking with a staff.

The Pilgrim Foundation, Amazon Division. My mind was starting to work again.

"Miss Jones," I muttered. "So nice to see you again."

"The feeling is mutual." She licked her lips. "But I prefer 'Ms.'"

To my surprise and no little horror I realized that her words were throaty and warm and she gazed at me with something that might have been desire.

Her face matched her body with a predatory, feline grace and feral blue eyes. I started to speak, but as I watched, the outlines of her face blurred and twisted...

It was like the Fallen... One moment she was an artificially beautiful human woman who would have been right at home on the cover of a hotrod magazine, then...

Then she was the thing I'd faced at the abandoned house in Canby. Without her disguise, she was naked and if possible even more voluptuous, with wide shapely hips and generous breasts, but her face was a twisted, skull-like thing with empty, staring eye sockets and flames for hair.

"*Shu-hadaku'idim,*" I growled. "Scythe-bearer."

She stepped back, her human features reasserting themselves.

"Well, well." Her perfect red lips curled up and the icy desire in her eyes seemed to deepen. "I'm flattered that you remember. Pity we can't renew acquaintances." She turned and walked away, striding confidently on white spike heels. "He'll be here in a few moments. Don't go anywhere."

The room was now in focus—all I could think of was the exam room at a hospital. It was all white, with sink, cabinets, dispensers for purple latex gloves and hand sanitizer, jars full of tongue depressors and swabs, a wheeled EKG monitor and all the other accoutrements I'd come to expect. There was, however, no calendar with cute picture of kittens or the doctor's kids.

My kidnapper stood beside the door with a bored expression. He was clad in fatigues with an automatic pistol nestled in a holster at his side. He watched in silence, his eyes greedily roaming up and down Bethany's body as she sashayed out the door, hips rocking to and fro in an exaggerated parody of human motion.

He obviously hadn't seen what I'd seen.

"Hey, soldier-boy, don't judge a book by its cover." My voice was frail but I felt strength slowly returning. "She'd just bite it off and swallow."

He didn't respond, but continued to stand, regarding me with an expressionless stare. I had a feeling that he'd seen and heard far worse than anything I could dish out right now.

I lay there for several long minutes, staring at the ceiling, head throbbing, feeling nauseous and wishing that all those chemicals would just pack up and leave.

Despite the hammering pain, I lifted my head and looked at soldier-boy.

"Hey, you. I gotta go the bathroom. Whatcha gonna do about that?"

Still no response.

Then the door handle rattled and Bethany returned, followed by Roger Dandridge.

"Jesus, Dandridge, do you *ever* take off that suit? Or is it part of your human disguise?"

Dandridge's face broke into an amused smile.

"I'm glad to see you're hale and healthy, Alex. It was important to me that you not be harmed."

"Oh, I've been harmed. Just unstrap me and I'll show you how much."

Dandridge stepped closer, leaning over the gurney rail and looking at me. The woman stood back a respectful distance, near the mercenary, who kept darting lustful glances at her.

"I doubt you're strong enough to rip a piece of paper in half, let alone fight, but I'm not going to take any chances. I'm sorry for acting so quickly, but after you'd left I realized that you might be very useful to us. You're an unusual man, Alex. I think you'll be able to make a substantial contribution to the Pilgrim Foundation."

"Sorry, Rog." I was drugged and sick, but defiance still burned inside me. "That requires my cooperation, and I'm not about to go along with any of your idiotic plans."

Dandridge stood up and placed a warm hand on mine. "Oh, I know that, Alex. I know you were only buying time. That's why I decided—reluctantly of course—to take action when I did. Heaven knows what you'd have gotten up to if we hadn't."

"Unstrap me and you'll find out."

"Oh, Alex. You really don't need to play macho here." Dandridge looked sympathetic. "I realize we've put you through quite a bit over the past few hours. I'm also hoping that your friends Loren and Anna will be joining us soon. That would make our job even easier. And oh, yes, that dog of yours. Beowulf?" He sighed and smiled warmly. "I love dogs. I've had many over the years."

"For lunch or dinner?" My voice seemed stronger. Maybe all the emotions I was feeling were starting to overwhelm the remaining drugs in my system.

Dandridge laughed at that. It was a sincere, hearty laugh.

"You know what else I admire about you, Alex? Your sense of humor. You're here, tied up and drugged, in the heart of what you consider to be enemy territory and you can still joke about it. That's a very rare quality, believe me."

I'd had about enough idle chatter. "What are you planning to do, Dandridge?"

"Well, of course I need to keep you in the loop, don't I? Well, Alex, I'll do that—I'll tell you all of the details of my evil scheme of world conquest and then I'll leave you suspended over the shark tank so that you can escape and blow up my secret lair. That sound about right?"

He laughed again. "See, Alex? You're not the only one with a sense of humor. I've heard too damned many jokes over the years, none of them seemed funny anymore. And now here you are, giving me a fresh perspective."

"Glad to help, Roger."

"You'll find out what I want soon enough. In fact..." He gestured at Bethany and the merc. "Get him unhooked and take him to the ritual chamber."

"Going to torture me for information, Dandridge?"

He made a face and waved his hand dismissively. "This isn't *Saw Part Eleven*, Alex. I hate those movies anyway. So much sex and violence in cinema these days, wouldn't you say? But we don't torture people, Alex. What's the point of that? We offer them what they want, and if they refuse, well..." He chuckled and spoke with a fake German accent. "Ve haff vays, if you know what I mean."

Silently Bethany disconnected my IV tube from the drip bottle and taped it to my arm, then the soldier pressed on a pedal and began to wheel me toward the door.

"So am I going to get one of your patented mind control tattoos?" I asked. "It may not work on me as well as you want."

"Oh, no," Dandridge replied as he led us out into the hallway. "As I told you, the whole tattoo thing is terribly crude and unsubtle. You needn't worry about that—we'll get this over as quickly as possible. Like I said, I truly hate inflicting pain, even when it's necessary."

* * *

Bethany wheeled me down corridors that wouldn't have been out of place in a European royal palace while the merc walked casually alongside. The floors were polished marble, black with white veins or white with black. Doors were elaborate and baroque, flanked by gilded columns. Overhead chandeliers twinkled and glittered, just coming on with the approach of night.

Twice we went past windows and I looked out to see the grounds of an extensive estate, illuminated by floodlights. There were manicured lawns and carefully-tended shrubberies, gravel walkways and an outbuilding surrounded by parked vehicles. Once I saw another wing of the mansion, plain Georgian style with decorative cornices and large, multi-paned windows. Thick trees surrounded us.

"Where..." I muttered, still fighting off the lingering effects of the drugs. "Where are we?"

"Family estate," Dandridge replied. "East of Seattle, right up against the Wenatchee National Forest. I'm surprised you didn't already know that, Alex. You're such a skilled researcher, even with your limited resources."

"Sorry to disappoint..."

"Think nothing of it."

At length we reached a small room with elevator doors. Dandridge inserted a key card and punched a code into the number pad beside it. The doors slid open silently and we entered.

Dandridge spoke as we descended.

"I told you that I'm about 5,000 years old, Alex. That's not entirely true. It's more accurate to say that my *essence* is that old. My spirit, my soul, my... well, my *self*. It's what lives inside our bodies and makes us what we are. A long time ago I gained the ability to trade my essence for another's. It's a complicated concept, but simply put I am able to place myself in another body and displace that other person into mine. Body swap. I'm sure you're familiar with it—it's been written about in many fantasy and science fiction novels, they've made horrible movies about it, even cartoons. Frankly, over the years I've decided that I prefer classic Warner Brothers cartoons to just about any other form of entertainment. They never get old, no matter how many times I watch them. *Bugs Bunny?* Coyote and Road Runner? Sheer genius if you ask me."

The elevator stopped smoothly and the doors opened. I was propelled into a narrow concrete corridor, lit by grilled industrial fixtures. It was cold and Dandridge's voice echoed flatly as he led us down the hallway, speaking all the time.

"I digress. Where was I? Yes, body-swapping. I'm not the only one who can—it's rare and most of the people who can do it don't understand how it works. Once you understand however, it's relatively straightforward. The only real problem is that it requires the total acquiescence of the subject—it took a long time to figure out an efficient way of doing it. Drugs help a bit—they can make the subject more amenable to displacement, but regrettably the most effective means is the infliction of pain. The catch is that it can't inflict permanent harm, or else the entire process is pointless. In the past it's proved very difficult to accomplish this, but lately... Well, modern medical science has come to the rescue."

Ahead lay another door with a keypad. Dandridge used his card and typed in the code again.

"As I said, I do hate pain." He stepped into the chamber beyond, and Bethany pushed the gurney after him. The soldier stayed outside and the door closed softly. "But again, necessity often trumps one's delicate feelings. I don't want to do what I'm about to do, but, well, I've come to the conclusion that I *have* to."

The room was circular with pastel-colored walls and a domed ceiling, gently illuminated by indirect lighting. On the floor, inlaid with a variety of colored stones, was the mandala-pattern and its strange letters that I still couldn't read. The room looked like the ritual chamber under the Pilgrim HQ building in Portland if it had been built by a real architect.

Near the center of the pattern stood a wheeled device that looked somewhat like the EKG monitor from the exam room.

A bundle of electrodes with adhesive patches hung from a hook on the side.

Dandridge gestured silently and Bethany wheeled me into the center of the pattern beside the machine. She pressed the pedal and the gurney dropped to the floor.

"Please accept my apologies in advance," Dandridge said as Bethany began to attach the electrodes to my forehead and temples. They were icy cold. "This really is an unfortunate necessity."

I stared. My heart was racing now and adrenaline was flowing. I still felt sick, but now I wanted to break free from the restraints and flee.

"You're..." I fought the insane torrent of fear that flashed through my head. "You're going to switch bodies with me?"

"Yes. Yes, I am." Dandridge stood a few feet away, watching the woman prep me with an approving glance. "I know who and what you are, Alex. You're the *Panigara*. The Shepherd. What the Fallen call *Hirdir*. You have a connection to other places. You have the ability to see things that normal humans can't. You have access to a very powerful weapon. And your friends trust you. If we can't locate Anna and Loren, you can do it for us. Or rather, I can, as you. Anna is quite fond of you, it seems, and she can still prove very valuable to us. Not as valuable as you, but valuable nonetheless."

He folded his arms across his chest. "I've done this a couple of hundred times over the centuries, Alex. It gets easier every time. And I'm not cruel about it, either. I've made arrangements to transfer control of the Pilgrim Foundation and all of its resources to Alexander St. John. People will wonder why someone as wealthy as Roger Dandridge would award control of his charity to an unknown journalist and publisher, but hell... It's a privately-held charity and I can do whatever I want."

"*You'll* run the Foundation as me? What the fuck are you talking about?" Desperation clawed at me, but I was helpless, weary and sick, unable to fight against what was coming. The scythe-bearer's soft touch on my head felt like crawling centipedes and worms.

"Well, someone has to, and if I'm you... Well, it just works out better. And you haven't heard the best part. You get to be billionaire Roger Dandridge. You'll have time to enjoy all of my resources. Except those I take with me to the Foundation of course, but our day is getting closer and we won't be needing the Dandridge fortune much longer. And when the master comes, Alex... Gods, what wonders you'll see!" Dandridge's eyes lit up and he stepped closer. Bethany left the circle.

Dandridge continued, and his voice became that of a true believer, exhorting me to follow him. "A mathematically perfect world, Alex! No more hate, no more crime, no more poverty. A world of law and order—literally. Mimma-Lemnu's order, and his law. Fair, equitable, merciful, just. All the sacrifices will be worth it, Alex. All the pain, all the suffering... It'll be over, and the people of the world will live forever in peace and joy. And there will be a place for Roger Dandridge if he wants—you'll see. It won't be so bad, Alex. When he comes, you'll see. You'll see the value of order, the value of faith, and the joy of submission."

He turned to the machine and pressed his thumb against a round red button.

"Again, I'm sorry, Alex. But this is for the best."

He pressed the button.

VIII

Once, while helping a woman whom I hoped to date assemble a bathroom shelf I managed to jam my thumb into the ragged end of a metal tube and pry my own thumbnail off. That was one of the most painful things I'd ever experienced.

This was worse.

There's a strange purity to real pain. Not the kind of pain that you feel when you accidentally rip off your thumbnail, or when you break your arm or a doctor sticks a needle in your eardrum to drain an infection—those are bad, to be sure, and you have every right to scream, curse, and carry on.

What Dandridge inflicted on me was beyond that kind of pain by several orders of magnitude. It was the kind of pain that made it pointless to scream or curse or carry on. It was pain that skipped all the intermediaries, and went right to the nerves in my brain that received the impulses. Without being filtered by proximity, by skin, by neural transmitters or even by an animal brain that could tamp it down to a manageable level. It was pure pain that didn't pause, didn't lessen, didn't change.

As it continued and my body clenched, spasming and straining against the straps that held me, I felt myself falling, tumbling into nothingness... There was no body to fall—it was only my mind, my consciousness, my essence...

This was the dark void between worlds. I had visited it once, briefly, during that last fight with Onatochee, when She Who Watches had spoken to me. I fell through shadowed chasms of freezing cold, burned in flames hotter than the sun, spun dizzyingly from impossible heights. I only glimpsed things as I went whirling past, but what I saw was terrifying.

I saw the yawning void between worlds, a place absent shape, color, texture, even empty space. I saw endless corridors where lost souls wandered, crying in despair. I saw ruined streets, reflections of human dreams and aspirations, crawling with black worms that cried out from hunger that could never be satisfied. I saw great dark shapes stirring in blue-black seas and legions of monstrosities that were neither fish nor man. I saw dragons and demons and plains of cracked, glowing stone. I saw the fearsome chaos that was the sentient cosmos called Onatochee. I even glimpsed something huge and terrible—a vast figure with four arms and a massive bestial face, three angry yellow eyes glowing at me with infinite hatred...

Then amid endless darkness I saw a single figure. I drew closer and it came into focus.

Annabelle Lee Moore stood naked, arms outstretched, head thrown back. Her tattoos flashed and fluoresced silver-blue and the wind blew her red hair. From her back rose the suggestion of soaring wings, sketched out in faint traceries of silver light...

She Who Watches called out, Her voice a soaring melody against a chorus of screams.

Then the pain faded, disappearing like water in the desert, replaced by a numb sense of shock and lethargy. Cold stone was underneath me, and dim light shone above.

I opened my eyes. I was on my back, staring up at the domed ceiling. Behind me rough hands seized my wrists and I felt the harsh metal of handcuffs as they snapped shut.

Through a haze, I saw myself... Alex St. John, weary and haggard but alive, stepping unsteadily from a gurney as the scythe-bearer unfastened the leather restraints.

"Well done, Alex," I said wearily, leaning against the woman for support. "That was quite a fight. Worst I've ever experienced. But it's done, and we..."

My voice faded into a roar of static. Faint glimpses of Anna and the silver-blue traceries on her skin flashed before my eyes, and I heard a voice...

You're the one who can resist. I felt it that night when She came. I know who you are. I know what you are.

Damien!

Damien Smith, the man who had gotten me into all of this, the one who had taken his own life in the face of the horrors he'd revealed.

My partner. My colleague.

My friend.

"Damien..." I mumbled.

Dandridge looked at me in surprise. Yes, it was Dandridge. Dandridge in my body. He wasn't me. He could never be me.

Will you take the weapon and stand in the doorway? Will you guard this world and all who dwell in it? Will you serve the sacred spiral?

"Yes. I'll take it. I'll serve."

Dandridge's confusion deepened.

"What?"

Something broke free inside me. The same fire I'd felt the night we'd fought Onatochee. The same fury that had possessed me at Hauser Butte. I didn't have the sword in hand, but part of its energy flashed though my muscles and I pulled my arms apart, straining against the handcuffs.

The chain between them snapped like a rubber band and I whirled. The mercenary stood behind me, eyes wide, momentarily shocked into inaction.

I drove my fist under his chin and he went tumbling, nerveless. I spun, glaring at Dandridge in his stolen body. Bethany Jones shifted, transforming into a naked woman with a screaming, fire-haired skull face. She held a scythe that sparked and glowed.

I didn't care. I threw myself at her, heedless of the swinging blade. I blocked it partially, but the burning blade passed through my arm, leaving a trail of agony behind it. Black blood gushed, splattering on the inlaid floor, but with my uninjured hand I seized the creature's throat, and brought my knee up into her abdomen, kicking as hard as I could.

She wasn't human, but her anatomy had the same vulnerabilities. She doubled over, the scythe clanging to the floor.

Then I was on Dandridge. One of my arms dangled useless, half-severed by the scythe, and I felt dizzy as more blood gushed. But I knew what I wanted.

My body was weak from the drugs and from the pain that they'd inflicted. Despite horrific injury Dandridge was still strong. I overwhelmed him and crushed him under my body, my hand around his throat, squeezing.

"Give it back, Dandridge," I snarled. It was his voice, but my words. "Give it up or you'll die before I do."

His eyes showed fear—perhaps for the first time in centuries he was facing death, and in the storm of terror that filed his brain only one alternative remained.

The room flashed black and red, and I saw some glimpses of the alien vistas that I'd seen before, flickering through the darkness between worlds. Then I was on the floor with Roger Dandridge above me, one arm nearly severed, the other locked around my neck.

I was back in my body, but I was still weak. I kicked and struggled, and at last the loss of blood seemed to affect Dandridge and he fell away, rolling on the floor in a sticky pool of crimson.

The room spun as I staggered to my feet. I was weak, yes, but I was back where I belonged, and with luck I could get out of here, get back to Portland, get to Loren and Anna...

There was still a chance.

Then a figure rose up in front of me—Bethany swung her weapon at me, blade reversed, the heavy blunt end crashing down on my head and sending me flying.

Then I heard alarms and the lights in the room blazed to full brightness and the door opened, admitting a squad of men in camouflage, weapons drawn...

I tried to rise, tried to bring my hands up to defend myself, but a rifle butt descended, sending me back down to the floor and back into cold oblivion.

* * *

Roger Dandridge looked a bit worse for the wear. He was pale, his bright eyes were dull and his arm was in a sling. Nevertheless, his tone remained friendly.

"That was quite impressive, Alex. Really."

We were back in the exam room and I was on the gurney. My friendly merc, also looking a bit beaten-up, stood guard at the door. I felt as if I'd been thrashed by the entire Russian national rugby team, but I managed to retain some semblance of defiance.

"Sorry about the arm, Rog. You just can't get good help these days."

He nodded matter-of-factly. "Touché. My medical team is excellent, however. They can do wonders with transplants." He sighed. "As I said, you put up quite a fight. We'll have to try again in a few days, but this time we'll hit my body with some heavy sedatives before you come around. It'll give me enough time to fully establish control."

"Jesus, Dandridge. You *still* want to be me? Is your life *that* boring?"

He indicated his wounded arm. "Oh even more so now, Alex. I'm sorry that you'll have to face life with a crippled arm, but to tell you the truth you have no one to blame but yourself. I don't hold grudges, though. We'll get it all sorted out. It's just a bump in the road, really."

All at once I felt my anger at Dandridge change. It didn't vanish—no, that wasn't possible. But in an instant I felt it change, and evolve into something else. Something a bit more subtle.

In a very weird way, I felt sorry for him.

"You still don't get it, do you, Dandridge? Five thousand years and two hundred lives, and you still don't understand humanity."

He frowned. "What are you talking about?" Shorn of its old heartiness, his voice only sounded weary and slightly annoyed. It was an improvement as far as I was concerned.

"We don't need Mimma-Lemnu to tell us what to do, Dandridge. Humans have to learn on their own. They have to make their own laws and fail on their own. That's where all religious fanatics like you come up short—you think that if the law and morality is handed down from on high we'll have no choice but to obey, and everything will magically fix itself."

Now for the first time he seemed genuinely flustered, like a kid being told that there's no Santa Claus.

"Don't be idiotic, Alex. People are imperfect. They always make the wrong choices. If the past five millennia have taught me anything it's that humanity needs a strong hand to guide it, or everything's just going to turn to blood and dust."

"We've gotten by pretty well for five thousand years despite our flaws, haven't we?"

"Yes. By the skin of your teeth. By narrowly avoiding disaster every few generations. If you leave people alone, it's only a matter of time. Bigger and bigger weapons, more and more power of their own environment. It's inevitable that one of these days you *won't* squeak by, and everything will collapse."

"Maybe it's our nature to survive by the skin of our teeth, Dandridge. Maybe it's our nature to collapse every few generations, then learn from it, and come back even stronger. Wisdom has to be *learned*, Roger. It can't be handed to us by an arrogant supreme being that lives up in the sky and tells us what to do. Humanity has to make mistakes. Otherwise we'll stagnate and disappear as if we'd never existed."

Dandridge snorted. "So it's better to burn out than fade away? Is that what you're saying?"

"Damned right it's what I'm saying. And over five millennia you've just gotten too thick and stupid to see it."

Now real anger flashed in Dandridge's eyes. "I'm not wasting any more words on you," he snapped and turned on his heel. "Next time I come in here we'll finish this."

He strode from the room, allowing the guard to open the door for him.

"I'm going to burn this place to the ground, Dandridge. That's a promise."

He didn't reply, but slammed the door behind him.

I fell back onto the gurney. I was weak and exhausted and my whole body hurt.

It was all just pointless defiance anyway. He'd be back in another day or two, and we'd go through the same exercise, only this time he'd be ready for me. I'd be drugged, restrained, taken away, unable to strike back and resist. Maybe as Roger Dandridge I'd be able to use my resources to fight him and the Foundation, but my guess was that they'd take precautions, build in fail safes that would keep me docile and unable to stop them. Maybe they'd hold Loren and Anna hostage, or threaten someone else important to me. Or they'd just decide that I was too much trouble and just waste me. I didn't know and right now I didn't want to think about it.

The guard turned out the overhead light and stood in the dim illumination of a single lamp. I watched him for a few minutes, feeling my eyelids grow heavy and sleep creep up on me, unbidden and unwanted, but irresistible nonetheless.

Long ago, Damien Smith had taught me how to have lucid dreams, in which I was conscious and in control of my actions. I credited the ability for the prophetic or clairvoyant dreams that I experienced, some of which had helped us track down the demon Onatochee and his followers. I also gave credit to She Who Watches, that otherworldly creature who had given me both sword and title, but She was a distant and almost incomprehensible being whose origin I could not even guess.

Yet I had seen something like Her while I tumbled through those endless cold canyons in the spaces between worlds when

Dandridge had tried to take over my body. It had been Anna, yet not Anna. Somewhere, far away, in a distant realm Anna's presence had reached out, and I'd seen her...

Now I dreamed again, and the sense of falling returned, of disconnection from reality and transition. Was this something new? Had Dandridge inadvertently awakened something inside of me, made me aware of the endless dark spaces that surrounded us, a conduit to and from those other worlds that Damien believed adjoined with our own? Could I see and hear down them? Could I call out and touch something?

Faint silvery radiance touched my face, cool and comforting. It was like when I hugged Beowulf or lay beside Anna—a profound essence of peace and stability, something that was beyond anything that I could discern from my familiar senses.

In the distance a figure sketched itself out of silvery lines—naked and female, something that was both sexual and at the same time sacred and untouchable. It wasn't Anna this time. No, it was Her, the one whom I'd seen and touched before, beckoning to me across the gulf.

She Who Watches, perfect and distant but at the same time familiar, Her skin covered with racing sparks of blue, Her wings tall and elegant, Her face gentle and kind...

I wasn't just dreaming—I knew it now. I had indeed managed to detach a small part of myself to roam and reach out, to communicate with something distant and alien, yet at the same time wise and familial.

"Is it you?" I asked. "I'm the Shepherd."

She nodded. "You who summoned me, who bears my sign, who guards the doorways and serves the sacred spiral."

My dream-hands were free. I reached out to Her.

"Help me."

The air around me flickered and flashed, as if from distant lighting. She floated amid black and violet clouds, the wind swirling around Her but not touching Her.

"They come, Shepherd. They have been summoned as well."

"Who comes? Loren? Anna?"

"The others come, Shepherd. Be merciful. They serve me, though they do not know it."

An image shimmered in my memory.

A craggy mountain peak rose into the ice-blue sky and white snow covered the ground. Near the summit rose a statue, the carved image of a graceful nude woman, arms raised, wings spread out from Her back. And on a small patch of ground that was free of snow at the foot of the statue, knelt a figure, clad in black leather pants and vest, head bowed...

"The Fallen...?"

"All living things deserve mercy. All deserve redemption. No sin is so great that it cannot be redeemed by sacrifice."

Pain jabbed at my brain and I thought I heard the roar of engines.

"Please..." I said, watching as She began to fade away. "Please, help me..."

She nodded again, and between us appeared the shining image of the sword, sketched in shining silver-blue, floating as it had the time that I had reached out and taken it.

I name you Nomeus. *Do not fear the darkness. Save those you can. Avenge those you cannot.*

I reached out again, and my fingers touched the hilt of the sword...

...And I was awake.

The bonds that held me had disintegrated as if attacked by some kind of fast-acting rot. I sat up on the gurney, the sword in my hand, shining like a blue-white sun. The guard looked up, hand reaching for his pistol...

An instant later he was unconscious on the floor and I was busy binding him up with surgical tape. Then, muffled by distance and several layers of walls, I heard the first explosion.

I knew better than to try to shoot out the lock with the guard's popgun of an automatic pistol, and instead hacked at the door with my sword as another blast rumbled through the building. Outside I heard shouted orders, the sound of running feet, shattering glass, and the pop of automatic weapon fire.

The door held out for a minute or two before I was able to cut a hole large enough to reach the handle. I kicked splintered wood away, took the guard's pistol, and stepped into the darkened corridor. Emergency lights had come on up ahead, casting red shadows, and a couple of dark shapes hurried by, so intent on the growing sound of gunfire that they ignored me completely.

Frantically, I tried to remember the mansion's layout—I'd only seen a few corridors while royally fucked up on sedatives, but I remembered the location of the other wing, near the garage where I'd seen the vehicles.

I hurried along, keeping low and hugging the wall. Ahead a squad of mercenaries in camouflage held a position near a tangle of shattered glass that had once been a multi-paned window. Periodically they would unleash short bursts, then duck back. As I slipped past a fusillade of gunfire erupted from outside, shattering glass and pockmarking the wall as I went.

Where to now? The mansion was in almost total darkness, and had dissolved into a nightmarish confusion of gunfire and shouting. I reached an intersecting hallway that seemed to lead the way I wanted to go. As I moved along I came face-to-face with a crop-haired guard in full battle dress, an H&K G36 rifle cradled in his hands, grenades clipped to his vest. When he saw me he shouted.

"Hey! Who the fuck are—"

I bashed his head with the flat of my sword, sending him crashing down in a heap. That would teach him to wear his helmet. I relieved the man of his rifle and grenades, then continued down the corridor.

From outside I heard another massive explosion and the roar of engines. As usual, they stabbed at my head like needles. This time I was grateful.

Ahead I saw a staircase, lit by flashes of gunfire from the floor below. I made for it, but as I did a tall shape emerged, both beautiful and horrific in the flickering orange light that surrounded her death's head visage.

"Bethany?" I said softly, moving on guard. "Is it you?"

"Hello, Alex." The husky, sex-laden voice echoed from the burning skull. "So nice to see you."

Totally shorn of any illusion she was just as imposing as she'd been at the house in Canby—seven feet tall, sleek and muscular, a massive glowing scythe held in both hands.

I shifted my grip on the sword. "After careful consideration I've come to the conclusion that we work better as friends. I'm sorry to disappoint you."

She laughed, a screeching, high-pitched sound, then launched herself at me.

I'd slung the rifle and it got in my way as I raised the sword to defend. Blue sparks flashed when it met the scythe blade, and the impact shivered down my arms, sorely injured and weary but also filled with the sword's unearthly energy. We stood chest-to-chest for a moment, pressing against each other, each blade seeking to overwhelm the other, then I pulled back and let the blade fall.

"Oh my," she murmured, flames rising in her eyes. "You certainly know how to show a girl a good time."

She shrieked deafeningly, the scythe descended and I swung at the back of her head. The blade bit bone and red flames burst out like blood. Her screams redoubled in volume and pitch and she released her grip on the scythe with one hand, slashing at me with curved bony claws.

I got the sword up in time to block the blow, then riposted, swinging the sword in a short arc and slashing at her arm. Again, the blade bit, and this time it sliced cleanly through her arm, eliciting a wild cry of both pain and—God help me—ecstasy.

"Oh, Alex..." Her voice was tight with barely-restrained passion, as if she was on the very edge of climax.

She still held the scythe in one hand and to my surprise managed to swing at me once more. I ducked, falling backwards and only barely avoiding her swing. She dropped the scythe and leaped on me, her good arm slashing at my face.

A throaty whisper emerged from the smoldering skull. "Mmmm..."

I brought the sword up and thrust desperately, catching her in the chest and running her through. Burning blue sparks scattered across the naked human body and I smelled the stench of burning flesh. She screamed again, not as loud this time—she'd taken horrific injuries but she was still alive, and she slashed at me once more.

"Oh, Alex..."

Her words of passion were almost worse than the violence she was inflicting on me. Now she was on her knees, trying to rise, black blood splattered all across her pale, flawless flesh. Her shrieks were now incoherent, sensual moans.

I swung downward as hard as I could and the blade chopped savagely into her flesh, slicing through her back and shoulders, leaving her cut into two bloody, twitching chunks.

"*Ahhhhh.*" I didn't want to hear the sound, but I had no choice. It was an orgasmic cry that faded into a deep sigh of satisfaction.

What was left of Bethany Jones lay still. Good God, I wondered. Did we just have sex or try to kill each other?

Nausea welled up and I fled. The stairs opened onto another corridor, this one full of smoke and dust. A squad of guards hurried past, carrying a heavy machine gun and a belt of ammo. Jesus, what kind of arsenal did these assholes have?

Ahead of me the hallway ended at a large marble-floored foyer. More mercs knelt at the windows, firing rifles or tossing grenades out windows.

I knelt and pulled up a grenade. These people were mercenaries who had hitched their wagon to the Pilgrim Foundation and its ruthless founder, so I shouldn't be feeling any guilt or hesitation. But they were human beings, no matter what offenses they'd committed.

I steeled myself and prepared to pull the pin. They wouldn't be expecting an attack from this direction...

My unseen allies were way ahead of me. With a deafening roar and a sheet of flames the main door and most of the wall beside it burst inward, sending mercs flying and filing the entire foyer with black smoke. Outside another storm of gunfire erupted, and the few remaining guards stumbled away.

The banshee wail of engines erupted again, and through the shattered entrance a massive motorcycle appeared, bearing a sidecar. I recognized Arngrim at the machine's helm even in the darkness and obscured by goggles and dust. And in the sidecar, grinning and brandishing the tube of a portable rocket-launcher...

"LOREN!"

I raced forward, heedless of the danger, even as another round of gunfire burst out a few yards away. When he saw me, Loren uttered a whoop and flung the spent tube away, leaping from the sidecar and running at me.

We met with numbing force, throwing our arms around each.

"Fuck, Alex! We found you!"

"You sure as hell did!" I waved. "Arngrim! It's me!"

Arngrim's expression didn't change, but he motioned at me.

"Get aboard, Shepherd! We've got to get out of here!"

I wasn't inclined to argue with that sentiment, and so positioned myself on the seat behind Arngrim, my arms around his chest.

"Now this doesn't mean we're going steady, right?" I asked, and got a dirty look in return.

"This is no time for flippancy, *Hirdir*. Hang on!" He gunned the engine as Loren jumped into the sidecar, and turned around, faster and more nimbly than I would have imagined from his mount's bulk. Of course I knew what it truly was, and it wasn't exactly a motorcycle.

With a roar, we surged from the room and out onto the mansion's grounds.

The scene outside was like a war movie. In the darkness, figures ran in all directions, illuminated now and then by muzzle flashes and tracer fire. A yellow-orange explosion silhouetted a pair of Fallen on their cycles as they raced through a knot of guards, cutting them down with black-bladed weapons. A scythe-bearer traded blows with a dismounted Fallen, flickering jarringly between his human and demon form. He slashed with his sword, cutting off the fearsome deaths-head, but with a final blow the bearer took his leg, and he tumbled to the grass, blood geysering. A Fallen on a cycle raced up to him, pulling him onto the machine, and racing away into the night.

At the controls of our cycle, Arngrim waved his hand, pointing away from the mansion and shouted an ululating war cry that resounded across the grounds.

"Away!" he shouted. "Fall back!"

In perfect unison, the Fallen that I could see disengaged and began to retreat, streaming along the gravel driveway past the garage. Most of the cars that had been parked outside were burning, and bodies of guards were scattered everywhere. As we approached, I saw a wrecked cycle and the motionless shape of a Fallen in human guise, limbs twisted, clothes soaked in blood.

"Gods," snarled Arngrim, slowing down as we got closer to the corpse. "It's Gæirmund. We've lost good fighters tonight, *Hirdir*. I hope this was worth it."

I didn't reply. After the night's appalling bloodshed I wasn't any more enthusiastic about Arngrim's crowd than I'd been before, but right now they were the only allies we had.

Arngrim gunned the engine and we picked up speed, heading toward the garage.

There was a rush of movement ahead, and a patch of darkness seemed to loom up and come at us. It resolved itself into the nightmare thing I'd seen in the shanghai tunnels— tall and rangy, a pale hairless body, canine face, muscular arms, clawed fingers, backward-bent animal legs...

"*Idimma-Xul!*" Arngrim bellowed, swerving to avoid her.

A single taloned hand swatted at Arngrim's motorcycle and we went tumbling, careening into a wrecked Jaguar. Loren swore, and I felt myself flying through space, landing in a painful heap nearby.

I struggled to my feet. Loren crawled from the wreck, drawing a pistol. Arngrim was nowhere to be seen.

From the gloom, illuminated by the raging fires, Idimma-Xul emerged, leaning over Loren, reaching out with her huge hands.

He fired once, twice, plugging her between the eyes. She fell back, making a noise like an angry jackass as Loren scrambled away.

I'd managed to hold onto the sword. My leg hurt, my shoulder hurt—hell, just about everything that could hurt did, and a few others to boot. But the weapon flared to silvery brilliance, infusing me with its energy.

"*Idimma-Xul!*" I shouted, limping toward her, sword on guard.

She caught sight of me and brayed in recognition.

"*Panigara!* Belet-Ili's faithful lapdog! Come at last to seal your fate!" She held out her arms as if to embrace me. "Come! Let us dance, little one!"

From the garage erupted a fearsome howling and a pack of shapes bounded from the flame-lit shadows. They were smaller versions of Idimma-Xul—pale and hairless dog-like humanoids, loping along on two legs or four, uttering ear-splitting howls that cut through the noise of battle. *Ghul.* Eaters of corpses. The ghoul-queen's subjects crawled up from catacombs and cemeteries.

Loren limped up beside me. "Give me the rifle! I'll hold 'em off while you deal with the big ugly."

We exchanged a quick glance and I handed him my rifle. "Don't get yourself killed, champ."

"Right, boss." He sounded weary but saluted as he accepted the rifle.

Idimma-Xul stood waiting in the firelight. I came on guard and advanced. Behind me savage howls erupted, punctuated by three-round bursts of rifle fire.

"You are the last to bear the sign," she growled, crouching slightly as I came toward her. "All the others are gone—Enlil and Lamashtu, Marduk and Pazuzu. The stone warriors, the black-headed ones. You are the last, and once you are gone the master shall come and my folk shall once more feed on the blood of infants, born and unborn."

"It's nice to have a hobby," I said. I began to circle. She was even taller than I'd guessed at the tunnels, topping me by a good three feet, and I couldn't see any weak points in her defenses.

"Laugh, little one." Her voice oozed contempt. "Laugh at the one who would drink your blood and feast on your entrails. Laugh, for I am despair. I am madness."

"Right. I don't think you're being pretentious enough. You should try harder."

She didn't reply to that, but lowered her naked canine head and began to regard me with an appraising gaze, as if she too was looking for an opening.

It came with almost blinding speed. One moment Idimma-Xul was crouched on her haunches, glaring at me from ten yards away, the next she was on me, massive hands ripping at me, clawed feet kicking.

I parried her swing, and the sword sparked violently as if protesting. I felt something batter itself painfully against my psyche, an overwhelming presence, more insistent and powerful than Onatochee and the creatures that had come with him. My original guess had been correct—she was no alien invader, no creature from another reality seeking to conquer. She and her kind were truly of our world—monsters who lurked in the shadow, worshipping their demon-god and waiting for the day of his coming.

Her talons raked at my abdomen, trying to split me open. I dodged, but the razor-claws slashed across my thigh, opening huge gashes, almost blinding me with pain. I struck out blindly and the blade struck her leg, cutting hairy flesh, then rebounding, still protesting.

Nearby Loren unleashed a burst of gunfire, cutting down a dog-thing as it leaped at him. A second came just behind the first, but it too fell, blood and bone bursting from its skull.

Idimma-Xul was on me again. The Sumerians had considered her a goddess, an evil demon that devoured babies and could only be held at bay by powerful magic. Now she faced me, an ordinary mortal armed with the sword of a goddess whom she thought long vanished. Up to this point most of my fights had been even affairs. For the first time, I felt completely outmatched.

I fell back in the face of another assault—clawed hands and feet, slashing fangs struck at me from every direction, and I could barely hold them off. Another blow struck my shoulder like a sledgehammer, sending another wave of numbing, irresistible pain through me. Then she kicked again and I felt myself carried up, spun through the air, crashing down on my wounded side, desperately holding onto the sword.

"Little man," she hissed, stepping closer. Gore streamed from a half-dozen wounds; I'd hurt her, but nowhere near enough, and nowhere near as much as she'd hurt me. "You will be Idimma-Xul's first sacrifice to the master."

I struggled to my feet, but my knee gave out and I fell. She rose above me, blotting out the yellow light of the fires. Her black eyes locked with mine and I felt the full weight of her presence, just as I had in the Shanghai tunnels. My instincts screamed to move, to defend myself, flee—anything, and the burning silver-blue fury of the sword still burned in my veins but I couldn't move, frozen in place, helpless as she raised her great, eviscerating claws.

"*Queen of the Dead!*"

A bellow sounded from behind her, accompanied by a feral howl that I knew all too well.

Before she could turn Arngrim had leaped onto her shoulders, grabbing her head from behind, yanking it back, exposing her throat, and Beowulf, incongruously clad in a heavy black harness set with several odd projections, his eyes covered by tinted goggles, rocketed out of the night, sinking his teeth into her muscular lower leg.

"*Hirdir!*" Arngrim shouted as Idimma-Xul thrashed and brayed, striking blindly at her back, trying to dislodge him. "Now, *Hirdir!*"

Idimma-Xul's paralysis thinned and shattered like rotten ice. Though pain lanced through every joint of my body I wrested myself upright and sprang, sword arm cocked, blade shimmering and glowing with almost blinding brightness. At the top of the arc I swung, my hand guided only by the power that coursed from blade to hand to brain, and the tip slashed through ghoul-queen's thick, corpse-pale neck, cutting flesh and muscle and veins and trachea, and whatever else lurked beneath her skin, unleashing a flood of hot, steaming black blood that splattered across me and down onto Beowulf.

Idimma-Xul's howl was cut off and fell into a dying gurgle as the massive body collapsed onto the ground with a booming thud.

Arngrim's eyes met mine. They were wild with anger and battle lust. He threw back his head and howled, as harsh and horrific as the *ghul*. With his blade he hacked Idimma-Xul's head loose and held it up, still howling, then flung it toward the burning garage.

Beowulf bounded over to me and I hugged him, getting my face licked in return. Nearby the last of the ghouls were retreating, howling in despair and loping across the grounds as Loren fired after them. He lowered the weapon and hastened to join us.

"Jesus, Alex, is she dead?"

I nodded. "Thanks to Arngrim and Beowulf."

"Beowulf!" shouted Arngrim. "As worthy as any warrior who ever bore the name!"

Beowulf barked happily. I petted him weakly, looking at his harness.

"Jesus, Loren. Body armor?"

He nodded, grinning. "You'd be surprised what these guys can turn up."

Arngrim's motorcycle lay nearby on its side. He wrenched it upright and climbed on, kicking it to life.

"Come, quickly, Shepherd! We must go now!"

I nodded, then looked back toward the garage. Nearby was a metal aboveground tank with the words "Gasoline—Flammable" stenciled on its side. The fire was getting closer to it, but I'd made a promise to Dandridge and I wanted to be sure I kept it.

I looked at Loren. Several grenades were still attached to his vest.

"Got some willy-pete?" I asked.

He nodded and unclipped a canister. "It's my last."

"Good. It's all I'll need." I took it and strode closer to the tank.

I pulled the pin and threw. It landed at the foot of the tank. Then I turned and ran back toward Arngrim. He sat astride his bike, impatiently gunning the engine. Loren and Beowulf had crammed into the sidecar.

I mounted up behind Arngrim. "Okay, let's go."

The grenade went off as we rode toward the trees, splattering the tank and surrounding ground with hot-burning white fury. A moment later it burned through the skin of the tank and a massive orange fireball erupted, washing over us with a wave of heat. The flames quickly spread to the mansion and by the time we were on the highway, a mile or so distant, a column of angry flames was climbing toward the sky.

"You should be more careful!" Loren shouted over the roar of the engine. "You could start a forest fire!"

I didn't care. The die was cast. Roger Dandridge had chosen war and by God we'd given it to him.

The rest of the Fallen were on a side road just off Highway Two, surrounding Yngwie and Beethoven like a Greek Phalanx. As we approached, Beethoven's sliding door flew open and Anna rushed out, leaping on me as I dismounted, frantically kissing my cheeks and mouth, making only incoherent happy noises. A moment later she was kissing Loren and then Beowulf, though thankfully with less passion than she'd kissed us.

"Thank God. Oh, fuck. I was so worried..."

I looked at her as she hugged Beowulf and he licked her face.

"It was you, wasn't it? You contacted the Fallen."

She nodded. "When you didn't come back, we got out as quick as we could. We found Yngwie at the garage and Connie said you'd never showed up."

"We knew something was wrong," Loren added as he unstrapped Beowulf's harness and pulled the armor free. "No way you'd have disappeared without telling us. We checked your GPS, and it said you were headed north on I-5 before they turned it off."

"Yeah." I leaned against Yngwie, and it felt as if I were embracing an old friend. My wounded leg throbbed and I didn't think I could stay on my feet much longer. "They got careless. They must have turned it off and thrown it away, but you'd already gotten a fix."

"I was so worried and so afraid." Anna hugged me again, though my clothes were filthy and stiff with congealed blood and my face probably looked as if I'd stuck it in a fan. She felt good, even though every touch hurt like hell. And damn. She smelled good too. "I couldn't think of anyone else who could help, so I decided I'd try to find them again. I tried to remember what I'd seen when I was a kid. That day by the highway, those dreams I had... I fell asleep and I dreamed I was floating in darkness, calling out to them."

"And I heard." Arngrim sat astride his machine. It was battered but still roared and grumbled. The Fallen's machines were as resilient as they were, apparently. "I heard her call. I'd been praying and meditating, thinking on what you'd said to us, Shepherd. If I hadn't been there I might never have heard her. But we heard, and we knew where you were. Our old oaths to *Hirdir* brought us to you. We came and brought war on the enemy once more."

Gunnar spoke up. He was the one who wore the triskelion.

"We've struck the enemy a blow, but he isn't defeated. Dandridge, the high priest—we didn't find him, and he has other places like this, all over the world. He will strike back. Count on it."

Arngrim looked gloomier than usual.

"We've forced the enemy's hand, Shepherd. They have no choice but to act. They do not have all the weapons that they wanted and their plans are not as certain as they had hoped, but that will not stop them. They will call upon their master, and he will come. Soon."

He kicked his machine to life, and a moment later all the surviving Fallen did the same.

"Follow us if you would stand with the Fallen. You were right, Shepherd. We have broken our oath to you, and for that we must pay. But if you would fulfill yours, and defend your world, ride with us."

Despite visions of flames and death and destruction, I nodded. "I will, Arngrim. You're the only ones who can help us now."

"So be it." Arngrim waved an arm. "Ride, Fallen! Ride, *Fordæmdur! Hirdir* rides with us, and our Day of Vengeance is at hand!"

A roar of approval greeted the words and the Fallen kicked their machines to life. Thunder rumbled through the forest as the lead elements moved out onto the highway.

As Loren and Beowulf climbed into Beethoven, I cast a glance at Anna.

"I don't think I'm up to it, love. You want to drive?"

She kissed my cheek gently. "I thought you'd never ask."

I collapsed onto the back seat as Anna fired up Yngwie's engine. On the floor rested the Foundation's brass lantern and the books I'd taken. I still didn't know what to do with them, but something told me I'd have to figure it out soon.

I was weary. My leg ached, and I realized that Idimma-Xul had banged me up a lot worse than I'd thought.

Anna guided Yngwie out onto the highway. Loren followed, and the Fallen formed up around us, thundering down the road like the knights that they had once been and might be again.

We drove east, into the rising sun.

PART FOUR

WHY WE FIGHT

"**S**o where the heck are we?" Loren flashed me a familiar and relieved grin as he approached me along the paved path that led from a cinderblock rest room building to the parking lot where I stood unsteadily beside Yngwie. The air was hot and dusty, the ground was arid and covered with shrubs, but beyond the little rest room I saw the blue glimmer of water.

"Welcome to Starvation Lake State Park in eastern Utah," he said as Beowulf bounded through scrub and sagebrush to join us. "And welcome back to the living, too. You've had a pretty rough trip."

"I don't remember much of it." I looked at my clothes. I was dressed in clean jeans and one of Loren's t-shirts—this one read "11 cheers for binary!" My leg ached dully where Idimma-Xul had slashed it, but it seemed okay. "I appear to have changed clothes."

Loren nodded. "We fixed you up at a rest stop in Idaho. That Fallen guy, Gunnar—he cleaned those claw-marks on your leg and stitched you up. You didn't like it very much."

I surveyed the parking lot. Through shimmering heat I saw Beethoven parked a few yards away and the bulk of the Fallen mounted up near the entrance, their engines rumbling impatiently. Anna was there, talking with Arngrim. When she saw me she waved and started to jog over to us.

"I honestly don't remember anything," I said.

"It's just as well. You bawled like a baby."

"I'm sure you'd have done the same. Hi, gorgeous."

That last was directed at Anna as she came closer, face wet with perspiration.

"So I'm back," I said, accepting a cautious hug. "It's good to see you."

"It's better to see you." She looked up at me. She wasn't wearing her glasses. "You slept all the way across three states."

"Good for the constitution. Has the gracious Arngrim told you where we're going?"

She shook her head. "Only that it's another 300 miles or so east and we'd better get a move on."

"Jeez, excuse the hell out of me." Loren sighed and rolled his eyes. "Unlike our new friends, we puny humans have to stop every now and then for food and gas and to take a leak." He waved at Arngrim. "Keep your shirt on! We're leaving!"

Arngrim waved in reply and rolled toward the entrance, the body of Fallen riders following.

"Nice going," I said. "Now we can't stay and admire the scenery." I opened Yngwie's passenger door. "At least we have AC."

"Yeah right," Loren grumbled, trudging toward Beethoven, Beowulf trotting along behind. "These damned Westphalias have shitty heaters *and* no AC. All I get is hot air blowing through the vents."

"You're the one who wanted a hippy van. Don't come crying to me."

Anna made Yngwie purr, and we followed our guides back onto the highway.

***

While we made our way across Utah toward Colorado, I unfastened my jeans to look at my wounded leg. The slashes had been huge, ugly, and painful, and Idimma-Xul's claws had been filthy, but now my wounds were neatly stitched shut and were neither swollen nor weeping. I briefly wondered whether there was some strange Fallen healing magic at work, or whether Gunnar was just a particularly good field surgeon.

The sun was just touching the distant slopes of Front Range when we veered off the main road, dipping down into a forested valley. We followed a narrow access road for several miles, then onto an even less inviting gravel road for several more. As shadows grew thicker and the trees seemed closer, the Fallen deployed single file, heading down a narrow, overgrown path.

"Shit, what the hell is this?" Anna muttered to herself as she slowly guided Yngwie along. The road was almost too narrow— tree branches brushed against us while behind Beethoven coughed and labored. Loren stalled twice, but caught up each time.

At last we came to a stop. The road had broadened slightly, and ahead of us was a granite cliff face. Arngrim and two others were dismounted and, in the glare of the Fallen's headlights, busied themselves with a heavy metal door, overgrown with brush and all but invisible. After a moment, the door rolled up, revealing a dimly-lit concrete passage beyond.

Arngrim shouted to us. "Follow, *Hirdir*! We must be quick!" Then he mounted up and led his riders into the passage.

"You sure about this?" I asked, looking over at Anna.

She seemed confident. "I'm okay if you are, Shepherd."

"Carry on, then."

The sound of two dozen engines echoed in the cement passageway as we entered. On the wall I saw in dark stenciled paint the words "Strategic Air Command Access C."

I suspected that our trip was almost over, though what lay at the end was anyone's guess.

The good news was that we were about to find out.

Unfortunately, that was probably the bad news as well.

* * *

We came to a stop in an echoing underground garage and at last the constant thunder of the Fallen's machines faded into silence. Harsh electric lights shone from overhead. There was a rush of soft sound as they dismounted—two dozen nearly identical riders, unpacking saddle bags, assisting wounded comrades from sidecars and seats, and reverently carrying away Gæirmund's corpse.

Anna and I stepped out of the car. The air was cool with the faint scent of oil and old concrete. Nearby Beowulf and Loren were likewise dismounting. Beowulf seemed impressed with the acoustics and barked several times before Loren shushed him.

My double vision kept phasing in and out as I watched. In the more familiar view, the Fallen were just what they seemed—blonde, muscular men parking massive, gleaming motorcycles. Then they blurred slightly and became what they truly were—red-skinned demons chaining up ferocious beasts crafted of flesh and metal. I shook my head and tried to focus on the less disturbing of the two visions.

"What is this place?" Anna asked, looking back and forth at the chamber and the dismounting riders.

"My guess is that it's an old Air Force missile base," I replied. "Right, Arngrim?"

The Fallen's leader was approaching. I fancied I could see the slightest hint of a limp in his gait, as if he was finally beginning to feel the pains of old age.

"You are correct, *Hirdir.*" He stood before us, nodding approvingly as his men stowed gear and began to move away, up a series of metal steps that led to gray-painted doors. "We've fought many wars, served with many nations. This base was closed down almost a quarter century ago, and when it was we made certain that it was removed from all records and documents. We have lived here ever since. As far as your leaders are concerned, this place does not exist and never has."

Loren looked impressed. "Cool. How's the food?"

"You'll find out soon enough. I'll have Gunnar prepare quarters for you, and we'll be dining in a few hours."

I grunted. "So you *do* need food."

"From time to time." Arngrim smiled. "Nowhere near as often as you, however."

"Keep flaunting your superiority with me and I'll take my sword and go home."

"I doubt you'll be doing that, Shepherd. Once you're settled we can meet and discuss how to proceed." He waved. "Gunnar! Show the Shepherd and his companions to their quarters!"

Gunnar nodded and stepped up. "Get your gear and follow me, *Hirdir*."

Arngrim turned and followed his men from the garage.

"We will let you know when food is ready, and we can meet later tonight. I will speak with you then."

Then he was gone.

"Is he always like that?" Loren asked.

Gunnar frowned. "Like what?"

"Like he has the world's biggest corncob up his ass."

"Oh, that." To my surprise, Gunnar laughed. "Yes, he's been like that since the Hundred Years War. He never got over the Battle of Agincourt."

I helped gather up our various possessions, looking at Gunnar with renewed respect.

God damn. They actually had a sense of humor.

* * *

A little more investigation revealed that we were indeed in a decommissioned missile base with a layout that resembled three large cylinders sunk into the ground. The first two were hollow shafts with a series of ring-shaped floors spaced along their length—these had once housed a pair of Titan II missiles, but they were long gone and the floors converted to other uses. The rest of the Fallen lived in the third cylinder, which contained quarters, mess, storage, armories, a machine shop and a variety of other facilities.

Loren, Anna, Beowulf and I were housed in one of the old silos, with lockers and folding military cots on harsh treadplate flooring, lit by mesh-covered sodium bulbs. As we stowed our belongings, Gunnar bid us good day and stepped back into the elevator that had delivered us.

Loren dropped a duffel bag and laptop case onto his cot, then stepped over to the flimsy-looking railing that surrounded the vast shaft in the center of the room.

"Jesus." He reached into his pocket and pulled out a penny, then flipped it into the darkness. It took several seconds to ping off the bottom of the shaft. "What have we gotten ourselves into, Alex?"

I reclined on my cot. It was covered with a scratchy gray blanket with old USAF stencils. "All I can say is that it's better than what Dandridge had in mind. Right now we've at least got a little breathing space, and we know we're on the same side as the Fallen."

"Is that a good thing, Alex?" Anna sat on the edge of her cot. She'd taken off her shoes and was wiggling her toes. They were painted red, of course. "They were the only ones I could think to call when we lost you, but are they going to turn out to be as bad as the Foundation?"

I shook my head. "Right now my instincts are telling me no. But I'll tell you for sure after we chat with Mr. Arngrim."

Beowulf, looking as tired as the rest of us, jumped up onto Loren's cot and curled into a ball.

"I think he's got the right idea," I said. "Let's all get some rest before we eat."

Neither Loren nor Anna needed any persuasion. It was a testament to the extent of our exhaustion that we were all asleep in a few minutes, despite our fears and uncertainties and the strange place we now found ourselves.

I dreamed, but they were confused and ominous, full of indistinct images and distant sounds. When Gunnar showed up to summon us to supper, it was almost a relief.

"Stay here and guard the place, boy," Loren told Beowulf, who was sitting looking at us expectantly. "I'll bring you back a treat."

That seemed to satisfy Beowulf, who returned to his place on Loren's bed.

I was glad to leave the jumbled, disturbing nightmares behind, but I was still groggy and tired as we rode the elevator down.

Gunnar ushered us down a corridor and into the big cylinder at the center of the complex, to what had once been the base's mess hall. There, a dozen or so Fallen had already seated themselves at long tables and were attacking their meals.

Loren sat down beside a pile of foil-sealed MREs and glanced over at the adjoining table where four Fallen, all nearly identical, still clad in their leather outfits, tucked away at self-heating goulash and sandwiches. They didn't seem to care what they were eating, putting food down in prodigious amounts without pausing between servings.

"Hell," he said, shaking his head. "Keep your extremities clear of their mouths while they're eating, huh?"

Gunnar laughed again. I was starting to actually like the guy. "We don't eat often, but when we do, small animals need to tread very carefully."

I prodded at a gray-green pouch marked *Pasta and Garden Vegetables in Tomato Sauce*.

"Where do you get all this stuff, Gunnar?"

"We have resources," he replied cryptically. "We've supplies here to last years if necessary."

"Is everything this classy?" Anna asked. She'd selected *Southwestern Style Chicken with Black Beans and Rice* and was reading the instructions on the flameless ration heater. "I mean, you're really serving us *haute cuisine* here."

"Our dining requirements are minimal," Gunnar admitted. He was already pouring water from a canteen into the heater bag.

"Hey," Loren said, looking at his own selected meal. "It says here not to eat the heater. That's really excellent advice, you know?"

We let our meals steep for several minutes, then chowed down with plastic utensils. It was better than I'd expected, but then again I didn't remember actually eating anything since breakfast on the day I'd been kidnapped.

We were just finishing our feast when Arngrim approached. "Are you well?" he asked. "Has Gunnar seen to your needs?"

I nodded. "Quite well. It's nice to meet a Fallen who can actually laugh once in a while."

Arngrim considered this. "Gunnar has a good heart."

Gunnar nodded gravely in reply. "You flatter me."

Arngrim fixed me with a steady gaze. "Come, Shepherd. We've much to talk about."

I glanced back at Loren and Anna. "My friends are coming with me. I'm not leaving them out of this."

Loren raised a hand. "No, it's okay. You guys go. We'll hang with Gunnar and the boys."

I turned to Anna. "You okay staying here with Loren?"

"Yeah." It was an uncertain sound, but she seemed determined nevertheless. She looked at Gunnar. "You guys got a PS4 here or what?"

* * *

Arngrim's quarters were what I expected—spare, neat, well-organized, with a small table, chairs, a cot and, to my surprise, an old and tough-looking computer terminal. On the wall hung several swords and axes, as well as a British Enfield rifle, an old German Schmiesser machine gun and an American M-14. I wondered if this was the same weapon I'd seen Arngrim carry in my vision, when he'd massacred the African Mimma-Lemnu worshippers.

Near the weapons was an armor stand, bearing knee-length Viking mail and an elaborate goggle helm. I stepped closer, gazing at it in wonder. There was a dragon crouched at the crest, bright and shining, chased in gold.

"Is this what you wore when you first came to this world?" I asked. I had to work very hard to keep from touching it.

"It is." Arngrim stepped up beside me. "I have kept it ever since, clean and polished."

"Fourteen hundred years is a long time, isn't it?"

I'd meant the comment lightly, but the words themselves seemed to press down on Arngrim like a great burden.

"It is indeed, *Hirdir*. And each one is longer than the last."

He gestured toward two chairs. "Sit. I can have refreshments brought if you like."

"No thanks." I seated myself on the hard metal chair and decided that the Fallen weren't really into creature comforts. "As you said, we've got some very important things to talk about."

"Yes." Arngrim sat and rested an elbow on the arm of his chair. For a moment his demon-visage flashed, strangely dark and troubled. He seemed to know I'd seen him. "You see us as we truly are, don't you?"

"Yeah, I do. Are you really the *Kussariku?* Benevolent demons?"

"We have been called that, Shepherd. We have been called other things as well." He looked away, thoughtful. "You were a prisoner of the enemy for several days. What did he tell you about us?"

"He said that you and the other Fallen were guardians of your world, but that you betrayed your trust and let Mimma-Lemnu's armies into your world. Then when you realized what you'd done, you rebelled. He said that you were the ones who burned your world, not Mimma-Lemnu."

Arngrim listened without emotion. "As always the enemy tells just enough truth to make his lies believable." He sighed. "No. More than a little truth I fear. Yes, we were seduced by the enemy's promises, his sweet words and oaths of peace. No doubt you heard them spewing from that sewer that Dandridge calls a mouth. Justice and plenty for all. An end to war, to suffering, to want. All that is required is absolute obedience to their demon-god."

"Yeah, that's about right. Sunshine, happiness, cute little puppy dogs. Just worship Mimma-Lemnu and Bob's your uncle."

Mentioning the enemy by name didn't seem to trouble Arngrim as much as it had on the road to Canby. He seemed different in other ways too—slower, quieter, less confident.

"Yes, and as far as that goes Dandridge is correct. The enemy will bring a world of perfect law and order. No crime, no violence, no unpleasantness is tolerated, and there is only one penalty for violations. It's a world where every rule is defined, every action measured. A world without variation, without expression, without individualism. The very concept of freedom is blasphemous to the enemy and his followers."

"And that's what he did to your world?"

"That and more, Shepherd. Yes, it's true. When we saw how we had been deceived, we rose up. We made war on the enemy. When Dandridge said that we burned the world, it was a lie, but it held a grain of truth. It was the enemy who unleashed the forces that destroyed what had once been paradise—to punish us for our transgressions, to defeat us utterly. Had we not risen, our world would have been as it had been before—beautiful and flawless." He looked down at his arms and chest with the expression of a man surveying a trash heap. "And so would we. You have no idea what we gave up when we rebelled, Shepherd. None."

I remembered my vision of Arngrim praying on the mountain, and of the brief flash of a winged, angelic creature. "Oh I have some idea, Arngrim. Believe me."

"We fled here. The doorways between this world and the other are one-way. They allow only entry, and once here we cannot return. That is one reason that the enemy has taken so long to come here—he is reluctant to abandon his other conquests in order to take this world."

"And you spent almost a millennium and a half in this world, killing Mimma-Lemnu worshippers wherever you found them. In the meantime, you served as warriors and mercenaries, and were never terribly particular about what side you were on, despite your oath to Pastorius to live in peace."

There was a look in Arngrim's eyes that I hadn't seen before—I could only describe it as shame. "We were warriors born, Shepherd. Our mother created us to defend Her world, and we betrayed her. War is the only life we know, and here in your world there is war aplenty. We appear as we wish, in guises appropriate to our time and place. And no, Shepherd, we did not care who we fought for. War was war, and it didn't matter to us if our army wore blue or gray or black or green." He passed a hand over his eyes, and his voice grew unsteady. "Your words cut me like a sword, that night on the road. Yet since then I have thought and prayed and contemplated what you said, and I can only say that you were right. We Fallen, we *Fordæmdur*, we who were once proud guardians… We served in evil causes and did not care. We served the enemy and did not know it. We broke our oath to Pastorius."

I didn't reply immediately but let the silence stretch out between us. There was something about Arngrim's tone that spoke more than his words.

"You've suspected this for a long time, haven't you?" I asked. "You felt doubt about what you were doing but could never give voice to it. You knew what you were doing was wrong and violated the Shepherd's oath."

Arngrim nodded. He looked miserable.

"What happened to you, Arngrim? What did you see? Was it just one thing, or was it just the weight of the world and all the years?"

He acted as if he didn't hear me, but was instead lost in his own world of sadness and regret. "Is it possible, Shepherd, that everything we have done since coming to this world was a mistake? That we truly are lost and damned? Oathbreakers in this world as surely as we were in our own? If that is true, then not even death can redeem us."

Then I remembered words, spoken softly in a dream, words that I had heard only a few days ago.

"All living things deserve mercy," I said. "All deserve redemption. No sin is so great that it cannot be redeemed by sacrifice."

Arngrim's head snapped around and he stared at me. "Where did you hear that?"

"She said it to me, Arngrim. She Who Watches. The one you call Belet-Ili."

There was a flash of recollection and Arngrim looked upward toward the ceiling, as if something long forgotten had stirred in his mind. When he looked back at me, his gaze had softened. "Then She is not lost to us. She still speaks through you."

"And others, Arngrim. There's still hope. There's always hope. This world doesn't have to die, and neither do you."

At last something was alive in Arngrim's dark eyes. It was the look of a man who had finally realized that two plus two is four. Something I had said had triggered it, but I still didn't know what it was.

"Very well, Shepherd. If there is a way, we will find it." He glanced back at the shadowy corner where his old armor stood. "The Fallen will ride with you to damnation or redemption." He looked back at me. "And I do not care which, just as long as it all ends. I am weary. We are weary. I ask only for an end to pain."

I couldn't think of anything I could say in reply.

The conference room reminded me of *Dr. Strangelove*, with a circular table in the center surrounded by old wheeled chairs covered in worn, cracked leather, a great situation map on one wall, portraying the world of the 1980s, and a big video monitor, now dark and dead-looking.

We were all there—me, Loren and Anna looking uncertain beside me, Beowulf at our feet eating enthusiastically out of a steel mixing bowl. Arngrim sat across the table, along with Gunnar and two other fallen that I didn't recognize—one was clean-shaven, his blonde hair done up in a topknot; the other was bearded and forbidding, an ugly scar across one cheek. In the middle of the table sat the junk we'd looted from the Foundation—the two blood-stained volumes from Hayes, and the leather-bound book and lantern from the shanghai tunnel.

We'd filled Loren and Anna in on our recent discussions and now Arngrim was holding forth about Dandridge and the Foundation's intentions.

"We came to this world through those openings that you call rifts. The doorways we used are called *Anaharani Alaktasa* in the old language—*roads whose course does not turn back*. They allow entrance to this world, but not return. Those who come here cannot go back, so Dandridge seeks the *Kadingir*—the Gate of the Gods. It allows free travel between the worlds, but its

257

creation involves elaborate rituals that can only be performed under very specific conditions and astronomical conjunctions, and these have not existed for many centuries."

Loren made a disgusted sound. "Who the hell *is* this Dandridge asshole, anyway? He says he's five thousand years old. He tried to take Alex's body so he could fool us and get to Anna. Has he really been swapping bodies for that long?"

Arngrim nodded, glaring angrily. "Yes. Dandridge. That's what he calls himself now. It's the name of the unfortunate whose body he stole years ago. Some wealthy wastrel or other. The one you call Dandridge is a monster, truly. He is indeed as old as he claims. He was a priest of the enemy, leader of the *ùĝ saĝ gíg-ga*, the Black-Haired Ones. They were driven from their places of power by the followers of the new gods—Enlil, Marduk, Hebat. Some of those gods dwelled in our world as well." He looked down at the table and his voice dropped a half tone or so. "Mother Belet, who made the *Kussariku* to guard Her world."

Anna spoke up. "He hasn't always been called Dandridge. What was he called back then?"

"It was well before we came to this world, child, but we know much of him. He was called *Azat Parzillu*, the Iron Serpent."

"Oh, Jesus." Loren leaned back, his hand on his forehead. "That sounds like the villain in a kung fu flick."

"I suspect that's why he changed his name," I said quietly. "No one would want to give to the Iron Serpent Charitable Foundation."

"So he wants this two-way gate but doesn't know how to get it." Loren looked at each of the Fallen in turn. "How do *we* fit into all of this? Alex? Anna?"

"He wanted to be the Shepherd," I said. "Or at least wield the sword. He was going to trade places with me, let me be the billionaire while he was busy serving Mimma-Lemnu. And he was planning on masquerading as me to get to you and Anna."

Anna suppressed a shudder. "God. What the hell was so special about me? What the hell makes *me* worth all that trouble?"

"All this time we've been thinking that it's just because Dandridge wanted to know how you resisted him," I replied. "But there's more, I know it. You can see the Fallen as they really are, and you can communicate with them. When I was knocked out at Dandridge's place, I saw you in the..." I stopped, trying to think of the right word. "The dark place between realities. I guess we should just call it the Between. You were shining pale blue and you had wings like Tsagaglalal. And I saw your tattoo flashing orange and blue. Mimma-Lemnu and Belet-Ili. You have some connection to both of them and I'll bet it explains why you can see the Fallen and how you can shrug off Dandridge's attempts to control you."

"I am called Wulfgar." The scarred Fallen spoke up. His voice was rough and gravelly. I idly wondered what his *real* name was and if I could even pronounce it. "Arms master and archivist. We are searching for answers—how you resist the enemy's influence and what your connection to the Fallen may be. If we find those answers, we may have new and powerful weapons against the enemy."

I nodded at the items piled up on the table. "Maybe there's an answer in those books somewhere. What are they?"

The clean-shaven Fallen spoke. His voice was smoother, almost melodic. "My name is Tjorkill. I am a historian and scribe. The two smaller volumes look like books of spells and rituals. The larger book is a holy volume that tells how to worship the enemy and provides history. Their letters are very old and hard to read, but I can help you translate them."

I nodded. "Good. Loren, how many laptops did you bring?"

"Three. One for each of us."

"Okay. Tjorkill, I saw a computer terminal in Arngrim's quarters. You still have electrical power here. How about data lines?"

Tjorkill nodded. "We do. This fortress is much as it was when it was abandoned, save for the removal of the great weapons. We rarely use the communications lines, but they are intact and functional."

"I'll see if we can tap in with the laptops," Loren said. "Your servers are still on at the house. Maybe we can VPN to them. That way we can check your surveillance and security systems to see if anyone's tried to break in."

Arngrim seemed a little taken aback at how quickly we had snapped into action. "And what will you be doing, Shepherd?"

I thought about it for a moment. "I'm going to be doing more research, seeing if I can get any more information on the Pilgrim Foundation and Roger Dandridge and what he wants with Anna. I'll look into his history, too. Maybe we can find some vulnerability back in his many incarnations."

"Very well. Gunnar will provide you both with any assistance you need."

Gunnar nodded and grinned. The contrast with the solemn-faced Arngrim and Tjorkill couldn't have been greater. "I will do what I can, Arngrim."

Anna looked nonplussed. "Hey, I don't want to interrupt this meeting of the He-Man Women-Haters Club, but what can Little Miss Fifth Wheel here do? Besides make coffee and take Beowulf for walks, of course? Need any veterinary assistance with your motorcycles? Alex says they're demons, too."

Arngrim inclined his head toward her and his voice took on an almost friendly timbre. "You may hold the key to defeating the enemy, young one. In fact, you may be the most important individual at this table, and the one most in need of protection. I propose that Wulfgar train you in self-defense and basic soldiery."

"Really?" She thought about it for a moment, then looked happily excited. "Cool. I get to really do all that Modern Warfare shit. Can Beowulf help?"

Beowulf's ears pricked up at the sound of his name.

I sighed inwardly as our meeting broke up and we moved toward our respective work spaces. Maybe she was a better fit for Loren than me. We'd have to sort it out later.

For the moment, we all had work to do.

* * *

Days blurred together in the sunless underground. The food was monotonous, the work was maddening, and the coffee was terrible. The lights burned constantly, for the Fallen seemed to have no need of sleep. Fortunately, we could retire to our quarters where we had control over the lighting cycle.

The base was full of unused space, all kept scrupulously clean, as if SAC personnel had just stepped out for a few moments. I had a small room that might have been an officer's quarters with a desk, chairs, and piles of the now-ubiquitous MREs. Our cellphones were useless under so much granite, so we communicated using the base's old closed-circuit intercom system.

Loren wired my room with Ethernet. The original network had been crude at best, but it was still live and with a little effort we got it working.

"It looks as if it's tapped directly in to the DoD network," Loren said as he connected my laptop to a switch. "Just pray to God they don't notice you in here."

I didn't plan on transferring funds or engaging in denial of service attacks, so it was likely I'd go unnoticed.

And so we worked, tapping away, making notes, scanning images, and discussing our findings until sleep overtook us and we crashed in our converted silo. Loren and I were connected to our servers in Portland through VPN, and periodic checks of the security system didn't reveal any attempted break ins. That at least was a relief.

I sent emails to Consuela through a spoofed IP address telling her that I was dealing with a personal emergency, and to go ahead and get the paper out as best she could. From what I was able to determine, she rose to the task quite admirably. That at least I didn't have to worry about.

It was a good thing, since I had plenty of other things to concern me. Something in my mind wanted to brood over where we were, and what this crisis had interrupted. I still hadn't worked out my feelings for Anna, her surprisingly equitable treatment of me and Loren, or how I really felt about it, but now wasn't the time. Once more, we were in crisis mode, assured by the Fallen that Dandridge and the Foundation would be making their move soon, though we had no idea what it would be.

Complicating matters was the fact that my suspicions about Anna had proved correct—she had access to abilities that no one, save perhaps Dandridge and the foundation, had suspected. She had entered into the dark space we now called the Between and called upon the Fallen. My encounter with her had helped me to break free of Dandridge's domination.

I'd also been able to summon the sword to my hand from over a hundred miles away. Had that been me, or had Anna helped? Either way it was a trick that I'd have to work on duplicating. Too bad I had no idea how I'd done it.

I forced myself to push such thoughts aside and bent myself to the task at hand.

I hadn't been entirely truthful with Arngrim. My research was indeed directed at Dandridge and his mysterious past, but it was also directed at Arngrim himself. Something made me want to know more about the Fallen's fearless leader—who he had been and what his history was, because once more my instincts were telling me that I'd missed something. This time, however, I was listening, and knew I had to find something.

Searching for the pictures was like finding a needle in a stack of other needles. Searches for images of 1960s white mercenaries in Africa, old west desperadoes, members of Quantrill's Raiders, and the 1943 SS all came up blank—either Arngrim's pictures weren't available on-line or I was just missing them due to the sheer volume of images.

I had to look at the clock and calendar to figure out how much time we'd spent down here among the Fallen, pursuing clues and desperately trying to learn more about an enemy that none of us really understood.

It was at 4:30 a.m., six days after our arrival, that I finally got a hit on my searches. There, in the saved image folder, was a picture that I recognized. It was a medieval portrait of a knight, clad in plate armor and bearing a shield with a golden dragon, rampant on a crimson field. Even over a half-dozen centuries, I recognized Arngrim.

"Holy shit." I looked at the page that displayed the picture. It was from a museum in Nice, France.

Portrait du chevalier anglaise (Walter Fitzhugh?) ca. 1460

A name at last. The hours of work were finally weighing down on me and despite my success, my eyelids were heavy and my limbs moved only sluggishly.

Bed first, I thought. Then we'll learn more about Sir Walter Fitzhugh.

* * *

The next morning Loren, Tjorkill, Anna and I sat down in the mess to bring each other up to date. I was eating from a pack labeled "Menu 10" which included a toaster pastry, hash browns with bacon, instant coffee and a tiny piece of dry wheat toast.

"Once this is all over and we're out of this damned underground detention facility," I said, looking disdainfully at a foil pouch with a tiny straw labeled "Lemon-Lime Beverage," "I am never going to eat another MRE as long as I live."

"You get used to them," Tjorkill said. "Eventually, you get to like them. Especially when they're all you have."

I made a disgusted sound. "Okay, guys. What's up? Anna?"

"I'm learning that everything you do on a car you do backwards on a motorcycle. Wulfgar gave me a wooden knife and has been busy not letting me hit him with it," she said, sipping at a paper cup filled with steaming hot tea. "Other than that, not much to report."

"Loren? Tjorkill?"

Loren set the big leather-bound book on the table with a metallic thud. "We've got our translation script working. We've come up with a pattern recognition program that is about eighty percent accurate at reading those hen scratches in those

Foundation books. We've managed to translate a few pages of the spell books and some of the big volume."

Tjorkill nodded. "Two books of spells and one of chronicles, rituals, invocations, and the like. Nothing we have found so far is useful, as much of it requires human sacrifice."

"The language is some kind of Akkadian dialect," Loren said. "I'm thinking that these Black-Haired Ones who first worshipped Mimma-Lemnu were transplants from the other world, brought here through a one-way gate. They brought their language with them, conquered a few cities and, presto, a new language. It combined with other local languages and drifted a bit over the centuries, so it has some pretty significant differences, but it's recognizable."

"It's the tongue of the old world," Tjorkill confirmed. "The alphabet is a secret script used only by priests, which explains why you were unable to find any examples of it in your records."

"That's all well and good," I said. The coffee was only lukewarm, but I needed the caffeine. "But have you found anything to suggest what the Foundation and Dandridge were going to do with it?"

Loren looked uncomfortable. "It's not good."

"I didn't expect good," I replied. "I just didn't want it to be overwhelmingly bad."

"I may have to disappoint you, dude." Loren flipped open the book. Its pages were leafed together with written notes and printouts. "There are references to the gates, and to the road that only goes one way that Arngrim was talking about. That Gate of the Gods—the *Kadingir*—is in here, but it could only be opened when the stars and planets are in a certain alignment, and that hasn't happened in over five thousand years."

"Loren, it sounds as if there's a *but* in there somewhere."

"Yeah," Loren said, his expression uncharacteristically serious. "It hasn't happened in over five thousand years, but it's going to happen again about..." He scanned the book, running his finger down the page. "Yeah. About now, give or take a few hours."

"Oh, shit."

"Yeah, that's what I said."

"And exactly how does this all happen? I'm guessing massive human sacrifice."

"Oh yeah," Loren said. "I don't think Mimma-Lemnu did anything that *didn't* involve human sacrifice. We did find one piece of good news."

"We sure as hell need some of that," I said. "What is it?"

Loren flipped to another bookmarked page. It was covered in the old symbols and surrounding an elaborate pattern that I couldn't quite make sense of. It looked a bit like a stylized tree, but I couldn't be sure. "Here. It says that while priests of evil can open the gate, the priests who serve the Lords of Sunlight—Marduk, Nabu, Belet-Ili—can close the *Kadingir* by calling on the..." He pronounced the next words very slowly and carefully. "The *Ngisma Tasinashkalim.*"

"What the hell does *that* mean?" Anna wrinkled her nose. "Alex and I don't speak Akkadian."

"The *Ngisma Tasinashkalim,*" Tjorkill said. "Its meaning is esoteric. But it translates roughly as: The Tree With Roots in Two Worlds."

I groaned. "A tree? And we have no idea what that means, do we?"

"We're working on it," Loren said. "I think it's allegorical. But at least it says that it's *possible* to close the *Kadingir* once it's opened. And if we could close it, they wouldn't be able to open it again for another fifty centuries. But I'm afraid that the closing rituals may need a sacrifice too, even with this tree thingamajig."

"So if we had this tree we might be able to do something, but we don't know what it is or how to get it?"

"Something like that."

"Mister Hodges, you have a very strange notion of what constitutes good news," I said.

Loren sighed. "I do my best."

* * *

We were in a somber mood as we returned to our respective projects, and I faced the prospect of another day of frustration.

When I got back to my work space however, I found that my engines in Portland had kept on slogging away, and had provided more information about the English knight Sir Walter Fitzhugh in the form of several historical articles and excerpts from scholarly books from England. I read it with interest.

A half hour later, I closed the last window and leaned back in my chair. I didn't say anything but whistled softly to myself.

Gunnar had dropped off copies of Loren's translations and the original book pages. I spent the next hour reading them and making my own notes in their margins.

Something was beginning to take shape in my mind. Something that might actually be an answer. Now I needed more information.

I dialed Gunnar on the closed-circuit phone.

"I need to talk to Arngrim," I told him. "Is he in his quarters?"

"No." Gunnar's voice was crackly and indistinct, but clearer than I'd expected through such an antiquated system. "He is meditating at the shrine. I can guide you there."

"I need to talk to him alone, Gunnar. I know my way around this place pretty well. Just tell me how to get there."

"Very well."

I listened, scrawling down directions, then thanked Gunnar and stood up.

I grabbed a few of my own printouts and stepped out of my office, my footsteps echoing in the lonely metal corridor.

* * *

The elevator bore me up and up on a ride that lasted several minutes. A shock of cool air hit me at the top when the doors opened and I stepped out onto a narrow concrete slab.

A low cement railing surrounded the slab and a narrow flight of steps led upward farther still. Below my perch was a sickening drop into talus and rugged ravines, but looking up I could gaze across the craggy expanse of the Southern Rockies, and in the distance rose the slopes of Gray's peak, almost snowless in the heat of summer.

Words were stenciled on the rock wall beside the elevator doors—the words "Weather Station" barely legible above a faded arrow pointing upward.

The steps were cut directly into the granite. It took several more minutes to climb and I had to stop and catch my breath twice, looking backwards at the vistas surrounding me. To the west the mountains faded into brown hills and beyond them into wrinkled tan desert, baked in the sun. As I got back to my feet, I reflected that I had never before felt quite so lonely and distant from my home.

Maybe this was what the Fallen had felt for almost a millennium and a half.

The stairs ended in a flat spot surrounded on three sides by rocks and open to the mountains on the fourth. This was apparently the location of the old weather station, but none of the equipment remained. It was high enough that there was still some snow here, and I abruptly remembered the place from my vision of Arngrim.

Sure enough he was there, kneeling, head down, before the graceful statue of She Who Watches, the alien entity that had given me my sword and title, and who had also, it now seemed, given birth to the Fallen, in whatever guise they wore in that other world.

"Arngrim?" My voice sounded small in this place.

"*Hirdir.*" He spoke quietly but did not move from his position of supplication. "You wish to speak to me, here under the eyes of Belet?"

"I do, Arngrim."

He rose slowly and painfully. Here, in the presence of his goddess, the centuries truly seemed to weigh down upon Arngrim. He was still the blonde, handsome biker I'd first seen on the slopes of Hauser Butte, but now he seemed older, weaker, and infinitely sadder. Here his demon-self didn't appear to me. Here he seemed entirely human.

267

"I have been praying to Her, Shepherd." He was introspective, a far cry from his old assertiveness. "Seeking guidance, but none has come."

I stepped closer. "Arngrim, I have some questions to ask you. They won't be easy for you to answer, but they're important."

Arngrim nodded slowly. "I will answer as best I can." He gestured at several stones that had been laid out like benches. "Sit. Ask your questions."

I nodded and we seated ourselves.

I shuffled through my papers and pulled out a printed image. It showed the medieval knight and his coat of arms, gold dragon on crimson field.

"Arngrim," I asked. "Is this you?"

III

As he looked at the picture, Argrim's eyes flashed with the old fire, and for an instant I felt a trace of fear. Then, to my surprise, his face fell and he looked down, still speaking in a humble, downcast tone.

"Yes, Shepherd. It's me. When I was called Sir Walter Fitzhugh."

"That's what I figured. I was searching for evidence of your previous identities and I got lucky. Then I looked you up based on the coat of arms and discovered that Sir Walter Fitzhugh was an English knight who fought beside King Henry at Agincourt in 1415."

"I did that. There were times when we Fallen walked alone, going our separate ways. I served in King Hal's army and fought the French." He looked up. "If you know that much, you've probably learned the rest of the story."

"I learned that Sir Walter was awarded an estate for his service to the king and went there to live out his life in peace." I pulled out another printout, text from an English history book. "I also learned that Sir Walter was married and had two sons, Robert and Henry."

I let my words hang in the thin mountain air, the very silence between us adding to their import.

"You had children, Arngrim. You took a wife." I waited a long moment before I spoke again. "You tried to live like a normal man."

Arngrim surged to his feet and turned to face me. But when he spoke, his words were sad, not angry.

"It was the war, Shepherd. All the wars. We had been here for eight centuries and had never had a moment's peace. War, bloodshed, conflict… At first we thought nothing of it. We were warriors. Our duty was to guard our realm against all enemies. Warfare was nothing new to us—it was our life."

He turned and walked toward the edge of the grotto, leaning on the old concrete railing.

"Yet after a time, after enough blood, even the most hardened killer can be forgiven for asking why. At Agincourt, I saw Frenchmen, nobles all, drowning in the muck, hacked to pieces by vengeful Englishmen. It was no more or less terrible than anything else I had witnessed, but it was finally too much. It was… It was just…" He seemed at a loss for words.

"The straw that broke the camel's back?" I asked. "We humans are very good at coming up with clichés, aren't we?"

"Yes. For want of a better phrase, yes. It was the final straw. I decided that I had had enough of the life of a warrior. I had lived among you long enough that I felt kinship, even affection. Eight hundred years is a long time, Shepherd. I was tired. When the king offered me an estate and title, I accepted. And when he suggested it would be wise to take Lady Roswynn to wife, I agreed to that as well."

The significance of Arngrim's words wasn't lost on me. "Had a Fallen ever done that before?"

He shook his head. "No, and none have since. I cannot say that I truly understood what it was to be a man. Yet when I was with Roswynn I was happy. And when she gave birth to Henry… I felt things that I thought were impossible for my kind to feel. Then Robert was born, and for a time I was truly at peace."

"What happened?"

Arngrim laughed humorlessly. "Henry became a soldier. He had grown up on tales of my glory and wanted to win glory for himself. He died at the siege of Orleans. Robert's ship sank in the Mediterranean several years later and he was lost to us. Roswynn could not live with the sorrow and wasted away. Soon I was alone again, and the house of Fitzhugh ended. I left England and rejoined the Fallen. I swore that I would never try to live as a man again."

Arngrim's voice was tight with emotion. My feelings for him as an individual were ambivalent—he had done terrible things without a thought, had advanced causes of unspeakable evil. Even so, I felt my own emotions welling up as I considered the plight of such an ancient creature, all but immortal in an alien world, seeking peace and finally finding it, only to have it all taken away.

"And so we *Fordæmdur* fought for whoever would pay us the most. And there were so many places to fight in those days, Shepherd. With sword, with bow, with musket and rifle. So many places. The Thirty Years' War. The Great Turkish War. The English Civil War. Then we crossed the water and came here for a time. The French and Indian War. The War of Independence. Of 1812. We helped storm Chapultapec Castle. Then we rode with the Confederate Raiders, killing and despoiling. Not because we cared for the cause, or even for the men we fought beside. We fought because we fought, and it was the only thing we knew."

"I saw. You were with the SS at Kursk."

"I was, Shepherd. Do not think I am proud of what we did? But do not think I am ashamed either? So many years had passed and so much blood had been spilled that it didn't matter anymore who we fought for and who died."

"Even innocent blood, Arngrim? Even the people who died in the camps or were butchered by the Nazis?"

When Arngrim didn't reply I went on. "You served the most monstrous evil this world has ever witnessed and you say it doesn't matter. That's bullshit, Arngrim. Blood matters. Innocent blood matters. Every human life matters, even to some red-skinned alien demon like you. It sickened you once, and when life as a man didn't suit you, you ran away, back to the blood and the horror." I stared at him, but he wouldn't return my gaze. "For all the years you've lived, Arngrim, you don't understand who we are. Because you don't want to."

To his credit, he took it without protest. He'd probably heard it before. Maybe from himself.

"I cannot gainsay you, Shepherd. You speak the truth. But if I do not understand your folk, you certainly do not understand mine, yet you see fit to judge us."

I ignored him. "Did others leave? Did they get weary of it all and go to live apart?"

He nodded. "A few. I can't tell you how their stories ended, or whether they are even still living. But they grew sick of what we were doing and left. Some returned. Gunnar was one."

It didn't surprise me. Gunnar was the only Fallen that I could genuinely say I liked.

I sighed. It was interesting information, but it didn't get us any closer to a way to fight the Foundation. One more question remained.

"You're not fighting anymore," I said. "You fight the Foundation and their people, but you're not mercenaries or soldiers now."

"No, we are not." He didn't explain further.

I persisted. "Something else happened, didn't it? Something made you start to believe again."

Arngrim didn't reply but stood at the railing, staring stone-faced across the mountains.

"What happened, Arngrim?"

The silence went on. As much as I wanted to press Arngrim for an answer, I didn't.

At last he spoke, still gazing out into space.

"I saw her, Shepherd. I saw the goddess Belet-Ili."

"She Who Watches? You saw her?"

He turned and sat down on the railing, his back to the abyss.

"When I went to live with Roswynn, I thought I was weary. I thought I could change myself, become something different. In the end, I realized that I was a fool and could never be anything but what I was. Yes, we fought. Any war, any battle, anywhere we were needed. We also hunted down the enemy's agents and destroyed them before they could do mischief in this world. Yes, many were ignorant of the evil they served, many were innocent. But the innocent are the enemy's most powerful weapon, for they do not believe that they are doing evil. As the years passed, I became convinced that the enemy would not come, and that Belet-Ili had forsaken us. Perhaps She perished on our old world. Perhaps She could not come here anymore. All I knew was that no Shepherd came to guide us or aid us. We remembered the sword and the man who wielded it, and were ever-vigilant for his return, for we knew that it would herald the coming of our Day of Vengeance."

I took this in calmly. I had figured out some of it already. "Then you saw me at Hauser Butte, and you realized…"

"That the *Hirdir* had come again, and that soon the enemy would stir. But now… Now, I wonder what difference we can make. Your words still shame me, Shepherd, for I know you are right. For years now I have doubted our cause, wondered whether we were the evil ones, not the enemy."

"What was it, Arngrim? How did it happen?"

He paused for a long time, as if pulling old thoughts back and putting them in order. "It was almost two decades ago, Shepherd. We were fighting in the desert, in that place where this world has always fought, where war is as familiar as night and day. What conflict it was, what side we fought on… I truly cannot say."

"It didn't matter at all?"

"Not at all. No more than it mattered when I wore that black uniform with the death's head badge. That day we were advancing against an enemy artillery position. We were supported by fighter aircraft and armored vehicles. Enemy shells rained down on us, and when a commander sent incorrect coordinates, our own aircraft bombarded us. We Fallen survived, for as you've seen we are very resilient and strong, far stronger than the folk of this world. But there were others advancing with us, motorized troops and foot infantry—they were struck by incendiary bombs and perished, screaming, horribly slain by their own aircraft."

"My God."

"It was like seeing those men die in the mud at Agincourt. I thought I'd grown jaded, that I didn't care anymore, but that moment it all returned to me. I've seen many horrible things, Shepherd. I've seen cities put to the sword, I've seen men drowning in blood, I've seen entire peoples massacred. Yes, I know—even by those whose uniform I wore, Belet have mercy. You speak to me accusingly, yet what we Fallen did was no worse than anything done by the folk of this world. They seem to revel in death and warfare, as if it is their natural state. If a nation or a people or a faith was to be exterminated, so be it—your folk think nothing of it, so neither did I."

I tried to protest, but I couldn't. My self-righteous words to Arngrim rang hollow as I remembered a quote someone had attributed to Stalin—"One death is a tragedy. A million deaths is a statistic." He probably hadn't really said it, but its truth was cold and undeniable.

Arngrim and the Fallen were more like us than I wanted to admit.

He went on. "But that day, Shepherd, almost six hundred years after my horror on that day at Agincourt, once more it was the straw that broke my back. I remembered the world we'd left, the paradise that had been crushed and burned beyond recognition. And as I heard the screams of the dying, and for the first time I wondered... These people, they have so little time, their lives are so short, they're so frail... Why do they fight? Why do they kill? Why do they seem so intent on their own deaths? What had I been doing for over a thousand years, save add to the carnage of a world that was as beautiful as mine, and drag it a few steps closer to the enemy?"

I swallowed, trying to think of some reply. Arngrim, after so many centuries of thoughtless, inhuman violence, was finally thinking like a human. And he didn't like it.

"The flames were all around me, and the screams of the dying and wounded rang in my ears. Something inside me broke, Shepherd. Something told me that it had to end, that I could no longer be what I once was. Yet I had tried to change, and failed. I could see only one way out. I threw down my rifle, I tore my helmet off, left behind my body armor, and raced at the enemy, screaming, crying, demanding that they kill me. The other Fallen, who knows what they thought, seeing the one who had led them for so long go mad and cast aside all, crying out for the peace of oblivion."

"Oh God, Arngrim… But you're here with me. Still alive. What happened?"

Arngrim looked up at the statue. "I saw Her, Shepherd. The goddess. Floating above the battlefield, serene and silvery-blue as She had always appeared to us in the old world. She gazed down at me with absolute compassion and perfect love, Shepherd, and She spoke to me."

"What did She say?"

"The same words She said to you. That all living things deserved mercy. That no offense was so great that it could not be redeemed by sacrifice. And I saw something, Shepherd… I saw…"

He broke off, and strode toward the statue, where he once more fell upon his knees.

"I saw a light, inside Her, cradled in Her belly like a child, as if new life grew within Her. I saw Her hands, I saw Her face, I felt Her mercy and…"

"And what?"

"And nothing. I awoke in a field hospital. We'd overrun the enemy position and broken through. The war, such as it was, had ended shortly after it began. We were free to go."

I stood up and walked to where Arngrim knelt, head down. After a moment's hesitation I put a hand on his shoulder.

"You knew that She was still here, Arngrim. You knew that there was hope, yet you still couldn't bring yourself to believe it, could you?"

"No, Shepherd." His voice shook. "I couldn't. I knew what She had said, but I didn't know what it meant. And those men, those lost, dead men. Their screams have haunted me ever since. But other voices joined them—the voices of those we have killed, those whose lives we took in the cause of evil. Slain, burned, gassed, stabbed, massacred, all because of their appearance, or their faith, or the flag they were born under. I'd felt it once, long ago, and it had failed to change me. But in that moment, on that battlefield, the idiocy and pointlessness of it all suddenly came back to me." He looked up. To my astonishment his eyes were bright with tears. "Why do you do it, Shepherd? Why do you fight? Why don't you treasure the short time you have? For so many years I have watched you, and I still don't know why."

Emotion welled up inside me as well. "I'll be damned if I can tell you why, Arngrim. All I know is that we do. All I know is that we're frail and small and alone and sad, and we have only a few years to try and understand what it all means. All I know is that we're not perfect. But I also know we're good, Arngrim. And I know that this world is good. And I know that I've sworn to guard this world and these imperfect, short-lived people. I know that all, but I still can't tell you why. I wish I could."

Then Arngrim was on his feet and his hand was on my shoulder, his old eyes staring into mine.

"You are *Hirdir*," he said. "You hold the weapon of our sacred mother, and you stand guard as we once stood guard. We failed, Shepherd. We betrayed our faith, we broke our oath, we lost what we once had." His expression grew strong again. "The *Fordæmdur* will not fail you. If sacrifice can redeem us, then let it be done."

I nodded. "Thank you, Arngrim."

IV

The situation room was tense. Loren had done a great job fixing it up; the big video monitor was alive again, glowing brightly with snow.

Anna sat between me and Loren, who was busy fiddling with a laptop, getting his link to the big screen working. The Fallen sat apart—a smiling Gunnar who seemed more like a southern Cal surfer dude than a demon-biker from another dimension, the grim-faced Tjorkill and Wulfgar, and finally Arngrim, reserved and contemplative in the days since our conversation on the mountain.

Loren fiddled with the touchpad and tapped a few keys. "Like I said, when we first got here, this facility is still connected into the NORAD and DoD networks. There's been no activity for years, so no one noticed." The big screen flickered, then displayed a black and white satellite image of Eurasia, with Russia's borders delineated in white. "For the past few weeks, I've been sitting here listening passively, and over the last couple of days there's been a huge increase in chatter about something big going on in Russia, near Lake Khantaskoye. I found a NORAD satellite feed and tapped in."

I threw up my hands. "Christ, Loren. You were warning me about attracting too much attention and you're tapping a goddamned top secret satellite feed?"

"It seemed important. Check this out."

The picture zoomed in on north central Russia and a lake with a large city on its western shore. Tags and topographic data appeared on the screen—the city was called Snezhogorsk. The terrain was a combination of forest and tundra.

"The Russians have been frantically transferring military units from the Ukrainian sector and into Snezhogorsk for the past three days. Motorized infantry, armor, even a couple of air wings. And if they're willing to let the Ukrainian situation go hang, it's got to be something important."

I frowned. "What the hell?"

Loren pressed a key and a black dot appeared west of the city. "A couple of thousand troops and several dozen tanks moved into this area yesterday. There were signs of fighting and today about five hundred infantry and no tanks came back."

"Shit."

The Fallen exchanged worried glances. They'd been soldiers for centuries and their instincts were telling them that something was wrong.

"Is it the enemy?" demanded Wulfgar. "Do you have any more information?"

Loren nodded, suddenly looking as worried as the Fallen. "Yeah, I just got a video feed. That's why I figured I'd call you. Watch."

The map was replaced by a fuzzy video image that bounced up and down as if it had been shot from a moving vehicle. It showed a forested landscape with the indistinct images of rifle-armed infantry moving through it. As I watched, a couple of big blocky T-90 tanks slid into view, their outlines blurry. Ahead was a thick stand of trees, and in the middle was a grainy black object that pulsated and shifted.

Abruptly the shape reared up, and the earth around it buckled, trees falling like toothpicks, and a series of towering figures emerged. Blurred, grainy, ill-defined, they were still clearly huge with wings and fanged, elongated heads. At first there were three, then four, then six...

"The Seven have come." Wulfgar's voice was grim.

"The *Sebitti*," Gunnar said. "The battle-lords, drinkers of blood."

I felt a chill run up my spine as I watched the video. It continued to shake and waver, sometimes swinging wildly so that I could only barely tell what was happening. Some soldiers fell back. Others fired weapons, but the great figures swept down, crushing them or flinging them into the air. A pair of tanks opened fire, but the Seven pounced, smashing the vehicles like toys. A figure towered before the camera—yes, it was horrific, even in this poor image—covered in scales and bony plates, winged, with a sinuous snake-like neck and the head of a huge leopard. It opened its mouth and fell upon the camera...

Snow filled the screen again.

Loren switched off the video. "That's all I got. It looks like the Russians got their asses handed to them."

"They've made their move," Tjorkill said. "The Seven have come to prepare the way for the great enemy."

"Shit." It was all I could say. "Do you think they've opened the Gate of the Gods?"

Arngrim's voice rumbled for the first time. "I do not, Shepherd. We are still bound to the old world. These are *Anaharani Alaktasa*, the roads that do not turn back. We would have felt it had Dandridge opened the *Kadingir*."

"What are they doing, then?"

"They are preparing the way. Seizing beachheads before the enemy opens the *Kadingir*."

"He has waited five millennia for this moment, *Hirdir*," said Wulfgar. "He desires this world. It is a nexus, with doorways to many others."

"Doorways that are coming open." I felt the old stab of helplessness, remembering my conversations with Damien about leaky screen doors and alien monsters lurking in the darkness between worlds, biding their time. I'd fought one of them—Onatochee. And from what I was learning now, creatures like Onatochee weren't even a blip on Mimma-Lemnu's radar screen.

"Is there anything we can do?" Loren looked toward the Fallen, but their faces showed no encouragement. "Any way to close that Russian gate? Keep any more of them from coming through?"

"Even if we could, the Seven have entered this world." Wulfgar clenched his fist. "Other doorways are sure to open, admitting even more terrible creatures. You saw what only one *lilitu* could do. You slew Idimma-Xul but only with great effort. There are others, as powerful as she was, and they will come soon."

"We will fight." Arngrim's voice was flat, emotionless, as if he was finally admitting to a long-denied truth. "We will fight and die as we swore we would. Oathbreakers we have been, but we will keep this last one." He stood. "Prepare for battle."

I felt a rush of alarm. "Arngrim, wait." I frantically looked back at Loren and Anna. They both looked scared. "There's still time. If we put all our resources into those Foundation books, get full translations, maybe we can find something we can use against the enemy. Some way to send the Seven back, some way to close the gates before anything comes through, some way to defeat them when they come here. I know there's not much of a chance, but you can't throw your lives away in a fight you can't win. Not yet."

Gunnar spoke. "If those broken oaths mean anything to us, we must help the Shepherd, Arngrim. For so many years we have fought for nothing. I left because I could no longer face the endless bloodshed, but like you I came back because there was nothing for me among men. We swore once to live in peace. Now at least we can use what little honor remains to us in service to something true. We must aid the Shepherd, Arngrim."

Fire still burned in Arngrim's eyes, but I also saw a hint of the emotion he'd shown me at the shrine. He drew a deep breath.

"Very well, Shepherd. We will wait. Continue to watch for signs of the enemy's coming, for there will be more, and soon. We have very little time before his forces have grown to overwhelming strength."

I felt a rush of gratitude, mixed with fear. We'd been battering our heads against a concrete wall for weeks now and had almost nothing to show for it. Now the clock was ticking—how much time did we have? Days? Hours?

I looked around the room, feeling an edge of desperation. "We've got to find something. We'll just have to brew a little coffee and..."

My gaze settled on Anna, sitting fearfully between me and Loren. She'd been silent for the entire meeting. Her eyes were surrounded by dark circles. I could tell she was trying to keep up a bold front but was on the edge of absolute collapse.

Something tickled at the back of my mind. Again, I'd missed something. Again, I felt as if I had all the right pieces but couldn't figure out how they fit together.

Ngisma Tasinashkalim. The tree with roots in two worlds.

I stood up. "Everyone, do what you can. Loren, keep translating and keep an eye on those DoD channels. Gunnar, Wulfgar, all of you... Please, please give him all the help you can. Anna, just try to stay sane and don't worry."

She gave me a tired grin. "I've been doing that since we got here."

There was a soft rush of movement as we all stood up and began to move toward the door.

"So what are you doing?" Loren asked.

I spoke in an even voice, suppressing the foreboding I felt. "I'll tell you later. I've got a hunch to follow."

* * *

Beowulf seemed to sense my unease and stepped gingerly into my quarters where I sat in semi-darkness, staring into my laptop's glowing screen.

"Hi boy," I said softly. "Come on, get some pets."

He padded over and sat beside me, dutifully accepting my attention.

281

"Just when the night seems blackest, there's nothing that raises the spirits like patting a dog on the head, you know that, boy?"

He looked up with wide eyes as if he truly understood me.

A bell sounded on the laptop, quiet but also somehow alarming.

I didn't want to open the search window, but I did.

For another two hours I read. Beowulf snoozed uneasily and I drank bitter coffee. When I finished, the clock said it was 3:35 a.m.

With numb fingers, I selected "print" and waited while the little ink jet that Loren had brought from the house slowly cranked out page after page.

As the last page settled into the paper tray, I picked up the intercom and rang Loren.

"Yeah, what is it?" His voice crackled through the closed circuit, tired and cranky, but awake.

"We need to meet again, Loren. You, me, Anna, and Arngrim."

Something in the tone of my voice alarmed him. "Shit, Alex. What did you find out?"

"More than we wanted to know." I picked up the stack of papers. "Meet me at Arngrim's quarters and all will be revealed."

"Right, boss."

He didn't sound as if he wanted to go.

To be perfectly frank, I wasn't sure I did either.

* * *

It had only been a few hours since our last meeting, but everyone looked even more haggard as we sat in Arngrim's quarters.

Loren spoke up first. "Things are going to hell very quickly, Alex. A huge forest fire came out of nowhere in Brazil, and the locals are telling stories about seeing flaming horsemen and winged monsters. A big thunderstorm in Australia, also out of nowhere, centered on Ayer's Rock—high wind, hail, lightning. Several towns washed out, power and communications are out, and a report about giant snakes flying through the sky, riding the lightning."

"Time grows short, Shepherd." Arngrim crossed his arms across his chest. "What have you learned?"

I spoke carefully. "I'll need to spill some of your secrets, Arngrim. I don't have time to be discreet."

He waved a hand. "Speak on, Shepherd. I will not take offense."

I launched into my spiel immediately, giving Loren and Anna the Reader's Digest version of Arngrim's history and his years as Sir Walter Fitzhugh. Then I told them about Henry and Robert.

"Wait. What?" Loren shot a suddenly puzzled look at Arngrim who sat, arms still crossed, looking uncomfortable. "You guys can have kids with humans?"

Arngrim gave Loren a hard glance. "Yes, we can. And I did." His expression shifted to the look of pain and regret that I'd seen at the shrine. "They, and their mother, brought me peace and surcease for a time. But it was far too short."

"So you were human enough to love a woman and have two children with her?" Anna's voice was quiet and compassionate.

Arngrim nodded. "Until they died and I was left alone again. Then I returned to my kind and tried to forget. And I had almost forgotten. I do not know whether to thank you or curse you for reminding me of the past, Shepherd. The past is dead and can never be brought back."

"The past isn't dead, Arngrim." I handed him a copy of an illuminated manuscript page. "It lives in all of us. This document reports that Robert Fitzhugh's ship sank in the Mediterranean in 1436, but he survived and was captured by the Ottomans. Your son didn't die, Arngrim. He lived."

Arngrim's entire demeanor changed as he stared at the page in frank disbelief. It was an expression I'd never seen one of the Fallen make before.

"My son lived? Robert? What happened to him?"

"It took a lot of digging, but I found what I was looking for. A man matching Robert Fitzhugh's description was said to have escaped from the Turks and served as a mercenary throughout Europe and the near east. He was called Robert Anglaise, or Robert the Englishman. He defended the walls of Constantinople in 1453 and fought against the Almohads in Spain in the 1480s. He was quite the swashbuckler, and he apparently left a number of illegitimate children all across the Mediterranean."

Arngrim didn't reply, still gazing, stunned, at the paper.

"I lost track of Robert after the wars in Spain, but I also found a number of people who claimed descent from him. One of them, a man named Aldo Bertini, ended up founding a successful trading house in Venice in the 1500s. His descendants migrated to England and changed their name to Bridges a century later. One William Bridges is listed as a passenger on the *Anne,* a ship that sailed for America in 1623. Then I lost the thread again, but finally found a Thomas Bridges who fought in the Revolutionary War whom I'm pretty sure was one of William's descendants."

Loren gazed at Arngrim in wonder. "Holy shit. Your family did all that?"

I nodded. "And more. The trail got easier to follow after Thomas. His great grandson Andrew was a member of the 20th Maine Volunteer Regiment, and fought at Fredricksburg and Antietam. On July 2nd, 1863 he and the 20th Maine held the end of the Union line at Gettysburg. They pushed back assault after assault and when they ran out of ammunition they fixed bayonets and charged down Little Round Top, turned the Confederate flank, and probably saved the Union Army. Andrew Bridges was wounded and lost an arm in the action but returned home a hero. Arngrim, while you were with Quantrell burning down Lawrence, Kansas, your descendant was busy helping save the Union and set other human beings free."

Arngrim didn't respond to my gibe, but stared at me with only the barest comprehension of what I had said.

"Your legacy on this world, Arngrim. Your descendants. Your family. So much that would never have happened without you."

I felt a swell of emotion, and was afraid that if I continued my voice would break. I drew another deep breath, composed myself, and continued.

"Andrew Bridges had a son, John, who died in 1933. John's son Francis grew up during the Great Depression, then fought in the Pacific during World War II. He worked for General Motors in Michigan after the war and *his* son Jason was born in 1960. I followed Jason's trail for quite a while—he wasn't very successful, moving from city to city, job to job. He enjoyed working on cars and reading. His favorite author was Edgar Allen Poe. He had a problem with alcohol. He was killed in 1997 when he fell off an el train platform in Chicago. The news report said he'd been drinking. Two years earlier he had abandoned his second wife in Portland. She moved to Arizona, took back her maiden name—Moore—and raised their daughter alone."

I paused for a long time, my gaze settling on Anna who stared back, realization dawning in her gentle eyes.

"And that daughter, Annabelle Lee, was *you.*"

For a long moment, the proverbial pin dropping in that room would have sounded like a rifle shot. Arngrim seemed to sway in his chair, as if I'd struck him in the face with a sledge hammer. Loren didn't seem to know who to look at but kept shifting from Arngrim to Anna to me and back again.

Arngrim stood like a man awakening from a bad dream.

"You?" He stepped toward Anna, reaching out a hand. "You? My kin?"

"Your great, great, great, great, great by several orders of magnitude granddaughter, Arngrim." I put an arm around Anna's shoulder. She was frozen and unmoving.

"Are you sure?" she whispered. "Are you really sure?"

"Not a hundred percent but close to. It's been centuries and I've only had a few days to research. But it sure as hell looks like it, and it explains how you could see the Fallen in their true form that day in Arizona."

"And how she could call on me," Arngrim's voice was quiet with wonderment. He looked at me and his eyes were bright. Another first. "If what you say is true…"

"It's true," Anna said. "I feel it. I've always felt it. I look at you and I know now. It's got to be true."

Arngrim knelt beside her chair. He took her hand and it disappeared in his calloused paw.

"When I saw Belet-Ili on the field of battle, She called on me not to despair. I didn't understand then, but I do now. I now know that it was your life I saw quickening inside her. You are blessed. You are a miracle. You give hope where there was none. Yet I…" His voice broke. "Yet I called you whore. I wished you dead. My flesh and blood, living remnant of what I loved the most. I called you…"

His head fell forward and his shoulders heaved with sobs.

"Forgive me. Please. Forgive the mindless rage of a lonely, foolish creature who thought all love had fled from the world."

Now Anna was crying too. "Arngrim… Arngrim, I…"

He looked up at her, eyes brimming. "Anna. Your father—my descendant—failed you, abandoned you, left you alone. Please let me make amends. Please let me try to be what he was not."

Anna reached out and embraced him. "Arngrim." She buried her face in his shoulder. "Grandfather."

That's what the Couch Park cult had called Dandridge. Then it has sounded sick and perverse. Now it was a joyful word, filled with both love and sadness.

Arngrim held her close, softly stroking her hair with one huge hand. "I never thought to laugh again, or feel joy. I thought that such things were for men alone, and not for my kind. I thought it was better to live briefly and feel what men feel than to live forever and feel nothing. But now…"

He locked gazes with me, his eyes overflowing with tears—real, human tears.

"I know now, Shepherd." His voice shook with emotion. "I know why you fight."

* * *

It was after six in the morning, but time had long since ceased to mean anything in the Fallen's subterranean home. I was tired and all the coffee and energy drinks in the world couldn't keep my eyes open. My fellow humans, even the normally indefatigable Loren, looked equally beat and we all staggered off to our silo, visions of the horrors in Russia and thoughts of our wondrous discoveries blending together in our heads.

I asked Gunnar to wake us in two hours. It wasn't much, but it was all I could justify with the outside world bursting at the seams. I was mostly asleep already by the time the elevator reached our quarters. I vaguely recalled mumbling "g'night" to my companions, even though it wasn't night, and realizing that it sounded kind of stupid, before throwing myself onto my cot and falling instantly to sleep.

This wasn't a lucid dream. I didn't see vast plains or demonic vistas, I didn't commune with gods or observe real-time horrors from afar. This was a real dream—my brain continuing to function, working out problems, fitting together puzzle pieces, reliving the past days as I slept.

Ngisma Tasinashkalim. The tree.

Roger Dandridge wanted to open the *Kadingir*, the Gate of the Gods. The thing that would allow him and his master to come and go as they chose.

He also knew that the gate was not invulnerable. That we could close it, lock his master in his self-made hell for another five millennia. But first...

Annabelle Lee Moore, standing on her porch, watching in fear as the Fallen thundered past. Annabelle Lee growing up with stories of her faithless father, living with an intolerant, bitter mother. Annabelle leaving home for a better life. Anna going to school, Anna getting her tattoos, taking a job as a dancer. Anna bowing and strutting. Anna naked to the world but as strong as a queen and as beautiful as a...

As what? As a goddess...?

Annabelle Lee alone in the nothing between worlds, her skin covered in the same silver-blue tracery as She Who Watches. Annabelle Lee calling across the centuries upon her kinsman, to one who prayed only for death and an end to an existence that had long since lost all joy and light. And to that one she brought hope...

She who bore the bloodlines of two worlds...

She who stood...

She...

Ngisma Tasinashkalim.

I was wide awake, gasping for breath.

V

It was 9:00 a.m. and the world continued to slide into the abyss.

"More reports of weird weather and monsters." Loren read the reports like an earnest but ill-groomed newscaster. "The Erta Ale volcano in northern Ethiopia has erupted violently, raining ash on surrounding communities and—guess what?—all but cutting Tigray province off from the rest of the region. Refugees report seeing faces in the ash cloud, flying serpents, yadda, yadda, yadda." He threw the papers down and they slipped off the table and onto the floor. Beowulf sniffed at them. "It's getting worse. How much longer 'til the tipping point?"

"Not long, I assure you." Arngrim sat beside Anna, holding her hand in his. "I hope you've learned something, Shepherd."

"I have." I spoke quietly, feeling a tone of reluctance creep into my voice. "It's just a theory, and it may be all we have."

For her part, Anna still looked tired, but when she looked at me her face was serene, as if Arngrim's presence lent her strength and calm.

"Spit it out, Alex. It can't be much worse than what we've already heard."

I wasn't sure of that, but I forged ahead anyway, feeling as if each syllable was being pried out of me with a crowbar.

"I think we all know *Ngisma Tasinashkalim* isn't literally a tree. I think we all knew that it's poetic, or a code phrase for something that the Mimma-Lemnu cultists already understand. I think it refers to a person. I think it refers to you."

It was another bombshell—the second in as many days, and it had about the same effect, throwing a blanket of silence across the room, prompting the others to stare at Anna, variously wondrous, curious or dubious. Anna herself listened without emotion as I went on.

"Not a tree, a woman. A woman rooted in two worlds. A woman of shared ancestry, both this world and the other. It sounds statistically impossible, but I believe that all of Walter Fitzhugh's descendants were male. Now at last you're here—a female descendant of the Fallen. The first woman born to the bloodline in six centuries. Chosen of Belet-Ili, with the power to close the gates of the enemy."

Now Anna showed emotion, her hand slowly rising to her mouth, her eyes widening slightly.

I forged on, despite her fear. "It's the only thing that makes sense. You can see the Fallen, you can talk to them, you had the dreams, and saw their past. You maintained a connection to their old world but you lived in this one. Dandridge must have known about the Tree, but he didn't know it was you. He just knew you could resist his control and wanted to find out why. It's the only mistake he's made so far, and we might have a chance to exploit it."

"Oh God." Loren looked horrified. "If we hadn't showed up in Canby that night..."

I nodded. "Dandridge would have Anna and we'd be screwed. She'd be dead or imprisoned or under his control. Or he'd have done a body swap with her and he'd have her power."

"It was destiny, Shepherd," Arngrim declared. "Guided by our mother's hand, you saved the one most precious to us."

"Jesus." Anna bowed her head and the sobs began to come. "Oh, Jesus. Please… Please don't…"

Arngrim put an arm around her shoulder. "Child, please. You've given us reason to go on, you've given me reason to hope. Don't despair now. You have the power that the enemy sought. If we can unlock it, we can use it against him."

She stood, pushing Arngrim away and casting a hollow, hopeless glance around the room, first at me, then at Loren, then at the Fallen.

"I can't do this anymore," she said softly. "I can't. Please don't make me."

I stood, reaching out to her.

"Anna, please, we don't..."

"NO!" she exploded. It was the loudest sound any of us had made. Beowulf jumped in alarm.

Anna turned and strode from the room shouting, her voice echoing in the hall outside. "I don't want to hear another word! Just don't fucking *talk to me!*"

The explosion had been building for weeks—maybe months. We had grown used to the quiet, cooperative Anna, willing to bide her time and wait for the rest of us to figure out what to do. Now all the patience, frustration and fear finally rose violently to the surface.

None of us wanted to follow and none of us spoke. Arngrim looked shattered, Loren confused. Beowulf whined softly. A few moments later, I heard the sound of the elevator doors opening.

"Where's she going?" Loren asked.

Arngrim listened to the sound of the elevator for a moment. "Up. To the shrine."

Loren was on his feet. "Oh, fuck. Is she gonna..."

"No." I raised a hand. My head hurt and I felt the terrible strain of sleep deprivation, but I tried to make sense of what Anna had just done. "She needs to think. None of us are acting rationally here. We've got to give her time, let her decide how to go on. We've been running the show since the beginning and she's just been along for the ride. Now it turns out that she's the key, she's the important one, and we need to let her do what she has to do. She's been waiting for us all this time, and now we need to wait for her."

Quiet assent from the others followed. Loren nodded and slowly sat down.

Arngrim composed himself with some effort and sat as well.

"We can't make her do this," Loren said. "I know what she's thinking. She could be killed, or worse. If we forced her to help us, we'd be just as bad as Dandridge. What do we do if she can't help us? What then?"

At least I knew the answer to that question. I'd seen other friends sacrifice themselves. And I'd sacrificed someone I loved, two years ago in an abandoned building in Brooklyn.

"Then we find another way," I said. "I won't sacrifice someone I love." I turned to Arngrim. "And you won't either."

It wasn't a question. I already knew his answer, too.

"No, Shepherd." Arngrim's voice was flat and final. "We spill no more innocent blood. And I will not harm my kin, or put her in harm's way if she is unwilling."

No one replied.

We sat in silence for a long time.

At last the intercom buzzed, and I answered.

"Alex?" Her voice was faint, as if she was speaking from a long distance.

"Yes," I replied. "Are you okay?"

"No. No I'm not." There was a pause, broken only by the faint hiss of static. "God, Alex. I don't know what to do."

"You want to come down and talk with us?"

"No. I want to talk to you. Can you come up?"

"Sure. I'll be right there."

I hung up. The others were looking at me with open concern.

"I'm going to go talk to her," I told them, rising slowly to my feet. All of my injuries were hurting—even the ones I'd taken from Onatochee, years ago.

Loren nodded, looking concerned but understanding. "Don't be too long, okay?"

Beowulf stood, tail wagging.

I looked at him indulgently. "Okay," I said. "You can come too."

* * *

The shrine was chilly as the late afternoon sun sank across the western plains. A few scraps of fog clung to the distant slopes. It was late summer, but the chill told me that autumn wasn't far off.

Beowulf happily explored the place as I sat on the bench beside Anna.

"You were the only one I could talk to," she said. "You told me about becoming the Shepherd. How you were offered a choice."

I sighed. "It wasn't much of a choice, really. If I had turned it down, well, everything we know and love would probably be a big infected hole and Onatochee would have his own reality show on A&E. Not really a great alternative."

She shrugged. "Yeah, but it was still a choice. Now I've got to make one too."

I reached out for her, but she moved away.

"No," she said. "Not now. Nothing personal, Alex, but I think I need to be uncomfortable right now."

I understood all too well.

"Yeah, I hear you. It doesn't seem fair, does it? Getting put in an impossible situation, told 'If you don't do the right thing here, millions will die, and the earth will be reduced to a cinder, but hey—it's your choice.'" I shook my head sadly. "Then when you do the right thing, suddenly everything you do is wrong, every choice you make is a misstep. Yeah, great. I got to be the Shepherd, and now *I* get to pass judgment on everyone."

"You mean like those kids on Hauser Butte?"

"Yeah, and those Onatochee cultists and the soldiers at Dandridge's estate... They're human beings, too. Maybe they're wrong, maybe they're evil, maybe not. But they're still dead and I feel like I'm responsible for their deaths. Anyone who thinks that doesn't weigh on my conscience is full of crap."

Anna paused for a moment, then looked into my eyes. "Since we're being so honest, what else are you responsible for? Any high crimes and misdemeanors I should know about?"

I took a long, deep breath. "After my girlfriend died of a heroin overdose I beat her dealer almost to death. I thought I was getting even, but it turns out all I was doing was destroying someone else's life, and tying a few more weights around my own neck."

She took a few moments to process this.

"Is that the worst thing you've ever done?"

"No," I said softly. "It isn't."

Her eyes bored into me like pale-blue lasers.

"You told me about your girlfriend, Alex. Trish. You said she didn't make it, but you didn't tell me what happened to her." She stopped, carefully considering her words. "What happened to her, Alex? What really happened?"

I couldn't keep looking at her. I glanced away, toward where Beowulf was busy grooming a paw.

"I did it," I said at last. "I searched for her for months and I finally found her in a burned-out tenement in Brooklyn. I tried to get her to come home. I tried to save her, Anna. But she was still..." Tears came now and I couldn't stop them. "She was still possessed. She tried to kill me. I stabbed her with the sword. Just like I'd done with the other cultists. She'd given herself up to Onatochee, and there wasn't anything I could do to save her."

It felt like that day, years ago when I'd confessed my sins on a windswept hillside, in front of my friends and under the eyes of an ancient being who was offering me an impossible choice. That day the truth had been bitter, but it had saved me. This truth was even worse.

What the hell would it do this time?

Anna let it sink in for a few moments before replying. "I guess I've known it all along, the way you told the story. I didn't want to think about it too much—that my knight in shining armor killed his last girlfriend."

I sat down heavily, head in hands. "Well now you know for sure. I'm not a knight in shining armor. I'm not anything. I'm just a stupid college drop-out who was in the wrong place at the wrong time."

There was a very long pause. So long I wondered whether she was still there or not.

"You made a choice, Alex. And you had to live with the consequences. I don't think you're a murderer. I know you too well by now. I know you've killed people, but you're not a murderer. It doesn't make it any easier to love you, but there it is."

I looked at her. I felt as if I was swimming in misery but tried to remind myself that she was the one who had to make an impossible choice.

"So you love me?"

She smiled bitterly. "Yeah. I do. And I guess you love me too, huh?"

I nodded. "Yeah. I love you. I didn't think I could anymore, but I do. More than I ever thought possible. And that's what makes all this so fucking hard."

She stood and walked over to the statue. Beowulf trotted up, grinning, and she petted his head.

"My other chosen companion." She smiled wistfully at him as he tilted his head up. "The one creature who doesn't judge me, who doesn't have an opinion about what I should do. Do you, boy? Do you?"

Beowulf's adoring glance answered the question quite eloquently.

Anna looked up at the statue.

"Is that what She looks like? She Who Watches?"

I stood behind her. "Yes and no. It's a good likeness, but She's a lot more than that. A stone carving can't quite convey what it's like to stand in Her presence and know that She's talking directly to you."

Anna hugged herself. "You know, in school I read about this guy. A hermit. He just wanted to live in his cave and be left alone, but one day a bunch of priests showed up and said, 'Hey, we need a new pope, and we picked you.' And he said, 'Screw you guys, I'm just a hermit. I don't want to be pope' and tried to run away. But they chased him down and dragged him back to Rome and forced him to be pope, whether he wanted to be or not."

I laughed. "How'd that work out for him?"

She shrugged. "He was a shitty pope. They threw him into prison and let him starve to death." She shivered. The chill was growing and she was only wearing a t-shirt and jeans. "I guess he was right, after all, huh?"

"Are you afraid that's going to happen to you?"

"Yeah, maybe." She turned around and looked up at me, and it was the most vulnerable and helpless I'd ever seen her. "You mean it, right? You really love me?"

"Oh God yes, Anna. I love you. And I know you love Loren too. He deserves someone like you."

"So if I say no to all of this, you'll go along with it?"

I nodded. "I swear, Anna. Truly. Besides, if I objected Arngrim would kick my ass right down this mountain."

She looked away. "Good. That's all I wanted to know."

"So you're not going to do it?"

"No," she said, looking past me, back toward the stairs. "I'm going to do it. Now come on, before I change my mind."

I whistled for Beowulf and we clambered down the steps.

"You sure about this?" I asked as the elevator doors opened and we stepped inside.

"No I'm not," she replied and looked up at me again. "Were you?"

* * *

More precious hours passed in the unending light of the base. Now that we had combined resources, revelations came quicker. The bloodstained books contained more horrific rituals and rites of sacrifice, the big leather book provided history and descriptions, along with the most important ceremony of all, sealing the Gate of the Gods.

Unfortunately, as Loren had feared, shutting the *Kadingir*— or, as became apparent, granting the Woman with Her Feet in

Two Worlds the ability to close such a gate—required blood sacrifice, just as opening it did.

Loren read the translation with growing disgust.

"The blood of one hundred goats, eighty ewes, forty mares, twenty stallions, twelve virgins, six infants, and one..." He broke off. "Holy shit. One king?"

"Where the hell do you get a king these days?" I stood up and began to pace the room. "To complete this ritual we'd have had to kidnap the king of Denmark and slit his throat. That really isn't going to work in the twenty first century."

"The Danes still have a king?" Gunnar asked. "It's good to know some of the old ways persist."

"I think his duties are mostly confined to cutting ribbons at shopping center grand openings," I said. "In any event, human sacrifice is out."

"Wait. Wait just a cotton picking minute." Loren read intently and with growing excitement. "It says here... That if you don't have sufficient sacrifices... Hmmm... That an object that has been sanctified in the proper manner can be used in place of sacrifice. An object such as the... The... It can't translate. It says *Dhalkhu'girru-quppu*. The..."

"Burning Cage of Demons," Tjorkill said. "I read of it long ago. The Black-Haired Ones built stone arches that allowed travel between distant cities and temples. They bound the spirits of wind demons to the stones, and used the demons' powers to carry them to other places."

A lightbulb all but appeared over Loren's head. "Could the demons be bound to other things? Like, maybe a brass lamp?"

In the silence that followed, our eyes swiveled to the table where the Foundation books stood in a stack. Beside them, set aside and so far impervious to our research, was the brass lamp I'd stolen from Foundation HQ in Portland.

"Holy shit," I said.

* * *

"So we've got a plan," Loren announced. "It's a lousy plan, I admit, but it's the best we've got."

"You're not selling this very well, Loren," I told him. I sat with the Fallen, petting Beowulf and feeding him MREs. The dog had taken the past few weeks in stride, but was clearly restless and as tired of endless metal corridors and windy mountain slopes as the rest of us.

He gave me a look. "We've deciphered enough of the ritual that I think we can do it safely, without sacrificing any kings or goats or anything."

"So when do we do this?" Anna asked. She looked uneasy, but her voice was more resolute than I'd have thought possible, given how little sleep any of us had gotten. "Now?"

Tjorkill shook his head. "That is the one flaw in the plan. The ritual can only be performed in the presence of the *Kadingir* itself. It is the energy of the open gate combined with that bound to the lantern that allows us to invoke the *Ngisma Tasinashkalim.*"

"God, this just gets better and better," I complained, leaning back in my chair and stretching. My joints ached and popped. "We have to wait until Dandridge opens this damned gate of his, *then* slam it shut on him? What if our ritual doesn't work?"

"Then, as you would so eloquently put it, we're screwed," said Tjorkill.

"Yeah," Loren added. "We're going to have only one shot at this."

"I hope I'm not being too much of a party pooper here," I said, "but do we even know where Dandridge is opening the gate? My guess is that your buddy and mine Mimma-Lemnu will be waiting on the other side with an army so we're going to have to close it in one big hurry."

"I think we've worked that out," Loren said. "At least I hope we have. It has to be in a thin place. In the book it's called an *Erset Zalazalag.* And there's only one useful thin place we know of that's anywhere close."

I frowned. "Hauser Butte?"

"It makes sense. It's close to Dandridge and we've already seen activity there."

I wasn't convinced. "Even if it's there, I imagine the Foundation will have it surrounded by scorpion wolves and demon women. We'd have to fight our way in."

Arngrim made a face. "They will fall like wheat before a scythe."

"We fled when last the enemy came at us in numbers," Gunnar said, eyes downcast. "We should have stayed and fought to the end."

"No!" Tjorkill was on his feet. "The enemy sent ten thousand times our number against us. If we had not fled, this world would have no defense. The enemy would have come and conquered, just as he conquered our world. Not even the *Hirdir* could have stopped them. Now your world has a chance to survive, Shepherd."

"Yes." Now Arngrim was standing too. "Each Fallen is worth a thousand foes." Then he looked at me. "And you, *Hirdir*, you are worth at least a hundred."

I wasn't sure whether to be complimented or insulted.

"Hey!" Loren exclaimed. "What about me? How many enemy am I worth?"

Gunnar laughed. "No more than a dozen or two, my friend. But your dog is worth fifty."

Loren shrugged. "I'll take that. Give me a magic sword and I'd kick ass, though."

Anna gestured at Loren's untidy pile of papers. "So you can do this? Give me the power to close the gate? Without killing anyone?"

Loren nodded. "There's a lot of chanting and inscribing, but I think we're up to it."

"Does it say exactly what it does to Anna?" I asked. "Jesus, Loren. It could... It could even...?"

"Kill me?" Anna asked.

"Yeah, kill you. That's not something I'm especially interested in doing."

Arngrim looked toward Anna. "Are you sure you want to face such dangers, Granddaughter? The thought that I have found you at last only to lose you again is too great to bear."

"We have to take the risk," she replied. "Alex told me what Belet-Ili said to him. If I can help stop those bastards, if I can help you and your people find peace, I'll do it."

For the second time in two days, tears gleamed in the big demon-man's eyes.

"Your words shame me, Granddaughter," he said softly. "We have lost much, we Fallen. But in you we have gained far more."

I tried to suppress the rush of emotion that I felt and spoke as calmly as I could. "Loren, does it say anything about what effects it would have on Anna?"

"Not really, but it sounds like she's still alive and still has free will, just a whole lot of power. There's a lot of stuff about what she can do once we've performed the ritual. She will close the ways, She will bring justice, She will reveal what is hidden and esoteric crap like that."

"Great." I rubbed my forehead. Anna had made her choice, but now I wasn't sure I liked it. "This all feels so half-assed it's not even funny. What if it's not Hauser Butte? Shit, Dandridge could be on a plane to Outer Mongolia right now, and we wouldn't have a chance in hell of catching him."

My laptop rested on the table in front of me. A soft ringing sound issued from it, telling me that I had received an urgent email. I frowned. Was Consuela having problems with the advertisers again?

I opened my mail client and stared.

"Jesus."

"What's wrong?" Loren asked.

"I think you're right about Hauser Butte."

The message was from *fmagrudr@easternOR.net*. The subject read "Alex—Urgent—They're back."

H Alex and Loren, hope Beowulf is in good health, etc., etc. It's been a rough couple of months for me—money's tight and Corey finally decided he wanted to go to school in Ashland, so I'm running the place by myself. Sorry, but this isn't exactly a casual message. Things have been getting strange out here again, and I thought you guys would want to know.

The weather sucks. This drought's been going on all summer and we're actually starting to get dust storms. Most folks have been staying indoors out of the heat, but I still have to drive out on the range to check on my cattle. One day I decided I'd drive out past Rafferty's place and check out Hauser Butte.

The first thing I found were fresh tire tracks on Goldfinch Road— lots of them. Now there is no reason on earth for anyone to go down there in this weather, given the dust and the heat. Yeah, I could see some damned extreme hiker type going down there and getting stuck in a ravine so he has to chew his own arm off to get out, but there were tracks from five or six big vehicles. So I was careful.

Good thing too. I parked behind an outcropping a couple of hundred yards from the place and checked it out with my rifle scope. At first I didn't see anything, but then I looked really careful and saw a couple of big military-style trucks covered in camo netting, and three black Hummers, parked so they'd be hard to spot unless you knew what you were looking for. I didn't see anyone, but I got the hell out of there, *moving slow so I wouldn't raise any dust, and I came back after dark with a night vision scope.*

They weren't as careful at night. I saw a couple more of those punk-ass kids hanging around. But they were with some guys in fatigues with rifles, and a couple of guys in suits, I shit you not. Then two of the soldier-types went over to one of the trucks and opened it up. They pulled out a bunch of bundles that looked like bodies wrapped in plastic, and something else climbed out—it was like a big dog the size of a horse, with wings on its back and a long tail that reached up over its back.

When I first saw those dumbasses up there I thought I should call Jane Enriquez and have her roust them out with a couple of deputies, but then I remembered what happened that day when we were up on the butte. No way Jane's equipped to deal with that kind of thing.

Then I remembered what you'd said, and I thought of all that bizarre crap that's happening in Russia and Ethiopia. The weather around here is getting worse and worse—too hot to move, dust everywhere. Something told me that those little shits on Hauser Butte had something to do with it, and I knew I had to get in touch with you.

I tried to call but all I got was voicemail, so now I'm emailing. I don't know whether you'll get this in time, or whether you can do anything about it. But it looks like those bastards are back, and they're up to something again. If you're there, come out as soon as you can. This looks pretty serious.

Frank's words repeated themselves over and over as I packed my bags and prepared to depart. Down on the loading dock the Fallen were firing up their demon-machines and the sound reverberated off metal walls, multiplying itself a hundredfold.

Things were getting worse out there—the dead zones in Russia, Brazil, and Africa were growing bigger, with more refugees and even wilder tales. The Russian military was frantic, and Loren had intercepted a DoD communique suggesting that Moscow was considering launching a nuclear strike on the region.

If you're there, come out as soon as you can. This looks pretty serious.

It did indeed, and it was getting more serious by the hour. Weather reports told of large dust storms and weather even hotter than normal in a region that was used to weeks of drought and 100 degree temperatures.

The Foundation had returned to Malheur County, and if one of those mysterious suit-wearing strangers turned out to be Roger Dandridge, then their intentions were crystal clear.

They were planning to open another gate, and they were going to do it soon.

I suppressed a shudder and took one last check of my possessions before heading downstairs.

* * *

The noise grew to deafening volumes on the dock. With my strange double-vision, I saw the Fallen and their mounts as both blonde humans with gleaming motorcycles and blood-red demons unchaining metal-skinned beasts.

"Are you ready, Shepherd?" Arngrim shouted above the roar of racing engines.

"Yes!" I popped Yngwie's trunk and threw my baggage in. Beowulf jumped in and seated himself on the passenger seat, while Anna threw me the high sign from where she sat at Beethoven's wheel.

Loren rolled down Beethoven's passenger window and shouted. "Next stop Hayes, Oregon!"

Ahead of us the great doors creaked open and I drove, leading the way with the Fallen escorting Beethoven and its precious cargo behind like a chrome-and-leather honor guard. Last of all, emerging from its hiding place deep in the missile base was one more Fallen vehicle—a huge HEMTT A3 hybrid diesel-electric truck, its bed covered in heavy tarps. I didn't bother to ask Arngrim where he'd gotten it or what it carried, knowing I'd only get stony silence for an answer.

By noon we were half way across Utah, stopping only to add fuel to the flimsy human machines and answer the puny humans' biological compulsions. By sunset we'd reached Winnemucca and turned north on I-95, bearing straight for the Oregon border. In three hours we'd be in Hayes and Frank Magruder would have some surprise houseguests.

* * *

It took considerably longer than three hours, for the dust storm closed in almost as soon as we crossed the border. It was no natural storm—that was certain—for hot yellow sand hissed against the windows, slithering across the asphalt in front of us like snakes, swirling ghostly in our headlights, blowing overhead in massive gritty clouds, blotting out both moon and stars.

The Fallen's machines didn't seem affected and Yngwie dealt with the dust reasonably well, but Beethoven's air-cooled engine and competition carbs choked up periodically, forcing several rest stops.

We passed stalled trucks and abandoned cars all along the route. GPS and cell phone service vanished, and the few towns we passed through seemed deserted and ghostly, their residents holed up inside as dust piled up in great drifts.

Anna had switched vehicles at the last rest stop. She peered out Yngwie's window forlornly. "God, it's the Dustbowl."

"Yeah." I carefully focused on the road ahead. It was easy to lose it in the swirling darkness and our speed had dropped to less than thirty. At this rate we wouldn't get to Hayes until well past midnight. "Our enemies always seem to bring bad weather with them."

I made a stab at changing the subject. "So how's it feel having a family again?"

She took a few moments to answer. "It feels weird. Especially since my new family isn't even human. But I guess it's typical of me—the kids in school always used to call me an alien. They called me Ms. Spock because of the glasses and because I was such a nerd."

"Ms. Spock? Very creative."

"Well it was more creative than the little shits who kept calling me a geek, or the ones who called me a lesbian." She looked thoughtful. "Come to think of it, they were half right. Just ask my first girlfriend."

It was close enough to relationship talk that I couldn't stay off the topic.

"When this is all over, Anna, I just want you to know…"

I started strong, but my execution was poor. My words trailed off as a dozen carefully-prepared speeches suddenly drained away into nothing.

"I mean, I don't want to stand in anyone's… I don't want you to think that I…"

Her old impish expression returned, though it was filtered through puffy, tired eyes. "Oh Jesus, Alex, spit it out. Are you trying to say you're okay with me and Loren?"

"Y… es?"

"But that you'd still like to be with me too? And that you're uncomfortable talking about it because you've never had a relationship like that and you're not sure if it would work, but you care about both of us and don't want it to damage our friendship?"

"Y… es?"

"See? How hard was that?"

"Uh…"

She reached out and touched my face. "Alex, I really love you, and I finally figured out that you've only had a couple of real relationships in your life. Underneath all of this demon shit, and this Fallen shit, and this Dandridge shit I'm really feeling bad for dumping this kind of thing on you when you've got so goddamned much else to worry about. And I will be as patient and understanding with you and Loren as I possibly can, just as long as you both promise to do the same for me, okay?"

"Uhh…" The vocabulary center of my brain had suddenly gone blank. "Okay?"

"Now maybe we should put this relationship crap on hold until we know for sure that there's even going to be a world that we can boink in?"

I felt a sudden wave of relief.

"Sure. Yeah. That sounds good. First thing's first, you know?"

"Yes, Alex. I know."

Damn. Demons, monsters and ancient evil sorcerers—those were the easy parts of my life right now.

Women, love, relationships… Those truly terrified me.

Slowly, doggedly we pressed on through the howling wind and the thickening dust. Ahead, I could barely read a road sign that said *Burns 100 miles*.

We were getting close.

But what would we find when we got there?

* * *

Night deepened around us. Our headlights barely penetrated the swirling yellow clouds and our speed fell to a crawl. Almost nothing was visible beyond the dust, and within an hour we had almost no idea where we were. It was only by chance and careful odometer reading that we found Local 72, the road out to Frank Magruder's ranch.

It was almost 2:00 a.m. when I caught sight Frank's mail box, alone and defiant in the dust, standing like a sentinel beside the access road to his house. I was alone in Yngwie; Anna was back riding with Loren and Beowulf. I suspected they probably made better conversation than I did. I looked down the access road. There were no lights, but the dust was probably too heavy to see them anyway.

All but blind, I nearly plowed into what was left of Frank's metal gate, slamming on Yngwie's brakes and stopping only inches away.

Behind me, the line of faint headlights that marked the column's location came to a stop as well. I struggled into my duster, wrapped a bandana around my face and pulled on a pair of goggles. Similarly bundled, Loren climbed out of Beethoven and hastened to help me. When I opened Yngwie's door, the wind hit me like a dry, gritty wall. The noise of wind filled my ears, rising in an instant from a banshee shriek to a bass rumble.

"Nice weather we're having!" Loren shouted, his voice muffled by a scarf and faint against the wind. "Maybe we should buy some property here after the war!"

"Yeah, I'll add it to our investment portfolio." I gestured at the heavy metal cattle gate, now a twisted ruin scattered across the sand. "Looks like someone got here before us. Let's get this crap out of the road."

Together we dragged the broken chunks of the gate away. It was good to have someone there to remind me I wasn't entirely alone in this hot, gritty maelstrom.

The wind slackened and the dust dissipated slightly as we turned toward the vehicles. In the brief lull, Loren looked back down the road.

"Hey Alex—you sure Frank's ranch is down this way?"

I shrugged. Anything was possible in this weather. "Relatively sure. Why?"

"Well that's bad, because I think I hear gunfire."

I whirled. The wind picked up again, rising swiftly to an angry wail, but before it did I heard the unmistakable crack of rifle fire from the direction of Frank's house. I felt the stabbing pain of a headache and the world around me seemed briefly to fluoresce and shimmer.

Loren heard it too and was in motion before I was.

I followed, racing toward Yngwie, hoping that the Fallen would hear my shouts.

"Arngrim! Boots and saddles! Frank's in trouble!"

VII

There was no plan, there were no tactics, and no thought save action. The darkness was now almost complete, and Yngwie's headlights illuminated only a fresh storm of grit and dust. Nevertheless, I jammed into gear and let out the clutch, plunging down the road in a spray of gravel.

How far to the house? Would I see it in time to stop? Would something else loom out of the storm before I got there? Jesus Christ—was I even at the right place?

It all jangled and clashed in my head, no one fear or question stopping long enough to even warrant consideration. All I knew was that there was gunfire, and someone might need us.

My ballpark estimate was that the house was about a quarter mile down the road. I had enough presence of mind to keep an eye on the odometer, watching as it ticked away one tenth, two tenths… Just as it began to change to three I swung to the right, feeling an ugly lurch as the road dropped out from under me and gave way to dust and grass and scrub. I ground to a halt and in a moment I was out, rushing toward the trunk. I still heard the staccato pop of a rifle, and—more alarmingly—a distorted, tinny howl carried on the wind.

Then Beethoven rushed past, engine protesting loudly, and an instant later Loren too pulled off the road, bumping violently into the brush. The driver door popped open, disgorging

Loren, still donning tac vest and night vision helmet. Then Anna leaped out the side door, zipping shut a heavy coat and slipping a pair of goggles on, followed quickly by Beowulf who took up station near the front of the van, staring anxiously into the maelstrom.

I located my own night goggles, sword, and a Glock in the trunk. Loren was busy slapping an ammo mag into the G36 rifle that he'd kept since the fight at Dandridge's mansion. I switched on the goggles and shoved a couple of frag grenades into the pockets of my coat. As I came back around the car I saw Anna racking the slide on a Glock.

"You stay here!" I bellowed over the wind. "We can't risk you getting hurt!"

Anna's expression was invisible behind goggles and a scarf, but she nodded, shouting something I couldn't hear.

I pointed. "Beowulf! Stay with Anna!"

Beowulf snapped to attention with a look of immediate comprehension and strode over to stand, legs apart, tail stiff, beside Anna. As Loren and I prepared to plunge into the storm, he looked at us with concern.

"We'll be okay, boy!" Loren shouted. "You take care of her!"

Beowulf seemed to almost nod curtly, then Loren and I were off, advancing toward the sound of gunfire and the fearsome howling, which grew louder as we approached in deafening disharmony with the screaming wind.

I ran, feet pounding on the gravel road, sword in one hand, pistol in the other. If I fell I'd either shoot or impale myself but nothing seemed to matter now save getting to the end of the road, to the house and to Frank Magruder.

The first thing that emerged from the green swirling light and dark ahead was the motionless body of a ghoul, its skull shattered by a rifle shot. Then a piercing howl cut through my head and a crowd of pale naked bodies rushed out of the dirt, all teeth and claws and angry yellow eyes.

I met the charge of the first ghoul with a single shot, pegging it in the eye, sending it tumbling, then swung into the second, slicing messily through its ribcage. Hot blood splashed across my hands and arms; I pivoted to the right, letting the sundered remains slide off the blade, and pounding the pommel into the face of a third, feeling bone shatter.

Beside me, Loren stepped back, unleashing one, two, three semiautomatic bursts, each one stitching the flesh of a ghoul. Two were down, but the third was hit in the shoulder and kept coming, its canine face distorted and snarling. Gathering itself, it pounced on Loren and the two crashed down together, but an instant later a pained shriek gurgled from the corpse eater's throat, and Loren stood, his combat knife black with blood. The creature lay twitching at his feet as he ducked under the attack of its fellow, disemboweling it with a single stroke.

Then a massive weight struck me from behind, a wet growling in my ear, something kicked the back of my knee and I went down. Our friends weren't stupid—some had circled around behind us as the others sacrificed themselves attacking from the front.

Rough hands encircled my throat; I managed to release my grip on the sword and jam my own hand in front of my windpipe keeping the thing from crushing it, but its grip was powerful. The ghouls were deceptively thin—this one seemed to outweigh me by a hundred pounds despite my desperate efforts to dislodge it.

For a long minute we struggled in painful stalemate—the creature was unwilling to relinquish its hold on me, but I was unable to push it back and my pistol was trapped beneath me. It snarled and snapped at me, jaws clashing together a millimeter or two from my head, splashing me with hot spittle; if I let off for an instant it would rip half my face off. Its breath smelled of rot and graveyards.

At last I gathered what strength I could and pushed upward, trying to force my knees under me so I could push it off. The ghoul pressed back down with renewed ferocity, but I'd gained an inch or two, freeing my trapped hand, brought it up beside my head and fired.

The report slammed me almost as hard as the bullet, filling my head with a harsh clanging, driving out even the screaming howl of the wind. But the creature jerked and convulsed, allowing me to throw it off, where it lay on the ground, blood spurting from its rent throat. Weaving, barely able to stand, I pumped two more rounds into the thing and it lay still at last.

Beside me Loren had finished dispatching the last creature, yanking his knife from the eye of a slain ghoul. Four more motionless bodies lay at his feet and he was splattered with blood, staring at me with wild eyes, panting and coughing in the hot, dirty air.

Oh God... My mind spun angrily as my stomach lurched and I tried to make my head stop ringing. *Oh God, Loren... You poor bastard, you poor geek gamer bastard... What have I turned you into?*

Then my twisted insides interrupted my reverie, rising up and overflowing. I fell to my knees, retching up the last couple of Fallen MREs that I'd eaten.

Loren knelt beside me, and I could see him mouthing the words "Are you okay?" even though I couldn't hear him through the ringing in my head.

I pointed to my ear. "I'm deaf! I can't hear you!"

He nodded, then looked up, alarmed. Distant and faint against the racket in my skull, I once more heard the harsh tinny howl, barely audible but all too real.

I struggled back to my feet, retrieving the sword and waved at Loren, shouting even though I could barely hear my own voice.

"Come on! Let's move!"

Again, we ran through the storm, toward the sound.

Jesus. Where the hell were the Fallen? And when would the horrific clanging in my head go away?

Dust rose and fell around us. I glimpsed the dark shape of a house, only a few yards distant, and a pair of muzzle flashes. Then it vanished into the storm again as the throaty, ringing shriek cut through the noise in my head and Loren looked up in sudden alarm.

Something enormous slammed into the ground between us, something that plowed up the hard-baked desert ground and knocked us both off our feet, rolling in opposite directions, lost in the roaring dusty void.

Then it lifted up and disappeared back into the dust, and I had the faint impression of a vast, fanged leopard's head attached to a scaled snaky neck, ugly and washed out in neon green and black.

The things from the Russian satellite feed. *The Sebitti.* Drinkers of Blood. This was one of the things that had massacred a battalion of Russians. The sword in my hand seemed suddenly inadequate for fighting something of such magnitude and malignance.

I'd lost all perspective when I'd fallen, but now panic stabbed at me, the panic of an animal confronted by a predator, of the tiny fish pursued by the shark. Through the haze I glimpsed Loren fleeing—he'd seen it too.

I turned to follow, only to have a massive black wall block my way—a hand, scaled and clawed, like the hand of the Statue of Liberty, sweeping through the dust, slamming into me, carrying me backwards, fingers closing to trap me, crush me...

Survival instinct flashed white-hot through my brain; I lashed out, swinging the sword two-handed, chopping down upon the giant hand, slicing through the scaled flesh of the clawed index finger, cutting flesh and bone and sending the huge member falling, spinning away, followed by a flood of blood that steamed and hissed, accompanied by an enraged shriek that once more penetrated the jangling torrent of noise in my skull.

The desert exploded again, a slap of pressure and hot dust washing over me, sending me falling, rolling, clinging desperately to the sword hilt. Another titanic shape loomed out of the dust like the hoof of an impossibly huge horse, rising up, dragging clumps of earth and dirt with it, then slamming down again, seeking to stamp me out like an annoying insect.

It rose up, then plunged downward once more. I swung at it and the sword bounced off, chipping fragments from the great dark hoof, but not hurting it, and then the hand was on me again, encircling me with its remaining fingers, crushing down on me, lifting me up into the roiling hot air. Painfully,

I wrenched my arm and the sword free as something loomed out of the clouds, that mammoth leopard's head, snarling, yawning, fangs like dagger-shaped monoliths, dark red tongue and gums dripping with hot saliva, squinting eyes pulsing red-green-yellow-red...

Screaming, cursing incoherently I struck again, slashing as I descended toward the nightmare giant's face, hacking at its contorted brow, the blade flaring fiercely, slicing through the strobing red-green-yellow eye. Thick fluid gushed, and another scream, louder and more terrible than the first emerged from its cavernous, yawning mouth.

I was spinning through space, tumbling end over end, flung away, battered on burning winds, whirling toward the ground...

A familiar warmth surrounded me, along with a bubble of silver-blue light, slowing my descent just before I made contact. I still hit hard, knocking the wind out of me, but I kept hold of the sword and staggered to my feet. My head still rang, but I could hear the wind and the chatter of gunfire, but it seemed to come from everywhere, and for an instant I was completely shaken and disoriented.

Then I heard the sound of engines... the Fallen's screaming demon-machines, and a deeper, basso roar like a real human artifact. A dark shape materialized, rolling toward me on eight rubber wheels, a wedge-shaped armored vehicle. On a swivel mount atop it sat one of the Fallen, manning a six-barreled autocannon that whirled with a harsh whine, spitting fire into the air. Now I knew what they'd carried on that huge truck, under that tarp.

I fell in behind the vehicle, looking up into the storm-tossed sky. The shape of the *Sebitti* was ahead, a towering shadow with a waving, sinuous neck and bestial head. A storm of fire from the cannon struck carved black furrows in its flesh and it recoiled, its screams rolling like metallic thunder. A pair of Fallen on their cycles took up a position beside the armored car, each with a shoulder-fired launcher, blasting two more charges at the waving, roaring form. Red-orange flames bloomed across its body and it stumbled, falling down onto one colossal knee that crashed down onto the ground a few yards distant.

Then the giant angry leopard head swung down at the end of a green scaled neck the thickness of a subway tunnel, its single remaining eye glaring, jaws clashing. It seized one of the Fallen and his machine, crushing them instantly even as the other slashed at it with his black-bladed axe and the cannon kept up its steady fusillade of burning metal.

It was hurt, but it wasn't dead, and not even the Fallen seemed able to overwhelm it... I kept remembering the ease with which its fellows had dispatched the Russians, and prepared to rush the thing, knowing even as I did that it would do no good...

Calm fell over me like a blanket, washing away the fear, and again the warmth grew inside me. The last remnant of the ringing vanished, along with the howl of the wind and the ugly blast of the dirt-laden wind. In a single instant, the night was still, dust and gravel rattling down like hot stony hail, the bright light of the moon shining...

The air around us cleared and at long last I could see my surroundings. We were twenty or thirty yards from a low ranch house, its walls deep in drifts of wind-blown dirt. Part of its roof had collapsed, and great rents had been torn in its side. Dark figures surrounded the place—*lilitu,* ghouls, and scythe-bearers, stunned into motionlessness by the sudden cessation of the storm.

Between us and the house stood the great *Sebitti,* even more fearsome in the natural moonlight, still down on one scaly bird-like knee, its reptilian body burned by explosions and torn by gunfire, its chest heaving, its neck drawing back as if to strike, fangs bared in an expression of mindless feline rage.

A shout echoed from behind me. *"Blood drinker! Kalbi-Amelnakru! Dog of the enemy!* Face the Fallen and perish!"

A chorus of engines exploded and the lights of twenty machines blazed, illuminating the wounded giant and eliciting another deafening scream. The line of machines began to move, weapons came on guard, swords and axes poised.

Something flashed in my mind, something bright and close, the touch of something warm, something loved... It was what I had felt when I'd been with Damien, when I'd kissed Trish or played music with Loren.

The sickness and fatigue that had been with me since Dandridge's mansion began to vanish, draining into nothingness and I stood without pain, raising my hand and shouting.

"Fallen! Wait!"

My voice echoed across the battlefield, over the sound of engines, and as one the line of riders paused.

The silver light around us grew in intensity as if the moon had suddenly loomed large, but it came from something closer, something here, in contact with the earth. I turned and saw.

Anna strode from the van, naked and etched with silver-blue, her tattoos glowing with an inner light. Beowulf marched beside her with the bearing of an armored knight. Darting fireflies of brightness swirled around her, sketching out intricate patterns like mandalas and alien runes in the air, drawing the outlines of wings rising from her back. She held aloft the brass lantern, the Cage of Demons and it glowed with the same blinding luminance. There was comfort in her presence that stilled the maelstrom and made the towering monstrosity above us cringe back in sudden fear.

She didn't need the ritual. All she needed was to be close enough to a doorway, and the energies would be absorbed, flowing into her through the sigil on her skin.

Dandridge had had our most potent weapon in his possession but hadn't realized it. We'd taken her from him, and now he was going to learn the cost of his error.

The lantern's light moved with her like a great dome, holding the storms at bay, clearing the skies, letting the clean light of moon and stars illuminate the land. As she strode, the radiance touched the gathered creatures, and with agonized shrieks they dissolved, crumbling into dust that shimmered for an instant then fell to the ground. Seeing their fellows' fate, the others began to flee, first by handfuls, then in great throngs, hundreds of dark bodies scattering across the desert.

The *Sebitti* crouched unmoving, an obscene statue, a monument of the enemy. Anna strode closer, looking up and into its single hateful eye.

She paused for a moment, then spoke, and the single word rang like a church bell on a cold and lonely night.

"Depart."

Beginning at its feet the battle-lord began to dissolve like the others, collapsing into glittering fragments that hung in the air, then rained down to the hard desert ground. A single agonized groan escaped from that nightmarish throat before it, too vanished into shimmering dust.

I stared at the shining thing that Anna had become. Over near the Fallen's battle line, I saw Loren, also staring dumbly, at a loss for words, possibly for the first time in his life. Arngrim dismounted and fell to his knees, mirrored a moment later by all of the other Fallen. For a long moment, the night was silent.

Then the blue light faded and Anna was Anna again.

"Alex…" She took a single unsteady step toward me, then fell forward. I hastened to catch her, bearing her gently to the ground and covering her with my coat.

"You're okay, honey. You're okay." I spoke quietly as the others rushed up to see to her. "You're gonna be okay."

She gazed at me, eyes heavy. "I felt it, Alex. I can do it."

As I struggled to reply, a weary voice sounded from the direction of the ranch house.

"Alex? Loren? Is that you guys? You took your sweet time getting here, didn't you?"

I looked up and saw a familiar figure limping toward us.

"Hi Frank," I said, rising and holding out my hand. "Long time, no see."

VIII

I realized that trying to hug Frank would probably earn me a punch in the mouth, so I accepted a grave handshake as the Fallen approached, on foot or mounted, engines rumbling. Even in the dim light of the moon it was clear he'd been through a lot. His clothes were rent, his rugged face was haggard, and there was blood on his shirt.

Frank was still old-school, however, and he knelt down beside Anna, gently taking her hand.

"Frank Magruder, Ma'am. I saw what you did. Thank you."

"You're welcome, Frank." Her voice was weak and sleepy. "Call me Anna."

Arngrim rode toward us, the APC rumbling behind. Frank looked at him without expression. "You'll have to introduce me to your friends, Alex. I remember 'em from Hauser Butte. I guess they're on our side now, huh?"

"For the moment." I waved at the approaching Fallen. "Jesus, Arngrim. A Stryker? Where the hell did you get it?"

Arngrim looked back at the vehicle with a matter-of-fact expression. "We have our sources, Shepherd." He dismounted and approached Frank, hand extended. "Frank Magruder. I am Arngrim. The Shepherd speaks highly of you."

Frank shook his hand with a slightly bemused expression. "Charmed, I'm sure."

317

From nearby, a wounded ghoul shrieked as Wulfgar dispatched it with a single sword stroke.

Anna sat up, looking uneasy, pulling my coat around her shoulders.

"Uh, guys, do you think we could continue the introductions inside? It's getting kind of cold out here."

* * *

There wasn't much left of Frank's ranch house. The roof was partly caved in, wallboard was cratered by bullets and shrapnel, most of the windows were broken and boarded up.

We seated ourselves in the remnants of the living room. Hot white light from a pair of Coleman lanterns illuminated three hunting rifles leaning against one wall. The floor glittered with spent shell casings.

"The weather set in about three days ago," Frank said as he lit a propane stove and set an aluminum coffee pot atop the blue flames. "Phones, cell service, power went down a few hours later." He nodded outside to where the Fallen were still mopping up the last few enemy survivors. "Then that bunch arrived. Rolled right over the town. Some of us hid, some of us put up a fight, but the rest of them… God only knows what became of them. I'd pretty much given up hope, figured I'd take as many of them with me as I could."

"You fought well, Magruder," Arngrim said. A rifle shot echoed from outside. He took a quick glance out the window and seemed satisfied. "Is there any assistance we can provide you?"

Frank shook his head. "No. But you can tell me exactly what the hell is going on and who the hell you are. I'm grateful for the help Alex, but I like to know who I'm dealing with. The last time I saw your gang, Arngrim, you were cutting a bunch of kids apart on Hauser Butte. Now you show up at my place with military vehicles and heavy weapons and expect me to just roll over and play ball?" He waved an arm. "Those bastards in Hayes, whatever they're doing to the people there—did you bring them? Are they here because of you?"

"No!" Arngrim's bark was emphatic. "*We* are here because of *them,* Frank Magruder."

"It's a good thing they are too," Loren added. He sat on the sagging couch, one arm around Anna, who was still wrapped in my coat. "That fucking sandstorm outside is going to be the whole world pretty soon if Dandridge and the Foundation have their way."

Frank frowned, perplexed. "Who the hell is Dandridge? What Foundation? Jesus, Alex. Does everything with you have to be so damned complicated?"

I rubbed my forehead. "It's a long and complicated story, Frank and we don't have a whole lot of time. I'll try to give it to you in fifty words or less."

Admittedly, it took a little more than fifty words, but by the time I had finished Frank was staring bemusedly, his gaze shifting from me to Anna, to Arngrim.

"Demons? Monsters? Dimensional doorways? Jee-zus Christ on a fucking bicycle." He looked at Anna. "Sorry for the language, ma'am. No offense meant."

She rolled her eyes. "None fucking taken, believe me."

The coffee pot was boiling and Frank poured into several chipped enamel mugs. "Hope you like it black. I'm fresh out of milk and sugar."

"No problem, Frank." Anna accepted a steaming mug and sipped eagerly. "Best coffee I've ever tasted."

I took my own mug and drank. Damn. She was right.

Loren looked toward the boarded windows. The screams and occasional gunshots had faded to nothing.

"Okay, so we've got coffee and we're all alive. Now what?"

I stood up with difficulty, using the sword for support. Idimma-Xul's healed slashes ached and my joints smoldered with pain and stress. Shit. I wasn't even thirty and I was already feeling old.

"We know where the enemy is and we know what he's planning. We've got our weapons, we've got your tank and your autocannon and two dozen of the biggest badasses who ever strode the earth, Arngrim." I turned and looked at Anna. My head throbbed. "Are you ready for this? I don't think we're going to need to do that ritual at all."

She swallowed and shook her head. "I felt it. I didn't understand it, but I felt it. I knew I could send them back. And I felt something else, like looking at a bonfire on the beach miles away. He's here, Alex. Dandridge is here."

"Good." It was something I'd both been fearing and expecting. "Then we need to move out quickly."

Just as I finished speaking the door flew open, admitting a cloud of dust. Wulfgar and Gunnar followed, dragging a struggling figure behind them.

"A gift for you, Shepherd!" Gunnar declared. He was filthy save for a large goggle-shaped patch of bare skin around his eyes. "One of the enemy's human slaves."

Wulfgar hoisted the figure and threw him, none too gently, onto the floor in front of me. "Do with him what you will, Shepherd. He is less than dirt to us."

Their captive was a man, ankles and wrists bound with zip ties. He wore a black tank top, and through the grime I could see an ornate "A" tattooed on one shoulder, a "J" on the other.

I squatted down beside him and yanked his head up by the hair.

"Well, well. If it isn't AJ? Nice to finally make your acquaintance. I think your late friend Bethany would have called me Shepherd."

He'd taken a beating, but AJ still managed to summon up a defiant glare.

"You're too late, Shepherd," he spat. "We've already won. The dead will rise up and consume the living. *Usella mituti ikkalu baltuti.*"

I was busy suppressing the urge to punch AJ in his arrogant face when the room was suddenly suffused with shimmering blue light. I started in surprise, letting AJ's head bang painfully to the floor.

Slowly and deliberately, Anna stood up from the couch, shedding my coat as Loren, Frank and even Arngrim drew back. Beowulf stood his ground, but still looked at her fearfully.

Light shone from her tattoos and her eyes were solid silver-blue, cold and merciless. She stepped toward AJ, who stared in growing terror.

"Hi, sweetie." Her voice resonated through the house like the noise of an oncoming train, and when she opened her mouth I saw bright silver-blue burning inside her. "Miss me?"

AJ's lips trembled, his eyes wide.

"Anna… Anna… I… I…"

Her voice seemed to echo inside my skull. "You're sorry about all those times you told Jammer I was a slut? You're sorry you tried to drug me at that party? You're sorry you're a pathetic little misogynistic prick? Is that what you want to say?"

She drew close, her shining face just inches from AJ's. His response was reduced to frightened gibberish.

"What did he offer you, AJ? Money? Women? Drugs? Did he tell you he'd make you a big man, and all those bitches who had ignored you would have to do what you told them to? I can see it, AJ. I can see it through that tattoo on your back. He can see you, but now so can I." She reached out a hand and touched his forehead. He shrieked and convulsed. A dark stain was spreading from his groin. "Feel it on your skin, AJ? Feel it crawling like worms, eating away at you? The mark of the enemy, consecrated to Mimma-Lemnu instead of Belet-Ili as the sacred words decreed? Perverted, twisted, rotting evil flesh, AJ. Feel it?"

AJ's body spasmed, straining desperately against his restraints. A tormented groan escaped from his throat, forced out through clenched teeth. Shaking painfully, he rolled over onto his stomach. The stink of burned flesh suddenly filled the air.

"Oh, shit." I stared in horror.

His black tank top was burning away, and beneath it his skin smoked and blistered in the shape of the enemy's mandala. AJ's groans transformed into an agonized shriek, dragged out for long seconds until at last the burning stopped and he lay still, panting and moaning softly.

The entire back of his shirt was gone, and beneath it his flesh was seared black and raw red.

"Oh, fuck!" Loren stepped back, his hand over his mouth. The stench was horrible. "What the hell did you *do* to him?"

Anna didn't reply, but instead reached out once more and, where her fingertips touched AJ's seared flesh, circles of silver-blue spread like ripples in a pond. As the light spread, his moans grew softer and his breathing slowed. His body relaxed, his head dropping again to the floor.

She stepped back, the light in her eyes fading until she was once more herself. She fell back onto the couch and pulled my coat over her.

"He's okay now," she said. "Roll him over."

We complied. Unresisting, AJ let us raise him to a sitting position. He looked at us with tired eyes. There was no more arrogance in his gaze, only exhaustion and hopeless fear.

"He's going to do it." His voice was laconic and sleep-drugged. "He's opening the gate at the Butte. Sacrificing people from the town. Mimma-Lemnu's coming. He's coming. He's coming. He's coming."

* * *

The moon shone brightly as we prepared to move out, but a mile or two distant the sand still swirled and raged.

Loren and I moved weapons and gear over to Yngwie. As admirable as Beethoven was, he wasn't suited for the kind of cross-country driving that lay ahead. In all honesty, neither was Yngwie—I'd avoided taking the big Camaro out when we'd been here last, but now I was going to risk it.

Frank and Anna carried cases and duffels while Beowulf trotted along, looking at us with concern. Loren had fitted him with his body armor and goggles, and he'd taken them without complaint, as if he knew how serious the situation truly was.

"You should stay here and keep an eye on AJ, Frank," I said, stowing a case of smoke grenades. AJ was free of Dandridge's influence and slept like the dead on the couch. None of us were inclined to bring him along, and Anna had reassured us that he was harmless. "It's going to get bad out there."

I wasn't at all surprised when Frank glared at me defiantly. "Like *hell* I will, Alex." He nodded back at his ruined ranch house. "There's nothing here for me now. Paula's gone five years now, and Emily and Corey are off doing what they want. I couldn't even afford to hire anyone to help me with the cattle and now the storm's killed 'em all." He shifted his gaze back to the towering storm ahead. "I'm sick of living here and I'm sick of standing still. There's a day when you get up in the morning and you look in the mirror and say to yourself 'God damn. What the hell happened to me?' Well, that day came a while ago. You understand what I'm saying?"

Strangely enough, for someone who was young enough to be Frank's grandson, I did understand, probably better than most.

I nodded. "Okay, Frank. I'm with you, always. And if you know any good prayers you should probably say them now."

He laughed at that. "I never took much stock in prayer. I figured God's never done much for me, so why should I bother asking?"

I understood that too. "You need armor, Frank? I've got some spare tactical vests."

He nodded. "Seems sensible to me."

While Loren was getting Frank outfitted, I located Anna. She was sitting quietly, leaning against Arngrim's motorcycle. Frank had found some of his son's old clothes that more or less fit, but I thought she looked a bit odd in rolled-up jeans and an oversized flannel shirt.

"I can see them now," she said as I approached. "I see them as demons and as humans, both at the same time."

"Yeah, I know." I put a hand on her shoulder. "I've been dealing with that for a while now."

"But it's different. I see them both simultaneously, and it just seems... well, normal. And I see something else. Maybe I can see flashes of what they used to be, before everything fell apart and they fought Mimma-Lemnu."

I remembered the brief glimpse I'd had of Arngrim, alone in the grotto, praying.

"What do they look like?"

"They're beautiful." She looked down. "That doesn't even begin to describe what they look like. Otherworldly. Ethereal. And sad. Very sad. Like those stories about war heroes who have to go work as security guards or janitors. They fought and fought and fought for so very long, Alex. But they never really *lived* here. There's still a thread that binds them to their old world, and here they'll never know peace. And even if they want to die, they have to really, really work at it. Arngrim tried and he failed. The one that the *Sebitti* killed—his name was Ulfred. I think that Arngrim envies him."

I followed her gaze to where Arngrim was helping to stow ammunition on the Stryker. His machine stood nearby, flickering between motorcycle and monster as I watched. Since the night when he'd rescued me from Dandridge's mansion, my sympathy for him had been growing, in spite of all the evil he'd done. Now for the first time I began to feel something close to pity.

"Are you sure you can do this?" I asked. "You can close the gate? Stop Dandridge?"

"I think so." Now Anna turned her gaze toward the distant storm. "It's out there. It throbs like an infected wound, like something I want to heal. Remember what I said to AJ? The mark of the enemy, the thing that the Fallen hate so much—it's not evil in itself. It can be consecrated to any purpose—Dandridge is just using it to control people. You were right—when we came close to the gate the energy passed through the symbol and into me because of my connection to the other world. Dandridge did the ritual to consecrate it to Mimma-Lemnu, but it didn't work. Because of my connection to Arngrim, I was able to resist. Now I've connected to something else. We didn't need the ritual—I just needed to be in the right place to make contact with... With Her. With that goddess that the Fallen worship. The one who gave you the sword. I'm connected to Her, too. I can feel Her, but I can't really understand Her or figure out what She is."

"She Who Watches," I said softly. "I don't fully understand either, but I think She's a friend." I glanced at the sword, now back in its place strapped across my back. "She gave us this, and She gave us you. But I'm still afraid for you, Anna. What's this going to do to you?"

She drew a deep breath. "I don't know, Alex, any more than you do. But it's what I've chosen and now I'm stuck with it."

I couldn't have put it better myself.

Before we departed, I returned to the house, where AJ crouched fearfully on the sofa.

"You," I said. "We're going to go do our best to spoil your boss' day. Now that that damned tattoo is gone, your connection to him is broken. You're no use to him."

AJ listened apathetically.

"I'm not sparing anyone to guard you," I continued. "I advise you to get the fuck out of here and never come back."

He nodded silently.

As bad as he was, I couldn't bring myself to hurt him anymore. Maybe leaving him alive was a mistake, but I didn't care. I opened the door, then delivered one last rejoinder over my shoulder. "And I suggest you pray that you never see me or Anna ever again, or you won't like the results."

* * *

The Fallen were assembled in line abreast; over two dozen angry, snorting machines and their grim riders, a vanguard for Yngwie and the Stryker.

I stood beside Yngwie and nodded to Loren.

"So are you coming with me?"

He shook his head. He was clad in tac vest, helmet, and night vision goggles. He carried a complement of grenades, two Glocks and his H&K. I thought about the skinny geek in the office and how much he'd changed.

"Nope. I'm riding with Arngrim."

As if on cue, Arngrim rolled up. His machine was fitted with the sidecar he'd carried during the attack on Dandridge's mansion.

"Mount up, Hodges!" he shouted over the growing roar of engines. "We've a battle to fight!"

Anna embraced Loren before he clambered into the sidecar, then kissed Arngrim on the cheek. The old warrior looked flustered for a moment then smiled.

"Granddaughter." His tone was soft but it still soared over the racket. "You have brought hope and love to a lost soul."

She held him close. "I love you, Grandfather."

"I love you, Granddaughter."

She stepped back, wiping away tears.

I forced back my own tears. "Arngrim."

He looked back. "Yes, Shepherd?"

"Why do we fight?"

"We fight for each other." He looked again at Anna who now stood beside me, and in his eyes I saw a range of emotion that I'd never seen in him before. "And we fight so that those who come after us will have a better world. And those are the only things worth fighting for."

I pulled the sword free and held it up in salute. "Hail, Fallen! The Shepherd rides with you!"

Arngrim nodded and roared away, toward his gathered host. His voice echoed as he went.

"Ride, Fallen! Ride, *Fordæmdur!* The Shepherd rides with us! Day of Vengeance! *Dagur Hefnd!*"

In response, I heard Loren shouting his own exhortation, faint against the crescendo of demonic screams.

"Up, Flamefang! For Melniboné! For vengeance!"

I shook my head slowly. I truly loved the man, but dammit he was weird.

I opened Yngwie's door to let Anna and Beowulf scramble in, and as Frank and I seated ourselves the Fallen took up the cry.

"Ride, the Fallen! Day of Vengeance! *Dagur Hefnd!*"

A chorus of metallic fury, the Fallen's host advanced across the desert, and we followed, into the roiling storm and the land of the enemy.

IX

The road ahead had never seemed so treacherous. Darkness competed with the boiling dust clouds to see which could piss me off the most. We drove behind the Fallen with the Stryker following, and most of the time Yngwie's headlights only reflected off the dust, leaving me alternately blind and swathed in a blanket of darkness.

Beside me Frank grumbled. He was wearing his ubiquitous Stetson which seemed a strange contrast to the Kevlar vest we'd given him. He'd refused a helmet. "Nothing's gonna be worth shit around this place even if we survive. This dust'll ruin everything. My dad told me all about it."

I frowned into the dust, trying to imagine what it had been like. "Did he come through the Dust Bowl?"

"Yeah. He migrated out here in '36. He was hoping for a better life and I guess he got it. For a while anyway." He turned and looked out the window. Almost nothing was visible. "And now... Shit. Now it's all blowing away again. He came here 'cause of the dust and now we're leaving for the same reason, almost eighty years later."

Anna spoke up. She still sounded tired but determined and hugged Beowulf close. "You don't have to give up, Frank. You've lived here all your life. You can't give it up now."

Frank chuckled humorlessly. "Who says I can't, Miss? I've been working practically since I was in diapers and what's it got me? My wife's gone, my kids' have turned their backs on me. Hell. People always talk about how much simpler life is out here, but it's all the same. No matter where you go, it's all the same. The politicians tell you they're in your corner, the preachers tell you to keep praying, but it's all the same. Behave yourself, do everything you're supposed to, work yourself to death and you get jack and shit."

Frank was weary, to be sure. He'd been up for days holding off a horde of monstrosities, so it wasn't surprising that he sounded tired and beaten down. Yet there was something different now—different from the man I'd first met only a few months ago. That Frank had had regrets, but he still had things to live for. Now everything he'd fought to build was gone, and not even his children were here to help him rebuild.

With an uneasy start, I realized that Frank Magruder was getting ready to die.

I focused on the dim red lights strung out ahead of us. Arngrim was there and my friend rode beside him. After centuries of pain and loss, Arngrim had finally found something worth fighting for.

And now, I thought, desperately trying to keep up and to come up with something to say to him, Frank Magruder was dying because he had nothing left.

We rolled through Hayes—perhaps some survivors lingered in hidden places, maybe they'd fled, but now the entire town seemed dead, its buildings dark, windows empty. Like the other abandoned settlements we'd seen, windblown dust was piled up against buildings and the street was thick with it.

"Jesus Christ." Frank mouthed the words, but I couldn't hear him. "Jesus Christ."

"There's still hope, Frank," I said. "They might still be alive."

"AJ said they were going to sacrifice the ones they captured." Anna's voice trembled, but in an instant I knew it was from anger, not fear. I risked a quick glance in the rearview. A faint bluish nimbus surrounded her, and glinted in her eyes and mouth as she spoke.

All canine silliness was forgotten, and Beowulf sat at attention like a soldier beside her, confident in body armor and goggles. I remembered how he had led us down the railroad tracks toward Onatochee's lair, and how he'd stood beside us in the last fight.

Unaccountably, I shivered slightly, thinking of Loren, bloodstained with a gory combat knife clutched in one hand. I'd taken a friend and turned him into a killer. Had I done it to an innocent animal, as well?

Shepherd. The word echoed in my head. *Nomeus. Panigara. Guardian of the Border Stone. You stand in the doorway with a candle, and they stand with you. You made a choice to serve, and they made a choice to stand beside you. You walk the razor's edge, Shepherd, but you do not walk alone.*

I shook my head, blinking away tears. The pain was there again, gnawing at my brain, urging me onward.

Ahead of us the lights of the Fallen peeled off to the right, roaring down Goldfinch Road.

"Here we go," I warned, downshifting and feeling Yngwie's low gear kick in. "It's going to get rough."

My passengers acknowledged silently. We were getting close, and now they were alone with their own thoughts.

The windows were closed, but there was a haze of dust inside the car. I coughed and tried to breathe shallowly, but with each bump and lurch I drew in deep breaths, fearful of what the terrain was doing to Yngwie's undercarriage.

We lurched downward, the Stryker grumbling along behind us.

"Rafferty's place," Frank said. "It looked abandoned when I came out here, but someone had been camping out in it. More of that blood and those letters on the walls."

I made an angry sound. "No surprise there, Frank. Those bastards need this place. If we can stop them here, we might be able to stop them everywhere."

Anna's voice issued from the back seat, deep and resonant, rising up above the wind, the Fallen's demon-machines, the snorting Stryker, and even Yngwie's laboring engine.

"I feel it. The enemy is here. They prepare the way. *Me amalatu babka.*"

Frank was staring at her, but I couldn't take my eyes off the column of tail lights ahead of me—they were my only point of reference as we continued to descend toward the desert floor.

"Holy shit, woman. What the hell are you?"

The blue glow filled Yngwie's interior. As it grew, my doubts and fears seemed to recede and drain away, replaced by warmth and confidence.

"I am Annabelle Lee Moore." She was calm, her voice filling our ears. "Consecrated of Belet-Ili. The Tree with Roots in Two Worlds. I bear the Cage of Demons. I am *Liruti* and *Petua*, Closer and Opener of the Gate. Bear me to the place, Shepherd. *Amelnakru ana simtim Alaku.* The enemy shall go to his fate."

The rearview revealed a figure crafted of blue light, her tattoos shining lines and curves of almost blinding brilliance. The lantern glowed on the seat beside her. Her clothes were gone again—had they simply been consumed by the light, I wondered?

I shuddered again but said nothing. Sure she *said* she was still Anna, but she didn't resemble anything of this world. To my eyes she was a living avatar of the being who had given me the sword and to whom I had sworn service.

Nemesis. Gaia. She Who Watches. Belet-Ili. How many other names did She bear and how many other worlds had She visited?

And what did She *truly* want of me?

The questions spun through my mind as we finally came out on the desert floor, leaving the Sheepshead Mountains behind.

All around us the dust cleared, as if we'd driven into the eye of the storm. The moon and stars shone down from overhead and the flat expanse of the desert was clear. The Fallen redeployed into a single line and slowed to a halt.

"Jesus Christ." Now Frank stared through the windshield, gaping at what lay ahead.

In the distance, Hauser Butte was lit up as if by an angry red sun. Motes of crimson light darted around it, spinning in a disturbing pattern that mimicked the mandala on the Foundation tattoo. In the center, around the stark granite prominence of the butte, the light seemed almost alive, pulsating and heaving, throwing out lambent red tendrils that reached into the air, then faded back into the main mass. The pain in my head suddenly redoubled.

"Behold." Anna still spoke in a deep voice that resounded inside the car, but even so she bore a tone of awe and respect. "The Gate of the Gods. The enemy comes."

A headlamp separated from the line of Fallen riders and Arngrim approached. Loren was still in the sidecar, his face hidden under a Kevlar helmet and a pair of goggles.

I rolled down the window. "What's up, Arngrim?"

He shouted back at me urgently. "Time is short, Shepherd! We must attack now! Are you ready?"

I started to speak, but Anna interrupted me, her voice soaring from the car and filling the air.

"We are ready, *Kussariku*. The enemy will bleed."

Arngrim caught sight of Anna's form, glowing in the back seat, and bowed his head.

"We will avenge our world, Granddaughter. Follow!"

He turned and headed back toward the Fallen.

Loren waved, shouting. "Take good care of my dog!"

I waved back. "No fear, brother! Stay safe!"

Arngrim bellowed an order and as one the Fallen's cacophonous battle-line leapt forward.

The Stryker moved out of column behind me and began to roll after them. Wulfgar sat atop the vehicle, manning the autocannon. He cast me a glance and motioned for us to follow.

"Here we go, folks," I shouted, shifting into gear and letting out the clutch. "Hang onto your hats."

The night was filled with noise and light, from the silvery glow of the moon overhead to the glare of headlights, now free of dust and the shining form of Anna, or whatever she had become, burning brighter as the desert rolled away beneath us.

The voice was back in my head, like Anna's but subtly different, issuing from a being far more ancient and incomprehensible.

Shepherd. Nomeus. Do not fear the darkness.

Hauser Butte grew closer, surrounded by its nimbus of almost-living crimson light. Muzzle-flashes sparked across the scrubland and I saw a few shadowy figures. A circle of mercs was deployed around the perimeter to slow down any attackers, but they hadn't reckoned on the Fallen, who shrugged off the gunfire like men bothered by mosquitoes, stabbing through the defenders like a lance, cutting them down or rolling right over them.

I haven't the strength to resist anymore, Alex. Life's beaten me down too much, I've failed one time too many. You're the one who can resist. I felt it that night, when She came. I know who you are. I know what you are.

Heavier weapons opened up. A pair of machine guns chattered in the night and an explosion burst in front of Yngwie, raining down grit and gravel. A Fallen machine plowed through a fireball, then tumbled end over end, sending its rider spinning, crashing to the hard ground. As we rolled past, he rose, dusting himself off and limped toward his undamaged machine.

I've doubted, I've loved, and I've seen how horrible vengeance is. I've failed. I've lied. I've hurt people. I've hated those I should love. I've hated myself. I've been human.

The butte was closer. All around me the Fallen shifted and changed—now they were armored knights with lances, now gray-clad riders with plumed hats and white gauntlets, now helmeted French cuirassiers armed with curved sabers, now blonde bikers, now demons on snorting monsters once more.

From the butte came the flash of mortar fire, and another pair of explosions buffeted us, each landing on either side less than ten yards away.

Those who have suffered know others' suffering. Those who doubt know others' doubts. Those who have failed know and forgive others' failure. Those who have loved know others' love. Those who have taken vengeance know its sadness. Those who truly know themselves have seen the darkness in their own souls. Only those can serve me, and know what it is to be Nomeus.

Two black Humvees rushed from cover at the foot of the butte. Each had a ringmount and a helmeted gunner—the first opened up with a heavy grenade launcher, the second with an autocannon, blasting great gouges in the desert around the Fallen. The autocannon ripped into a demon-machine, tearing it to pieces and rending the rider. Four grenades exploded amidst a knot of Fallen, and they went flying in different directions.

Will you take the weapon and stand in the doorway? Will you guard this world and all who dwell in it? Will you serve the sacred spiral?

Beside me, the Stryker rushed forward, and Wulfgar triggered the autocannon. Twenty millimeter shells slammed into the lead Humvee and it exploded, shrapnel raining down. An instant later its ammunition cooked off, dozens of smaller blasts tearing up dirt and gravel. The second Humvee tried to pull back, but Wulfgar zeroed in on it flawlessly even as his Stryker bumped and shuddered over the uneven ground, and a moment later it too was burning scrap metal.

We're all human, Alex. All of us. And that's the most powerful weapon we have.

Arngrim had learned what humans fought for and in doing so had become more human himself. Now, amid flames and battle as Frank grunted angrily and the patterns on Anna's skin grew to near-blinding brilliance, I understood too.

Our world was still green and blue and alive—the Fallen's was a ruin of rock and fire. We rode to save one world and avenge another. And the enemy was here.

We serve the sacred spiral. We ride for salvation and vengeance both.

The Fallen had reached the base of the summit and were dismounting. A moment later, we rolled up behind them and slammed to a halt, dust rising.

"Last stop!" I shouted, popping the trunk. "Everybody out!"

Frank complied without a word. He followed me toward the rear of the car as I pulled on my coat and levered open the trunk, arming myself with sword and Glock as Frank grabbed a Colt M14 rifle.

"Nice weapon," he said, slapping in an ammo mag. "You ready?"

I strapped the sword across my back and clipped grenades to my vest. "I'm ready if you are."

He nodded curtly. "Let's move."

Anna stood in front of the car as we came. She was something else entirely now, an ethereal figure of blue light, surrounded by bright dancing motes, silver-blue in contrast to the burning red sparks that filled the air around the butte.

"Alex." For a moment her voice was human again, soft and fearful. "Alex. Please don't leave me. Please stay alive."

I touched her face and my fingertips tingled with static electricity. "I'll do my best, love. Don't you leave us either."

The Fallen were advancing into the rocks. They were all demon now, their old Viking disguise gone. The motorcycles were monsters too, bounding along after their masters. Ahead I saw Arngrim—he was a red-skinned alien thing, but I recognized him nevertheless. Loren waved frantically then raced along after him.

"Follow!" I shouted. "Follow them!"

There were more mercs among the rocks, but the Fallen made short work of them, slicing them apart with black-bladed weapons or gunning them down. It was strange to see demons bearing automatic rifles and pistols, but I was used to strange by now.

A shriek echoed as we scrambled along the trail and a pair of *Shu-hadaku'idim* sprang at Frank, scythes whirling. He'd seen these things before and responded instantly, pumping three quick rounds into each one, knocking them to the ground.

It didn't kill them—they were up again in an instant, shrieking and ravening.

Anna stepped up beside me. Actually she seemed to glide more than step, her feet barely touching the ground.

"Begone," she intoned, and the demon-women screamed with pain, falling back into the rocks, panting and snarling, scythes at the ready. They were hurt, but they were still very much alive.

"They're drawing power from the gate. I can't fully banish them," she said, voice a mix of uncertain human and unearthly goddess. "You may need to fight them."

I drew the sword. "I'm ready. You okay, Frank?"

He nodded. "I already bagged three of those things at the house. Bring 'em on."

Beowulf rushed beside us as we charged, and threw himself at the lead demoness, dodging under her swinging weapon and latching onto her calf, snarling as his fangs tore at her flesh. As she struggled to dislodge him, I swung, slashing through her neck and sending her head spinning away.

Beside me, Frank avoided the enemy's scythe-swing, rolling then springing up, rifle blazing. A half-dozen rounds struck her under the chin, blasting through the top of her head, splashing fiery blood and fragments of bone. Then Beowulf was on her, again ripping at her leg, and I finished her off with a single sword stroke from behind.

Frank and I breathed heavily as we exchanged glances. Before either of us could speak, a torrent of gunfire erupted from the other side of the ridge. Loren appeared a moment later, hurrying toward us, carrying his rifle in patrol ready mode. He was filthy and already looked exhausted, but when he saw us he motioned.

"Come on! You're missing the party!" Beowulf bounded up toward him, panting and grinning. "Hi, boy! Kill lots of monsters?"

Beowulf barked. Another rush of gunfire sounded, along with the fearsome scream of a *Sebitti*.

Loren looked suddenly worried. "Come on! Quick!"

I hurried along, Frank and Anna close behind.

Then we were over the top, looking down on the place where Jack Rafferty and the kids had been opening their gate in the heat of early summer so long ago.

The Fallen were there, blazing away with automatic weapons, hacking with swords and axes, struggling with a horde of *lilitu*, scythe bearers, and scuttling leaping ghouls. The towering form of a *Sebitti* loomed above them, swinging great clawed hands, knocking the Fallen and their beasts aside, crashing down on them with massive hoofed feet, leopard-jaws clashing.

Beyond the battle front was the huge boulder where they'd opened the first portal. Or where it *had* been—now it was a chaotic jumble of flashing red sparks and tangled black tendrils, blurring together and breaking apart, pulsating and quivering to some alien rhythm. And standing nearby was a circle of *Shu-hadaku'idim* and *lilitu*, surrounding a tangled mass of human bodies, lying still on the ground.

As I watched, two men dragged a body from the pile as a third stood over it, raising a knife that gleamed red in the pulsing light and stabbed downward, slicing through the helpless victim's neck. A minute spark of red rose from the twitching corpse and joined the swirling mass of red nearby.

"God damn it!" Frank had seen it too. "What the hell are they doing?"

I glared down the slope, past the struggling demons. It was a hundred yards distant and lit only by the moon, but I recognized the figures—kids from the Couch Park Family, a few mercenaries in black battledress, Father Tom lurching along on his clumsy beast-leg, dragging bodies from the pile and nearby, wielding the knife…

I felt the old rage fill me, the hatred of those things that didn't belong here, that came to kill and consume and destroy, and of those turncoat humans who did their bidding. In my hand the sword glowed brighter, and beside us Anna's skin grew brighter still.

Raising the sword, I rushed down the slope, my voice rising above the din of battle, shouting a single, hateful word.

"Dandridge!"

X

The air was hot, unnaturally so, filling my lungs with almost tangible anger and hostility, resisting my best efforts to expel it. My heart hammered inside my chest, my legs and arms ached, my head screamed in protest, but on I rushed, an automaton, dragged along by the glowing alien thing that now seemed like part of my hand.

The Fallen were ahead, contending with the hordes of scythe-wielding demonesses, pale dog-human monstrosities and winged, scorpion-tailed wolves. Above the fray towered the battle-lord, snarling its deafening metallic snarls and striking down with its titanic clawed fists. Wherever it struck, the earth buckled, sending combatants flying, Fallen and monsters alike.

I dodged as a machine-demon went flying past, shifting between animal and cycle, crashing to earth, bending and breaking, then dragging itself to its feet and rushing back at the enemy. It gathered itself and leaped over the battle line, landing on a scuttling ghoul, crushing it into the dirt, then scrambled forward, metal claws digging into the flesh of the *Sebitti*. The machine-demon clambered up the monstrous leg like an insect, gouging and tearing until the battle-lord swatted it away. It went spinning through the air and disappeared into the fray.

Arngrim and Loren were ahead of me, fighting side by side. Arngrim swung a huge curved black axe, caving in the skull of a scorpion wolf. It yowled and fell, twitching, and Loren was on it, stabbing with his combat knife, sawing through its neck, triggering a gush of hot black blood. For a moment, he stood over the corpse, panting and staring as Arngrim advanced against another foe.

I rushed toward him. "Loren! Dandridge is here! He's sacrificing the people from Hayes!"

Loren nodded. His expression was strange, like the thousand-yard stare of a combat veteran.

"Yeah, I know. Arngrim says he's trying to open the gate before we get to him."

A mass of earth erupted nearby as the towering demon crushed one of the Fallen and his machine.

"We're getting our asses kicked, Alex!" Loren crouched, knife on guard. "Mister fucking Godzilla up there is killing us!"

Arngrim fought on, dismounted, axe whirling. The battle-lord was just ahead of him, rising like an unclean monolith above the field. It looked down and screamed, reaching toward Arngrim.

Arngrim struck at the huge hand as it came at him, nicking its flesh. It drew back, then screamed and aimed a furious foot-stomp at the Fallen leader. It crashed to the ground with another seismic shock; Arngrim dodged, but fell heavily to the ground, struggling to rise.

I looked back. A blue nimbus marked where Frank, Beowulf, and Anna advanced through the carnage. Enemy and Fallen alike fell back before her.

I turned, shouting. "Anna! Help us with the *Sebitti!*"

Her countenance and manner were even more alien than they had been. Despite the blood and death around her, she walked with serene steps, gliding like a ghost, looking up at the towering form of the battle-lord with an almost loving expression.

When it caught sight of her, the *Sebitti* froze in mid-reach, its claws once more extended toward Arngrim.

Anna's new voice echoed across the battlefield.

"*Barra.* Begone."

A cloud of the blue sparks swirled around her and I gaped as she rose into the air, one hand extended, almost as if she was reaching out to caress the great demon.

"*Barra.*"

The sparks shot from her and swirled around the battle-lord, burrowing into it, searing flesh. The demon stumbled ponderously backward, its piercing screams tinged with agony, clawing at its face to rid itself of the burning motes.

Loren pointed up. "Arngrim! Alex! Now! Now!"

Like a rising tide the Fallen around us galvanized into movement.

A metal beast rushed up, bellowing. I recognized it as the one I'd seen before—the one that the *Sebitti* had flung away. Now it was back, its yellow eyes burning with anger.

My synapses were on fire from the otherworldly energy of the sword. In a single motion, I reached out, seizing the creature by one horn and hoisted myself onto its back, settling against its thick sinews as it bounded toward the stricken battle-lord.

Fire blossomed up and down its scaly hide as the Fallen opened up with heavy weapons, but I didn't care. My blood burned and my senses sang, and my mount seemed to dance gracefully across the desert floor, leaping toward the demon's leg, sinking in its claws and again dragging itself up the monstrous body. But now the battle-lord was distracted, stumbling, screaming as gunfire rent its body and Anna's blue motes ate away at its face, searing skin and muscle, leaving burnt flesh and bone.

I held the beast's horn in a one-handed deathgrip, feeling gravity drag me back as it pulled itself up by its claws, higher and higher even though the demon shook and writhed against us.

Closer... The machine-demon ripped its way along the beast's abdomen, leaving black weeping gouges behind, then at last reached its chest. I felt its life energy, pulsing painfully, felt its alienness and its hatred... Its mind was a twisted song of chaotic impulses and aggression—the same thing I'd felt in Onatochee.

It did not belong here. It had to be banished.

I reversed grip on the sword, still clinging to the machine-demon's horn and stabbed down into the greenish, scaled flesh, thrusting the burning blue-white blade below the monstrous ribcage where its heart should have been.

Then the night whirled madly, and I felt myself and my mount flung away once more, dropping sickeningly through space as a deafening shriek of tortured metal and otherworldly agony split the night and slashed across the battlefield.

The rocky ground rushed up, but before we struck, the blue radiance of the sword surrounded us and we crashed heavily to earth, bruised and battered, but alive.

I dragged myself to my feet. Everything hurt, but I was used to that sensation by now.

The machine-beast was on its four feet, shaking its head and snorting.

"Good job, brother," I said, putting a hand on its head. "You okay?"

It nodded. "Yeah, pretty much."

I stared. The voice was deep and guttural but I understood it clearly.

"You can talk?"

It nodded. "Yeah. We just don't normally have much to say." It bared its fangs. Several were broken, but it didn't seem to mind. "Nice job, Shepherd."

"Don't mention it."

Without another word the beast leaped away, bounding across the desert, back toward the battle.

The great *Sebitti* had collapsed and now the Fallen swarmed all over it, hacking and stabbing. Moments later the huge body was still, disintegrating into the same shimmering dust I'd seen at Frank's ranch.

I hastened to follow. Only a handful of defenders remained, falling back now to the inner circle that surrounded the crimson bubble formed by the opening rift.

Arngrim was nearby, splashed with gore. Unlike the other Fallen, he still shifted between human and demon form, and it hurt my eyes to look at him. Loren was beside him, down on one knee, panting while Beowulf looked at him with concern. Frank held his rifle at the ready, gazing at the pulsing red blister a hundred yards distant, and nearby Anna floated a foot or so off the ground, still calm and serene. The blue motes danced around her, forming the outline of wings rising from her back.

"Arngrim!" I shouted. "We've got to move! He'll have the gate open any second now!"

Anna's voice interrupted me, echoing in my head as well as through the burning air.

"We must wait. We must allow him to open the gate before I can seal it."

"Oh fuck." Loren didn't sound too good. "I forgot that part."

Anna didn't reply.

I swore. "He's killing those people! We can't wait for the gate to open!" I pointed forward. "Arngrim! Fallen! Come on!"

I didn't care what Anna wanted now—she was the pawn of something greater. Maybe it was something good, but it was something alien, and it didn't seem to care that Dandridge was killing innocents to open his fucking gate. I was determined to take him down before he could kill more of them.

The surviving Fallen gathered into a single group, flanked by their demon-mounts. There were perhaps a score surviving now, but they moved without hesitation, advancing toward the circle.

Ahead of us, the defending scythe-bearers came on guard, their weapons gleaming in the sick red light of the gate. Inside the circle, two mercenaries seized another victim—I recognized Mary Bolling, the rancher who had lost cattle to the mutilators—and without hesitation Dandridge slashed her throat. She didn't make a sound—thank God they all appeared to be unconscious—but her body twitched and shook as her lifeblood drained away and her red spark rose to join the others.

Dandridge looked different now. His Armani suit was in rags and his face was drawn and haggard, much of his middle-aged good looks sucked away. The arm I had wounded was different—it wasn't even human, but was a black segmented insectile limb ending in a wickedly serrated claw. Apparently Mimma-Lemnu's limb-replacement technology still had a few bugs in it.

We charged into the circle of defenders, swords and axes swinging, guns blazing. The sword still guided me—in a single movement, I shot a scythe-bearer between the eyes then decapitated her, charging over her still-convulsing corpse to engage a pair of *lilitu*.

Undeterred, focused on his task and ignoring us completely, Dandridge dispatched another victim. Around him the remaining mercenaries all looked fearful, clutching their rifles with growing uncertainty.

Loren had armed himself with a sword now, and traded blows with a demoness, ducking and stabbing. His vest was rent in numerous places and I saw blood on his arm, but still he fought, and beside him Beowulf dove in, tearing at the enemy, then falling back before she could strike him. Loren's blade caught her in the midsection, gutting her, but still she fought.

Ten Fallen have perished, but we're still alive, I thought. Why? Why are we still alive?

Exhaustion warred with the sword's mystical energy inside me, driving me on like a zombie, dead but hungry for flesh. The world was red-lit, garish, out of focus.

Ahead of me, the mercenaries had taken up positions around Dandridge, who continued on alone, pulling victims from the pile of bodies and slashing their throats open. Now I saw him with Chet Graham, the mayor who had run the dry goods store before the Walmart opened in Burns Junction. Blood jetted as Dandridge stabbed and hacked with his dagger, black in the harsh illumination of the gate. Dandridge still ignored me, obsessively focused on his murderous task.

Two mercs blocked my way. Out of ammunition, they stabbed at me with bayonets. I shot the first one in the shoulder and swung my sword at the second, knocking the rifle from his hand. He fumbled for a sidearm, but I kicked him in the face and overbore him, yanking his combat knife from its sheath and throwing it away. He stared up at me with wide, terror-filled eyes.

"Looks like you backed the wrong side," I said, voice ragged. "You think?"

He nodded. "Yeah. Please… Please don't…"

I stepped back, my pistol trained on him. He looked as if he was about twenty years old and had no idea what he'd gotten himself into.

"Run," I said. "Run now and don't look back. This is your only chance."

He stared for a moment then turned and dashed away into the sea of struggling combatants. Whether he made it out or not was up to him.

The fight still raged behind me, amid gunfire and screams of the dying, but I felt suddenly alone. A few yards across a short stretch of ground was a slight rise, and atop it stood Roger Dandridge, surrounded by a grotesque tangle of bloody corpses. In his insect claw-hand he held the hair of a young man with a pierced nose and a dirty leather jacket. I recognized him as one of the Couch Park kids, but I didn't remember his name. Dandridge had just finished slitting the boy's throat and dark gore welled up on the already blood-soaked earth beneath him.

A handful of other Couch Park kids huddled near the pile of unconscious townsfolk, trembling and terrified. Father Tom stood over them, orange threads pulsing from his forehead to the tattoos on the kids' backs. The enormity of what they'd done was finally sinking in, but it was too late to turn back now. As I watched, Tom seized a girl by the arm and began to drag her toward Dandridge.

New energy and determination flowed through me and I raised the sword and an incoherent bellow of rage burst from my lungs.

Tom turned at the last moment, dropping the girl's arm, glaring at me with eyes that sparked red.

"*Panigara!*" he shouted. "Motherfucker!"

More red sparks flickered, forming the shape of a fiery blade in his hands, and he met my attack with screaming ferocity. Our weapons clashed together cacophonously, sending up a mass of red and blue fireworks.

"Fuck you, Shepherd!" he growled. *"Usella Mituti Ikkalu Baltuti! Mimma-Lemnu..."*

For several long moments we stood face to face, glaring with mutual hatred. This was another turncoat who had given up his humanity in exchange for promises of power—promises that I knew were empty, that would be forgotten the instant Mimma-Lemnu set foot in our world, but Tom was too far gone to even consider such a thing—after so much booze, so many drugs, so much violence and hatred and neglect... Like all the others he would be pitiful if he wasn't so utterly depraved.

With a heave, I shoved him backwards. He stumbled, falling over the body of the girl he'd seized, crashing to the rocky ground, more sparks flaring.

He was stunned for only an instant, then rolled, trying to get back on his feet. My sword descended, trailing blue light and struck him in the shoulder, sundering flesh and shattering bone and the red sparks fled along with Tom's rattling scream.

I leaped over him, leaving him writhing on the ground. The sword dragged me along, toward where Dandridge stood, dispatching another victim.

"Hi, Roger," I said. "Seen any good cartoons lately?"

He looked up as if seeing me for the first time, his eyes blazing with madness, lit by dancing crimson light. At the sight of me his expression abruptly changed, and he broke into a huge, friendly smile, made monstrous by the blood that covered his face.

"Alex! My God, it's good to see you!" His voice hadn't changed—it was still hale, hearty, and friendly. He spread his arms in welcome—one human, one monstrous. "I never got a chance to thank you for your visit. I have to say that you really brightened the place up, Alex. Everyone is always so grim and serious all the time—you were like a breath of fresh air."

He glanced behind me, where Father Tom lay on the ground, motionless now, his blood soaking the dry earth.

Roger clicked his tongue. "Oh, Tom. It really isn't working out very well is it? Frankly Alex, Thomas was always a big disappointment to me. I think he might have exaggerated a few things on his resume. Do you think you could handle his job? It's yours if you want it."

It threw me. I honestly couldn't tell whether he was yanking my chain or whether he was so far gone that he truly believed what he was saying.

In the end, of course, it didn't really matter; I was through bantering with the bastard. I charged, firing off the last of my Glock's ammo and swinging the sword, letting its energy guide my arm. He was only a few feet away now—one blow would end it all.

Then I felt as if I'd slammed into a concrete wall. My face went numb with the impact and I fell backwards, staggering and falling to my knees.

The red sparks had formed a shimmering barrier between us, and Dandridge looked down on me with a strange combination of sympathy and smugness.

"I take it that's a no. I'm sorry to hear that, Alex. You could have brought a lot to the organization, but I think it's time to close the loop on this deal, don't you?"

I struggled to rise. The old pain was back, worse than before, bearing down on me like an angry foot stomping on a bug. He'd taught his kids to do it, but their attacks were infinitesimal compared to this. Something else pressed down on me, and with growing terror I realized that it could easily crush me. It just didn't want to right now.

Dandridge turned toward the bubbling red glow of the rift and shouted, his voice taking on a keening shriek, like the screams of the *Sebitti*.

"Gatekeeper, open your gate for me! *Ati me peta babka!* Bring forth the *Kadingir! Ana harrani sa alaktasa la tarat!*"

Each word stabbed through my brain like his damned torture machine. My head threatened to explode from the pressure. I felt blood running from my nose and mouth, darkness clouded my vision, swirling angrily, but still I watched.

The rift changed, its lambent crimson color fading to transparency, opening like...

Yes, like a door...

...And beyond it a scene from my nightmare.

Broken plains, streams of molten rock, jagged prominences, a darkly burning sky, and...

And...

And through the gate came the enemy.

Blurred and indistinct through waves of heat and the distortion of the rift itself, it was the horde that had pursued the Fallen, or one very much like it. Black horsemen rode in the lead, wreathed in flames, their mounts the size of trucks, striking sparks upon the stony ground as they went. Behind were rank on rank of *Shu-hadaku'idim* and ragged crowds of ghouls, black as roaches scurrying along the ground. Other things writhed there too—huge snakes soared and twisted in the sky, *lilitu* flew on leathern wings, dark purple clouds flashing with violet lightning moved with purpose and intelligence, iron beasts ten times the size of the Fallen's machine-demons strode along with great spiked towers on their backs, spewing flames. And behind it all, in the distance, tall and fearsome...

I could barely perceive what I saw. Certainly I was the Shepherd, and the weapon I carried granted me senses beyond others, but my mind and heart were still very much human, and humans were probably never meant to gaze on the foul gargantuan glory that was Mimma-Lemnu.

Outwardly he resembled the statues I'd seen—roughly manlike, with four long slender arms and a triangular alien face with three yellow eyes and great sweeping horns like an antelope. But there was far more to him than mere senses could perceive—a palpable aura of doom and despair radiated from him like a cloud, something that I could neither fully see nor comprehend.

This wasn't like Onatochee—he'd been a confusing mass of impulses and extradimensional energy, something incomprehensible that my feeble brain could only guess at. Mimma-Lemnu was a real thing, flesh and blood, infused with horror and unimaginable power. If he set foot in our reality, his very presence would drain all will to stop him, and all humanity would be able to do was cower and hope for mercy.

Now he strode behind a phalanx of demons and monsters, and even with Anna's newly-found powers our handful of defenders seemed utterly outmatched.

In my throbbing brain I once more felt a gentle touch, calming and comforting. It was far off, nowhere near as strong as it once had been, but it was enough to clear my head and focus on what I saw.

Save those you can. It was my voice that spoke in my head this time, not hers. I focused on the words, repeating them to myself, feeling my strength return incrementally as I did so. *Avenge those you cannot. Do not fear the darkness. Shepherd. Shepherd.*

From my constricted throat I formed the words, and with almost blindingly painful effort I forced them out.

"*Nomeus. Panigara. Shepherd.*"

On my feet now, struggling forward, feeling the fell energies from the rift obstructing me, pressing me back. The sword burned like a brand, glowing hotter and whiter as I ground ahead, step by step.

Ahead of me, the first of the horsemen approached the rift. In an instant he'd be through.

"Dandridge." It was almost inaudible, guttural, an animal sound. Ahead of me, he stood, his back still turned, staring in wonderment as his master's legions advanced.

"Dandridge." A step closer now. My arm was like lead, but I raised the sword, gripping it with both hands.

The horseman was only a few feet distant. Black armor wreathed in flames, spikes and chains, an evil helm with two burning yellow eyes staring through the slit, a lance of flames, a snorting demon-horse clad in black iron barding, its coal-black surface crawling with burning yellow-orange spirals and runes, flaming hooves that sparked and burned...

"Dandridge."

I swung back. Invisible hands plucked at me, seeking purchase, but I wore the *aegis,* the shield consecrated by the one who had called me Shepherd. They tore at my face. I felt my skin blister and peel. I smelled the stink of burning hair. My eyes stung and burned.

Suddenly the chains that held my limbs seemed to shatter, as if the forces that held me had finally surrendered, and I shouted, giving voice to the anger and hatred I now felt.

"*Dandridge! Azat Parzillu!* Iron Serpent!"

He whirled, staring in shock, eyes wide at the sound of his ancient name, his insect-arm thrown up in surprise.

"Alex, what..."

The sword moved by itself, whirling through the burning red air, a shaft of blazing white, cutting effortlessly through Dandridge's alien limb and into his ribcage, down through his abdomen and to his hip, sending the master of the Black-Haired Ones falling, collapsing into bleeding pieces.

I felt something rush past me, like a sudden gust of wind, and the pain in my head vanished. From nearby I heard a groan and a scream as the mass of surviving townsfolk began to stir, free from whatever spell Dandridge had cast over them. There were dozens left and they all looked alternately confused and terrified.

The pain was gone, but my body was still a mass of aches and stabbing agony. I sought out the figure of Jane Enriquez, the sheriff—she was still alive, thank God. I shouted as loud as I could, waving frantically.

"Enriquez! Get these people out of here, *now!* Run, for fuck's sake! *Run!*"

Neither the sheriff nor any of the survivors needed further encouragement. As one, without question, the crowd broke up, individuals running, helping each other, or urging others to go. Before she went one of the Couch Park kids, a blonde girl with a shaved, tattooed head, cast me a glance, alternately angry and sorrowful.

"Go!" I shouted. "Get the fuck out while you can!"

Her face softened, and in an instant she was a scared little girl, looking at me gratefully before turning to vanish into red-lit shadows with the others.

From the gate came a sound like stone shattering as the transparent red barrier stretched and disintegrated, and the lead horsemen galloped through, hooves leaving a trail of flames. A moment later another emerged, then a third.

My legs threatened to collapse under me as I turned and made for the place, sword on guard. Its energy was the only thing holding me upright and I moved like a puppet. Despair grew inside me. Dandridge was dead, but he'd achieved his master's goal—the gate was open and the enemy's vanguard was through. Was it too late? And where the hell was Anna?

"Dagur Hefnd! Day of Vengeance!" The shout cut through the night, and Arngrim was there, afoot and covered in blood from head to toe. He was human again—a vision of the Æsir at Ragnarok, swinging his black axe at the lead horseman. The flame lance stabbed at him, but disintegrated as it touched his chest, then the axe's blade chopped into the horse's armored neck, sending it tumbling, falling in a wreck of tormented metal and flesh.

More Fallen surged toward the gate as it continued to disgorge riders. The wounded machine-demon that I'd ridden against the battle-lord raced up, pulling down a rider in a tangle of metal and spikes and chains and blood.

A series of explosions cut through the riders as Wulfgar opened up with the Stryker's autocannon. The horsemen crumpled and fell, one after the other in the face of the Fallen's onslaught. In their world, they may have been invincible, but here they were bound to the laws of earth, and vulnerable to the weapons of man. But even as their vanguard collapsed, more and more surged through, and the ground around the gate became a chaotic nightmare of chopping, hacking weapons, blazing guns and flames. Horsemen, ghouls, scythe-bearers and *lilitu* fell by the score, hacked and bloody, but still they came. The Fallen fought tirelessly, cutting down scores of enemy, but even they were beginning to fail, their ranks dwindling in the face of overwhelming numbers.

"Alex!" It was Loren. He looked badly hurt—his face was bruised and swollen. He held a sword in his right hand, but seemed too weak to use it. Beowulf ran up behind him. His body armor was gone, and he limped along, his front leg held up painfully.

"Jesus." I leaned against a rock, still trying to muster up the strength to wade into the fray and try to turn back the enemy, even as more poured through the gap. The sound of metal and bellowed war-cries was almost deafening. "Are you okay?"

It was a stupid question of course, but Loren nodded. "Right as rain. Where the hell is Anna? Isn't she going to close this fucking thing?"

I scanned the field—she was nowhere near. Then I looked back into the darkness behind us.

"There! Look!"

Silver light glowed among the tumbled rocks, and a moment later Frank emerged, leading the shining figure that both was and was not Annabelle Lee Moore.

I waved, shouting. "Anna! Frank! Here!"

Frank saw me and hastened over. Anna came on at a more leisurely pace, her feet a few inches above the ground, gliding serenely toward the fray where black horsemen and scythe-bearers contended with the remaining Fallen. Half of Arngrim's warriors and their beasts lay slain, but they had already accounted for hundreds of the enemy.

Unfortunately, I'd seen what lay beyond the gate, and there was easily enough there to overwhelm even the Fallen.

"Jesus Alex, you look like shit," Frank said.

"You don't look so great yourself," I replied. He was almost as battered and bloody as we were. His rifle was gone and in its place he carried one of the Fallen's black swords.

He forced a tired smile. "It's nothin', Alex. Hell, they just mussed my hair a little."

"Shit." Loren pointed. "She's doing it, Alex."

I looked. Anna stood back from the fray, her body now transformed into a silver-blue statue, holding the lantern aloft. A sphere of whirling sparks issued from the lantern, and she began to rise into the air—six feet, ten feet, twelve...

The lantern shone brighter and the sphere expanded and as it did, it sent the enemy reeling, staggering, falling, to be cut down by the surviving Fallen.

And something strange happened to the Fallen as well—as the lantern's light illuminated them, their bodies shifted and changed, transforming from red-skinned horned demons into angelic figures, inhumanly beautiful, with graceful white wings, then flickering back to their Viking forms, to demons and back into angels.

See what they gave up, I thought. *See them as they once were.*

Anna's voice rose, and the battlefield grew quiet.

She held the lantern aloft and it flared like a nova. "Behold me, gatekeeper. *Me amelatu!* Seal this gate for all time! *Babka darisam liru!* Awaken, goddess! *Ilati Negeltu!*"

Each syllable rang and resonated, striking the legions of the enemy like a hammer. Horsemen and scythe-bearers were lifted up and thrown down to the ground, flopping like dolls and dissolving into shimmering dust. The rift flickered and flashed, blue motes chasing red around it in a growing cyclone. Dust rose and the wind began to pluck at my clothing.

In an instant I saw what was happening. "Oh shit! Hang onto something!"

Loren and Frank stood frozen as the wind grew to a howling gale, rushing from the dusty desert into the still-yawning gate. Beowulf whined and looked nervously at Loren.

I grabbed Frank by the shoulders and shook him. "For fuck's sake, Frank! We've got to get..."

Before I could finish, a wall of grit struck us, bowling us all over, sending us sliding across the ground, inexorably pulling us toward the collapsing rift.

I struggled to maintain my grip on the sword and heard myself shouting over the wind.

"Jesus Christ! Anna! Stop! Anna! *Anna! Stop it!*"

For all the good it did, I might as well have been shouting at the moon. Anna too glided toward the gate, blown along with the dust as all around us the howling gale picked up dirt, rocks, corpses and the still-living forms of the Fallen, drawing them in like iron filings to a magnet.

My voice rose to an incoherent scream as the wind lifted me up and I sailed helplessly along, tumbling, falling, twisting, and the familiar desert vanished, replaced by red-lit, burning rock. Anna's shining body was at the center of the storm, carrying along everything that wasn't attached to the earth in a whirling, titanic mass. Fallen spun on the wind, helpless for all their strength, along with corpses of their fellows and those of the enemy that had not yet collapsed into dust. I saw the big shape of the Stryker, pulled along as effortlessly as the rest of us.

Then the near-solar light of the lantern plunged through the gate and vanished, its brass rivets popping, the entire device flying into pieces. I saw tangled masses of darkness, flecked with specks of bright light emerging from the wreckage—the demons it had held were escaping their prison at last.

Behind us, the gate winked out, vanishing into red-black shadow, and abruptly the wind stopped. I felt myself falling, and this time the sword's energies did not slow my descent. With numbing force, I struck the ground, and an instant later a crushing weight fell across my legs and lower body, trying to drive me into hard, burning rock. I felt bones break, and my brain struggled to deal with the sudden onslaught of pain and injury. There was a roaring in my ears, the world was a red-lit blur, and after a moment even it began to fade, vanishing under a blanket of numbing, unthinking darkness.

XI

Consciousness returned only with difficulty, stabbing through the fog of uneasy shadow that covered me. When at last I managed to hold onto a spark of awareness and drag myself back, I suddenly wished I hadn't.

We were on a rocky rise in the middle of a burning, endless plain. In the distance rose craggy mountains that belched fire and magma, streaming down their slopes to form a vast branching network of burning rivers. The sky was black with smoke, and a red sun shone through only feebly. The air smelled of ash and the scent of seared flesh burned in my lungs.

We were on the other side of the gate. Mimma-Lemnu's world, the place of burning that I'd seen in my dreams.

I was pinned beneath the huge form of an armored demon-horse and its rider, and clutched the sword in an unconscious deathgrip. I couldn't feel my legs and the thought that I might lose both of them even if I survived briefly flashed through my mind.

Some Shepherd I'll make rolling around in a wheelchair. The thought was mad, incongruous, fearing for the future when the present was such a horror.

Battle raged around me. There were few Fallen left, maybe a dozen or so. Only one or two of the machine-beasts still fought, the rest lay sundered and bloody. Overhead, great flying snakes coiled and slid along the winds, periodically vomiting gouts of flame at the ground. Black clouds churned, lightning spearing down into the battle below. In the distance the towering metal behemoths advanced slowly like nightmarish armored elephants, spewing fire and smoke.

A Fallen warrior leaped from the ground, rising up like a soaring bird to land on a flying snake's back, stabbing and cutting with his sword, sending them both writhing to the ground in a burst of angry flames. Beside them lay the wreckage of the Stryker, on its side and burning, and lying motionless in the gunner's position was the body of Wulfgar.

Metal clanged from a few yards away, and I heard a familiar voice shouting. In their red demonic forms Arngrim and Gunnar stood back to back, holding off a rush of enemy warriors. As I watched, a scythe-bearer rushed up and Gunnar struck, cutting it in half. In its death throes, the demoness lashed out, catching Gunnar in the neck, nearly decapitating him. His great red-skinned body collapsed to the ground.

He'd been our friend. The only one of the Fallen I'd liked from the start. I wanted to feel sorrow, anger, and loss, but my body refused to cooperate, endeavoring to simply stay alive.

The clash of weapons rang uncomfortably nearby. Straining to look over the bulk of the fallen horse, I saw Loren engaged in close combat with one of the armored warriors while Beowulf darted around its legs, barking and snarling, his broken paw held gingerly as he leaped this way and that.

The warrior was unhorsed and its armor was battered, but it moved with mechanical precision, swinging a great sword that gleamed green-black like obsidian. Loren blocked the blow with his scavenged Fallen sword, then jammed the blade in beneath the warrior's helm and stabbed upward. Black vapor spewed from the rent, and the armored creature stumbled, collapsing to its knees, and finally disintegrating into a pile of rusting metal.

I shouted feebly, waving to Loren. He was a mess—bloody with one arm hanging limply, his sword held weakly in the other. But he continued to fight, battering away the assault of a ghoul, pressing it back and chopping off an arm. Beowulf leaped, overbearing the thing and tore its throat out.

"Loren," I mumbled, my voice cracked and tired. "Loren. Jesus."

"You want him, bastards?" The shout came from only a few feet away. I twisted back, feeling my injured legs ache dully, and glimpsed a pair of pointed western boots projecting from torn, bloody blue jeans. I craned my neck, looking up. Frank Magruder stood over me, sword in hand, slashing and stabbing as enemy after enemy threw themselves at him.

"You want him?" he demanded again as a *Shu-hadaku'idim* swung at him. He blocked the blow and stabbed her through the throat. "Come and get him!"

"Frank..." My voice was too weak for him to hear me. "Frank, get away... Don't..."

He didn't hear. He was covered in blood, some of it his own, but most of it his foes. He stood, legs apart, sword on guard, swinging and whirling as if he had been born with it in his hand. He was more warrior now than I'd ever been, fighting with only a scavenged sword in defense of a man he barely knew.

How? How does he know what to do? Frank Magruder, Oregon rancher, holding off the enemy hordes like Conan the Barbarian...

It didn't matter now. We were in the enemy's world now. Their gates were closed, the high priest slain, and the lantern destroyed. They attacked us with the fury of the damned, denied their rightful destiny, at least for the moment.

Beyond the knoll where the Fallen fought and died, the enemy stood above the battlefield like the Colossus of Rhodes, towering even above the armored behemoths. Despair still rolled from him in waves, but it no longer seemed to affect me. He gazed down at us with an inscrutable expression, not deigning to join the fray, but allowing his minions to dispatch the impertinent enemy.

I felt anger radiating from the monstrous demon-god, but confidence also. We'd closed this gates, but he could open others. He was impossibly ancient and impossibly patient. Our attack had delayed his triumph, not thwarted it.

And now we were doomed.

Unless...

In the sky a point of light grew, the radiant blue counterpart to Mimma-Lemnu's angry red.

She hung there, quiet and detached in a great oval of light, untouched by the violet lightning that the storm-demons unleashed against her. She was more Belet-Ili than Anna now, tall and unearthly, winged and radiant.

Her voice echoed in my head, softly speaking in a hundred languages at once, some familiar, some utterly alien.

I am stronger here, Shepherd. In your world I could only act through others like you, but here I can share the spirit of another, one who has been consecrated, and who had roots in both worlds... Here, I can do this...

Overhead, the circle of light that surrounded Anna exploded silently, bursting out in all directions, rolling across the land like a wave, and where it struck the creatures of the enemy they fell, melting into the burning ground beneath them. *Shu-hadaku'idim* and *lilitu* scampered away but were overtaken, torn into burning pieces and scattered. Ghouls fell, shrieking and convulsing. In the distance one of the behemoths tottered, stumbled and fell, exploding in a black and orange inferno as a second crawled to a stop and collapsed on its knees, motionless and inert.

The demons who fought us fled or were destroyed. A demon-wolf vanished in mid leap as it threw itself at Frank. His sword swung through empty air, sending him off balance and making him stumble. Loren had fallen and the scythe bearer who had struck him down was still contending with Beowulf when she too dissolved into nothingness.

"Loren!" My voice was weak. "Loren! Talk to me, Loren!"

He stirred feebly, waving an arm as Beowulf licked his cheeks, then looked at me, his jowly face a mask of concern.

The field nearby was littered with enemy corpses. Of the fallen, only Arngrim and three others still stood on the field, black with gore, breathing heavily. He was in human form, but his three fellows wore their demon bodies, staring reverently up at Anna. Then Arngrim fell to his knees, followed by the others.

"Belet-Ili!" he shouted. "We have failed you, mother of us all! Look down on your Fallen children and have mercy!"

Frank stepped back and collapsed against the bulk of the fallen warhorse. He looked down at me wearily. He seemed frail now, the lines on his face deeper. It was as if he had just expended the last energy in his body to defend me.

"You still alive?"

I nodded. "Barely. Thank you, Frank."

"Just doin' my job, Alex."

I pointed my chin toward Loren. "See if he's okay."

Frank nodded and hastened over to Loren's side, stopping to give Beowulf a quick hug.

On the plain below, a swathe of bare stone appeared, free of enemy warriors forming a broad corridor between us and the mountainous shape of Mimma-Lemnu. On either side, the legions of the enemy milled in confusion and fear, their ranks collapsing into chaos.

For an instant, I felt something besides despair radiate from the great demon-king, something that was unfamiliar to him.

I felt surprise and fear.

Anna hovered above me, almost close enough to touch.

The enemy is vulnerable, Shepherd. You must use the weapon. You and my Fallen can return the enemy to the darkness. Go now.

I waved at the horse that lay across my legs. "Are you fucking kidding? I'm trapped and I can't walk five feet. I'm human, and I have fragile bones, remember?"

She seemed surprised and rose up a foot or two.

Shepherd?

I struggled, trying to pull myself free. The pain in my legs grew brighter and more piercing, throbbing and pulsating. "I can't move, goddamn it! I can't even fucking crawl!"

The goddess who lived in my friend's body seemed puzzled, as if She didn't fully comprehend human frailty.

Along the bare corridor of stone, Mimma-Lemnu advanced on us, moving a quarter mile with each stride, his hoofed foot crashing to the ground and shattering stone as he did. Magma welled up where he walked, and behind him the mountains began to belch forth more fire and soot. The streams of glowing lava grew to floods, bursting their banks and overflowing.

Confusion and doubt spread from Anna, replacing the gentle comfort I'd felt.

Shepherd, you must.

"I fucking *can't*, you stupid alien!" I gestured with the sword. "Go find someone else to carry this thing!"

Peace again radiated from Anna, falling over me like soft rain.

Be at rest, Shepherd. You do not walk alone.

As I struggled to comprehend what She meant by that She spoke again. She moved, floating toward where Loren lay.

Francis Magruder.

Kneeling beside Loren, Frank looked up in sudden surprise. "What?"

You sacrifice to no gods, you bow to no king, you obey no chief, you offer no tribute.

Suddenly I remembered what Frank had said to me.

I never took much stock in prayer. I figured God's never done much for me, so why should I bother asking?

Anna continued to speak with the voice of a goddess. *In each world, I may choose only one. One Shepherd to stand for all. Called by many names, wielder of my weapon, bearer of my aegis, rider of my dark steed.*

Oh, God. Frank...

Will you take the weapon and stand in the doorway? Will you guard this world and all who dwell in it? Will you serve the sacred spiral?

Frank Magruder, Oregon Rancher. All his life, depending only on himself, unbowed, unwilling to trust either king or priest. His words returned to me.

No matter where you go, it's all the same. The politicians tell you they're in your corner, the preachers tell you to keep praying, but it's all the same. Behave yourself, do everything you're supposed to, work yourself to death, and you get jack and shit.

Frank stood, staring open-mouthed. In the air between him and Anna, the image of the sword was forming, a gleaming framework of darting blue sparks.

"I don't…" He faltered. "Jesus. I don't know… What do you want from me?"

Serve the spiral, Francis Magruder. Bear my weapon. Stand for this world and its people.

For what was probably the first time in decades, Frank Magruder was at a loss for words.

"Frank!" I shouted and my chest hurt. Fuck, had I broken my ribs again? "Frank, listen to her!"

He turned toward me, and in his eyes I saw a lifetime of sacrifice and disappointment, decades of sadness hidden away deep inside a weary soul.

"Alex?" His voice trembled. "Alex, I don't know what to do."

The same fear had tormented me when She had first offered me the sword. That time I had failed. I didn't want to lay the same burden on Frank that I had borne ever since, and the pain and loneliness that came with it. But as the ground shook once more and the enemy moved another step closer, I realized that we had no choice.

"Take it, Frank! Take the sword!"

Deliberation filled Frank's weary eyes, banishing fear and hesitation. He turned back to Anna and reached up, his fingers touching the sword's hilt and his voice rang out across the shattered plains.

"I'll take it."

Light flared, a blue-white star raging between the two beings, goddess and champion, growing to encompass them both.

I name you Nomeus. *Shepherd. Panigara. Guardian of the Border-Stone. Stand in the doorway and do not fear the darkness. Save those you can. Avenge those you cannot.*

For a moment, I was blinded, and when the glare finally cleared, Frank Magruder stood in the light of Anna's radiance, a dazed look on his face, a sword clasped in one hand that was twin to my own.

It was indeed Frank Magruder, but he was different. His hair was dark, his face unlined, his body that of a man of twenty, lean and agile—just the type that I could imagine bounding about on stage with a Les Paul Special, screaming out Motley Crüe covers. But when he looked at me his eyes were still those of the old Frank Magruder, weary and wise, but also bright with the realization that he had been given something that no one else had.

Frank Magruder had been given a second chance.

Again, the ground leapt up beneath us, sending painful shockwaves through my injured legs. Hey, at least I could feel them. Nearby Loren groaned as Beowulf licked his face.

"Fuck, Alex, why does this keep happening to me?" His voice was frail, but the Loren I knew and loved was still there.

"Because you run in and start shooting like a dumbass," I replied. "You really have to be more careful with yourself, dude."

He nodded. "Point taken." He rose painfully to his feet. "Frank, you look different."

Frank didn't reply as another shock rumbled through the ground. Mimma-Lemnu was only a few hundred yards distant, his monstrous form filled the sky, a mountain poised to fall upon us.

Anna rose into the air, a bubble of pure shining light illuminating us all.

Shepherd. My Kussariku. The enemy comes.

Without a word, Arngrim and the Fallen were on their feet. From the rocks nearby emerged a single machine-demon, and I recognized the wounded one that I had ridden. As Arngrim mounted up, it transformed into his old motorcycle, roaring angrily, and the other Fallen rose into the air with slow, graceful wingbeats.

Arngrim's gaze sought us out, and at the sight of Frank, standing with sword in hand, he nodded as if the rancher's transformation was the most natural thing in the world.

"Come, *Hirdir!*" he shouted. "Our vengeance is at hand!"

Frank looked over me and Loren, his face a mixture of hope and fear.

"Alex, I sure as hell hope I don't screw this one up."

"If a loser like me can do it, you can too, Frank!" My throat was raw and my broken ribs stabbed at me as I shouted. "Get going!"

He grinned at that and nodded once decisively. Then he scrambled down the slope, mounting up behind Arngrim. The roaring demon-mount shot away, straight ahead, leaving a trail of glowing molten rock down the middle of the corridor that Anna had cleared. Above them the three surviving Fallen flew on the burning winds, their once-black swords now shining with white light.

Loren and I were on the sidelines for once. Anna rose higher into the sky, darting toward Mimma-Lemnu, a firefly attacking the leviathan. A crackling, static sensation filled the air, and from the bodies of the slain Fallen, lines of blue light appeared, connecting them to Anna's shining sphere, swirling around her in a familiar spiral shape, spirits rising in union with their creator.

No sin is so great that it cannot be redeemed by sacrifice. You are redeemed, my Kussariku.

Mimma-Lemnu saw her and threw open his mouth, revealing a double-row of wicked fangs and a black, shiny tongue. Clouds of black smoke and a deafening braying sound emerged, rolling across the landscape, disintegrating the stone, sending up geysers of glowing lava. On the plains, the surviving legions were swallowed up in a sea of yellow-orange and a wave of unbearable heat washed over us, singeing my already-burned skin. Below us, molten stone welled up, and in a few moments we were on an island in a burning sea.

The corridor between us and Mimma-Lemnu remained clear as Frank and Arngrim roared down it, the tide of fire lapping at its fringes. The flying Fallen swooped down, slashing with their swords. As they drew closer a bolt of jagged lightning exploded from Anna's bubble, crackling around Mimma-Lemnu's massive triangular head, searing his flesh as she'd burned the *Sebitti*.

He shrieked, and the sound ground the stone around us to dust. A granite outcropping nearby disintegrated, falling into the bubbling magma that surrounded us.

"This is getting bad, Alex." Loren struggled to push the dead demon-horse's body off me with his good arm. "Fuck, this asshole is heavy."

I couldn't help much, neither could I give him much encouragement. Our little island was getting smaller by the moment.

Now the Fallen whirled around Mimma-Lemnu's head like enraged crows, cutting and stabbing. Black wounds sprang open on the demon-lord's face, his jaws snapped ponderously as they passed. He snatched at them with four titanic clawed hands and caught one, swatting him out of the air like a mosquito, sending him flying into the sea of lava.

Melted stone flowed around Mimma-Lemnu's feet as he strode toward the stone road down which Arngrim and Frank raced.

Anna's voice echoed in the distance.

Shepherd! Use the weapon! Break the enchantments that protect the enemy!

The words rang loudly in my head, but they must have rung even more loudly for Frank. Small in the distance, Arngrim's cycle raced up a craggy slope at the end of the stone road and leapt into the air, rising as if propelled by a rocket. Frank's sword shone blindingly as he sprang from his seat behind Arngrim, flying through the air toward Mimma-Lemnu's great elongated head and three burning eyes.

He struck squarely between them, the burning blade vanishing as it plunged into the monstrous skull, eliciting another deafening shriek.

The demon stumbled, falling down to one knee, then tottering over like an impossibly huge tree, splashing into the lava, his flesh rent and vulnerable, the molten stone searing him to the bone.

Only Arngrim remained, his machine plunging down to land upon the demon's heaving chest, transforming back to demon-shape as it did, claws sinking into now-vulnerable flesh. Then he was out of the saddle, black blade plunging into the center of Mimma-Lemnu's chest, catching, and ripping down, sending up a geyser of yellow-black blood. At the demon-king's throat, Frank swung his sword, and more blood gushed out.

"Perish, enemy!" Arngrim's shout echoed across the burning yellow sea. *"In the name of the Fallen!"*

Then all was still. The titanic corpse began to sink into the sea of molten rock, the tiny forms of Frank, Arngrim and his mount still clinging to it.

"Hey dude." Loren sounded terribly worried despite our victory. "Did we just win or are we gonna die?"

"Maybe both, brother." The heat from the rising tide of lava was fearful, and it was only a few feet away, lapping up like friendly waves at the seashore. I was trapped and couldn't move, and there was nowhere to run in any event. Beowulf stood beside me, holding up his wounded paw and whining.

Her voice was in my head once more.

Shepherd of earth. What was hidden shall be revealed. Let my Kussariku's sacrifice heal their world.

I felt a sudden tension in the air, like static electricity before a thunderstorm.

"My God." Loren's voice was hushed and, for once, free of anything resembling sarcasm. "Look, Alex."

Across the land around us, wonder unfolded.

Blue light radiated from Anna where she floated in the sky and spread out like a pool of water. In the light, I saw the reflections of the Fallen, and felt their presence. When it touched the stricken land below, the light changed, and burning stone transformed into gentle green and gold.

From this land you came, my Kussariku. And to it you return, to live forever in peace.

All around our little island, the heaving sea of yellow-orange solidified into hills and ravines of dark granite or rich dark earth. Shoots and seedlings began to grow, rising up as if in time-lapse photography, into plants and trees that were at once strange and familiar, spreading faster and faster. Trees were multi-branched, delicate, with multicolored flowers and leaves of red, green, and gold. Plants and shrubs bloomed in a rainbow of strange colors, violet puffballs and fungi popped up in bunches, long thin leaves waved in a cool breeze that banished the furnace-heat of Mimma-Lemnu's realm, other plants sprang forth like striped parasols.

In the distance, the angry mountains calmed and grew cold, snow springing forth, and the great falls of lava transformed to rushing blue water, spreading across the healing land. Overhead the sky cleared, black clouds dissolving, replaced by white billows lit by a greenish-white sun.

"I'll be damned," I said softly. "She will reveal what was hidden."

Vast forests spread across the golden-green landscape and from them rose slender towers. Buildings appeared along the winding rivers, and from the trees issued flocks of flying creatures—colorful avians with multiple wings and long, flexible tails. Small creatures crept from concealment, things like foxes and badgers, and green-and-black striped deer with elaborate antlers and soft black eyes.

I felt the ground around us rising. As it shifted, the horse's corpse grew lighter, and collapsed into dust, melding into the rich black soil beneath me. There was a stab of pain as it did and I saw my right leg bent back unnaturally. Then the sacrificed Fallen's life-force passed through me; broken bones drew back together, moving without pain to a normal position, sore and tortured but whole once more.

White columns rose around us, and a domed roof appeared over our heads, woven of light that solidified into pale stone. A shining polished floor coalesced out of raw rock, leaving us on a curved balcony that rose higher into the air. Gold and green spread out in the distance, the black shapes of forest rising from nothing, along with more buildings.

Loren helped me to my feet, and Beowulf trotted along, his broken leg healed. I was still sore as hell and used the sword for support as I hobbled to the stone railing. Below us the world continued to grow and mend. From a nearby cluster of buildings, I saw a group of figures emerge, tall and slender, clad in colorful silken robes. They were outwardly human, but with flat, almost expressionless faces and large black eyes. Their skin was pale violet, and they looked about themselves in frank, undisguised wonder.

"Alex?"

I looked toward the voice. Frank was approaching, bearing the sword in one hand. He was uninjured, his wounds healed by the same power that had fixed my leg, but looked as exhausted as Loren and me. Arngrim and two Fallen strode behind him. He still looked like a Viking biker, but his companions were now back in their old form—tall, sculpted bodies with graceful white wings, their hairless flesh pale violet like the creatures in the cities below, sexless and alien, but beautiful nonetheless.

"My God, Frank." I threw my arms around him. At this point I was willing to risk a punch in the mouth, but he returned my embrace with enthusiasm. "My God. What have we done?"

"You have helped restore our world," Arngrim said, his voice quiet and humble. "When Mimma-Lemnu burned, Belet-Ili preserved, hiding the land in another place, frozen in time and safe from the enemy, concealing its energies inside the *Kussariku*, awaiting their sacrifice to bring it forth once more." He strode to the railing and gazed down. "Now the Fallen live again, their spirits nourishing a world reborn."

A shining blue light heralded Anna's approach. She glided through the air and alighted on the balcony beside us.

"It is done," she said. Her voice was fading back to mortal levels, and the light that surrounded her grew softer, revealing more of Anna's body. Her wings vanished, melding back into her flesh. "My *Kussariku* are *Fordæmdur*—Fallen—no longer. Their sacrifice has restored their world and sent the enemy back into darkness. No more will he threaten this land."

Arngrim and his fellow *Kussariku* dropped respectfully to their knees. Frank seemed about to do the same, but I stopped him with a hand on his shoulder.

"No," I said. "We don't kneel."

Anna turned her eyes on me. "Nor should you, Shepherd. Your faith is in all living things, not a single being, and your duty is to guard against the darkness. Frank Magruder, this world needs heroes. Will you serve it as Shepherd?"

Frank glanced at me, and I marveled at his face, young and vital but also quiet and wise.

"It's your call, Frank. You always have a choice."

Frank looked back at Anna then nodded gravely. "I will."

Anna turned to Arngrim and his two angelic companions.

"What would you do, Arngrim of the Fallen? You too have a choice."

Arngrim raised his head.

"I will return with the Shepherd of Earth, mother of all. I will live as a man and do no harm. I will be a father to the one who redeemed me, and no more will I fight, no more will I take human life. I will only work to save life, and do penance for my fourteen centuries of blindness. This I will do in the name of all those Fallen who gave their lives in your name."

Anna nodded and seemed pleased. "And so it shall be, Arngrim, Fallen no longer." She addressed the other two. "Tjorkill and Sæmund, will you remain here and aid the Shepherd in defense of this world?"

"We shall," they said in unison. "We will not fail in our charge again, mother of us all."

Anna turned back to me. She was almost herself again. Her voice was the same one that I'd first heard on a rainy night in a sleazy bar, months ago.

"We're going home, Alex. All the other gates are closed and locked. Mimma-Lemnu's armies on earth were destroyed when he fell. At dawn, one last gate will open, and we'll go back."

I nodded. "Good."

The last of the luminance faded and Anna stood there, naked, human, and vulnerable. I took off my coat and put it around her shoulders.

"You did all this, Anna. You're the best of all of us."

Loren hastened up and put his arm around her. "We love you, Anna."

It was a simple statement of truth, and I let it stand.

She looked first at Loren, then at me.

"I love you too."

We stood together on the balcony for a long time, watching as the newly-born inhabitants of the world wandered about in a daze, awake from an impossibly long nightmare. Lights twinkled from their exotic, onion-domed buildings as the sun sank below the horizon. In the forest, insects danced, sparkling in multiple colors like earthly fireflies, and the cries of night birds echoed across the newly-reborn canyons and rivers.

Time didn't seem to pass at all as we watched the night unfold and felt the cool breeze of a new world. We were still standing there when sunlight paled the sky and mist crept from the rivers and birds sang in the forest below.

It was dawn of the first day.

***

The passage back shimmered on the balcony, soft blue and green and so unlike the monstrous wound that the Foundation had opened on Hauser Butte. The green-white sun crept over the horizon. Strange cries cut through the chill morning air.

Frank and I stood together, gazing out at the winding river below, and the exotic spired city that rose beside it. Lights were coming on all across it and I saw tiny figures moving.

"They'll be here soon, Frank," I said. "Your people. Are you ready?"

Frank chuckled. His voice was younger too but his words were still the old Frank. "Hell no I'm not ready, Alex, but what can you do?" He held out his sword, gazing at it in fascination. "Sometimes you just have to use the tools you're given."

I watched a flock of four-winged birds flitter out of the mist, shining red and gold. "This is your world now, Frank. I envy you."

"You sure you don't want to stay, Alex? I could use the help."

I agreed. He'd meet them soon—those beautiful violet-skinned beings who had built their cities, whose lives had been torn apart by Mimma-Lemnu and his legions. He'd learn who they were, what they believed, how they spoke. He'd learn their stories and their songs and their fears, and he'd learn to be their friend.

Part of me wanted to stay, to see these new beings, to learn with Frank and to see his story unfold. But in my heart I knew that I shouldn't. I was bound to the earth and it to me. And so were Loren and Anna, now inexorably tied to the Shepherd and his work. I thought of all that had gone before, of Michael and Trish, of the people of Hayes and the Couch Park kids, now scattered and lost. I thought of Damien—how amazed and delighted he'd have been to see light shining in a dark cosmos.

"No, I can't," I said at last. "Only one Shepherd per world, remember? This is your world, and the earth is mine."

Frank laughed again. "I don't even know what this damned place is called."

"You will, Frank. And they'll all know your name soon."

"Hey, guys!" Loren's voice echoed from nearby, accompanied by an impatient whine from Beowulf. "You going to stand there sightseeing all day or are we going to go *home?*"

I turned. "Jesus, Loren. You finally get to be Buck Rogers and see a whole new world and now all you want to do is go home?"

He grinned. "Oh yeah. This place is beautiful, but I don't think I could ever get used to living in a world that looks like a prog-rock album cover."

"That's our Loren," Anna said. She was still bundled in my coat and my guess was she wanted to get back someplace where the clothes actually fit her. "Always putting things in perspective."

Arngrim stood beside the gate, gazing back at Frank.

"Serve this world well, Shepherd," he rumbled. "Do not fail as we failed."

"Don't worry," Frank shot back. "I'm here for the duration."

"It is good, Shepherd. I will remember and honor your name for as long as I endure on the earth, Frank Magruder."

"Same back to you, Arngrim. You take care now."

There was a motion in the shadows between the graceful white stone columns, and a bulky figure emerged, limping on four massive clawed legs. It was the machine-demon that I'd ridden, the same that had borne Arngrim into battle with Mimma-Lemnu.

"Hi, guys."

I felt my face break into a relieved smile. "Holy crap. You're alive. Any others?"

The great head, its metal horns battered and splintered, shook back and forth. "Nope, I'm the last one." Only one of his yellow eyes remained, and that turned toward Frank. "I'm pretty beat up, and you've already got a couple of friends to help out, but you want another? I'm not as fast as I used to be, but I can get you where you need to go pretty quick."

Frank's grin widened. "Damn, mister. I always wanted a talking horse."

The demon looked slightly offended. "I'm no horse, buddy. I've got a hell of a lot more personality."

Frank stepped up and patted the thing on its craggy red forehead, between its horns.

"Fair enough, then. You got yourself a job."

"Deal."

"Hey, guys, I hate to interrupt this touching scene, but that gate's not going to stay open forever." Anna gestured toward the blue-green portal. "We really need to get going."

I sighed. She was right. I slung my sword and turned away.

"Goodbye, Frank. Keep shouting at the devil."

He raised a hand and waved. "You do the same, Alex."

* * *

A few moments later, we stood on the slopes of Hauser Butte—Anna, Loren, Beowulf, Arngrim, and I. The last blue-green shimmers of the gate vanished and all around us the light of real dawn grew. The sky overhead was pale blue with a few wisps of cloud, and of the carnage that had visited this place—the blood and death and sacrifice—there was no sign.

"Hey, Alex," Loren said. "What's that over there?"

I looked toward where he was pointing and felt a renewed rush of emotion.

The rise where Dandridge had opened the *Kadingir* was covered in lush green grass, sprinkled here and there with blue, white, and yellow flowers.

We walked toward it slowly and reverently. In the center of the space were several small seedlings, only a few inches tall, but reaching eagerly up toward the sun.

"They're trees," Anna said, her voice heavy with something that was both joy and sadness. "Ten of them."

"The Fallen," I said, softly. "The ones who died here."

Anna was on her knees, gently touching each of the little trees.

"I feel them, Alex. They're not dead. They're still with us."

As the spirits of the *Fordæmdur* nourished the land of their birth, so did their spirits nourish the world where they had sacrificed themselves. In my mind, I saw the entire wasted desert around Hauser Butte bloom and grow green. Was it a real vision of the future, I wondered, or just my own wishful thinking?

"Farewell, *Fordæmdur*," I whispered softly. "I won't forget you."

Anna stood. "We'll come back here, won't we?"

"You couldn't keep us away," Loren said. "We'll be back, don't worry."

I drew a deep breath. "Unless someone did some vandalism last night, Yngwie is probably on the other side of the butte. Shall we go home?"

Loren nodded, slowly and wearily.

"Hell yeah, Alex. Hell, yeah."

Epilogue

ANNA

I wonder what Frank would have thought of all this, Anna mused as she walked down Hawthorne, letting the crowd carry her along, snapping pictures as she went. Beowulf trotted happily at her heels, excitedly taking in the sights, sounds, and especially smells around him.

The Hawthorne Street Fair was in full swing, filling Portland's most Bohemian neighborhood with tents, booths, food carts, singers, dancers, and performers. It was like a grand medieval tournament, but with lattés and organic produce instead of ale and turnips. Anna floated along like a bright, tattooed butterfly, as much a part of the city as its trees and sidewalks, a girl raised in the desert but now a woman made of equal parts rain, trees, and earth.

This year's street fair seemed especially bright, noisy, and joyful—a sign of recovery and the rejection of past tragedy. There were other reporters here of course, relieved that the world was finally getting back to normal, after the strange disasters that had suddenly visited the far corners of the globe, the wild tales of fantastic monsters, and their equally abrupt cessation. A few went so far as to compare the events in Africa,

Russia, and Australia to the still-unexplained Christmas Storm, but they were mostly ignored.

Tragedy had hit close to home as well, with the horrific deaths of twenty-two residents of the small town of Hayes, all apparently victims of the same serial killer. Authorities were seeking Thomas Kingman, aka Father Tom, aka Terrance Caine, aka Ted Rice in connection with the killings, but so far he had eluded capture. People remained nervous but seemed willing to at least temporarily forget about the demons in their midst as summer came to a hot, pleasant close.

Anna smiled at the thought of Frank Magruder. *I don't know,* she thought. *He'd probably just say something like "Get a job, you hippies."*

That was Frank for you. Living proof that you could disagree with someone and still love them. She felt a swell of affection and loss at the memory of her friend that was testament to the power of friendship over ideology.

Maybe Frank would have looked down his nose at these people, but I'm one of them, and I still cherish Frank's memory.

A woman stopped for a moment, dropping down to one knee to pet Beowulf and receive a polite kiss on the cheek. She was pretty in a punk-rock fairy kind of way, with a pale green Mohawk and a variety of piercings. Her t-shirt had a picture of Kermit the Frog in the style of Korda's portrait of Che Guevara, and she wore shorts, fishnets, and scuffed combat boots.

She grinned up at Anna. "Sweet dog," she said before disappearing into the crowd.

She cast the woman an appraising glance as she went.

Very cute. A little young for my tastes, but cute.

She took some more pictures. The details of her very first byline for *The Ranger* were still a little vague, and she would have to get it finished and submitted to Loren before her next appointment with the tattoo artist rendered her back tender and made typing an agonizing chore.

The mandala pattern on her back was gone, vanished with the closing of the final gateway. The outlines of a pair of inverted angel's wings now occupied the blank space, soon to be filled with feathers and other details, a tribute to the Fallen who had given their lives to restore a lost paradise, and to their leader, the being who had forsaken his immortality for her and her world.

Arngrim was off on his own now, vanishing into the wilds on a motorcycle after a solemn promise to return soon to check up on Anna. At first she had thought that he saw becoming human as some kind of punishment, but at that moment, as he dwindled into a tiny spark on the highway and finally vanished altogether, she realized that in reality it was a reward. He'd been given a child to fight for and a world to help defend—what better reward was there for a man like Arngrim?

As for Alex and Loren, they seemed content with the situation and relieved to return to a somewhat normal existence. She'd hitched her wagon to a very unusual star, but if it meant having the love and loyalty of two very different, but also very smart, very brave men, it was worth the complications.

It was a beautiful day, probably one of the last before winter closed in, and she had more than enough photos. As she looked down Hawthorne toward the forested volcanic cones of Mount Tabor and Rocky Butte, she felt a strange stirring inside her, and a faint but nagging itch radiating from her tattoos and piercings.

Abruptly, without effort, she remembered what Alex had said to her while they both sat in the old weather station, weeks ago.

It doesn't seem fair, does it? Getting put in an impossible situation, told "If you don't do the right thing here, millions will die, and the earth will be reduced to a cinder, but hey—it's your choice." Then when you do the right thing, suddenly everything you do is wrong, every choice you make is a misstep.

It was all about choices, wasn't it? Alex had made his choice, and so had she, even though it had seemed as if there were no good alternatives.

Just because all your choices are bad doesn't mean you don't have a choice, she thought. *Sometimes you just have to go with your heart and hope for the best.*

Compulsion filled her—a warm, urgent sensation that drove her on, making her walk determinedly eastward, toward the forested slopes ahead.

"Come on, Beow," she said, gently tugging on the dog's leash. "Let's take a walk."

* * *

She stands alone on the crest of Rocky Butte in the last rays of the setting sun. To the north lies the mighty Columbia River and beyond, past a blanket of green-black trees, the truncated cone of Mount St. Helens, all but bare of snow. To the south, the lights of Portland are slowly winking on in the gathering dusk. Beowulf sits on his haunches nearby, watching her with rapt fascination.

A voice that is not a voice echoes in her mind, forming words that are not truly words.

Daughter of the Fallen. Handmaiden of Belet-Ili. Bearer of sacred fire. Sorceress.

She feels every molecule of her body sing and vibrate in perfect harmony, and senses the warmth as it radiates through her tattoos—the blue peacock feathers on her back, the winged hourglass on her chest, the shadow of the old mandala on her back, and the unfinished angel wings that replace it. She looks down, seeing them burn faintly. Motes of silvery-blue swirl around her like a snowstorm, forming a shining spiral.

Surrounded by a cloud of dancing sparks, Annabelle Lee Moore rises slowly into the air, her face a mask of joy, fear, and wonder.

About the Author

During the day Anthony Pryor helps keep computers running at a large school district, but by night and on lunch breaks he's been editing, developing and writing for more years than he cares to admit, producing fiction and support material for popular games like Battletech, Dungeons and Dragons, Pathfinder and A Song of Ice and Fire, and working for publishers like Wizards of the Coast, White Wolf, Paizo Press, Green Ronin and others.

He lives in Milwaukie, Oregon with an overweight cat, plays more games than is strictly healthy and tries with minimal success to master the bass guitar in his copious spare time. With a mom who used to hang out with Diego Rivera and Frida Kahlo and a daughter who attends graduate school while fighting injustice and poverty in her spare time, Anthony's actually the boring one in his family. His greatest ambition is to be a world-famous rockstar, but being a writer is okay, too.